A LOVE MATCH LEGACY BOOK

THE *Sebastian* GUARANTEE

USA TODAY BESTSELLING AUTHOR

KRISTA SANDOR

CANDY CASTLE BOOKS

The Sebastian Guarantee

Copyright © 2022 by Krista Sandor

Candy Castle Books

Cover Design: Qamber Designs

Cover Model Photography: Wander Aguiar Photography

All rights reserved.
ISBN: 978-1-954140-15-8
Visit www.kristasandor.com

Chapter 1
PHOEBE

"Phoebe Gale, I'm cutting you off."

Oh, hell no! Phoebe pushed up her glasses, adjusted her beret, and gathered her resolve. Today was not the day for moderation. For the moment, she was the toast of the techies, and this was the day she'd learn if she was on the cusp of digital greatness or a breath away from being another one-and-done in the breakneck-paced tech world.

She glanced at her overalls and spied a dried glop of mustard. This stain didn't help her plead her case, but she couldn't allow it to deter her either. She swished the tail of her braid over her shoulder and let her chestnut-brown locks cover the crusty evidence.

She lifted her chin. "No, Hank, you can't cut me off. Not now. Not when I need it the most."

The grizzled Hank crossed his muscled arms, swirled with ink, and eyed her closely through the food truck's order window. "This would be your sixth today. Don't think I haven't kept track." The guy checked his watch. "And it's not even five o'clock."

Those were factual statements. Nevertheless, a gal needed

what a gal needed. She inhaled the heavenly scents wafting from the truck. "Desperate times call for desperate measures. And my desperate measure consists of a six-inch Hank Dog with ketchup, mustard, and a healthy sprinkling of shredded lettuce . . . for luck." She pressed her hands into a prayer position and gave the man her best puppy-dog eyes. This was not her first hot dog emergency, and Hank was no stranger to this expression. The man often parked his food truck near her Denver apartment, which also served as her home office.

A year ago, she'd left her position at her uncle's tech company to start her own business. She would have quit sooner had she known there was a hot dog food truck in her neighborhood.

Hold up! That wasn't exactly true.

She'd loved working at the company her uncle and late father had started. But she wanted to make a name for herself on her own terms and forge her own path—a path that, so far, had been blessedly dotted with a plethora of food trucks.

In the last three hundred and sixty-five days, she'd hit up Hank's mobile kitchen three or four times a week, and the pair had become fast friends. But she couldn't allow the gourmet hot dog chef's concern over her daily intake of processed meat to cloud his ability to sell her what she needed.

Since she was a little girl, hot dogs had always been her go-to comfort food. Scratch that. Hot dogs were her *anytime* go-to food, but today, her nerves had her ready to jump out of her skin.

She glanced at her cell phone. No new emails. The nervous energy pulsing through her kicked into overdrive as it mingled with the nitrates from her five previous hot dogs.

She ignored her frazzled disposition and flashed Hank her most endearing smile. "Pretty, pretty please, hook me up with a little hot dog perfection."

Luckily, she was pretty, pretty sure Hank understood that

she possessed a dogged determination when it came to getting her frankfurter fix.

The food truck vendor sighed dramatically, shook his head, then picked up a pair of tongs.

Sweet victory!

"Yes," she whispered and pumped her fist.

"What's with the lettuce today, Phoebe? It's not your usual order," Hank asked as he plucked a hot dog from the grill, nestled it into a toasted bun, then dressed her delicious dog.

"It's something for work. You're familiar with Zinger, right?"

"Who isn't?" Hank remarked. "It's the top internet search engine. I would've loved to have bought stock in that company thirty years ago. I'd be a gazillionaire."

"Yeah, they're huge," Phoebe agreed. "And that's why I'm so amped up. They sponsor an event, and it's a big deal if you get invited," she explained, trying to play it cool. And no, she wasn't losing her mind. The lettuce that had driven her to hoover hot dogs all day long wasn't the green vegetable.

Spelled *L-E-T-I-S*, the *LETIS* that had her popping and fizzing like a shaken-up can of soda, stood for Lifestyle Entertainment Technology and Innovation Symposium. You couldn't simply sign up for it. LETIS was an invitation-only conference. It brought together up-and-coming creators in the lifestyle, tech, and entertainment fields and eagle-eyed investors looking to fund the next big thing. The event was set to take place, starting tomorrow, at a mountain lodge in Colorado. Due to the exclusivity of the conference, that was all the information they'd provided. The invitations went out in waves, and the LETIS website reported that the final batch of invites were set to go out today.

And why did she think she had a chance of being invited?

Because of a match—a Munch Match app.

Eleven months ago, Hank had the audacity to park his

truck across town. This wasn't a huge inconvenience. Most food trucks posted their location on their website, and it wasn't hard to track him down. But as she noshed on her lunch, an idea popped into her head. What if she had been in the mood for noodles or street tacos? What if she'd been jonesing for food truck falafel? What if she didn't even know what she wanted, but she wanted it from a food truck? Her need to know the location of every food truck in the Denver Metro Area and her desire to craft an application that matched a person to precisely what they didn't know they wanted had morphed into the Munch Match app.

She'd put her tech skills to work and created an algorithm that, after answering a series of questions, directed the user to the closest food truck to meet their specific craving. She'd done it for Denver, then decided to expand it exponentially. Why not? People needed to eat across the globe, and the code that strategically scraped location data and menu selections worked anywhere.

But that wasn't everything it did—and this was the part that had plucked her one-woman tech company, Foot Tap Studio, out of obscurity and splashed it across the internet's tech sites.

A month after she'd released the app, an influx of emails had clogged her inbox. Emails with *thank you so much* and *your app changed our lives* written in the subject line. Munch Match didn't only connect people with exactly which food truck they should visit. It had facilitated a significant number of love matches.

Yep, love matches.

People would show up to grab a quick bite to eat and end up meeting their significant other as they waited in line. And when one of the editors at Techy Times, the preeminent news organization for super tech nerds, met her significant other using the app, the woman had written an article about her experience. Within minutes of the piece going live, Munch Match downloads had skyrocketed. The hashtag #Munch-MatchLoveMatch had hovered in the top ten tags over the last few months. As the developer of the hyped app, she'd have to be considered an up-and-coming innovator, right? Not to mention, in addition to Zinger, Techy Times was a LETIS sponsor. They'd surely want her there.

Hank held up the bin of shredded greens. "I'll take your word about lettuce being a big deal."

"I'm all about the lettuce, Hank," she replied. "Let us eat lettuce," she proclaimed, like the nerd she was.

"You sure are one lovable odd duck, Phoebe Gale," Hank replied with a toothy grin.

She glanced over her shoulder at the line snaking down the block. "I might be an odd duck, but I'm the odd duck who tripled your business."

"No," Hank countered, wagging a finger at her. "You quadrupled it. And I'm not the only food truck operator who's seen a jump in profits. Your little Munch Match thingamajig has boosted profits for all of us." He wrapped her Hank dog in tinfoil and handed it over. "This one is on the house."

She blew her favorite hot dog slinger a kiss and accepted the free meal. Someone tapped her shoulder, and she turned to find a slim man with slight features holding the hand of a woman with her hair in a bouncy blond ponytail.

"We're sorry to bother you," the woman began, "but we couldn't help overhearing your conversation. Are you really Phoebe Gale?"

Phoebe had a good idea she knew what was coming. "I am."

"I'm Delia, and this is Roderick," the blonde continued. "We have to thank you. Roderick and I met at the Mr. Cheesy Forever food truck three months ago. I didn't even know I wanted grilled cheese, but I trusted your app."

"Me too," Roderick added. "I thought I wanted pizza, but your app said grilled cheese. I ended up in line behind Delia. I listened as she ordered extra cheese, then I ordered extra cheese, and the rest is history."

Phoebe swooned. Who couldn't love a romance sparked by a chance food truck encounter?

"I fell head over heels in love with Delia as I watched her chomp away on a super-cheesy sandwich, and yesterday, we returned to that food truck, and I asked her to marry me," Roderick added as Delia raised her left hand, revealing a sparkling diamond.

Phoebe pressed her hot dog to her chest. "Congratulations! My dear friend's dad launched the Mr. Cheesy Forever food trucks back when I was a kid. I'll be sure to let him know. I'm so happy for you guys."

It wasn't a lie. She was genuinely excited for the couple, but when she saw the way Roderick looked at Delia, she could only wonder if anyone would ever look at her like that.

"Could we get a picture with you, Phoebe?" Roderick asked, pulling his cell from his pocket.

Phoebe snapped out of her morose relationship musings and plastered on a grin. "I'd be honored."

Roderick handed his phone to Hank, and the vendor snapped a photo of the trio.

"And I want one of you guys, too," Phoebe said, juggling her cell phone and the hot dog. She'd never been the most graceful of gals, and thanks to a pervasive case of butterfingers, she dropped her phone but saved the hot dog. She peered up at Hank. "I'll protect this hot dog with my life."

The man chuckled. "Gotta have priorities."

Delia was quick to help and retrieved the phone. But before handing it over, the woman got a glimpse of the screen and gasped. "Is that a picture of you and Sebastian Cress—the social media hottie, Sebastian Cress?"

At the mention of Sebastian Cress, Phoebe's heart swelled. She gazed at the image of herself and Seb sitting side by side on a pair of swings, clinking beer bottles. The picture had been taken only a few weeks before the Techy Times piece came out. That night, she'd been completely unaware that her life was about to take on a new trajectory. But her career prospects weren't the only thing that changed after the Munch Match piece was published. Come to think of it, since around that time, she'd heard less and less from her friend. Sure, Sebastian was busy. Like her, a year ago, he'd broken away from his family business to make a name for himself. But soon after the Techy Times piece came out, his social media feed had veered from fitness tips, style commentary, and life hacks to late-night partying with a string of different models and socialites. When was the last time they'd talked? It had to be going on a month —maybe more.

She drank in his endearing half-smile and sparkling eyes. "Yes, that's Sebastian Cress and me."

"All my friends follow him," Delia gushed. "He was named the sexiest man on the internet."

Phoebe sighed. "Yep, he sure was."

"Are you guys together?" Delia asked, wide-eyed.

Phoebe froze. Her mouth wanted to say yes, which was a bonkers reaction. There was no way she and Sebastian could ever be together. "No," she replied, forcing the syllable. "Sebastian Cress is my best friend—one of my best friends. I've known him for years."

Just as the words passed her lips, she recalled the day they'd met years ago, when she was a girl. She'd peered through a car window and gazed at the skinny boy with blue-green eyes. And then Sebastian spoke. His crisp British accent had left her seven-year-old self utterly enchanted. Alas, growing up in the good old U.S. of A had washed out his prim accent. The guy sounded as American as apple pie. Still, every now and then, a word would slip into their conversations, and she'd hear the echoes of the British boy who'd built pillow forts in her bedroom and snuck her extra chocolate chip cookies and hot dogs at get-togethers with their families.

Delia's eyeballs looked ready to pop out of her head as the picture disappeared and a carousel of photos flashed across the screen. "In this one, you're with Sebastian Cress and Aria Paige-Grant, the singer. Do you know her, too? She's famous."

"She's my other best friend," Phoebe answered.

The image disappeared and her favorite quote by Eleanor Roosevelt flashed across the screen. *The future belongs to those who believe in the beauty of their dreams.*

"I love that quote, too," Delia remarked.

"It's a good one," Phoebe said, feeling a kinship with those thirteen words. Back when she was in high school, she'd chosen it for her yearbook quote.

The picture changed again and flashed a shot of her, Aria, Sebastian, and Oscar.

Roderick gestured to the screen. "Who's that guy?"

"That's Oscar Elliott. He's a talented artist and photographer. His dad is the one who launched the Mr. Cheesy Forever Food trucks. The four of us have been close since we were kids."

Close was an understatement. They were more like a patchwork family—and their families had a unique beginning. Their nannies had been best friends. And thanks to a nanny love match, their nannies had married their caregivers. Her uncle Rowen had married her nanny, Penny Fennimore. Sebastian's dad, Erasmus Cress, had married Libby Lamb. Oscar's dad, Mitch Elliott, had married Charlotte Ames, and Aria's uncle Landon had married Harper Presley. The four families had been brought together by a renowned nanny matchmaker, and they remained close to this day.

A flush graced Delia's cheeks as another shot of Sebastian illuminated the screen. "Sebastian Cress is . . ."

The gal didn't need to go on. It wasn't uncommon for women to melt into pools of swooning goo in Seb's presence. It was weird how, one day, they were kids horsing around in the backyard, and the next, the gawky, knobby-kneed Sebastian had bloomed into a beautiful beefcake of a man. Six-four and built like a brick house, it was no wonder the guy had millions of online followers. Yesterday, he'd posted a picture of himself with the New York City skyline framed in the window, wearing nothing but a towel around his waist, and she absolutely hadn't had the sudden urge to lick his abs. Nope, it didn't even cross her mind because he was her friend. Her best friend. Her lifelong childhood friend. Her friend, friend, friend, friend, friend. Not to mention, she had a boyfriend. Jeremy. Jeremy Drewler.

Jeremy wasn't exactly her boyfriend, officially. But they'd met at a food truck a few days after the Techy Times article had been posted. Had their Munch Match turned into a love match? She wasn't quite certain. Things were going well. Like most of the guys she'd dated, Jeremy was in tech, but something had happened that made her think the universe wanted them to be together. Last week, he'd been invited to LETIS. It had to be a sign. She wasn't one hundred percent sure if he was dating anybody else, but if she were to also snag an invite, their time at the symposium could bring them closer. Then she could see if her Munch Match had the potential to be a love match.

"Hey," came a sharp voice from the middle of the line. "Could you hurry it up? We're hungry."

"Cool it," Delia chided. "We're in the presence of tech greatness. This is the Munch Match app lady, Phoebe Gale."

The low hum of conversation stopped as the food truck patrons leaned from side to side to get a better look.

Phoebe turned redder than a bottle of Hank's organic ketchup. "Yep, that's me, Phoebe Gale."

A guy behind Roderick and Delia gave her a once-over. "I read online that your uncle is Rowen Gale, the tech billionaire, and your aunt is Penny Fennimore, the genius behind the narrative for the video game AI-77. Is that true? That game has been out more than fifteen years, and it's still at the top of the charts."

"That's right. AI-77 was the first game my aunt and uncle worked on together."

Phoebe braced herself. Here comes the deluge of delusions the public had held about her life. She should be used to it by now. After her parents had passed away when she was barely three years old, she'd lived with her grandmother for a couple of years before her uncle gained full custody. Her uncle Rowen and Aunt Penny had raised her in Denver. It was no surprise people knew their names. The pair were a powerhouse in the tech and video gaming industries. Undoubtedly, their celebrity status would pique people's interest in their niece's life as well.

But she wasn't complaining. Growing up with famous and wealthy caregivers had its perks. While she thought about her parents every day and often wondered what life would have been like if they hadn't passed away, their loss hadn't directed her down a darkened path. She'd had a glorious childhood. She was loved and never wanted for anything. Still, it also led people to have wild misconceptions about her and her finances.

A scruffy guy with a mop of golden hair standing about five people back stepped out of line. "You must be crazy rich."

Case in point—the money curiosity.

Mr. Golden Mophead eyed her outfit, then cocked his head to the side. "Why do you walk around looking like that?"

Phoebe assessed her clothing choice. Besides a stain she'd covertly covered with her braid, she couldn't figure out what the dude was talking about.

"Like what?" she lobbed back.

"Like a nerdy French farmer. Who pairs glasses and a beret with overalls and sneakers?"

No, no, no! She could not allow this mophead to disrespect her clothing.

She narrowed her gaze. He'd messed with the wrong nerd. "Someone who requires bifocals, studied French in high school, loves the look of a beret, and is practical enough to appreciate the functionality of overalls." She stared the man down, then tapped her foot twice, taking advantage of a secret way to insult him without him being any the wiser.

"You've got to be loaded," the guy pressed, oblivious to her foot tapping. "Everyone I know has the Munch Match app on their phones."

The situation wasn't as cut-and-dried as one would think.

"Munch Match was kind of a fluke. I'm not even sure how the algorithm works. I don't charge people for it, so I don't make anything off it. But it gets my name out there. The funny thing is, I never set out to develop food apps. What I want to do is create an online community to empower and connect girls and women online through a myriad of entry points. I'm calling it Go Girl."

This was her dream, but it was in no way even close to a reality. She needed organizations to agree to partner with her and more resources, aka investors who could supply her with cold hard cash, to make it happen. Hence why she needed to snag an invite to LETIS.

Mophead yawned, clearly not interested in her career plans or female empowerment. He shrugged. "I figured you had a trust fund stuffed with billions of dollars."

She had a trust fund but couldn't access the money until she was thirty-two—not that it was any of this random dude's business.

She restrained herself from rolling her eyes. "I plan on making my own way in tech."

A woman standing behind Mr. Nosy Mophead craned her neck to look past the man. "Did you meet your perfect match at a food truck?"

Had she met her perfect match?

Phoebe pictured Jeremy. With his strawberry blond locks twisted into a low man bun and horn-rimmed glasses, he was a mix of trendy nerd meets hipster app developer.

"I met someone a while back at a food truck, and things are . . . good," she answered as a prickly sensation worked its way down her spine. That was odd. Jeremy could be her perfect match. It was possible, right?

"Do you have a sexual fetish for hot dogs?" Mophead asked, staring at his smartphone.

What the hell?

Her jaw dropped at the crazy question. "Why would you ask me that?"

He held up his phone. "It's on your Info Darling page."

This had to be a joke.

"I didn't even know I had an Info Darling page." She tucked her hot dog under her arm, then opened the internet browser on her phone. Info Darling pages were for famous or infamous people. She was a twenty-four-year-old small business owner trying to make it in tech. Who would make an Info Darling page for her—and post that she was a frankfurter freak?

Wait a hot second! She had a pretty good idea of the culprit. She schooled her features. "You can't believe everything you read online. I simply enjoy eating hot dogs."

"Because they make you horny?" Mophead pressed.

That earned him another set of foot taps.

"Because they taste amazing," she barked, when her phone pinged an incoming email. She stared at the screen and forgot about the ridiculous Info Darling page as she gazed at the subject line.

Invitation to LETIS, RSVP ASAP

This was it.

She opened the email. There, in digital glory, was her ticket to what could be a life-altering event. "Hank, it's the LETIS people. They want me."

"Tell those leafy-greeners your answer is yes," the man replied and gave her two thumbs-up.

She skimmed the message.

Tap the accept invitation button, and you're in. Details will be sent in a follow-up email.

She tapped the button. Not two seconds later, her phone pinged. But it wasn't the incoming email with more info on LETIS. This time, the ping alerted her to a text—a text from Jeremy.

Are you free to grab a drink now? I'm not far from your place. I need to ask you a question—an important question.

An important question?

Did Jeremy want to take things to the next level? Did he want to date her exclusively?

Maybe Jeremy Drewler was her perfect match.

She hammered out a reply.

Sure, ping me the address.

Another chime cut through the air.

Jeremy was at a bistro six blocks away.

What a day!

"Food truck brothers and sisters," she cried as a tingly warmth spread through her body. "After today, my life will never be the same. Hot dogs are on me!" she exclaimed and waved her arms like a benevolent hot-dog-obsessed overlord.

Everyone in line cheered, and even Mophead nodded approvingly.

Hank waved her in. "There are at least a hundred people in line. At eight dollars a pop, that's eight hundred dollars in franks. Are you good for that?"

Phoebe switched to her banking app.

Balance $869.69.

She peered at the people cheering and holding up their phones, snapping her picture. There was no turning back now. She switched to her money transfer app, tapped the Hank's Food Truck icon, and sent the payment of eight hundred big ones.

Hank's cell pinged with the hefty infusion of cash. "You're one of a kind, Phoebe Gale."

She glanced at the grill. "Do you think you could find it in your *kind* heart to hook me up with another hot dog on the house? I'd like to bring one to a guy I'm dating to solidify our connection with my favorite food. I'm feeling lucky, Hank. That last ping was him. He said he had an important question to ask me. I think he might really like me."

The man narrowed his gaze. "Do you promise this Hank dog isn't for you?"

Hank knew her well.

She pressed her hand to her chest. "Cross my hot-dog-loving heart and swear to die. The man who eats this love-match hot dog will be the person who'll hold my heart in his hands. He'll be the one. He'll be my match."

Chapter 2
PHOEBE

Hank tossed his tongs in the air and caught them like a pro. "One on-the-house love-match Hank dog to-go coming up."

"Thank you," Phoebe gushed. Jubilation fizzed through her veins. Everything was falling into place.

Hank plucked another dog from the grill, dressed it in a toasted bun with ketchup, mustard, and an ample sprinkling of lettuce, then wrapped the delicacy in foil and handed it to her. "If anyone deserves a love match, it's you, Phoebe Gale. You've got a heart of gold—or a heart filled with gold and processed meat," he added with a sly grin.

The joy in her heart had her ready to burst. "That means a lot to me, Hank."

"Good luck, kid," he added.

"I don't need luck," she replied, meeting his sly grin with one of her own. "I've got LETIS." She slipped the wrapped delight under her beret, then eyed Mophead. "Another excellent reason to wear one of these," she said and gestured to her head covering. "Hands-free hot dog storage."

With a walking-on-sunshine spring to her step, she set off in the direction of the bistro. Things were looking good—

damned good. She peeled the foil of her sixth hot dog of the day, reveled in the first divine bite, then tapped her cell phone's video icon and invited Aria, Oscar, and Sebastian onto the call. It was time to share the news with her besties.

Aria was the first to join. "Hello to my favorite hot tech diva. Is this the LETIS call?"

"It is," Phoebe chimed. "I got invited. I RSVP'd yes."

"Pheebs, I'm so happy for you. Is that a sexy celebratory hot dog in your hand?" Mischief danced in Aria's eyes.

"Wait a hot-diggity-dog of a second," Phoebe snapped and pointed her partially wrapped hot dog at the camera. "Did you make an Info Darling page about me and say I was sexually attracted to hot dogs?"

Aria beamed. "I was wondering when you'd see that."

"What were you thinking?" Phoebe pressed, then took another bite.

"Oh, come on, it's funny. And aren't you proud of me for flexing my tech skills? Aria Paige-Grant, singer, songwriter, tech genius."

"I think you're more of a . . . " Phoebe shot back. She stopped walking, angled the camera toward her foot, and tapped twice, one tap for each syllable of her insult of choice since she was in first grade.

Aria gasped. "Did you bust out our secret foot tap language and call me a *butt-hole*?" her bestie asked with mock indignation.

"You bet your piano-playing ass I did," Phoebe replied, but she couldn't stay angry.

"And I bet," Aria countered, "that you've got a hot dog under that beret."

Dammit! There were many pros to having lifelong friends. This, unfortunately, was one of the cons.

Lifelong friends had all the dirt and knew every secret.

In third grade, she and Aria had been assigned to write a

report on France. That was when she'd discovered the delightful beret and learned she could hide a considerable amount of junk food—even a hot dog—atop her noggin while wearing the stylish head covering.

Phoebe cleared her throat and continued down the street. "I don't have a hot dog hidden beneath my beret," she lied.

"Prove it, bitch," Aria demanded playfully. "And remember who you're talking to."

Oh, Phoebe knew who she was talking to. She and Aria were thick as thieves, and the reason their uncles had wisps of silver and gray threaded in their hair. To say they'd been a sassy handful as kids might be the understatement of the century.

But it was time to change the subject. As much as she loved reflecting on the past, today was a day to look forward. Except, when she looked forward at her friend on the screen, something was off. With a mess of makeup spackled onto Aria's face, the singer looked more like a fabulously done-up drag queen than an edgy rock star.

"What's happening with your beauty product situation? I'm for women embracing whatever makes them feel powerful, but you look ready to deliver the five o'clock news with enough rouge to put a clown to shame."

Aria pinched the bridge of her nose, then cringed when she peered at her fingertips caked in tan-colored goop. "My record label suggested I freshen up my look. They flew in a new stylist and a new makeup artist. Plus, I've got a possible new sponsor. Some makeup company wants me as their spokesperson."

Phoebe could hear the exhaustion in her friend's voice. "Are you okay with the changes?" she asked, softening her tone. "And where are you? What are you doing at this exact moment?"

Aria glanced off camera, then massaged the back of her neck. "Tour stuff." She angled her cell to show a stretch of piano keys. "We're doing the sound check before the concert. Then I've got a meet and greet with the local press." She smiled, but it didn't reach her eyes. "Honestly, Pheebs, I don't know what city I'm in, and it doesn't even matter. It's the same script every time. Smile, play the piano, belt out the songs, then smile some more before I haul my exhausted ass onto the tour bus and drive to the next place to do it again. I'm the rock star version of the directions on the back of a shampoo bottle, except my regimen is: perform, deflate, repeat," she finished, then knocked out a cascade of notes on the piano. "But I'm so proud of you. Your news has made my day." She cocked her head to the side as a curious expression bloomed on her face. "What else is going on? I'm getting a feeling the LETIS invite isn't the only thing making you vibrate with excitement."

"I've got news about Jeremy." Phoebe took another bite of her hot dog.

"The drooler?" Aria shot back and proceeded to open her mouth and mimic what looked like a drooling zombie.

"His last name is *Drew-ler*," Phoebe corrected.

The spark of mischief returned to Aria's eyes. "Yeah, that's what I said. *Droo-ler*, like, 'Oops, look at that *drool* on the pillow. I'm a *drooler*.'" Aria dropped the zombie drooling act and pursed her lips. "I don't like him."

"You've never met him."

"True," her friend replied with a little shrug, "but you've told me that he never texts you first and most of your dates consist of him stopping over at your place after the bars close."

Aria wasn't wrong, but he had texted her first this time.

Phoebe swished her braid over her shoulder as she continued down the sidewalk. "I'm meeting Jeremy for drinks now. He invited me," she added with a tinge of harrumph to her tone.

Her phone pinged as Oscar Elliott joined the video call.

Oscar brushed his dark locks out of his eyes. "Hey, Pheebs! Hey, Aria! What's up?"

"Phoebe got invited to that LETIS thing," Aria crooned.

A wide grin split Oscar's perma-brooding expression. "That's great news, Pheebs. We should celebrate. I'm just outside the city, and Seb's supposed to be in town—or maybe he already is. I'm not sure."

"You've talked to Seb recently?" Phoebe nearly tripped over her own two feet.

Aria and Oscar nodded.

"I haven't heard from him in ages," she replied, losing the spring in her step. Why had Sebastian told Aria and Oscar he was returning to Denver but not her?

"When he's not banging airheads," Aria huffed, "he calls to check in and say hello. But those calls are getting fewer and farther between. Do you guys know what's going on with him? I've tried to ask him if he's okay, but he always changes the subject. I don't get it. Last year, he was stoked about doing his own thing and building a life-coaching empire. The guy earned an MBA in eleven months. We know he's smart as hell. He had everything going for him. He was a fitness phenomenon, living with a purpose and sharing his tips and tricks. Then six months ago, his social media went from inspiring people to be their best selves to guzzling Grey Goose with bimbos like an entitled playboy. I love Seb like a brother, but what the hell is he doing—vying for douchebag of the century?" She glanced away, then groaned. "I've got to go. The new makeup lady is headed my way with a bottle of tan goo. Give me strength to fend her off. Love you guys. Congrats again, Pheebs." Aria blew a kiss, then left the video call.

Phoebe took another bite of her hot dog and focused on Oscar. "Will Seb be okay?"

"It's Seb," Oscar answered, not really answering. "What else is going on with you, Pheebs?"

"I met a couple who used my Munch Match app. They told me they fell in love in line at a Mr. Cheesy Forever food truck. Your dad's businesses are rocking."

"Yep, too bad his son can't get his shit together," Oscar replied, then shook his head. "Let's not talk about my dad and me."

"Okay," she said, switching gears. "I've got more news. Remember how I told you about Jeremy, the guy I was seeing?"

"The drooler?" Oscar shot back.

Phoebe huffed. "He's not a drooler. Well . . . he does drool, but who doesn't? Anyway, he texted me. He says he's got something important he wants to ask me. It has to be about taking our relationship to the next level. That's got to be good, don't you think?"

Oscar grimaced like he'd stepped in a pile of dog crap. "I don't know, Pheebs. A while back, Aria mentioned she had a bad feeling about him, and Seb thinks the guy sounds like a real tool."

"Sebastian discussed Jeremy with you?" she blurted. She'd only mentioned Jeremy to Seb a handful of times. And thinking back, when she'd spoken of him, Sebastian's countenance had hardened, and he'd ended the call abruptly. She'd wanted to press the subject with Oscar, but the bistro came into view before she could get more details. She'd have to pick Oscar's brain later. She had a date with destiny. Her pulse kicked up. This would be the place where true love would strike. Her match was about to reveal itself. She could feel it in her bones.

Years ago, she'd asked the famed matchmaker Madelyn Malone if she, Aria, Oscar, and Sebastian would find their love matches. The woman's response had stayed with her to this very day. It came to her every night before she fell asleep. The matchmaker said that matches are a matter of the heart and don't always reveal themselves. And then she'd gone further. She'd waved them in, and with the air of mystery and magic sparking between them, she'd divulged that their matches had already been made. It was a beautifully romantic notion. As a girl, she'd imagined it as a love seed just waiting to bloom and grow in her heart. Was that seed about to sprout?

She studied the bistro. The happy hour crowd was in full effect. The restaurant's doors were propped open, allowing the patrons to mingle and move between the patio and the indoor seating and bar area. Music and laughter carried on the cool fall breeze, calling to her as if Mother Nature herself knew a life-altering event was about to take place.

Phoebe exhaled a slow breath and spied Jeremy sitting at a table on the patio. The guy was talking to a woman—a woman with her breasts spilling out of her top. She wore sky-high heels, and her ensemble didn't leave much to the imagination. Phoebe glanced at her overalls and sneakers, then looked up and caught Jeremy squeezing the woman's hand before she strolled away.

Why would he do that?

Self-doubt twisted in her belly, but she couldn't jump to conclusions. She was here at his request. He'd reached out. This well-endowed woman could be an old friend or an acquaintance.

"Your match has been made," she whispered like an incantation, mimicking the nanny matchmaker's rich, Eastern European accent.

"What did you say, Pheebs?" Oscar asked.

And OMG! She still had Oscar on the video call.

That could be a good thing.

"Oscar," she blurted, "I'm at the bistro, but don't hang up. I'll record the rest of the call so you can hear everything Jeremy says to me. It's not like I'm being sneaky. To be fair, I'd end up telling you. This gets the info to you firsthand. Then I'll have video proof that Jeremy Drewler might be my love match."

Oscar raised an eyebrow. "Do you really think the drooler is your love match?"

"There aren't a whole lot of guys lining up for the job." She jammed the hot dog into her mouth and took a colossal bite. Why had she said that? She didn't need a boyfriend. Sure, she'd fantasized about finding *the one*. But it wasn't her only goal in life.

Since she was a girl, she'd dreamed of becoming a savvy entrepreneur. She wanted to be a force in the tech world and bring women to the forefront of the industry. Still, she couldn't deny that she liked the idea of working with a partner. She'd grown up watching her aunt and uncle collaborate. Their love had fueled Gale Gaming's success, and it still did. It was hard not to pine away for a love that lifted you up and always had your back. A love worthy of a true love match. She and Jeremy were sort of like her aunt and uncle. They were both in tech, and while he hadn't shown much interest in her idea to create Go Girl, he might warm to the idea—especially if an investor from LETIS signed on to fund the project.

"Shit," Oscar mumbled.

"What is it?"

"A news alert about Seb popped up on my phone."

"What does it say?"

Oscar's brows knit together. "It doesn't make sense. It says Sebastian Cress, son of British boxing champion Erasmus Cress and yoga guru Libby Lamb-Cress, leaves children in the pouring rain while he snaps selfies and steals their cab. It also says tap for pictures and video."

That didn't sound like Sebastian. He adored kids. He was crazy about his eight-year-old sister, Tula. This must be a misprint or a case of mistaken identity. She was about to convey this to Oscar when Jeremy waved to her.

Her pulse kicked up. "The Sebby news alert is probably clickbait. Just hang tight and listen. You'll have access to the recording along with Aria and Seb." She hit the record button, then headed toward Jeremy's table.

Her maybe Mr. Love Match took a sip of beer. He stood, then sat, then stood again. He glanced away. "Thanks for meeting me on such short notice."

She leaned in, thinking he wanted to kiss her hello, but he dropped into his chair as she presented her cheek. *Ouch!* She mustered a grin. Jeremy looked as if he were sitting on pins and needles. That had to mean he was about to take a leap. Butterflies—or five and three-fourths hot dogs—fluttered in her belly. She settled herself in the chair across from him, set her nub of hot dog on the table, and angled her phone, so she was in the frame and Jeremy couldn't see that she was recording the encounter.

"I have great news," she began to get the ball rolling. "I got invited to LETIS. The invite came in right before your text. We can go together. And before you say anything, I know why you messaged me."

Confusion marred his expression. He twisted his strawberry blond ponytail into a man bun and adjusted his hipster horn-rimmed glasses. He was clearly nervous. *Oh my gosh!* This could be her love match reveal.

He glanced at the group of women making duck lips and taking selfies. The boobalicious woman sat with them, yucking it up for the camera.

Another tinge of jealousy hit Phoebe's system.

Ignore it! He's anxious, that's all.

Jeremy cleared his throat, then drained his glass of beer. "You know why I texted you?"

She checked her phone. It was still recording.

Here goes everything.

"You want to take our relationship to the next level. You

want to do the whole boyfriend-girlfriend thing. My answer is—"

"Phoebe," Jeremy blurted, "don't say another word."

With her lips parted, she froze. Was this bigger than just proclaiming they were a couple? Did he want to ask her to move in with him, or was this the precursor for a marriage proposal? Did she want to marry Jeremy Drewler?

Jeremy leaned forward. "You're an interesting person, Phoebe, and your tech skills are pretty good, you know, for a chick. But you're not the type of girl a guy would want to have as a girlfriend."

She blinked. The nitrates from those hot dogs must have messed with her mind.

"What?" was the only thing she could get out.

He gave her a once-over and cringed. "You've got mustard on your overalls."

She touched the spot. "You don't want to be with me because of a mustard stain?"

Jeremy's features morphed into a syrupy expression. "I don't want to date you because you're you. You're a computer nerd."

Was she hallucinating?

What he was saying didn't make sense. She peered at the red recording light on her phone. "But you're a computer nerd, too."

He shrugged. "Yeah, but it's hot for a guy to be a tech nerd."

"I don't understand," she stammered, hating how pitiful she sounded. And she wasn't pitiful. She was a force of nature. Granted, she was a quirky force of nature who loved hot dogs, dancing in fuzzy socks, and curling up in front of her computer, but she was a force, nonetheless.

"You're decent to talk shop with, but you're not what I want.

I asked you to meet me here tonight because I had a feeling you might get invited to LETIS, you know, because you're a woman, and they probably have to fill some bullshit quota and invite a certain percentage of female innovators. I didn't want you to think we'd hang out if you got in. I couldn't have you by my side ruining my prospects. I've got to be on my A game, especially since you wouldn't connect me with the tech power players in your family. The truth is, you brought this on yourself, Phoebe."

What?

She wrung her hands. "I thought you liked me. You slept with me—many, many times."

He glanced over his shoulder at the busty woman posing for selfies with her friends. "Yeah, that was a mistake."

She looked between Jeremy and the chick making duck lips as another girl filmed the gaggle of women, and the pieces came together.

This horn-rimmed glasses-wearing butthole had only gotten close to her because of her last name.

"I'll do you a favor and tell you something you need to know," he said with a smug air. "I know most of the guys you've dated. They only hung out with you because they thought you'd introduce them to—"

"My uncle Rowen and my aunt Penny," she supplied, confirming her suspicion.

He shrugged. "Yeah."

A coppery taste invaded her mouth. She swallowed the bitter humiliation and schooled her features. It was time to throw some sass his way. "What do guys want in a woman, Jeremy? You seem to be an expert, and I'm dying to know."

"Honestly?" he tossed back, surprise coating the word.

And then it hit. Maybe she needed this information. She'd never had a long-term relationship. Perhaps there was something wrong with her in the girlfriend department.

She willed her voice not to shake. "Yes, honestly. Explain it to me."

He traced his index finger around the rim of his glass. "Guys want someone who's sexy and alluring. They want to look at the woman on their arm and say, 'Damn, I'm a lucky guy.'"

A part of her couldn't deny that she wanted someone to feel that way about her.

"Let me ask you this," Jeremy continued. "Do you even own a pair of high heels?"

She shrugged. "There's got to be a pair somewhere in my closet."

"When was the last time you wore them or put on lingerie?" he shot back like this was a deranged dating game show.

She ripped a sliver of tinfoil from the hot dog wrapper and twisted it. "I like fuzzy socks."

Jeremy barked a condescending laugh. "News flash: those aren't sexy."

She dropped the foil. "I think I get it. What you're saying is that guys want—"

"The opposite of you," he finished, cutting her off like the butthole he was.

She leaned forward, ready to pounce, when the treat beneath her beret slid past her forehead and plopped onto the table with a dramatic thud. This foil-wrapped deliciousness was supposed to have solidified her connection with her perfect match. She adjusted her beret, then cradled the wrapped Hank dog in her hands as one salient fact became crystal clear. Jeremy Drewler was not worthy of this hot dog. How the hell could she have thought he was her match?

Jeremy reared back in his seat. "That's disgusting! Why do you have a hot dog under your hat?" A smirk returned to his lips. "Wait, let me guess. Is it a snack for later when you're alone in your apartment, staring at your phone, hoping I'll send you a one a.m. booty call text?"

This jackass had gone too far. Little did he know he'd never gotten her off. Nope, she always had to go into the bathroom and finish up with her trusty Wham Bam battery-operated boyfriend.

She clenched her jaw and glanced at her cell. Oscar waved his hands wildly. The sound was muted, but she could tell the guy was yelling for her to stop.

Moment of truth—her friend was correct to be worried. But there was no turning back now.

It was time to throw down—frankfurter style.

She stood, slapped a deceivingly demure smile on her lips, and batted her eyelashes. "You're partially correct, Jeremy. It is a hot dog—but not just any hot dog." She wrapped her fingers around the foil-clad frank, raised her arm, and prepared to launch a wiener at an even bigger wiener.

Jeremy sprang from his chair and shrieked like a preteen girl at her first boy band concert.

Vibrating with fury, she pulled her elbow back another inch as the light from the setting sun glinted off the foil. She flicked her gaze from Jeremy and observed the wrapped masterpiece. She couldn't defile a hot dog. This misogynistic prick wasn't worth it. She set the wrapped delicacy on the table and gently stroked the warm wrapper.

"Good luck ever getting a guy, you crazy hot-dog-obsessed girl nerd," Jeremy mumbled.

Now she really couldn't let him leave unscathed. She surveyed the table and spied a metal rack with plastic bottles of fancy-pants gourmet condiments. *Jackpot!* Just because she couldn't pelt him with a food truck hot dog masterpiece didn't mean she couldn't retaliate. Thinking fast, she plucked a compact container of Dijon mustard from its resting place.

Like an expert connoisseur of hot dog condiments, she assessed its weight. The bottle was nearly full.

"Excellent," she whispered, then slapped an evil computer nerd genius smirk to her lips.

"What are you doing with that mustard?" Jeremy squeaked.

She flipped the cap like she was disengaging the safety and pointed the loaded condiment at the King of the Tech Douchebags.

"This crazy hot-dog-obsessed girl nerd is about to test a theory," she answered coolly.

Jeremy stared at the bottle. "What theory is that?"

"Let's see how *sexy* you are covered in spicy Dijon." She glanced at her cell and found Oscar staring back at her. She caught her friend's eye, winked, then zeroed in on her target.

"You don't have to do this," Jeremy pleaded like they were engaged in a showdown, which they kind of were.

A dead quiet set in. All eyes were trained on them. Even the duck-lips crew had stilled. Phoebe tightened her grip when, somewhere in the distance, a crow cawed like they were in an old Western gunslinger flick.

This shit was on.

She narrowed her gaze. "Oh, Jeremy, I have to do this."

Harnessing the rage of every woman who'd been jerked around by a drooling douche nozzle, she let the Dijon rip. Like a mustard-bottle-wielding Annie Oakley, she nailed the lens on his horn-rimmed glasses.

Take that, wannabe tech-savvy hipster!

The man gasped, giving her the perfect second target. She lowered her aim and filled his stupid pie hole with the tangy delight.

Adrenaline flowed through her. "I am Phoebe, Princess of the Hot Dog Fairies, Bearer of Cookies, and Eater of Pizza," she proclaimed like Athena, the Greek goddess of war, as she resurrected the title she'd given herself in first grade.

And then she ran out of mustard. The bottle was empty, but one fact remained indisputably true: she'd utilized those mustardy ounces like a boss.

Jeremy spat and sputtered like a seizing car engine as he removed his mustard-laden spectacles. He wiped his wrist across his mouth. "You're nuts, Phoebe Gale! If it wasn't for your last name, nobody would give you the time of day. No LETIS investor will finance your girl power bullshit idea," he snarled. The man turned toward the duck-lip brigade. "Let's go, Tina."

"May the best nerd win LETIS funding," she hurled back as Jeremy disappeared down the street with the boobalicious Tina teetering behind.

As if she were waking up from a dream—or in this case—a nightmare, Phoebe sank onto the chair. She picked up her cell and stared at the pulsing red light. It was still recording, but she didn't see Oscar in the corner frame. His screen was black, but not black like they'd been disconnected. The fuzzy darkness moved like Oscar had pocketed his phone. She tapped the screen, ending the recording, then set the empty Dijon bottle next to the love-match Hank dog. Jeremy was a creep, for sure, and deserved his condiment bath, but could there be a sliver of truth to what he'd said?

She was twenty-four and hadn't had a serious boyfriend.

Did men truly want the opposite of her? Was she undateable? Was undateable even a word? Her posture stiffened. Was she being watched? Dumb question. She'd unloaded a container of Dijon on a man in the middle of a crowded bistro. She looked around, and yep, all eyes were trained on her. She had to get out of there. She had to grab her Hank dog, slip it under her beret, then start running and keep going until she ended up somewhere north of her current location—possibly Canada or Greenland.

Slowly, she reached for the hot dog, just as a waiter placed a martini with three olives in front of her.

She froze. "What's this?"

The man gestured to the drink. "It's a dirty martini with three olives. A woman at the bar asked me to bring it to you. She also mentioned something about Eleanor Roosevelt, but it was pretty loud inside and I didn't catch it."

Phoebe glanced past the open doors and surveyed the line of stools dotting the bar. "Where is she?"

"She left shortly after the . . . incident," the waiter answered, taking in the splatter of mustard on the patio. "She also asked us to leave the tab open and not disclose her name."

Phoebe removed the olive-laden toothpick and pointed it at the waiter. "A mystery woman watched me douse a man with mustard, then decided to pay for me to get hammered?"

The man suppressed a grin. "That appears to be the case."

She nodded when a flash of mustard caught her eye—not the condiment, this time, but the color. An attractive young woman with a marigold-colored scarf walked by the bistro. Her hair bounced in perfect blond highlighted waves as she sailed down the street in a cloud of put-together perfection. And she wasn't the only one who'd noticed. The male bistro patrons seemed to forget about the insane woman with the mustard. Every man on the patio drank in the blond goddess gliding down the sidewalk. The woman glanced at the salivating dudes, and a self-assured smile bloomed on her lips. She could have her pick of anyone in this place—and she knew it.

What did it feel like to wield that power over the opposite sex?

Phoebe sighed and scratched at the stain on her overalls. She wouldn't be finding out tonight. She plucked the martini glass stem between her fingers and downed the liquid in a single gulp.

Not bad.

She eyed the waiter. "Can you do me a favor?"

"Of course."

Phoebe studied the blond stunner, and an absolutely ludicrous notion popped into her head. A buzzy euphoria took hold. She glanced at the love-match hot dog, and for the second time in five minutes, she knew what she needed to do.

She tapped the rim of the martini glass and eyed the waiter. "Keep these coming. I've got a plan to flesh out, but I'll need to be good and drunk to figure out a way to pull it off."

Chapter 3
SEBASTIAN

Ping, ping, ping!

Ping, ping, ping!

Sebastian Cress burrowed beneath the covers.

Ping, ping, ping!

He groaned. What the hell was making that racket? It wasn't his cell. He knew that for sure. He'd turned the damned thing off yesterday before he'd boarded his flight from New York to Denver, and he hadn't turned it back on.

That had been a conscious choice.

What hadn't been a conscious choice was dropping it seconds before he'd quickly jumped into a cab outside Denver International Airport in the pouring rain to evade a gaggle of tittering fans. It had cracked down the center, but he'd pocketed the damaged device, then ordered the driver to hit the gas and get him the hell out of there.

He'd been in no mood to engage with the public. The minute he'd stepped off the plane, he'd caught a handful of people filming him. By the time he'd left the terminal, a dozen giggling young women wielding smartphones had followed him to the taxi line.

And why were members of the fairer sex trailing behind him like he was the Pied Piper?

A couple of months ago, an online publication dubbed him the sexiest man on the internet, and this fan club melee had become a staple in his life. At first, he'd basked in the adulation. It wasn't like he *hadn't* gone looking for attention. He was the one who'd shifted from posting exercise tutorials and healthy eating tips to flooding his socials with shirtless pictures of himself partying with a cast of women whose names weren't worth remembering, along with a string of sweaty, bare-chested shots of him fresh out of the shower. Every image highlighted his muscled body and rock-hard abs. Legions of ladies had called him man candy. His DMs were chock-full of marriage proposals and requests to carry his child. For a spell, he welcomed the distraction. But his time cavorting around the globe like a pampered man-whore was over.

He scrubbed his hands down his face, tried to swallow, then groaned again. His mouth tasted like crap tequila, which wasn't surprising. After he'd landed in a wet and stormy Denver, and before he'd headed to his parents' house, he'd hit up a hole-in-the-wall bar near the airport and guzzled a ton of —that's right—crap tequila.

Ping, ping, ping!

The incessant sound sliced through his brain like a buzz saw gnawing through a block of cheese. It was as if the noise was coming from beneath his pillow. Could he still be drunk? Why would his bed be pinging? He pushed onto his elbow and cracked his bloodshot eyes open. He glanced at his bedroom window, trying to get his bearings, but the curtains were closed. From the slim slice of light coming in, he could deduce that the sun was either setting or rising—most likely setting. It was no surprise he'd slept through the day. He'd arrived at the house at two a.m. and was relieved to find it empty. Had his father been home, the former heavyweight champion and British boxing sensation, Erasmus "The British Beast" Cress, would have scowled, then described his twenty-four-year-old son as a wobbly git. And the man would have been right. When the British Beast's only son finally stumbled through the door in the wee hours of the morning, he'd clutched the railing and hauled his drunken ass upstairs before crashing face-first onto his bed.

Ping, ping, ping!

He shook his head, working to clear the cobwebs, when a few items on the bedside table caught his eye. A lump formed in his throat as he took in an old pocket watch, a smooth aquamarine stone, and a framed photo of the pint-sized version of himself. Dressed in a red and green Christmas sweater, he stood arm in arm with the people who had been his best friends since he was a kid: Aria Paige-Grant, Oscar Elliott, and Phoebe Gale. He allowed his gaze to linger on the little girl in braids with a hot dog in her hand, then returned his attention to the watch and the stone. A wave of shame that couldn't be mistaken for nausea washed over him as he recalled the type of person he used to be.

Ping, ping, ping!

It was too early or too late—he still didn't know which—to wax poetic over his poor choices.

Ping, ping, ping!

With his head ready to explode, he tossed the pillow onto the floor and spied the source of the sound. In the hazy light, he could barely believe his eyes. "Why is there a random cell phone here?" He blinked. It wasn't only a cell phone. A wrinkled piece of folded paper with *Seb* scribbled across the top sat next to the device. He picked it up, shook it open, and read the succinct message.

Answer me, Big Foot.

He recognized the handwriting and the insult that had become an inside joke. Despite a screaming headache, a grin stretched across his parched lips at the thought of his raven-haired eight-year-old little sister. How he adored Tula Meredith Cress.

Not long after he and Oscar turned sixteen, they'd become big brothers. Tula and Ivy Elliott entered this world a day apart, and it was safe to say the girls had their brothers wrapped around their fingers. The Big Foot reference came from a game they used to play when the girls were toddlers and loved comparing the size of their chubby feet to their big brothers' honking hooves. But hiding a charged cell phone under his pillow that aggravated his already hellacious hangover was pushing the limits of his brotherly affection.

Ping, ping, ping!

He grabbed the device and answered the call. "Tula Cress," he barked, "why is there a phone under my pillow?"

"Because," came the eight-year-old's sassy squeak of a voice, "I left it there, dingbat. Did you think a phone fairy put it there? News flash: there's a tooth fairy and maybe a hot dog fairy because Phoebe told me she wanted to be a hot dog fairy when she was a kid. But I know for a fact there isn't a smartphone fairy."

He pinched the bridge of his nose. At the mention of Phoebe, a perplexing tsunami of emotions hit. Over the last six months, she'd left him a mountain of messages. But he couldn't muster the strength—or perhaps it was that he couldn't muster the courage—to have more than a fleeting conversation or a generic text exchange with his best friend.

"Sebby, are you there, or did you fall asleep?" Tula pressed. "And don't you tell me you're super busy and have to get off the phone."

He massaged the kink in his neck. "I'm here, T, I'm here."

Phoebe wasn't the only person he'd been avoiding. He hated how long it had been since he'd spoken with his sister. Along with being a shit friend, he could add being a shit big brother to the list of his failures over the last one hundred and eighty days. With the phone pressed to his ear, he dragged his ass out of bed and into the bathroom. He flipped on the tap and bent down to slurp a few mouthfuls of water.

"How do you like my burner phone, Seb?" Tula tossed out nonchalantly.

Burner phone?

He lurched forward, choking on the liquid. "Why do you have a burner phone?"

"So I can talk to Ivy after Mibby and Dad put me to bed. Why else?"

This spunky, slightly frighteningly devious kid.

He caught his breath and wiped his wrist across his mouth. He still got a kick out of his sister calling Libby, Tula's biological mom, and his stepmom, *Mibby*. That had been the nickname he'd given to Libby when she was still his nanny. Mibby was the mashed-up version of *my* and *Libby*. Wanting to be like her big brother, Tula had picked it up instead of *mom* or *mommy*, and to his great pleasure, it stuck.

He used to love that Tula wanted to be like him. Now it was probably better that he'd distanced himself from the child. Still, he was her older brother, and in this situation, he could act like it.

"Where did you get the burner phone, T?"

"Do you promise not to tell Dad and Mibby?"

"Tula," he chided.

The girl huffed. "Ivy and I asked Phoebe to get us secret phones after she brought us to a Girls in Tech Expo downtown a few weeks ago. We were on our way home and told her we needed secret phones to play super-secret spy agents. We weren't lying, Sebby. We play secret spy agents, and sometimes we play after our parents think we're asleep on school nights but then end up talking about normal stuff. You have no idea how busy the life of an eight-year-old girl is these days."

He pressed his lips together to suppress a chuckle. "When Phoebe and I were around your age," he said when he was sure he wouldn't bust out laughing, "we were into playing super-secret spies, too."

"That's what she said!" Tula exclaimed.

He cleared his throat. "Did Phoebe say anything else or mention a boyfriend, some guy named Jeremy Drewler?"

He cringed. What was he thinking, asking his kid sister about Phoebe's love life?

"She didn't say anything about a drooling Jeremy," Tula answered to his absolute delight.

Jeremy Drewler was wrong for Phoebe. Granted, he'd never met the guy, but from what little he knew, the dude sounded like a tool. As her friend—no, as her *best* friend—he needed to look out for her. That's what he was doing. Yep, that was it. Totally it. Done and dusted.

"Want to know what else Phoebe said?" Tula asked like she was dangling a bit of meat in front of a lion.

His brain screamed *hell yes*, but he had to play it cool. "If you want to tell me, you can, I guess. Whatever. It makes no difference to me. Unless you want to tell me, then you might as well say it. We are on the phone." Jesus, he sounded like a moody preteen.

"Phoebe said a lot of things about being a strong woman. She wants Ivy and me to follow our dreams, and then we stopped at a food truck and ate hot dogs and cookies. Lots of chocolate chip cookies." Tula paused. "But I don't have time to talk about Phoebe. We need to talk about you, Sebby."

Yowza! That couldn't be good.

"I left my super-secret spy agent phone in your room and took Ivy's with me to Rickety Rock so I could call you. You know it's our family's fall break-break," Tula added, lowering her voice.

His family had started doing this back-to-nature break

when he was in elementary school. Mibby insisted they take time away to connect with their inner selves and each other. During the school year's fall break, they'd head south to their mountain home, a few hours away in Rickety Rock, Colorado. They'd put away their phones, laptops, and tablets to recalibrate, reconnect, and find balance. He loved that time, and he should have been there with them. But he had a legitimate reason to skip out this year that also allowed him to breathe a sigh of relief. His absence in Rickety Rock meant he wouldn't have to come face-to-face with his dad, who wasn't impressed with how his son had been conducting his life. Little did his dad know, that made two of them.

Despite his fall from grace, he was determined to succeed. He'd returned to make a change—and to make good on the promise he'd made to himself and his deceased mother. His publicist, Briggs Keaton, who also managed his father's PR and business dealings, had scheduled a slew of meetings for him in Denver.

But before he could get on with turning his life around, he needed to hear out his sister. She was breaking the rules for him. He owed her his utmost attention.

"What do we need to talk about, Tula?"

"*Boyo*," the little girl answered, mimicking their father's gritty, East London accent.

And *boyo*, it was never a good sign when Erasmus Cress dropped that word to describe anyone.

"What did Dad say, T?" he asked, but he had a good idea he already knew what his old man was rumbling about.

"I heard Daddy and Mibby talking when they thought I was asleep the day before we left for Rickety Rock. Dad said, 'that *boyo* of ours is acting like a right plonker, showboating around the world like a lazy sod.'" Tula perfectly imitated their father. "And then Mibby said she felt a shift in your aura six months ago, and she was worried your chi was out of balance.

But then she said she felt another shift a week or so ago. Our Mibby is good at telling when we're out of sorts or have big changes coming our way."

His sister wasn't wrong. Libby Lamb-Cress was blessed with an intuition like no other.

"That's why I left the phone under your pillow, Sebby. Dad and Mibby said you were coming home, and I had a feeling you'd wait until we'd left."

He flinched. Her words sliced through him like a knife straight to his heart.

"The only time I see you is when I look at your social media stuff. But it makes me sad to look at your pictures," Tula continued.

He cleared the emotion clogging his throat. "Why does it upset you?"

"I can tell you're pretending."

He stared at his reflection in the bathroom mirror. "Pretending to be what?"

"Happy."

Dammit.

Tula Meredith Cress had inherited a good chunk of her mother's spot-on insight.

His eyes burned, and it wasn't from an abundance of alcohol or lack of decent sleep.

"Are you okay, Sebby?" his sister asked softly. "What happened that made you sad and made you forget to put on a shirt in your posts?"

It was a valid question, but he'd spent the last six months trying to forget the answer, and it wasn't an answer he could share with Tula.

He hadn't always been like this.

A year ago, he'd set out to make his own success. And he hadn't been alone. He and Phoebe had left their positions at their family's companies to chart their own course and start their own businesses. They'd talked or texted multiple times a day and cheered each other on. Phoebe wanted to use her talents to unite women and girls in tech, and he wanted to employ his fitness and business skills to create a program that helped people attain their goals through positive lifestyle choices.

He'd been a machine for the first six months, working from early in the morning until late at night. It took time and research to craft an in-depth business plan. He knew this. And he'd wanted to get it right. He'd used his savings to travel the world, gathering information on the benefits of different types of diets and exercise habits. He'd met with fitness professionals, motivational speakers, and scientists. He wanted to harness the information he'd amassed to create a system that would encourage—no, guarantee—a harmony-infused existence. Boiled down to one succinct goal, he wanted to become a motivational life coach who transformed lives. He dreamed of writing books, creating a media channel, and guiding the masses toward better, more fulfilling choices.

That's when Project Confidence was born. But it still needed work—and probably a better name.

Here's the thing. He understood the ins and outs of business development. After graduating with a business degree, he'd spent a handful of years expanding his family's Pun-chi yoga franchise. This form of exercise married precise yoga positions with the intensity of boxing moves. While it seemed like an unlikely match, his stepmom and dad had proven the two disciplines created a workout that provided heart-pumping aerobic exercise with a dose of soul-cleansing mindfulness, and he believed in it.

He'd opened Pun-chi yoga centers in the Middle East, Eastern Europe, and Asia. He hadn't just stuck to the spreadsheets and presentations with investors during that time. When it came to the business side of things, he could talk the talk, but when it came to the fitness aspect of the business, he could also walk the walk.

He'd taught Pun-chi yoga classes and begun sharing fitness and health tips on his social media accounts. That's where he'd gained a following and realized it was time for him to break away from the family business and make a name for himself. He'd been well on his way until he'd woken up to the salty air on the Spanish island of Ibiza six months ago. He'd grabbed his phone off the bedside table to review his appointments. That was when he'd read a text from Phoebe that knocked the wind clean out of him. Instead of meeting with experts that day, he'd crawled back beneath the sheets, then hit the clubs that night.

After that day, his life had become a blur of booze and one-night stands. He'd distanced himself from the people he loved. He'd abandoned his research and flitted from one luxurious locale to the next, living the life of a rudderless playboy until a dream and a date on the calendar had stopped him dead in his tracks last week. That must have been the shift in the universe Mibby had felt.

Instead of making plans to party, he'd texted Briggs. He'd told the man he was returning to Denver and asked him to set up meetings with potential investors.

And his "come to Jesus" hadn't come a moment too soon.

He'd neglected his finances over the last six months. His stomach had dropped when he'd logged on to his savings account. He'd burned through most of it, and he wasn't about to ask his father and Mibby for cash. Sure, they'd give it to him, but that wasn't how he wanted to make it in this world. If he was going to set out on his own and build a business, he'd need to secure funding. And he needed it quickly. His last name helped. It opened doors, but it also brought immense pressure to succeed. Just by virtue of being the son of a former heavy-weight champion and a yoga phenomenon, a certain sect of this world pegged him as a spoiled rich kid and was gunning for him to fail. His choices over the past six months certainly hadn't done anything to dissuade the perception. That's why he had to turn his life around now. Failure was not an option. Not when his last name was Cress.

He left the bathroom, returned to his bed, and sank onto the edge. He had so many good memories in this room. Sleep-overs with Aria, Oscar, and Phoebe. Rocking a tiny, teething Tula in his arms in the dead of night to give his bleary-eyed parents a break. He returned his attention to the watch. He picked it up, taking comfort in its familiar weight, then pressed the latch. It popped open, and he looked from the delicate timepiece to the small, circular photo of his mom—no, his mum. That's what he'd called her back when he was a wee lad and still spoke with a prim British accent.

"Sebby?" Tula asked softly. "Are you still there?"

He closed the watch and exhaled a shaky breath. "Yeah, Tula, I'm here. I was just thinking." He had to get out of his head and put the kid at ease. It wasn't her fault her brother had screwed up. "You don't have to worry about me. I'm home. I've got meetings set up. I'm getting back on track."

It wasn't a lie—exactly. Regrettably, his neglected business plan wasn't looking too hot, and he hadn't decided what he would present to the investors. Still, his dream had been abundantly clear. He had to start somewhere, and that began at home.

"Do you promise that you're okay, Sebby?" The worry in Tula's voice twisted the knife in his heart.

"Big Foot always lands on his feet, kid," he answered with as much reassurance as he could muster.

"Will you take me to get ice cream when I get back from Rickety Rock?"

If Phoebe's vices were hot dogs and cookies, Tula's was the ice-cold dairy delicacy.

He grinned. "We can get double scoops."

"Triple scoops," she countered. His smart cookie of a sister clearly knew she held all the cards.

"Done. Triple scoops."

"Want to see something?" Tula asked, excitement threaded through the question.

The tightness in his shoulders loosened. "Sure, I'd love to."

"Look inside your closet."

He walked over to the door, turned the knob, then paused. "Wait a second. If I open this door, I won't find a pile of your dirty socks in there, will I?" he joked, feeling more like himself.

"No," she giggled.

"Or a bunch of moldy, brown banana peels?"

"Ew!" the girl squealed. "Just open the door, Sebby."

He did as his sister asked, then raised an eyebrow. "Is this what I think it is?"

"It's a hot dog costume," she announced.

That it was.

With a hole in the top of the hot dog portion for the wearer's face to peek out, the costume sported a stuffed spandex hot dog nestled in a bun with red and yellow fabric squiggles racing down a painted frankfurter. He ran his hand down the puffy fabric making up the bun portion. "It's huge. It looks like it could fit me."

"They had a zillion of them at the store but only in adult sizes," Tula replied. "But that's how I like it. It goes to my ankles. I saved up my allowance and bought it. It's my Halloween costume. I think Phoebe's gonna love it."

He could hear the joy in her voice. "I agree. Phoebe had hot dog headbands and shirts growing up, but she never dressed up as an actual hot dog, which is fascinating."

"Don't tell Phoebe when you see her. I want it to be a surprise."

Would he see Phoebe?

He wasn't even sure how long he'd be in town.

"I'll—" he began but stopped.

Tula cut him off with a gasp.

"Everything all right, T?" He could hear her fumbling with the phone.

"What did you do to the Tech Tweens?"

Tech Tweens?

He racked his brain. "I don't know what you're talking about."

"A news alert popped up on my phone about you and tweens . . . bloody hell," his sister whisper-shouted, again perfecting their father's rollicking British accent. "It's Daddy. I hear his footsteps. I told him I was meditating with the donkeys."

That was another quirk he loved about his family. They'd adopted two donkeys right after he'd come to live with his father and Libby in Colorado. To everyone's delight, the pack burros were still alive and kicking.

"How are good old Plum and Beefcake?"

"They'll get more treats than me if Dad catches me with this phone. I better go, and when you see Phoebe, remember, Sebby, she's the one."

The one?

He opened and closed his mouth a few times before he could respond. "Phoebe's the one?"

He held his breath as neither of them said a word.

"Phoebe's the one that you can't tell about my costume. What did you think I meant?" Tula tossed back with a curious bend to the question.

"Right, that's what I thought you meant," he blathered. Jesus, maybe he was still hammered.

"And turn on your cell phone, Sebby."

"Why?" he got out on a woozy breath, still reeling from their exchange.

"Because the universe wants you to do it," the kid answered matter-of-factly.

"The universe is sending you messages, T?" He shouldn't have been surprised. In most cases, when somebody said something like that, there was a decent chance they were a few slices short of a loaf. But with an aura-reading yogi for a stepmom and an insightful spitfire of a little sister, it was par for the course in his household.

"More like Briggs is sending a message," Tula clarified. "He called the house's landline last night and told Daddy he was sorry to bother us during our break but that he needed to talk to you. And Daddy said, 'now the *boyo* isn't answering your calls either?'"

Sebastian flinched. His father had every right to be mad. Last week, his playboy son had blown off a call—a damned important call.

"Mibby told Daddy to take five big breaths," Tula continued. "You better be careful, Sebby. You've been double *boyo-ed*, and you've got some crazy energy, *and* you should probably eat something. And about Phoebe . . . there's something else I need to tell you."

What else did Tula know about Phoebe?

His heart hammered. "Okay, Tula, I'm listening."

"Oh no!" the kid whisper-shouted. "It's Daddy. Gotta go."

And then she was gone.

What a way to end a call.

Lightheaded from the whirlwind of an exchange, he set Tula's super-secret burner phone on the bedside table and picked up his cracked device. He pressed the button, not even sure if the banged-up piece of tech would work, but miraculously, the phone came to life.

"Look at that," he remarked, then damn near dropped it again when a message blinked across the splintered screen. He'd missed seventy-three calls from his publicist. Barely a second had passed before the phone dinged and Briggs Keaton's name flashed across the damaged screen.

Tula wasn't kidding. The man appeared to have one hell of a bee in his bonnet, but he couldn't understand the guy's urgency. The meetings Briggs had set up weren't for another day—and the rest of the appointments were scheduled for next week.

Play it casual.

Briggs was a good guy—a little on the high-strung side, but a good man, nevertheless.

Sebastian picked up the call. "Hey, Briggsy, how are you?"

"How am I?" Briggs fired back in a puffed-up British accent coated with blistering exasperation. "I'm bloody terrible. I have a client on the verge of pissing away his chance to make a name for himself. Oh, and it appears he's also a misogynistic wanker who steals cabs meant for little girls."

Sebastian's jaw dropped. "What are you talking about?"

Chapter 4
SEBASTIAN

Misogynistic wanker?

Stealing cars meant for little girls?

Sebastian's mouth hung open like a perplexed flounder. Had Briggs lost his mind?

Wait! Maybe the man hadn't.

First, Tula had mentioned a news alert about tweens, and now Briggs was making wild accusations about kids and cabs. Could they be related? Too bad his addled mind couldn't connect the dots.

"Briggs, I can't make heads or tails of what you're saying. I took two cabs yesterday. One brought me home from . . ." He couldn't say *the bar*. "From a restaurant near the airport," he continued. "And before that, I'd hopped in a cab at the airport in the pouring rain with a gaggle of people chasing me. It was a bloody circus," he lobbed back, falling into the cadence of his childhood accent. He took a breath. "And I sure as hell didn't *steal* an automobile from anybody—let alone little girls. Help me understand why my publicist would call me a misogynistic wanker."

"Stand by," Briggs snapped.

A series of chimes dinged on Sebastian's cell as text after text stacked up like planes lining up for takeoff. He scrolled through the mix of pictures and headline screengrabs.

Internet's Sexiest Man Leaves Girls Crying in the Rain

British Beast's Playboy Son Snubs Children

An unsettling heaviness set in as he thumbed through picture after picture. He seemed to be guilty of what the headlines had proclaimed. He hit play on a video, and a knot twisted in his belly. Looking like the King of the Playboy Douchebags, he stared at the screen, watching as he strode past three girls carrying a bulky cardboard box. They looked a little older than Tula—probably eleven or twelve.

Tweens! *Shit!*

Now the alerts made sense. The muscles at the base of his neck tightened. The video caught him ignoring the struggling kids. Instead, he'd shielded his eyes from the rain and dropped his cell. The recording caught him swearing under his breath as he scooped up the phone. He'd been assessing the damage when a cab pulled up to the curb. The girls started for it, but he'd bypassed the queue. *Dammit!* He hadn't even noticed the line—or the girls.

"You cut off the kids and their chaperone and nicked their cab," Briggs supplied. "It made them late to their Tech Tweens Fall Festival."

Sebastian pinched the bridge of his nose. "Who are the Tech Tweens?"

"It's a robotics club for tween girls aged ten to twelve. The older girls, the twelve-year-olds, gather every year. They work on projects and sell cookies to try to earn enough money to go to Disneyland. The box they were holding contained their project. They were supposed to be in a video with other Tech Tweens and missed out because you took the last cab before a bus had a tire blowout. It skidded and came to a halt, blocking traffic into the airport's arrivals area."

This incident had to be plastered on every celebrity gossip site. He could picture the video views skyrocketing and his reputation tanking.

"Briggsy, I didn't mean to take their cab. I was being chased through the airport. I barely knew up from down. I just wanted to get out of there." He watched the video again. "Bollocks," he rasped, again sliding into his old accent.

"*Bollocks* is bloody spot-on, lad. Nearly everyone I had scheduled to meet with you canceled."

Sebastian braced himself. This couldn't be happening—not when he was on the cusp of turning over a new leaf.

"Who's left?" he asked, manifesting positivity. That's what Mibby would want him to do. He pictured his stepmother's serene expression. If she were here, she'd tell him to breathe, center himself, and set an intention toward fulfilling his destiny.

"That's why I've been trying to get ahold of you, Seb," Briggs replied, his voice rising an anxious octave. "I was able to talk one group of investors into meeting with you."

Hallelujah! It only took one.

"Thank you, Briggsy," he gushed while mentally high-fiving his killer manifestation skills.

"But your meeting is in twenty minutes."

Sebastian fell over as his whole world went topsy-turvy.

Goodbye, killer manifestation skills. Hello, Panic City.

He got himself upright and broke out into a cold sweat. "Twenty minutes? I don't think I could even make it to the kitchen in twenty minutes. I'm—"

"Still sloshed," Briggs challenged.

Shit.

Sebastian tugged at his collar. "I'm not drunk. I might have had a few drinks last night at the restaurant to take the edge off. But there's nothing wrong with that. I wasn't partying."

Briggs didn't reply.

Could the man have believed him?

Sebastian hoped he was in the clear. He'd nearly breathed a sigh of relief when his phone chimed with an incoming text. He stared at a picture of himself—a picture of himself seated at a table littered with empty shot glasses. That would be bad enough, but this photo caught him the moment some drunk chick plopped onto his lap for her friends to snap a pic.

He dropped his chin to his chest and closed his eyes.

Welcome home, Sebastian Cress. The world thinks you're a playboy screw-up, and you're not doing a hell of a lot to prove them wrong.

"You've got to make this meeting, Sebastian," Briggs said, his tone sharpening. "My credibility is on the line just as much as yours, mate. I'll send you the address."

Sebastian opened his eyes as his phone pinged the location. He stared at the map on his screen. The appointment wasn't far from Phoebe's place. That had to be a good sign. He could pop in and see her after and, hopefully, share some good news. He could apologize for being a real prick these past six months. He pictured her smiling the smile that only graced her lips when he made her laugh. The smile that was for him and him alone.

"Sebastian," Briggs clucked like an angry hen.

"Yeah," he replied, pushing aside thoughts of Phoebe's chestnut-colored hair and sparkling blue eyes. "I see the address, Briggsy. I'll leave now."

"And before I let you go, I should tell you there's some good news—a possible backup plan."

"Let's hear it."

"I pulled some strings and snagged you an invitation to the Lifestyle Entertainment Technology and Innovation Symposium. Suppose things don't go well at the meeting. In that case, the symposium will allow you to bump elbows with investors in a secluded environment. It's being held at a luxury lodge in the mountains a few hours from Denver. It's the real deal. Several start-ups and entrepreneurs have secured funding after attending. It's your chance to show people who you really are. It starts tomorrow and runs through the weekend. Just don't act like a—"

"Misogynistic wanker," Sebastian lobbed back in his father's cheeky accent.

Briggs chuckled. "I see we understand each other. Let's hope this *LETIS* event is everything people say it is. It wouldn't hurt to have multiple investors partnering with you."

Sebastian gasped as Briggs's words penetrated his muddled brain. "Briggsy, are you talking about LETIS, spelled *L-E-T-I-S*?"

Phoebe had mentioned this event. He hadn't even realized his life-coaching field could collide with her tech world. But they were both innovators in their respective fields.

"Brilliant, mate, you know it," Briggs answered with a little less dread in his tone. "I'll forward you the email with the details. And Sebastian?"

"Yeah, Briggs."

For a beat, his PR agent remained silent. "You're a good lad."

Sebastian held his breath. "And?" he asked, waiting for the other shoe to drop.

"And . . . I know things have been strained with your father. Just remember, he wants you to succeed, Sebby. He probably wants that more than anyone else."

Sebastian swallowed hard. Briggs was right. His father loved him fiercely. He knew this with every fiber of his being. That's why he had to make this work.

"I better get going. I don't want to be late." He paused. "Wait, there's one more thing." Sebastian pinched the bridge of his nose and paced the length of his room. "Thank you. I owe you, Briggs."

"Bloody right you do. Now, don't muck it up, lad," Briggs replied, then ended the call.

Don't muck it up should be his new motto.

Sebastian glanced at his bedside table. Knowing he could use all the positive juju he could get, he gathered the aquamarine stone and the watch with his mum's picture and slipped the items into his pocket. He turned, trying to figure out what he needed, caught a glimpse of himself in the mirror attached to his dresser, and . . . *yikes*. He raked his fingers through his honey-brown hair, grateful he'd had it cut short. It might not look like a rat's nest, but it also couldn't hide his scratchy, red eyes. Decent hair. Bad eyes. Maybe they'd cancel each other out.

Forget about the negatives. Manifest positivity.

He schooled his expression. In the dim light, he peered at the man in front of him. At least he was dressed—wrinkled and slightly disheveled but dressed.

Score a point for passing out fully clothed.

He scanned his room, spied his oversized pack, and slung it over his shoulder. He hadn't even opened it since he'd gotten home, but his notes were somewhere inside, and he should have them, just in case. More likely than not, he'd have to wing it. But he could do that. He believed in helping people. The dream that had rocked his world and plucked him from the brink made that clear to him. This was what he was supposed to do. Now, he had to articulate his passion and prove he had the drive to make it happen.

And not waste another second.

He raced into the bathroom, squirted a bit of toothpaste on his finger, and rubbed it around his mouth. He wouldn't be earning high marks on hygiene, but he couldn't go into a meeting with his breath smelling like a cantina.

With his appearance and scent passable, he bolted downstairs and headed for the garage. But he came to a screeching halt when he reached the door and found a light blue note taped to it.

Hello, my sweet Sebastian,

When you read this note, I hope the color blue brings you peace and tranquility. Also, I wanted to let you know your car is in the shop.

Namaste,

Mibby

He'd have to take another car. Mibby's SUV should be in the garage. There was a good chance his family had driven to Rickety Rock in his dad's car. He glanced at the rack that held their car keys and frowned. There wasn't a set of keys in sight.

Oh no!

He swung open the door and found it like the rack. Empty.

Shit! Mibby and his dad must have driven separately.

He pressed the button to open the garage door, praying he could manifest a car to materialize in the driveway.

Yeah, that didn't work.

He didn't have time for this. Even if he called for a car, it could take twenty minutes before it arrived. He paced around the cavernous space when a splash of hot pink caught his eye. He turned to find Tula's electric kick scooter.

"Dammit," he whispered, knowing what had to be done.

He whipped the matching pink helmet from where it hung on the glittery handlebars, smashed the damned thing onto his head like he was stuffing a watermelon into a thimble, then eyed the completely ridiculous and totally inappropriate form of transportation for a grown-ass man.

"This meeting better be worth it." He positioned his big foot on the slim board, turned on the power, then zipped off into the sunset, looking like a goddamned lunatic.

♥♥

"DUDE, you're too big for that kiddie scooter."

No shit, Sherlock.

Sebastian struggled to remain upright as he clutched the electric kick scooter's sparkly handlebars and ignored what had to be the tenth person to call out to him. And it wasn't like he could make a speedy getaway either. He'd be surprised if he were going twenty miles per hour. He tightened his core muscles. His toned abs were the only thing that kept him from wiping out. He glanced at his feet. Tula's nickname for him had never been more spot-on than it was at this very second. He could barely fit one of his size fourteen feet on the kick-board. That left the other foot cocked in the air the way actresses kicked up their heels when being kissed by their Prince or Princess Charming in the movies.

Forget about big feet and focus.

He trained his gaze on the road and buzzed by a restaurant. And for the eleventh time in a little under twenty minutes, he ignored another round of "Dude, that scooter is too small for you" bullshit.

"Hang on. You're almost there," he murmured, opening his pie hole, which was a mistake. His body heaved as something small and crittery entered his mouth. He spat out a gnat or fly. Hell if he knew what creepy winged insect had temporarily resided in his mouth. "Damned bugs," he eked out, only to suck in another. *Ugh!* He stuck out his tongue and blew a raspberry to disperse the unwanted flying visitor just as his stomach grumbled.

Christ, he was hungry, but he wasn't about to start eating insects. The last thing he needed was to present to a group of investors with a moth or a mosquito stuck between his teeth. *Double ugh!* The thought of that vomit-inducing image had his belly doing somersaults.

He pressed his lips into a hard line and thanked the universe when the building he was looking for came into view and his phone pinged his arrival. He cut the scooter's power, and the ridiculous mode of transportation stopped. A few people passing by did a double take, but blessedly, they didn't comment.

Forget about them and get your head in the game.

He propped the tiny scooter against the side of the structure and arched his back. His spine crackled and popped like a bowl of rice crisp cereal the second the milk hit. It would take a solid ninety-minute yoga session to get him back into alignment. He slipped his phone from his pocket and checked the time. He didn't even have two minutes for a restorative stretch. His meeting was in sixty seconds.

He barreled up a trio of steps, burst through the door, and spied a smartly dressed man seated at a glass desk surrounded by a sea of creamy white walls with a cursive *M* printed in gold.

Gracefully, the man folded his hands. "Sebastian Cress?" he purred in a French accent.

"That's me. I'm here to meet with the . . ." He glanced at his phone. It was a French word. Phoebe had studied French in high school. She'd know how to pronounce it. All he could do was hope he didn't butcher the word. "The *Marieuse* Group," he stated as an alert popped up. Five missed calls from Oscar. Then a text flashed on the screen.

WHERE ARE YOU, MAN? CALL ME!

What was going on with Oscar? It wasn't like him to slide into all caps.

Sebastian looked up from his phone and offered the man at the desk a weak smile. He couldn't bang out a text in front of this guy. It would be rude. The best he could do was ping Oscar his location. He tapped the icon, then turned off his phone.

The elegant man cleared his throat. "May I take your head covering?"

Sebastian stuffed his phone into his pocket and eyed the man. "Head covering?"

"Your helmet," the man clarified, coming to his feet. "Might I say the color suits you?"

Shit! Sebastian reached up and tapped his fingertips against the hardened plastic. How could he have forgotten to take it off? First impressions mattered a hell of a lot, and he couldn't screw this up.

Donning what he hoped was a pleasant expression and not the look of a deranged psychopath, he undid the chin strap and proceeded to inch the damned thing off, which was no easy endeavor. Had his brain swelled in the nineteen minutes it took to get there? He twisted and coaxed the hard plastic until . . . *pop*. He was free of the binding like an elephant emerging from an acorn.

He glanced at the helmet, then forced himself to project confidence—well, project as much confidence as a man could who'd rolled in with a hot pink dome molded to his noggin. He widened his stance, taking up more space—a full-on alpha move. "I'll keep the helmet with me. It's no trouble."

The hint of a grin pulled at the corners of the man's lips. "But of course."

Sebastian couldn't blame the guy for being amused. If he wasn't so desperate, he'd be laughing about the helmet, too. But he had to exude strength and composure. That's why he was there—to sell an image, personify a balanced life, and model success. He was there to be the poster guy for what people aspired to be. There was about to be a hell of a lot of fake-it-before-you-make-it. But that was okay. It was part of the process.

"This way, Monsieur Cress." The Frenchman led him down an ivory hallway decked with chic modern art on the walls and brass light fixtures adorned with crystals.

So far, so good. This Marieuse Group appeared to be the real deal.

"Through there." The man gestured to a frosted glass door with Claudette Marieuse and Bernadette Marieuse printed in swooping gold letters.

He nodded to the man and watched him head back to his desk.

This was it.

Sebastian smoothed his shirt, then slipped his hand into his pocket. He brushed his fingertips against the watch and the stone, gleaning their energy. "Manifest success. Trust that what's meant to be will be," he whispered to himself when his belly growled.

Dammit! Maybe he should have eaten a bug.

Stop screwing around.

He inhaled a cleansing breath, willed his empty stomach to shut the hell up, then opened the door. The room mirrored the chic white décor of the hallway. Two women, who looked to be in their forties or early fifties, sat at the end of a long rectangular table. He blinked. He wasn't sure he could believe his eyes. Was he seeing double thanks to shit sleep and a raging hangover? No, he wasn't. The women were identical twins. Dressed in matching black blouses with their dark hair piled on top of their heads in tight buns, the women had a Prima Ballerina don't-mess-with-me air about them. A young woman dressed in white with her dark hair in the same style stood in the corner with a cell phone pressed to her ear.

"Sebastian, please, come in. I'm Claudette, and this is my sister, Bernadette. Welcome to the Marieuse Group," the woman said in a breathy French accent.

This had to be a good sign. His aunts were identical twins. They were married to Mibby's brothers, who were also identical twins. He had a strong connection to the twins in his life.

Okay, universe, this was promising.

Bernadette made eye contact with the lady in white, and the young woman nodded.

Bernadette flicked her gaze to him. "Why should we invest in you? What sets you apart, Sebastian Cress?"

Diving right to business. That was another positive development. Not to mention, while Claudette and Bernadette weren't smiling ear to ear, these women didn't glare at him like he was a misogynistic wanker who enjoyed making twelve-year-old girls cry. Maybe they hadn't seen the unflattering coverage.

Look at that—another boost from the universe.

He relaxed a fraction, then glanced between the sisters. "I want people to live happier, more satisfying lives. I'd like you to invest in my life-coaching business to do just that. With proper funding, I can share my expertise through multiple outlets, such as online venues, print and e-book formats, and in-person events. It's a lucrative endeavor. Self-improvement is a fifteen-billion-dollar industry with eight percent yearly gains. With your help, we can carve out a piece for ourselves while doing real good for real people. In essence, we'll be changing lives for the better."

Boom! Succinct and to the point.

"Why do you need our money, Sebastian?" Bernadette pressed. "Your parents are rich and famous. Your father is a former champion boxer, co-creator of Pun-chi yoga, and now a philanthropist, and your stepmother, Libby Lamb-Cress, is not only the other half of creating Pun-chi yoga, she's also the face of female sexual empowerment."

He was ready for this question. "That's true, but I'm committed to building a business independently, without using my family's connections."

"Do you recommend sex toys in your life-coaching business model?" Bernadette pressed, then raised an eyebrow.

"What?" he stammered. He hadn't even considered anyone asking this question.

He almost dropped the helmet as a memory resurfaced. In it, he recalled the day after he'd turned thirteen. Mibby and his father had asked him to join them at the kitchen table. His parents then explained he was old enough to learn the true purpose of the toy Mibby's company made. He'd thought it was a submarine water toy—and a cool one at that! When they'd explained it was a sexual gratification device called the Wham Bam Thank You Libby Lamb Deluxe Vibrator, his brain exploded. Okay, it didn't exactly explode, but sweet Jesus, it felt like it had melted into a pile of mortified goo.

"No bloody way," he cried in a mish-mashy British-American accent, which was also the exclamation he'd blurted after his parents had asked him if he wanted to talk more about sex toys.

Claudette frowned. "You do not believe in women empowering themselves sexually? You say you want to help people live better lives. Does that not include one's intimate life?"

Had it gotten hot in there?

He hadn't delved into the sexual empowerment side of life coaching, per se. But he had to address the question. He shifted his stance. "I support people enjoying sex. I've had sex with many, many, many women. Tons of them. They've all left satisfied. Believe me, I didn't need to seek out experts to know what to do in the bedroom to help people gain more confidence in that area of their life."

Claudette and Bernadette's gazes dropped below his belt.

He might have gone overboard with that explanation. And more than that. What was he doing—persuading them to invest in his life-coaching business, or had he switched fields in the last five seconds and plunged into the male escort arena? He had to get this meeting back on track—a track where he didn't sound like a womanizing man-whore.

"My philosophy for maximizing confidence and empowerment," he continued, doing his best not to sound like a gigolo, "can be utilized in every aspect of a person's life—professional and personal. I grew up steeped in fitness and mindfulness. My master's degree in business has afforded me the knowledge to strategically target a broad audience. It also assists me in guiding those wanting to start their own companies. The sky's the limit. I guarantee, I'm presenting a worthwhile investment. You just have to believe in me."

That certainly sounded good, but did he believe in himself? He was currently working overtime to make it seem like he did.

Claudette narrowed her gaze. "Is there a unifying theme to your life-coaching plan? Something that hasn't been offered. A fresh take, if you will."

Despite being grateful for transitioning away from vibrator talk, this topic might be even worse. He had volumes of knowledge, but he hadn't distilled the information as succinctly as he'd wanted. Project Confidence was too vague. But he couldn't say that. "I can cite articles and expert opinions. I've traveled the world, meeting one-on-one with researchers at the top of the health, fitness, psychology, and business fields."

Bernadette shared a look with her sister and pursed her lips. "Have you seen the results of your particular style of life-coaching with a test subject or subjects?"

A lump formed in his throat.

The short answer to Bernadette's question was no.

The day he'd read Phoebe's text and his life had gone to shit, he was supposed to meet with a chef that morning. In the afternoon, he'd scheduled time to work on recruiting subjects. He'd bailed on the former and blown off the latter. But he couldn't divulge that info.

Asserting confidence, he looked between the women. "That piece of my program is in progress."

It wasn't a complete lie. He'd planned on testing his theory. He just hadn't gotten there yet.

Claudette frowned and jotted a note on a pad of paper.

Dammit! He needed to assure them he was the real deal. What he needed to do was accentuate the positives. That's what he'd coach a test subject to do—play their strongest card.

"Along with my knowledge base," he began, "I should mention that I have quite a following on social media. My brand has generated tremendous interest and awareness. The desire is there."

"We've seen your social media pages," Claudette answered as her gaze dropped below his belt again. "There is, as you say, significant desire."

Was he there so they could ogle him? Had one of these women—or both—messaged him about carrying his baby? It sure seemed like it. And dammit, he was back to the gigolo zone.

The woman in white on the phone, who he'd completely forgotten was there, stepped forward. "*Madame Bernadette, Madame Claudette, le partenaire silencieux*."

He didn't have to speak French to understand that the woman had mentioned a silent partner.

Bernadette held out her hand, and the woman in white slipped her the cell phone. "Our associate, Angelique, is on the phone with a member of our investment group who chooses to remain anonymous." She pressed the cell to her ear. "*Oui?*" She nodded as whoever was on the other end of the call spoke. The conversation was brief. Barely ten seconds had passed before she returned the phone to the ivory-clad associate.

Bernadette folded her hands on the table and shared a curious look with Claudette, who mirrored the position.

"You have a week, Sebastian Cress," Bernadette announced.

"A week to . . ." He trailed off. He had no idea what she was talking about and sure as hell didn't want to sound like an idiot or say something that would make him—again—sound like a male escort.

"A week to produce data or a case study. A before-and-after transformation, thanks to your life-coaching expertise," Bernadette explained.

"That should not be a problem since your testing is in progress, *oui*?" Claudette quipped.

With the investors in black staring him down, he pictured his mother. This was his shot. She'd come to him in his sleep and had led him here. She'd want him to take this opportunity. She'd want him to be the man he was supposed to be. A week ago, he'd gotten her message loud and clear.

His heart pounded, but he maintained his composure. "It won't be a problem at all."

"Excellent!" Bernadette remarked with a wave of her hand. "My sister and I have a busy schedule over the next several days. We can meet when we return and evaluate your data."

As if on cue, the Frenchman who'd led him to the meeting room opened the door.

"We'll be in touch. Giles will see you out," Claudette directed.

Holy shit! And there it was—the break he so desperately needed.

Sebastian nodded to Giles, then returned his attention to the sisters. "Thank you for taking a chance on me."

The twins shared another curious look.

"Don't thank us yet, Sebastian Cress," Claudette answered with a twist to her lips.

She was right. Everything hinged on his ability to produce results. How the hell was he going to do that in a week?

"Right, I'll have that case study polished up and ready for you to review." With his thoughts swirling and his heart pounding, he left the room and followed Giles down the hallway.

The man glanced over his shoulder. "Your friend is here, Monsieur Cress."

A friend?

The cyclone of questions and possible solutions ricocheting through Sebastian's brain came to a crashing halt. "I'm not sure I understand. I'm not expecting anyone."

Giles walked around his glass desk and took a seat. "Someone quite agitated, who calls themself your friend, entered the building looking for you. I told them you'd be out shortly."

Who could it be?

Sebastian thanked the man, then opened the door and got his answer.

Oscar Elliott paced in front of the building. Sebastian had pinged him the address, but he hadn't expected the guy to rush over. This, however, wasn't a casual how-are-you-doing visit. With a cigarette hanging from Oscar's lips, that meant one thing. Shit had hit the fan, and his best friend was stressed to the max.

"That's a terrible habit," Sebastian called, descending the trio of steps and trying to get a read on the guy.

Oscar exhaled a stream of smoke, then held up the cigarette. "I wouldn't have to do this if you'd answer your damned phone."

"I was in a meeting. And by the way, hello! It's great to see you, old pal. It's been a while," Sebastian deadpanned. And then it hit. Oscar had to be there because of the negative press. "If you're here because you read about me stealing a cab from a bunch of little tech-loving girls, rest assured it was a huge misunderstanding. I'd never—"

Oscar waved his hand and cut off his explanation. "I'm not here about that. We don't have time to discuss that clusterfuck of a video." His friend pointed to the scooter. "That's Tula's, right?"

Sebastian eyed the tiny mode of transportation. "Yeah, how'd you know?"

Oscar touched the sparkly handlebars. "Ivy has the same one. What are you doing with it?"

Sebastian held up the helmet. "I rode it here." He waited for Oscar to burst out laughing, but the man didn't even crack a smile.

His agitated friend took another drag off his smoke, then dropped it onto the sidewalk and ground it out with his foot. He paced in front of Tula's scooter. "Okay, we can deal with that."

Had the guy lost it?

Oscar Elliott could be the epitome of the moody, brooding artist, but something else weighed heavy on the man. His friend paced like a caged animal and nodded like he was going over a plan in his head. He gestured toward the street. "I've got my truck. I'll drop the scooter off at your house on my way out of town."

Sebastian looked the guy over, trying to assess if he had head trauma. "You're here to return my sister's scooter because you're leaving town?"

Oscar stopped pacing and met his gaze. "No, Seb, I'm here because of Phoebe."

"Phoebe," Sebastian whispered as a burst of adrenaline coursed through him. "What about her?"

Concern welled in Oscar's eyes. He raked his hands through his tangle of brown hair. "It's not good, man. She needs you. She needs your help. And she needs it now."

Chapter 5
SEBASTIAN

The muscles in Sebastian's chest tightened. "Is Phoebe okay? Is she in danger? Is she hurt?" He barely knew what was going on in her life. He hated himself for putting distance between them these past six months. He'd been an ass and a terrible friend. If she needed anything, he owed it to her to do whatever it took to make sure she was all right.

"First, I need you to turn on your damn phone," Oscar quipped.

His phone?

Sebastian shook his head in disbelief. "You're going to show up at my appointment like a psycho ex, lob a *Phoebe-needs-help* bomb at me, and then insist I turn on my phone before you say anything else?"

"Yes," Oscar shot back with a distinct edge to his voice. "And give me Tula's helmet."

Sebastian handed him the hot pink head covering, pulled his cell from his pocket, and powered it up. Vibrating with anxious energy, he stared at the screen.

MISSED GROUP VIDEO CHAT WITH PHOEBE GALE,
OSCAR ELLIOTT, AND ARIA PAIGE-GRANT.
RECORDING AVAILABLE.

He looked up from his cell. "I missed a group video chat. That's the Phoebe emergency?"

That couldn't be it. The cigarettes and the rigid set of Oscar's jaw told him that much.

Oscar set Tula's scooter in the bed of his truck, then released a heavy sigh. "What you missed was Phoebe recording and basically livestreaming Jeremy, the drooler, dumping her in the worst way possible. Aria had to get off the call before Phoebe met up with Jeremy. I was the only one on with her. I heard everything. I was in the foothills photographing the fall colors when I heard it go to shit. I drove like a maniac to get back to Denver to be with her. But I can't stay. That's why I need your help."

Sebastian's stomach dropped. "I'll do whatever you need me to do. But Phoebe and Jeremy weren't together like together-together, were they?"

Phoebe couldn't have given this guy her heart, could she?

Oscar threw up his hands. "I don't know what they were. Phoebe was into him. He'd texted her and said he wanted to meet. She thought he was going to ask her to take things to the next level—whatever that meant. Instead, he told her he was only with her because he hoped he could get in with her uncle and aunt at Gale Tech."

"He used her?" Sebastian spat.

Oscar ran his hands down his face. "Yeah."

"Dammit," Sebastian hissed under his breath. "I knew that guy was a wanker. I could feel it."

"The guy is a grade A asshole. But—to be fair—you've never liked anyone she's dated," Oscar replied, then glanced at his phone.

Sebastian scoffed. "That's not true. I liked . . ."

Shit! Oscar was right.

"It gets worse," Oscar continued. "Jeremy couldn't take the high road and tell her some bullshit like they were better off as friends."

"What did he say?"

Color rose to Oscar's cheeks. "He told her she wasn't the kind of girl any guy wanted to date."

"He said that? That's bloody bullshit," he shot back, anger slicing through his reply as he slipped into his old accent.

"It's a mess," Oscar continued. "She was excited because she'd been asked to attend that LETIS retreat. Jeremy had already gotten in, and she thought her getting invited would be a sign that he was her . . ." Oscar paused. "Her match."

Match.

The word dropped like a lead weight.

Being another person's love match had real meaning to them. His life, along with Aria, Oscar, and Phoebe's, had been inextricably changed—for the better—thanks to nanny love matches. And the matchmaker had told them that their matches had already been made. Sure, it had a kooky hocus-pocus ring to it. But the four of them knew firsthand that the matchmaker's prediction was about as undeniable as one could get when it came to falling in love with *the one*.

The one.

That's what Tula had called Phoebe.

"Jeremy was a douche about LETIS, too," Oscar continued.

Sebastian pushed aside thoughts of Phoebe being the one. "What did he say?"

"He told her he didn't want to hang out with her there, and then the asshat went further and blathered that she probably only got in because they had to fill some women quota."

Sebastian saw red. This dude deserved a one-two punch to the gut. He balled his hand into a fist, then willed himself to cool down as he focused on the other bomb Oscar had dropped. "Phoebe got into LETIS?"

Oscar nodded. "She was over the moon about it."

Sebastian tapped the email icon on his phone and found the email Briggs had forwarded. He held up his cell for Oscar to see. "I got invited to LETIS, too."

Oscar's expression brightened. "That's great news, Seb. You can watch over Phoebe. She'll need it with Jeremy being there."

"Where's the drooler now?"

A smirk pulled at the corners of Oscar's lips. "The guy took off after Phoebe squirted a bottle of Dijon mustard on him."

Sebastian couldn't help but mirror his friend's expression. Jeremy might have broken Phoebe's heart, but he couldn't stamp out her spirit. That was Phoebe Gale. Nobody burned brighter.

Oscar's phone pinged. He glanced at it, and his demeanor darkened. "Listen, you need to get to Phoebe. She's at a bistro a few blocks south of here. You can't miss it—or her. She's on the patio. I'll warn you now, she's hammered. She's been rambling about some random woman who walked by the restaurant, and she kept going on about how she has to come up with a plan and it has to be big."

Sebastian raised an eyebrow. "She's not planning on hacking into the FBI again, is she? She could easily sic them on the drooler."

Oscar chuckled and shook his head. "Jesus, I hope not. I'll never forget when the agents stormed our classroom. But no, I don't think we need to worry about her hacking into any government agency. But she did mention stilettos and duck lips."

Sebastian crossed his arms. "Stilettos and duck lips?"

Before Oscar could reply, his phone pinged. He glanced at the screen again, and a muscle twitched on his cheek.

Sebastian took a step toward his friend. "Who's texting you? They've got you worked up, man."

Oscar exhaled a tight breath. "It's not important. Listen, Phoebe's all over the place. Do whatever it takes to get her home. Thankfully, she doesn't live far from here. I wish I could stay, but I have to go. I have to . . . get somewhere." He held up his phone, but his palm covered the screen.

"You're talking in riddles. And you didn't answer my question. Who's sending you messages?"

"A friend who needs a little help. That's all. It'll be fine." Oscar mustered a grin. "It's good to see you, Seb. We've missed you. And if you see Jeremy, don't kill him. I might be off the grid for a bit, and you won't have anyone to bail you out of jail." His friend was trying to lighten the mood, but the guy was wrecked about something besides Phoebe's situation. He started to open the door to his truck, then stilled. "And don't let Phoebe do anything too crazy."

"This is Phoebe we're talking about. It's bound to be a little bonkers," Sebastian replied as warmth radiated through his chest. How he missed Phoebe's signature sense of open-hearted wonder. From the moment he saw her years ago, staring at him through the car's window with a mischievous sparkle in her eyes, he knew his entire life was about to change.

"True enough, my friend." Oscar gave him a quick salute and hopped into his truck.

And just like that, it was Phoebe or bust time.

Gripping the straps of his pack to steady the load, he jogged down the sidewalk in the direction of the bistro. It only took a few minutes to get there and a few seconds to zero in on Phoebe.

Oscar was correct. She wasn't hard to miss.

Wearing her beret, she sat at a table on the patio littered

with empty martini glasses. She held up her phone and snapped a picture of herself making a face like she'd stuffed her mouth with lemons.

"Phoebe," he called, striding toward her.

She dropped her phone on the table, nearly knocking over a trio of glasses. "Sebby, you're here! You're really here!"

"Yeah, are you okay?" he asked and surveyed the scene.

"I'm more than okay, Seb. Come here." Phoebe waved him in, then took off her glasses and pressed up onto her tiptoes. She rested her hands on his shoulders. "I've got something to show you."

A tingle danced down his spine as her warm breath tickled his chin. "What are you doing, Pheebs?"

"This," she purred. She batted her eyelashes like she'd been caught in a sandstorm, then busted out the lemon-sucker face.

"What am I looking at?" he asked, his voice growing hoarse. What was up with that? They'd been best friends for over a decade and a half. She'd touched him hundreds, no, probably thousands of times over the years. Why was this different?

"You, Sebastian Cress, are basking in my hot-girl face. I've been working on it. The more I *better* the *drink* it gets," Phoebe purr-slurred.

Oscar wasn't kidding. This wasn't tipsy Phoebe. This bordered on hold-my-hair-back, I'm-about-to-part-with-the-contents-of-my-stomach Phoebe.

"The more you *drink*, the *better* it gets," he corrected.

Her face lit up. "You agree."

"Pheebs, Oscar told me what happened with Jeremy. I'm so sorry."

She lowered herself, then wobbled. He gripped her waist and steadied her as she regained her footing.

"Jeremy Drewler is a . . ." She glanced down and tapped her foot five times.

She was bringing out the five-tap big guns.

"You remember what that means, right, Sebby?"

Hell yes, he did.

"Butthole douche nozzle," he whispered conspiratorially.

As a girl, *butt-hole* had been Phoebe's go-to foot tap naughty word of choice, while Aria had gone with the three-syllable *douche noz-zle*. Put them together, and you've got what the girls had deemed the crème de la crème of foot-tap insults.

She abandoned the slightly terrifying hot-girl face. Staring up at him, her bottom lip trembled. Pain flashed in her blue eyes. *Damn that drooling creep*. He stroked her cheek. "Phoebe," he whispered gently.

She held his gaze, and her lips tipped up, gifting him with the ghost of a grin before she shook her head like she'd just snapped out of a trance. She slipped on her glasses. "We're not talking about Jeremy. I'm a woman on a mission, Seb, and the mission is to be more like that." She returned to the duck lip eye-seizure expression. "Look at them," she said, then gestured with her chin toward a table of stylish young women—stylish young women who were pointing their phones toward the beret-wearing woman contorting her face like she was experiencing an exorcism.

He had to get his drunk best friend out of there. "We should go, Pheebs," he suggested, playing it casually.

Phoebe cocked her head to the side. "You don't like my face?"

"It's not that I don't like it. I love your face. I always have. It's—"

"My nerdy French farmer outfit?"

"Your what?" he eked out.

She glanced down the street, eyeing the different businesses' awnings, then snapped her fingers.

"Phoebe, are you sure you're all right?"

She looked around the patio. "Hold on, Seb. Before we leave, I need to say goodbye."

Say goodbye?

He did a quick check of the outdoor dining area. Every pair of eyes was glued to them.

He leaned in and lowered his voice. "Do you really know these people? Maybe we should forget the goodbyes and make a quick exit."

Her eyes welled with tears. "Sebby," she replied, conviction laced into the two syllables, "these people shared a transformational moment with me."

"Yeah, okay." There was no use fighting her. The only thing he could do was brace for the awkwardness impact.

Phoebe picked up a tube-shaped item wrapped in foil—most likely a hot dog—and extended her arms. "Happy hour friends, today you were with me when my dreams of finding my match with my love match hot dog went down the drain."

Sebastian grimaced. Forget awkwardness. This was pure mortification.

"Mustard was squirted, and hearts were bruised but not broken." She paused, possibly for effect, or maybe because she was hammered and had forgotten what the hell she was doing. Recovering, she pressed the wrapped hot dog to her chest. "I want to let you know that I'm okay. You don't have to worry about your girl, Phoebe. My best friend, Sebastian 'Mr. Lickable Abs' Cress, is here."

"Mr. Lickable Abs?" he repeated.

Phoebe blinked, trying to hold his gaze. "What?"

"You called me Sebastian 'Mr. Lickable Abs' Cress."

Her eyes widened. "No, I certainly did not."

Murmurs rippled through the air.

"I thought that was him."

"Did you see that video where he totally snubbed those tech girls?"

"The guy might be hot, but he's a jerk in real life."

Sebastian swallowed hard. The last thing either of them needed was to go viral. They had to hightail it out of this bistro.

"Fine, you didn't call me Mr. Lickable Abs, but it's time for us to go," he conceded, hoping that would get her moving.

"Okay, Seb, but I have to say one last thing."

He scanned the area. Now they had people stopping on the sidewalk to gawk.

"Make it quick," he murmured and scooped up her cell phone and shoved it into his pack.

She lifted a nearly empty martini glass. "Happy hour friends, I raise a drink to you. And . . . please don't believe what it says on Phoebe Gale's Info Darling page. Right here, right now, I'm setting the record straight." His loquacious best friend eyed the foil-wrapped item in her hand, then held it above her head. "I am not attracted to hot dogs."

Oh, fuck.

This would be an excellent time for Mother Nature to send in a few lightning bolts. Instead, a nervous waiter approached.

Sebastian waved the man over. "If it's not patently obvious, I need to get my friend out of here. Does she have a tab I can settle?"

The waiter shook his head. "The bill has been covered by another patron."

"Somebody else paid for these drinks?"

"Yes."

Sebastian glanced inside the bustling bistro. "Who?"

"The person asked to remain anonymous."

That was weird but welcomed.

"What about a tip?" Sebastian reached for his wallet.

The waiter waved him off. "That was taken care of as well. And . . ."

"Yeah?"

"Your friend—"

"Will be fine," he assured the waiter. "I've known her since we were kids. She's in good hands. I'll make sure she gets home safely."

The waiter glanced past him. "That might be easier said than done."

"Why?"

"She just ran off toward the kids selling—"

"Cookies, Seb!" Phoebe called over her shoulder, tearing down the sidewalk with her foil-wrapped hot dog in one hand and a martini glass in the other.

Chapter 6
SEBASTIAN

Sebastian stood there, gobsmacked, watching Phoebe get farther and farther from the bistro. He wasn't sure he could believe his eyes. But one salient fact could not be denied. For a woman who had appeared to have nearly consumed her weight in martinis, she was damned quick on her feet.

And that meant he had to be damned faster to catch her.

He leaped over the low iron railing separating the outdoor eating area from the sidewalk and sprinted down the block. "Phoebe, hold up!" She was headed toward a group of girls seated at a table with stacks of boxes—presumably, the cookies. One girl held up a sign that read Tech Tweens Cookie Fundraisers.

Tech Tweens!

Panic tore through him. He'd have to be the last person they'd want to see.

He kicked up his speed. Running like his life depended on it—because it just might—he caught up to Phoebe. He hooked his arm around her waist and hoisted her into the air as the Tech Tweens looked their way.

"Sebastian Cress," Phoebe squealed, "what are you doing?"

He was saving their asses from a little girl beatdown. That's what he was doing.

Half a block away, the girls came together like a squad of computer-savvy Navy Seals.

"It's him," a blond girl cried.

Trapped, his heart hammered as he scanned the area. He spied a boutique. Surely, the kids wouldn't follow them inside, would they?

He plastered on a grin. "Hey, Pheebs, let's check out this shop."

Tightening his hold on her, he swung open the door, and they crashed into the store. He'd barely recovered when a sharply dressed woman with blond hair sailed toward them.

"Welcome to Denver Diva Day and Night. Are you shopping for day or night apparel?" she pressed, staring down at them like it was normal for shoppers to dive into her store like stuntmen filming an action movie.

"Um . . ." he stammered. He had to play it cool. He needed to buy them some time. He looked back and forth, taking in the unique space. One side of the shop was painted white with an array of stylish women's clothing, while the other side was jet-black with—*holy hell*—some damned hot lingerie.

Phoebe wiggled against him. "Night!" she chirped, her feet still dangling. She tugged on his shirt. "This place is perfect, Seb. Put me down."

He glanced over his shoulder. Blessedly, there weren't any irate twelve-year-olds clawing at the door. He breathed a sigh of relief and complied with Phoebe's request.

She handed him her hot dog and the empty martini glass, then dusted herself off and adjusted her beret. She gifted the saleswoman with a sloppy grin, then gasped. "Mustard scarf," she announced, pointing to the saleswoman's accessory like she was caught in a solo drunken game of *I Spy*.

The woman touched the fabric with a quizzical expression. "Are you in the market for a scarf?"

"I was at the bistro down the street. I saw you walk by. This must be a sign. You're the person I need to help me pick out something super-duper sexy to go with my new hot-girl face," Phoebe explained, then flashed the duck-lipped eye seizure expression.

"Oh my," the saleswoman yelped, clearly taken aback—and rightly so. That face should come with a warning.

Thanks to being nice and liquored up, Phoebe didn't seem to notice. She made a beeline toward a display of silky lingerie and plucked a pink negligee from the rack. Holding it against her body, she turned toward a mirror and assessed the garment. "What's this called? It reminds me of a sexy minidress."

The clerk came to her side. "That beauty arrived the other day. It's what we call a baby doll. Billowy on the bottom and fitted on top to accentuate the breasts. It's sweet and sexy, wrapped up into one sensual number. It's an excellent choice for your frame. The bow will accentuate your bust, which is quite enviable."

Phoebe lit up. "Did you hear that, Sebby? My new lingerie friend says I have an enviable bust."

Oh, he heard it. He nodded. It was all he could do as he observed his friend shop for sexy lingerie.

Phoebe. Sexy. Lingerie.

He'd never put those three words together in his head. And why would he? He could never, ever think of her like that. Still, he couldn't look away or stop the rush sweeping through him as the blood in his brain diverted to the south. *No, no, no!* Dammit, he couldn't help himself. Unable to stop biology—or in this case, sex ed—he pictured her wearing the skimpy number. He could see her now, smooth silk clinging to her body. Lace tracing her curves and giving a teasing glimpse of her round, ripe, oh-so grabbable—

"Hey, Sebby?"

"Uh-huh?" he shrieked like a prepubescent schoolboy, almost dropping the hot dog and martini glass. So damned grateful he was wearing loose-fitting jeans, he shifted his stance. "I wasn't thinking about what you'd look like in that," he blathered like an idiot.

She dangled the negligee in front of him. "You don't have to imagine, Seb. You'll know soon enough."

"I will?" he yipped, his voice rising like a choirboy.

Her lips curled into a naughty little grin. "Oh yeah, because . . ."

He took a step toward her. "Yes?"

"I'm going to try it on," Phoebe cheered like she'd just won the lottery. She took a few wobbly steps, then stopped in front of a pair of pink glittery high heels. "With these," she exclaimed, uprooting the alluring footwear from the display.

The saleswoman led Phoebe to the back of the shop, and the women disappeared behind a black velvet curtain.

Deflating like a punctured balloon, he sank onto a display cube next to a headless body sporting a chic tan trench coat. He exhaled a weary breath and set the glass and hot dog next to him. *Jesus, what a day.* Still, he needed to pull himself together and be there for Phoebe. A question percolated in his head. How would he coach a client in his situation? He drummed his fingertips on his thigh, then snapped his fingers. He knew what to do. To be at one's best, he'd encourage the client to focus on the positives—only then could the person get out of their head and be able to focus on their goals.

And what were his positives? He had a potential investor. That was no small feat. Everything hinged on his ability to generate a case study in a matter of days, but he'd figure it out and manifest his destiny.

Other positives? He couldn't stop a smile from blooming. He was back in Denver, and he was with Phoebe. *He was home.* Fizzy joy bubbled from within, but it came with sound effects. His stomach growled. Gnarly and frighteningly guttural, it sounded like a ravenous bear emerging from hibernation.

"Is that you, Seb?" Phoebe called.

"No, it must have been a motorcycle or something outside," he white-lied, then eyed the wrapped hot dog.

His stomach emitted another rumble. If he didn't get something inside it, he could look forward to a wicked bout of dry heaving. He glanced at the closed velvet curtains and then returned his attention to the portable meal. Was it the healthiest of choices? Not really, but Christ, it smelled damned delicious. With his belly on the verge of spasming, he kept one eye on Phoebe's dressing area as he quietly peeled back the foil.

One little bite would do the trick. Just one. Phoebe wouldn't mind. She'd probably forgotten about the wrapped delight in her current state.

He gazed at the food masterpiece. This wasn't your run-of-the-mill frank in a bun. No, this was a gourmet hot dog, probably from an acclaimed Denver food truck. This city nailed it when it came to killer street food, and Phoebe's app made it easier for his friend to find her beloved favorite.

Eat me, Sebastian.

He licked his lips. It appeared he'd hit the hallucination portion of his hangover-meet-hunger condition. His mouth watered. He was no drooler, but he'd be slobbering like a Saint Bernard if he didn't get this beauty past his lips. With another quick check of the curtain, he peeled the foil back farther. His stomach was on the verge of launching into a series of somersaults. "Come to papa," he murmured like a creepy weirdo. He opened his mouth and attacked that dog the way a great white shark tears into whatever the hell great white sharks ate—probably fish or seals. He was too damned hungry to care because, hello, he was in the midst of a food orgasm.

He'd eaten a lot of hot dogs in his day. Anyone in Phoebe's orbit had. It was like a pre-req to gaining her friendship. But this hot dog was like tasting the treat for the first time. The flavors melded together, marrying scent, taste, and touch into one hot-doggity-delicious symphony of sensations. He'd eaten the world's finest cuisine, but nothing compared to this.

"Sebastian?"

"Mm-hmm," he hummed and bolted upright. It was near impossible to talk with six inches of hot dog bliss crammed into his mouth. And was that a brioche bun? It had to be. It tasted damned delicious!

Focus! Phoebe is calling.

He went to work, chewing like a voracious Great White Shark, then swallowed the meal in one giant gulp. He stared at the foil wrapper that left no trace of the delectable hot dog it had once housed. He stuffed the wrapper into his pocket with the watch and stone.

"I need your opinion, Seb. Can you come back here?"

He looked up as the phone near the register rang, and the clerk departed the changing area, leaving Phoebe alone.

"Okay," he answered, running his tongue across his teeth, feeling for speed-dash-dinner remnants.

Phoebe pulled back the curtain, only revealing her head and bare shoulders. She'd removed her beret and shook out her braid. Her loose chestnut locks kissed her collarbone. "You can't laugh," she slur-threatened.

"Pheebs, you know I won't."

She chewed her lip, then whipped the entire curtain out of the way . . . and good God! She was . . . she looked . . . He couldn't form a cohesive thought to save his life.

"Is this what you like—I mean, what guys like?" Phoebe asked. Her bottom lip trembled just as it had at the bistro.

"What guys like?" he stammered, parroting back her words.

Moment of truth. He'd slept with glamorous models and socialites. He hadn't lied when he'd garbled that admission at his interview with the Marieuse sisters. But he'd never been rendered speechless by a woman's beauty . . .

. . . until now.

Clad in pink, Phoebe Gale was an absolute goddess.

A goddess who was his friend.

His childhood best friend.

He could not think about sleeping with her.

Shit! He'd thought about it.

It had to be his addled mind and killer hangover making him forget that she wasn't meant for him—not like that.

"Seb?" she breathed. "Do you think it suits me?"

He stared at a smudge on the wall just past her shoulder. "Generally speaking, or are you talking color or choice of fabric?" Baggy jeans were not going to hide the evidence of how he felt about this sexy ensemble. He went the objective route. "It looks like how lingerie is supposed to look."

Phoebe wobbled out of the dressing room, teetering on the sparkly shoes, and caught a glimpse of herself in an ornate mirror leaning against the wall. She raised her hands in the air. "I've got the Sebastian Cress seal of approval. I'll take the baby doll and the shoes, too."

He turned to find the clerk with a tablet in her hands standing behind him. "That'll be four hundred sixty-nine dollars even. How would you like to pay?"

Phoebe blinked.

"Do you need your phone, Pheebs?"

Phoebe grimaced. "Four-six-nine is greater than six-nine. I have sixty-nine—like wine me, dine me, sixty-nine me."

Putting the whole sixty-nine nuttiness aside, he could barely believe that Phoebe must be lower on cash than he was. But he wasn't about to let her leave empty-handed.

"Pheebs, I saw some earrings over there by the entrance that might work with your outfit. Why don't you take a look, and I'll sort out your sixty-nine situation."

Phoebe patted his cheek. "Sebastian Cress, you are a peach," she finished, then hiccupped before teetering toward the front of the shop.

He flashed the clerk a weak grin. "My friend is feeling a little—"

"You're Sebastian Cress from the internet," the saleswoman interrupted, giving him a once-over.

"Yeah," he answered warily. If someone had asked twenty-four hours ago if he was *the Sebastian Cress*, it would have most likely come with a request to take a picture or get his autograph. Now, he wasn't so sure. Hopefully, this store didn't sell cookies.

"I own this shop," the woman explained. "I'll comp your friend the clothing. In fact, I'll give her anything she wants. But I'd like you to do something for me in exchange." She handed him her business card.

"Such as?"

"Post about my store. It doesn't have to be much. A few lines. You have a massive following, and I could use the publicity."

"That's a generous offer, and I'm happy to do it. But are you sure you want me to post about your business?" He checked on Phoebe and found her near the front by the entrance. He lowered his voice. "I've had some recent negative media coverage."

The owner waved him off. "I saw it, but don't worry. Some singer in a boy band got caught cheating on his girlfriend. It hit the internet thirty minutes ago. It's blowing up online. I haven't seen one post about you hating twelve-year-old girls since the latest online scandal du jour started filtering in."

He stood there, dumbstruck. "Okay."

She checked her watch. "We close in two minutes. I'd appreciate it if you made that post."

"Yeah, all right, sure." He slipped his cell out of his pocket, grateful that, despite it being cracked to hell, it still worked. He banged out a message about finding a gem of a shop that his best friend loved. And look at that. This had to be another sign that his situation was improving. If anyone could use some good juju, it was him.

"I'm craving cookies, Seb," Phoebe called from the front.

He shook his head and chuckled. "You've been craving cookies since you were six years old," he answered without looking up as he tagged the business in his post.

A bell chimed, and he grinned. Another good omen. If Mibby, in her cosmic, spiritual know-all, was there, she'd mention that the random ringing of a bell could be the universe's way of letting one know a new journey was on the horizon.

"Sebastian?" the shop owner said.

"Yes?"

"About your friend."

"Uh-huh." He added a few hashtags to get the shop more exposure, then tapped the post icon to spread the word through his social media accounts.

"She just ran away."

Not again!

He pocketed his phone and the business card as the good juju evaporated.

Wildly, he checked the store. "Phoebe left in nothing but lingerie?"

The woman looked past him out the large front window. "That appears to be the case."

He plucked her beret from the dressing room bench—he didn't have time to gather the rest of her clothes—and started for the door. What the hell was she thinking? Then again, the woman loved cookies almost as much as she adored hot dogs. He darted past a rack of frilly panties and spied the trench. "Do you mind if I take this for my friend? I'll post about it."

"The sexiest man on the internet with over a million followers can take whatever he likes," the owner replied.

As much as he hated that title, he was thankful to have it today.

He burst out of the store . . . and immediately hit the brakes. Standing not five feet from the entrance, a lingerie-clad Phoebe wobbled precariously, holding out her arms for balance.

A guy in a flaming red sports car drove by and whistled. "Hey, hot stuff!"

Sebastian stared down the driver. The prick hit the gas and disappeared down the street.

Good riddance!

He tapped his foot twice and mumbled under his breath. "Butthole." But he didn't have time to worry about some wanker. Putting the guy out of his head, he attended to the matter at hand: a basically naked-in-public Phoebe. The situation's only saving grace was that the sun had set. He looked her over. In the glow of the streetlamp, she was utterly luminous.

"Seb, it's a little chilly out here," she said, rubbing her arms.

He snapped out of his staring stupor. "Late September isn't outdoor lingerie weather in Colorado." He wrapped the coat around her shoulders like he was dressing a doll. She may be hammered, but he needed to lay down some ground rules. "You can't keep running off. Did you forget what you were wearing?"

She slipped her arms into the sleeves. "Oops, I did," she

cooed and bit her lip, and dammit, there she was again, acting ridiculously adorable. She held on to him for balance. "Have you ever tried walking in heels this high? It's like wearing ice picks while tiptoeing across a tightrope. As much as I like the sex-kitten vibe, they can't hold a candle to sneakers and fuzzy socks."

He double-knotted the belt. "I couldn't agree more. Fuzzy socks are bloody comfortable."

She grinned mischievously. "You did it."

"Did what?"

"Fuzzy socks are *bloody* comfortable," she slurred back in a God-awful British accent.

"It slips out when I'm feeling strong emotions." Without thinking, he wrapped his arms around her and rested his chin on the crown of her head. For a sweet slip of time, his worries melted away. That is, until something whizzed by his head.

Phoebe hummed a sweet little sound. "I had a dream about this."

Was that a drunk confession? Could she have feelings for him that went beyond friendship?

"Me too," he replied, tightening his hold on her, but before he could fully comprehend what he'd copped to, another object flew by.

Phoebe pulled back a fraction and pointed upward. "You had a dream about cookies raining from the sky, too?" she asked in a wispy, singsong voice.

Cookies raining from the sky? She hadn't dreamed of him holding her?

And then he put it together—just as something small yet solid struck the nape of his neck. *Pop!* It didn't hurt, but it certainly didn't feel good. Confused, he looked over his shoulder.

"That's him! Get him," came a little girl's squeak of a voice.

Dammit! How could he have forgotten the cookie-peddling Tech Tweens? And it appeared that they weren't only good with computers. With military precision, the girls got into position. Two launched cookies from behind a trash can while another pair pelted him from behind a mailbox.

"Seb, this is amazing!" Phoebe cried, oblivious that they were under heavy cookie assault. A cookie hit his temple, then dropped into her waiting hands. She took a bite. "And *delicious*."

What the hell was he supposed to do? Of course, he wanted to apologize to the kids. He owed it to them. Now, however, didn't appear to be the right time to wave the white flag. He dodged a chocolate-chip-laden treat and cupped Phoebe's face in his hands. "Phoebe, we need to run."

She shrugged, then caught another cookie. "That's not gonna happen in these." Like they weren't under attack, and she had all the time in the world, she took a bite and kicked up her foot.

A bead of sweat trickled down his back as cookies bounced off his pack and shattered on the ground in a smattering of cookie carnage. Then it stopped. Was it over? The scrape of cardboard being ripped cut through the brisk air. He knew what that meant. The girls were tearing into a new box and loading up on more cookie ammo. He quickly checked and confirmed his suspicion when two empty boxes dropped to the ground. He and Phoebe didn't have another second to lose.

He eyed his friend, who'd amassed quite a haul. "Hold on to your cookies, and don't lose your cookies."

Confusion marred Phoebe's expression. "Why?"

"Commence the second wave," a girl called.

He tensed as the cookie barrage resumed. *Pop, pop, pop, pop!* Golden-brown crumbs and tiny chocolate chips littered the ground. He hoisted Phoebe into his arms. "Because we're making a break for your place."

Phoebe shoved the cookies into the trench's pockets and wrapped her arms around his neck. She looked over his shoulder and pursed her lips. "Wait a second. It's not raining cookies. Those sweet little girls are throwing them at us. It's like dodgeball—the cookie version. And from the look on their faces, they are in it to win it. Do you think that's what's going on? Is this some new trend?"

He didn't have time to explain. "Something like that. Now hold on." With the crack of cookies striking the pavement, he broke out into a sprint.

"It's amazing! People are just drawn to you, Seb," Phoebe remarked, munching away as he hightailed it down the sidewalk.

He looked over his shoulder. Mercifully, the girls hadn't followed them. He slowed to a walk as the scent of hot dogs drifted in the air.

A tattooed man leaned out of a food truck parked across the street with *Hank's Franks* emblazoned on the side. "Hey, Phoebe, it looks like you got what you wanted. Congratulations!"

It came as no surprise to him that Phoebe was on a first-name basis with a food truck chef. But instead of responding, she curled into a ball and scratched his chest like a possessed badger digging a burrow.

"That guy seems to know you, Pheebs. Do you want to say hello?"

"I can't talk to Hank. I don't have the heart to tell him what happened," she murmured against the hollow of his neck.

"How'd you like the hot dog, man?" Hank called.

That was odd. How would this guy know he'd eaten Phoebe's spare dog? Perhaps it was just a guess since they were together.

"It was delicious. Probably the best I've ever had. It was

seriously everything I'd ever wanted in a hot dog and didn't know I needed," he hollered back, answering honestly, which, while it was the truth, was still a weird-ass way to respond about eating grilled processed meat.

Phoebe's burrowing stopped. "You ate the hot dog?" she asked against his shoulder, her question rippling through him.

"I did. Sorry. I was so hungry, Pheebs. I can get you another one."

She shook her head against him. "No, it's okay. Let's get to my place."

"Yeah, all right. We're nearly there."

He walked another half a block, and Phoebe's complex came into view. It wasn't a large building. Shaped like a two-story letter *C*, the apartments were on the periphery, with a courtyard in the center. He opened the gate, followed a path through the garden, then carried her up the stairs to her second-floor unit.

"Pheebs?" he said gently, but she didn't reply. "What's the code to your door? Is it still—"

"*A-I*-seven-seven. Yeah, it is. I haven't changed it."

Sebastian smiled. "After the video game."

She finally looked up at him. "It was the first video game my aunt and uncle worked on together. They fell in love creating that game," she answered, her voice taking on a faraway quality.

"I know, Pheebs. Your uncle Rowen and Aunt Penny were our group's first nanny love match. It started with them."

She nodded. "A true love match."

The words *love match* floated in the night air, mingling with the hint of grilled hot dogs. It was oddly comforting.

He entered the code, and the latch released. Pushing the door with his back, he carried Phoebe over the threshold.

"You can put me down, Seb," she said, her words taking on a monotone edge.

He knew this voice. She sounded like her uncle. The man was a tech genius, and his tone and mannerisms took on a robotic quality when he was working something out. What was going through Phoebe's head? Then again, it was as if they'd lived a thousand lives in the space of the last hour.

Running on autopilot, Phoebe slipped off the heels and flicked on the light. She looked up at him. "Want some water?"

"Water would be great."

Her place was just like he'd remembered—decorated in bright colors with an eclectic, whimsical vibe. Pictures of their multi-family get-togethers were tacked to her fridge and graced picture frames. He walked into what would be the main gathering space in most apartments—but not at Phoebe's place. "Still using the living room as your office, I see."

"Behold Foot Tap Studio and, hopefully, the birthplace of the wildly successful Go Girl Female Empowerment Hub," she replied as she grabbed a pair of glasses, then turned on the tap.

He studied the room, taking in her charts, sticky notes, and a myriad of whiteboards filled with tech mumbo-jumbo. Most of it didn't make a lick of sense to him until he saw one labeled *funding structure* with more than half a dozen ideas for creating revenue.

She came to his side and handed him the glass.

"You're making it harder than it has to be," he said, tapping the board before taking a sip.

"What do you mean?"

"The way to build up something like Go Girl is to start by offering a select number of customers a one-time fee giving them lifetime access to the service. As you grow, you'll phase that out and offer new customers a subscription plan. That'll ensure a consistent revenue flow while giving your first and presumably most loyal customers an incentive to stay and grow with you."

She sighed a weary little sound. "Add that to the list of things I need to figure out."

He watched her closely. "Are you having trouble with your business?"

She downed the water, left the glass on her desk, then padded toward her bedroom. "Let's talk and lie down at the same time. This day and the many, many martinis I consumed are catching up with me."

He followed and watched as she removed her glasses, then flopped onto her bed. The ghost of a grin tipped the corners of her mouth as she reached beneath her pillow and removed a pair of fuzzy socks. Twisting her body, she attempted to remain prostrate while struggling to put on her wooly foot coverings.

"You'll throw your back out moving like that. Let me help," he chided, taking the socks. He slipped one on. "What's going on with Foot Tap Studio?" he asked, turning his attention to her other foot.

She closed her eyes. "I have to nail down my sales pitch and figure out how to become . . . different."

"Why do you need to be different?" he asked, taking off his backpack and setting it on the floor.

"I've got to make a radical change." Phoebe pushed up on her elbow and glanced at a small calendar on her bedside table. "And I only have a handful of hours. I leave for LETIS tomorrow afternoon."

LETIS! In all the hubbub, he'd neglected to share his news.

He settled in next to her. "I got invited to LETIS."

She shot up and pounced on top of him like she was a cat and he was a plate of tuna noodle casserole. "You're going to LETIS to find an investor, too?" she trilled, then wobbled, losing her balance.

"Easy," he said, helping her lie back down. He rested his head on the pillow and rolled to his side to be eye to eye with her. "I'm going, but I got some good news today. I'm pretty sure I've already got an investment company lined up."

At first, she didn't reply, but he could see the wheels turning in her head. "Sebby," she breathed, "I'm so happy for you and me. You're the man every woman wants."

Where was she going with this? He tried to read her. "Every woman?"

"Your socials are filled with women who adore you. You have them wrapped around your finger."

"What?" He was not expecting that.

Color rose to her cheeks. "I'm sure Oscar told you about what happened with Jeremy. He heard it all."

"Yeah, he told me."

"So you know that Jeremy will be at LETIS."

Sebastian tapped his chin theatrically. "Want me to mess him up? I am the son of a boxing champion. Or I could follow your lead, go the condiment route, and rig a bucket of ketchup to fall on his head—or maybe sriracha. That would burn." He expected her to laugh, but she didn't.

She hardened her features. "I want Jeremy Drewler to rue the day he met me. I'm done falling for jerks and wearing my heart on my sleeve. You can help me change that. It's like the universe meant for us to attend LETIS."

"What do you want me to do?"

"Turn me into a . . ." A devilish grin spread across her face. "A man-eater."

A man-eater? Was she kidding?

"You've been drinking. You're talking rubbish." He tried to roll onto his other side.

She stopped him and scooted in closer. Pain welled in her eyes. "Yes, I downed a bunch of dirty martinis, but this is the problem I've been trying to solve all evening. Behind the keyboard, I'm a barracuda. In real life, when it comes to men, I'm a mess. I don't want the Jeremy Drewlers of this world to keep getting the best of me only to cast me aside. Please, Sebby, I need your expertise."

"You want me to transform you into a better version of yourself?" he asked softly.

That grin that only appeared for him bloomed on her lips. "Think of it as Phoebe 2.0. Take me from computer nerd to show-stopping vixen," she said, then glanced away and chewed her bottom lip.

"Are you having second thoughts?"

Her smile returned. "No, my thoughts are about skin."

"Skin?" He touched her cheek. "Your skin is fine—luminous, actually, which is surprising since you've inhaled processed meats like a ravenous hyena since you were six years old."

"Not skin-skin," she chuckled. "My style and outer appearance. Skin is a gaming term for what a character looks like—their clothing or costume. Often, as you progress through a video game and earn more coins or whatever currency the game employs, you're offered the chance to upgrade your skin."

She wanted a life upgrade.

The breath caught in his throat. This was precisely what he needed: a person demanding a rapid-fire makeover. Phoebe Gale could be the before-and-after test subject. Her transformation could prove his methods weren't some pie-in-the-sky ideas.

"Come with me to LETIS and coach me through it," she pleaded, taking his hand. "I want investors to see me as strong and capable, not nerdy and disheveled. And when it comes to men, I want to be in charge, but I also want to show those jerks who dated me because they wanted to meet my aunt and uncle that I'm . . ." She swallowed hard.

"What?" he pressed.

"That I'm someone a guy would be proud to have by his

side. I want them to want *me.* I want them to look at me and think, 'Phoebe Gale is out of my league.'"

This could work. If he wanted to succeed, it had to.

He held her gaze. "You've got to follow my instructions to a T. Will you consent to that?"

"Yes!" she cheered. "I knew you wouldn't let me down. Make me bold and persuasive. Make me irresistible so I can go in with confidence. An investor will see me and know I'm capable of making Go Girl a success." She squeezed his hand. "You're nothing like those butthole guys who only wanted to use me, Sebby."

His heart nearly stopped. He wasn't one of those buttholes, was he? If he succeeded, they'd both win. He wasn't using her—exactly. He was answering a friend's call that just happened to serve two purposes. Should he tell her? No, he didn't want to muddy the waters. It might make her nervous if she felt like a lab rat. He'd keep the case study to himself. He would tell her everything after they succeeded. That made it okay, right?

He ignored the gnawing feeling in his chest. "Phoebe Gale, I'll help you become the person you want to be."

"You'll do it? You'll help me?"

A tingle worked its way down his spine. "I'll do more than that. I'll give you a guarantee."

Energy pulsed between them. The possibilities in the air were palpable.

She cuddled into him and sighed a dreamy little sound. "Say that again, Sebby. Except, this time, use my title from back when I was a girl and do it in your old accent."

He exhaled and pictured seeing her for the first time through the car window when he was nothing but a scared, knobby-kneed kid. All chestnut braids, and sparkling blue eyes, Phoebe Gale was sunshine, pure and wondrous.

His pulse kicked up. He had a sneaking suspicion that

agreeing to help her would either be the best decision he'd ever made or the worst.

He exhaled a slow breath. Hoping the universe knew what it was doing by throwing Phoebe into his lap in his time of need, he wrapped his arms around his best friend. "Phoebe Gale," he began softly in a British accent, "Princess of the Hot Dog Fairies, Bearer of Cookies, and Eater of Pizza, I give you the Sebastian Guarantee."

Chapter 7

PHOEBE

Phoebe rolled over and hugged her pillow to her chest. Half-awake and half-asleep, she inhaled . . . what the hell was that? *Vegetables?* She couldn't remember the last time she'd bought something from that food group. Could her neighbors be cooking? That had to be it.

She rubbed her temples, and holy martini-binge aftermath, her head pounded. She slapped the pillow onto her face, reveling in the coolness, when muted voices caught her attention.

"These are brilliant pieces. You've really come through for us. Thank you."

She sighed, listening to the cadence of Sebastian's voice. *Brilliant*—another one of the British words that crept into his dialect every now and then.

And then it hit.

Sebastian was in her apartment because her life had become a giant shitshow. Wait, her life wasn't a complete shitshow. As if she were rewinding the tape in her mind, she went over the events that had led her to this moment, curled up in her bed wearing—she touched the sleeves—yep, a trench coat.

From Hank's Franks to learning she'd gotten into LETIS to the Jeremy debacle, followed by a kind soul footing the bill for her to drink her weight in martinis, and then Sebastian showing up like a white knight, it was safe to say she'd been caught in a whirlwind of absolute insanity.

She tossed the pillow onto the end of her bed, then rested her hand in the empty space next to her. Like the pillow, it was cool to the touch, but it hadn't been like that all night. Sebastian had slept there. With him at her side, she'd fallen asleep listening to him recite the title she'd given herself in first grade.

It wasn't a big deal that they'd shared her bed. She'd been having sleepovers with the guy since she was a girl. They spent their Christmases at his parents' place in Rickety Rock. Despite being in their twenties, she, Seb, Oscar, and Aria still insisted on whipping out sleeping bags to bunk on the floor in the same room, pillow-fort style. Sleeping near each other hadn't been anything more than best friends hanging out.

Except last night had been different.

Sure, she'd been drunk, but she wasn't so far gone that she didn't remember the last thing Sebby had said—no, guaranteed. Then again, it wasn't as much what he'd said but how he'd said it. His whole demeanor had changed. He'd looked at her as if, by asking for his help, she'd held the keys to everything he'd ever wanted. The conviction in his gaze and the earnestness in his voice had left her breathless.

But that wasn't the only thing she recalled.

Slowly, she sat up, put on her glasses, and peered at Sebastian's backpack. It rested on the floor next to the clothes he'd worn yesterday. Her pulse kicked up as she slipped out of bed, then knelt near his stuff. As if she were being driven by an invisible force, she picked up his jeans, reached into the pocket, and removed three items. She couldn't stop herself from smiling as she admired the pocket watch with his birth mother's picture, the aquamarine stone

Libby had given him, and a rolled-up ball of tinfoil. Breathless, she returned the stone and watch but kept the tiny silver ball. She rested her free hand on the ground, steadying herself as a light-headedness took over that, she was relatively sure, had nothing to do with her martini bender and everything to do with Sebastian eating her love-match hot dog.

Cross my hot-dog-loving heart and swear to die. The man who eats this love-match hot dog will be the person who'll hold my heart in his hands.

A hot dog prophecy of sorts, she'd spoken those very words to Hank.

A sinking sensation set in. What did it mean that her best friend had devoured the very item that was supposed to point her in the direction of her love match? It couldn't be Sebastian. She wouldn't allow her mind to go there. He was her best friend, and she couldn't—no, she wouldn't—jeopardize their friendship. She couldn't picture what her life would look like without him. Sure, he'd been hella MIA for the last six months, but there had to be a reason he'd spiraled into a playboy existence. Not to mention, thanks to their families being so close, he'd always be in her life. And yet, that dormant love seed buried deep within her yearned to find *the one.*

She shook her head, banishing the ridiculous thought, and concentrated on the wadded-up metallic ball. Carefully, like an archeologist extracting a priceless artifact, she peeled back the wrapping and smoothed the silver foil on her lap. Rays of sunlight glinted off the surface. It was oddly beautiful. Overcome with emotion, her eyes welled with tears. What was going on with her?

"What's going on with you, Pheebs?"

She shrieked and flicked her gaze to the doorway, finding Sebastian standing there.

Confusion marred his expression. "Phoebe, seriously, what

are you doing?" Needless to say, he was confused. He'd caught her genuflecting in front of a square of tinfoil.

Oh shit, oh shit, oh shit!

How was she supposed to answer? She couldn't say, *hey there, BFF, I'm a little shaken. You polished off the hot dog meant for the man who's supposed to adore me forever and ever like some bizarre reverse Cinderella situation where, instead of the shoe fitting Cinderella's foot, the prince chowed down on the damsel's mincemeat pie—or whatever they ate in a quasi-medieval Fairy Tale World.*

Think, woman! What would be a non-weird explanation for him finding her like this? Wait, she was weird—super weird. Score a point for Team Awkward.

She picked up the foil, and like a total weirdo, licked it.

Sebastian's eyes widened as confusion made way for full-on disbelief.

"Darn," she lamented, feigning disappointment. "You're probably wondering why I'm licking tinfoil?"

"That's exactly what I'm wondering," he replied, eyeing her closely.

She cleared her throat. "I wanted to see if there was any hot dog left on the wrapper or a bit of bun."

"Pheebs, I don't think you should be eating bits of hot dog that have been wadded up in somebody's pocket for over twelve hours."

She slapped a grin on her face, balled up the foil, and placed it back in the pocket. "Excellent tip. You're already delivering on your Sebastian Guarantee. Man-eaters don't lick used hot dog wrappers. Lesson learned. Suggestion noted," she replied with a touch too much enthusiasm as she rose to her feet. "Look at that. Phoebe Gale 2.0, here I come." She raised her fist in the air, widened her grin, and flashed her pearly whites, hoping Seb's next action wasn't making a call to request an urgent psychiatric intervention on her behalf.

But something was up with him. He had a brazenly self-satisfied air about him, and one of his hands was behind his back. What was he hiding?

"Drink this," he directed, revealing a glass of green glop.

She gagged. There were the vegetables she'd smelled. "What in God's name is in there?"

"Your Sebastian Guarantee breakfast," he answered with his signature super-cocky and damned-endearing crooked grin.

She sniffed it, then retched again. "It smells—*and looks*—like wet moss doused in toad urine."

"Aren't you perceptive, Phoebe Gale," he sang, clearly enjoying himself. "That's what this is. And you should thank me for it. Do you know how hard it is to get a toad to hand over a vial of piss?"

She pinched her nostrils. "I'm not ingesting that."

"I could always pour it on my torso and let you lick it off my abs because they're oh so lickable—your words, not mine," he shot back like a self-assured scoundrel.

Heat rose to her cheeks, but she wasn't blushing because she was embarrassed. She was amped up. Endorphins flooded her system. Oh, how she'd missed this over the last six months—the back and forth, the playfulness, the challenge of going toe to toe with her best friend. And speaking of toes, she peered down at her fuzzy-sock-clad feet and lifted her left foot.

Sebastian zeroed in on the floor action. "If you're about to tap out what I think you're about to tap out, I'm making you drink two green smoothies." Mischief danced in his eyes. It couldn't be denied—he enjoyed butting heads with her, too.

She looked from her foot to the murky green drink, then lowered her foot.

"That's what I thought," he purred with a deliciously arrogant grin in place as he handed her the glass. "Drink up, hot dog fairy princess. Let's get some food into you that doesn't have a shelf life of ten thousand years."

She held up the glass. "What is this, really?"

"It's a Greek yogurt smoothie with spinach, kale, cucumbers, chia seeds, and a spritz of fresh lemon juice."

She tilted the glass from side to side and grimaced as the contents oozed around. "Can I have a moss and toad piss smoothie instead?"

"No," he barked, "and may I remind you that you agreed to follow my instructions precisely."

"Bossy Brit," she mumbled as she sniffed the concoction.

"Bloody right about that, lass," he quipped in his dad's loose, rollicking accent. "We're doing this properly, not getting it cocked up on day one, aren't we?"

What had gotten into this man?

"You're wired," she remarked, then noticed a slim pocket notebook with a pen sticking out of the spiral on the ground near the end of the bed. "What's *New Data*?" she asked, reading the words printed on the cover in Sebastian's handwriting.

"It's nothing," he answered like the wind had been knocked out of his sails. "My phone's a little banged up. It's easier to jot down notes I'd like to share with the investment group who showed an interest in funding my life-coaching business. Don't even worry about it. Like I said, it's just work." He plucked the pad off the floor and stuffed it into his pack.

Now she was the one sporting a confused expression. "Are you okay?"

He waved her off. "Yeah, of course."

"How long have you been up?" she asked, switching gears as she rolled her head from side to side, attempting to jump-start her brain. After last night, it would take a lot more than green glop to wake her up. Maybe she could borrow some of his get-up-and-go energy.

Sebastian's troubled air disappeared, and the spark returned to his gaze. "I got up early to make some calls, then I borrowed your car. I went to my place to grab a few things.

After that, I hit the market to purchase the healthy items for your breakfast smoothie." He checked his watch. "Which is looking more like a brunch smoothie. And," he glanced over his shoulder, "while you drink that, I'd like you to say hello to our guest."

Her heart nearly stopped. "Someone is here?" She'd heard him talking but thought he was on a call.

"Mara's here."

Mara? Had he brought a woman back to her place?

He had been cavorting around the world, banging whatever beautiful woman drifted into his orbit. He probably met *Mara* at the grocery store. She must have batted her eyelashes at him across a crate of cantaloupes. Had the two of them got it on in her apartment?

"Pheebs?"

"Am I supposed to know who this Mara is?" she asked with a distinct edge to her tone, when a movement beyond Sebastian's shoulder caught her eye.

An impeccably dressed woman with an asymmetrical platinum bob strode down the hallway and stood next to Sebastian in the doorway. "I'm Mara. You met my wife, Janelle, last night."

Janelle?

Phoebe chewed her lip. "I'm sorry, I can't place you, and I don't think I know anyone named Janelle. Yesterday is a bit of a blur for me."

"Janelle helped you in the dressing room," Sebastian explained. "She and Mara own the clothing store Denver Diva Day and Night."

Phoebe exhaled a frantic breath. "Oh, thank God." She paused and grinned vacantly at the woman. That was all well and good, but why on earth would the wife of a lady who helped her in a dressing room show up at her apartment?

Mara slipped her cell phone from her pocket. "Look at the

time. I should be getting back to the store. But first, I need you to approve a few things, Phoebe."

Phoebe's gaze ping-ponged between her best friend and Mara. "My approval?"

The woman looked her up and down. "That's right," she answered, then met Sebastian's gaze. "What did I tell you about that trench?"

Sebastian nodded approvingly. "She slept in it all night, and there's not a wrinkle to be found."

These two were going on like there was nothing completely bonkers about this totally bonkers situation.

"Hello," Phoebe sang, waving her hands. "I'll need you two to tell me what's going on here."

"I called Mara's wife this morning and explained the Phoebe 2.0 plan," Sebastian offered, which still didn't help her connect the dots.

"And that involves . . . ?" Phoebe asked slowly.

"New clothing," Mara supplied, taking her hand and leading her down the hall.

"I don't need . . ." Phoebe began, then shut the hell up. Her living room/office looked more like the inside of a celebrity's closet, with designer digs hanging from racks and luxurious scarves folded over the back of her sofa. She walked up to a midnight-blue beaded cocktail dress. The garment screamed sophistication. She touched the sleeve, then spied the price tag.

Eight hundred dollars.

Eight hundred dollars!

Not knowing what else to do, she lifted the glass of glop to her lips and started chugging.

"Phoebe," Sebastian said warily, "you don't have to drink it in one gulp."

Yeah, she did. She needed the time to think. She swallowed the last bit of the gag-reflex-inducing drink, set the drained cup on her desk, then wiped the back of her hand across her lips. "I'm awake, right? This is happening?"

"Yes," Sebastian answered again, looking like he was weighing the need to request psychiatric services on her behalf again.

In her defense, it wasn't every day a gal woke up to a room teeming with designer digs. She surveyed the luxurious fabrics and stylish patterns. Clothing ranging from sporty outdoor hiking apparel to sleek business casual numbers and a few chic dresses were intermingled with lacy lingerie and accessories like purses, earrings, necklaces, and bracelets. A stylish leather jacket hung on the back of her desk chair, and multiple pairs of shoes were lined up beneath each clothing ensemble. There had to be tens of thousands of dollars' worth of beautiful merchandise crammed into her modest apartment.

"You wouldn't catch a nerdy French farmer in any of these," she murmured.

Mara cocked her head to the side. "I'm not sure I heard you correctly. Did you mention farming?"

Phoebe shifted her stance. *Pull yourself together, woman.* "Everything is stunning and so incredibly beautiful, but I can't afford any of this."

Mara crossed her arms, and a ghost of a grin tipped the corners of her mouth. "I didn't ask if you could afford it. What I want to know is if you like it. Is there anything you'd change? Or is it a match?"

"Match?" Phoebe breathed, her body tingling as she spoke the word.

"Yes, does it *match* the look you were going for?"

Phoebe turned in a slow circle, taking it in. "I love everything. But again, these pieces are way out of my budget."

Mara raised an eyebrow. "Is free out of your budget?"

"Free?" Phoebe exclaimed for everyone in Metro Denver to hear.

"I've got this, Mara. I know you need to get back to the store," Sebastian said and walked the woman to the door. "Give our regards to Janelle. I'm happy to hear you've already seen a bump in your online sales."

Why in the world would Sebastian know anything about the sales of a women's clothing boutique?

"Good luck at your retreat, Phoebe. My wife and I wish you the best," Mara called before sailing out the door.

"Um . . . thank you . . . for everything," she replied, still not quite sure if she was actually awake.

She padded around the room and picked up a pair of chocolate brown riding boots rocking a six-hundred-dollar price tag, then returned them to the floor. Before she could inspect another gorgeous piece, butterflies flitted around inside her belly. She froze as Sebastian came up behind her. She could feel the heat of him and smell his clean, earthy scent. Every cell in her body begged for her to lean back and melt into his warmth, but she remained stock-still. "I must be dreaming."

"It's not a dream, Pheebs. I guarantee you're fully conscious. This is all for you."

All for you.

He was talking about the clothes, but did she want him to be talking about himself? Did she want all of him? Goose bumps rose on her skin. She blinked, snapping out of it. Holy don't-think-of-your-best-friend-like-that. Could she still be drunk? Pushing aside the crazy thought, she turned on her heel. There had to be a catch.

She pegged Sebastian with her gaze. "Boutique owners don't show up and gift people an entire wardrobe."

His crooked half-grin returned. "This is part of the Sebastian Guarantee. I believe you called it *upgraded skin*."

"I don't owe them a kidney, do I? They didn't already take it, did they?" She started to undo the knot on the trench's belt to see if a jagged line of Frankenstein monster stitches adorned her abdomen, but Sebastian stopped her. He rested his hands on hers, and she inhaled sharply.

What did those martinis do to her?

Sebastian took a step back and broke their connection. "You don't owe them anything. I agreed to give them some publicity on my socials, and in return, they comped the clothes. That's how you ended up with the trench coat, and," Sebastian glanced away, "what's beneath it." He pulled at the collar of his button-up. "Janelle gave me her card last night and said to reach out if you needed anything else."

"I hadn't put it together." Phoebe took off her glasses and rubbed her eyes as she recalled bolting out of the boutique without paying a cent.

"This morning, I went online to check the itinerary for LETIS. It was somewhat vague, probably by design, but they did reveal that there's a cocktail event tonight, then some outdoor activities, and a fancy dinner. I called Janelle and asked if she could hook you up with some outfits for a retreat at a posh Colorado lodge. I told them I'd be happy to tag them in more posts in exchange."

Every muscle in her body tensed. "LETIS! I can't believe I forgot about it. It starts this evening. I RSVP'd, but I haven't even checked my email to get more info on location and lodging."

Sebastian dusted off his shoulders.

This man.

"I took care of that, too. It's being held at the Glenn Pines Lodge a few hours northwest of Denver," he replied as his cell phone rang. He pulled it from his pocket.

"What happened to your phone?" she asked, taking in the cracked screen. Then she read the caller info. *Ivy Elliot's Super-Secret Spy Phone.* "Why is Ivy calling you with . . ."

"The burner phone you bought her?" Sebastian supplied.

"I wouldn't buy eight-year-olds burner phones. Tula and Ivy wanted to ride their kick scooters to school. Your parents and Mitch and Charlotte wanted the girls to have phones with them and asked me to help the kids pick them out. I suggested they let the girls play secret spies like we used to before they let on that they knew about the new phones."

"The girls think it's their little secret."

She sighed. "Our whole foot tap language was our secret. It inspires creativity and closeness. I love that my aunt Penny taught me the tap trick, and then I taught it to you, Oscar, and Aria. It's harmless."

Sebastian narrowed his gaze. "You're okay with secrets?"

"I guess, if you're focused on semantics, you could call the phones safe non-secrets," she countered, then chewed her lip.

"What is it?"

"You better answer the call. The girls might need something. I thought Mitch, Charlotte, and Ivy were leaving this morning to join your family in Rickety Rock for the rest of their break-break, back-to-nature week."

Sebastian's cocksure demeanor waned. "I have an idea why Ivy and Tula might be breaking the rules to call."

She watched the man. "Why?"

"They saw something online—something terrible that . . ."

"That what?" she pressed.

He bowed his head, and his shoulders curled in around his chest. "Something terrible that I'm at fault for. And it's bad, Phoebe. It's really bad."

Chapter 8

PHOEBE

Phoebe pegged her best friend with her gaze as a prickling sensation took over. "Sebastian, what happened? What could you have done that's so terrible?"

He ran his hands down his face. "Is it awful I'm relieved you don't know? You're probably the last person on the planet who hasn't seen it."

"Talk to me," she said, her heart breaking for him.

He stared at his cell. "If I'm right, you're about to get an earful." The color drained from his face. He mustered a grin that didn't reach his eyes and answered the video call. "Hey, Tula! How are you, Ivy? I see you're in the barn tending to the donkeys," he said, then swallowed hard.

"Sebby," Tula whisper-chided, "Ivy and I watched the video of you at the airport with the Tech Tweens."

"It had over a million views. People in the comments were calling you . . ." Ivy paused. "I have to tap it out with my foot because I'm not supposed to say really, really bad words."

Phoebe's pulse kicked up. She couldn't see the screen, but she could hear the disapproval in the girls' voices, loud and clear.

What Tech Tweens video were they talking about?

The fog in her brain lifted, and she pieced it together. The girls who'd showered them with cookies had been seated at a table with *Tech Tween Fundraiser* written on the sign. And then she recalled Oscar talking about some crazy alert—something about Sebastian stealing a cab and leaving kids in the pouring rain.

She'd written it off as clickbait. But had it happened?

"Girls, it's not what it looks like," Sebastian rasped. "It was a misunderstanding. I wasn't paying attention when I was leaving the airport. It was pouring rain. I didn't even know I'd taken their cab until Briggs sent me the video. I feel awful about it."

He did. She could tell. His shoulders slumped forward as his posture crumpled.

"You left them in the rain, and they started crying. Did you tell them that you're sorry?" Tula pressed with heartache in her voice.

"I haven't gotten a chance, T."

"Our teacher says you've got to take responsibility for your actions," Ivy added.

"And if you don't, it's super-duper bad for your karma," Tula continued.

Sebastian rubbed the back of his neck. "Yeah, I know."

Phoebe stared at the man who hadn't been himself for six months. Sure, he'd been acting like an aloof man-whore, but purposefully snubbing children wasn't in his DNA. No matter what happened, she had to set the record straight.

She slipped Sebastian's cracked phone out of his hand and eyed the girls. "Hello, ladies," she said with a sharp twist to her greeting.

"Phoebe?" the girls exclaimed, wide-eyed.

"You guys need to go easy on Sebastian. He hasn't been able to apologize because he's been busy helping me."

Speechless, the girls stared at her.

"And, if I remember correctly, you two are supposed to be taking a tech break and not sneaking around making calls in the barn. It's one thing to play super-secret spies when you're apart. But you're together. You need to enjoy that time. It's special. I enjoyed every second I spent with Sebastian when I was your age." She tossed a glance his way. "And Oscar and Aria, of course."

Tula hung her head. "I needed to talk to Sebby after I saw the video. I was mad because I've missed him, and my parents are always talking about how they're worried about him, and then Ivy and I saw what he did to the Tech Tweens, and—"

Sebastian flinched.

"And," Phoebe interrupted, "you know your brother is a good person. He'd never intentionally cause anyone harm." As the words left her lips, a tingle ran down her spine. She could feel Sebastian drinking her in. "Now," she continued, forcing herself to focus on the girls, "take a hike or pick some wildflowers. Commune with nature."

The kids nodded like they'd been read the riot act.

"We promise to follow the break-break rules from now on," Ivy said with a resolute nod.

"Wait," Tula yipped, her jet-black braids swinging from side to side as she leaned in. "Before we end the video call, can you tell us how Sebby is helping you? That might help clear his terrible karma."

Phoebe glanced at Sebastian. Gratitude radiated from the man, but it was mixed with something darker, as if he were conflicted. She returned to the girls. "He's helping me get ready for a special conference. It's where I hope to meet someone who wants to invest in the Go Girl community. He even helped me get some fancy new clothes to wear while I'm there. I don't know what I'd do without him." With her heart ready to beat itself out of her chest, she met Sebastian's gaze.

Her mouth grew dry. Her limbs lightened. It was as if gravity had shifted, and she was about to float away. This was not her normal reaction to her best friend. What had happened? What had changed that had her emotions all over the board?

Now Ivy leaned in. "What are you going to do about your makeup?"

Phoebe flicked her gaze to the screen. "What about it?"

"Aria showed us how to do our makeup before the school talent show last year when we sang one of her songs," Tula supplied. "We're good at makeup."

Phoebe focused on the tiny square with her image in the corner. *Yowza!* Maybe she did need some help in the cosmetics department. "I've got makeup. I just don't wear it that often."

"You don't have to wear a lot of makeup. It's how you wear it," Tula replied.

Ivy nodded and brushed an errant lock of auburn hair behind her ear. "You want to pop. Eyes and lips are what I'd recommend."

Oh," Phoebe uttered. Eight-year-olds knew more about being put together than she did.

Tula leaned in, edging Ivy out of the frame. "You've got nice lips, Phoebe. You should play them up. Don't you think, Sebby?"

Sebastian stared at her mouth. "Phoebe's lips are nice, yeah. Very inviting," he rasped.

Phoebe pulled at the collar of her trench. Had it gotten hot in there?

"Inviting?" Tula repeated and cocked her head to the side.

Unable to stop, Phoebe darted her tongue out of her mouth to moisten her lips.

"Not inviting. *Bloody kissable*," he said, slipping into his old accent.

The breath caught in Phoebe's throat as another reflex took over, and she clenched her core.

Stop that! No core clenching around Sebastian.

"Kissable?" Ivy and Tula said, then made grossed-out faces.

"No, not kissable . . . *capable*. Yes, Phoebe has capable lips," he corrected, then tugged at his collar.

My God, there was a lot of collar tugging going on between the two of them.

"How are lips *capable*?" Ivy pressed.

Phoebe had the same question. She parted her very capable lips, not sure what she would say, when she was saved by the bell—or in this case, her laptop that she'd left on the kitchen table. It pinged, alerting her to a video call.

Another one?

How many video calls was the universe going to throw at her and Sebastian this morning?

Then again, anything to end the kissable-lips topic was a godsend.

"Girls, someone's calling me. Sebastian and I need to go. We love you both very much. Now get off this phone, enjoy your break, and . . ." She racked her brain. "Go supercharge your chi."

"You can't supercharge chi, Phoebe," Tula remarked. "Chi just *is*. It's either balanced or imbalanced but always present."

"How about this?" Sebastian suggested, sounding more like himself. "Go take your balanced chi and muck out Beefcake and Plum's stall. You do that, and the next time I see you, instead of getting triple scoops at the ice cream shop, we'll defy gravity and ask for quadruple scoops."

"Quadruple scoops!" Tula exclaimed.

"You'll be a third-grade legend, Tula. I don't know anybody who's gotten four scoops on one cone," Ivy insisted.

Phoebe and Sebastian exchanged a knowing look.

"After you're done in the barn," Sebastian continued, "grab a yoga mat, get into child's pose, and reflect on what transcendental harmony means to you. Think about where you are in the metaphysical world and center yourself around that."

Phoebe nodded, not understanding a lick of what the man said, but it sure sounded good. "Yeah, do that, too—all the metaphysical stuff," she agreed as her laptop chimed again.

"One more thing, Sebby," Tula trilled.

"Yeah?"

"Your face looks better."

Sebastian touched his cheek. "My face?"

The girl's amber eyes sparkled. "It's not your pretending happy face."

Pretending happy face?

Phoebe looked up and basked in the glow of a Sebastian Cress boyish grin.

"No, T, it's not," he answered softly.

Tula's expression darkened. "You haven't told Phoebe about my you-know-what, have you?"

Sebastian's smile twisted into a mischievous smirk. "Your secret's safe with me. Love you, kiddo."

"Bye, Big Foot," Tula replied and blew a kiss.

Phoebe ended the call and handed Sebastian his phone. She had a million questions. What were they keeping from her, and what had him so frazzled that he'd taken a cab meant for a bunch of kids? But she held back and waited for him to speak.

He pocketed his cell. "Thanks for saying that, Pheebs. It was kind of you to bail me out with Tula and Ivy."

"I wasn't being kind. It's the truth, and I meant it," she answered as the air grew charged with whatever crazy vibe pulsed between them.

"Pheebs, I . . ."

"Yes?" she breathed, but her laptop pinged again. Dammit, she'd forgotten about the video call.

He glanced at the table. "You better get that."

"You're right." She crossed the room, entered the kitchenette, then opened her laptop. She stared at the name of the caller. "You know how I just bailed you out?"

"Uh-huh," he answered warily.

"You might be bailing me out on this call."

"Why?"

She sat down at the table. "My aunt and uncle are calling."

"What's so bad about that?" he asked, taking the chair to her left, out of the camera's view.

She glanced at a picture on the refrigerator taken the day she'd helped her uncle propose to her aunt. "Nothing, they're great. I just look at them and see . . ."

"What you want?" he supplied.

This man knew her inside and out.

"Yeah," she agreed, surprised at how emotional it made her to acknowledge the statement out loud. She exhaled a shaky breath and accepted the call. They'd barely been connected for a fraction of a second before her aunt started in.

"How's our favorite lady boss tech entrepreneur?" Penny asked, grinning from ear to ear.

"I'm plugging away." Phoebe studied the video feed. "Are you guys on your plane?"

"We're on our way to California for a quick getaway, but we wanted to call and see if you'd gotten into LETIS. We've been on pins and needles," Penny said, nearly vibrating with excitement.

Her aunt had a bubbly, fun-loving personality—Phoebe had picked up on it the second they met, back when she was an ornery six-year-old raising hell in first grade, and Penny was a nanny candidate. That energy was why she'd chosen her. On a scale of one to ten, the woman's excitement level usually hovered around a seven and a half. Today, she was off the charts—a solid twelve.

"Your aunt's been on pins and needles. I, however, have

managed to contain my excitement," Uncle Row added in his signature muted style.

"And by containing his excitement, he means he's been checking the security system on every device in the house—repeatedly. He's been an absolute manic mess," Penny said, calling out the man.

Her uncle bit back a grin as he met Penny's gaze.

Phoebe knew that look well. Her uncle had fallen for Penny, hook, line, and sinker.

"You can never be too careful when it comes to cybersecurity," the man answered, absolutely mooning over his wife.

"He was up until one in the morning. I even made him a sticky note letting him know he's supposed to check the devices in the house on the first Wednesday of every month." Penny held up an appointment book with stray multicolored slips of paper sticking out haphazardly.

"You know how I feel about sticky notes," her uncle replied, still biting back a grin.

Penny plucked a sticky note from the notebook and stuck it to Rowen's chest. "You adore them."

He shook his head and chuckled. "Enough about us," he said, removing the hot pink square. "Any word on LETIS?"

Penny leaned forward as her expression grew somber. "And even if you weren't invited this year, there's always next year."

Phoebe sat a little taller. "Don't freak out, but . . . I got in."

"She got in!" her uncle hollered, clapping his hands as a wide grin overtook his subdued demeanor.

Her aunt Penny tore up the pink note and tossed the scraps like confetti.

Phoebe caught movement out of the corner of her eye. Off camera, Sebastian silently mimicked her aunt and uncle, acting like a complete idiot, pumping his fist and mouthing *woo-hoo*.

"We're so happy for our hot dog fairy princess. That's a huge accomplishment, honey," Penny gushed.

"It is. Your mom and dad would be very proud of you, Phoebe," her uncle added.

Mom and Dad.

Phoebe nodded and blinked back tears, hiding her reaction to the mention of her parents.

"Where are they holding LETIS this year?" Rowen asked.

Phoebe steadied herself. "In Glenn Pines, Colorado."

"Glenn Pines?" her uncle repeated, wide-eyed.

"Do you know it, Uncle Row?"

"Your parents got married in a tiny chapel in that mountain town."

"They did?" She'd had no idea. It seemed like an odd thing not to know. At the same time, she couldn't remember ever asking about her parents' wedding. She looked away from the camera, again blinking back tears as the weight of the LETIS opportunity hit. She wanted to succeed for them. The wave of emotion nearly overtook, but then a tingling warmth radiated through her body, soothing her turbulent soul. She didn't have to look down to know that Sebastian holding her hand was the source of the comfort.

"It was an intimate ceremony. Just family. I was your dad's best man, and your grandma Cece stood in as your mom's bridesmaid. The ceremony lasted twenty-nine minutes."

Phoebe chuckled at her uncle's quirky comment. Of course, he'd remember a minute detail like the ceremony running time, but she was grateful he'd lightened the conversation.

"Last we spoke," Penny said and twisted a lock of her dark blond hair, "you mentioned Jeremy got invited. Are you two going to LETIS together?"

At the mention of Jeremy, Sebastian tightened his grip.

She squeezed his hand, trying to convey she was okay, but she wasn't. Searing anger pulsed through her at the thought of the man. "No, Aunt Penn, we aren't seeing each other, but I won't be alone." She turned to Sebastian.

Getting the message, he scooted his chair over to join her in the frame. "Hello, Rowen. It's so nice to see you, Penny. I'm back in Colorado and attending LETIS as well. So, Phoebe and I will keep each other company," he finished, settling in next to her—and *not* releasing her hand.

Penny gasped—an action that was a little over the top, even for her emotive aunt. "Sebastian! Hello, sweetheart." She beamed, then pressed her hand to her heart and turned to her husband. "Oh, Rowen, isn't that wonderful news? Sebastian and Phoebe are together."

"Yes, yes, wonderful news. So very wonderful," her uncle replied with an odd lilt to the words. It was as if he and her aunt were role-playing or reading from a script.

What was up with them? Did her aunt and uncle think she and Sebastian were dating?

Phoebe shifted in her seat. "Sebby and I aren't together-together. I mean, sure, we're physically together in my apartment, but I'm also physically with"—she glanced around wildly and zeroed in on the first thing she saw—"a cucumber," she announced, spying the vegetable on the counter next to the blender. "Yes, I am also in the company of a cucumber," she reiterated, wishing a sinkhole would crack the ground beneath her apartment building and swallow her whole.

"I think Phoebe is trying to say that we got together yesterday to talk shop," Sebastian added.

He glanced at her, and in the second their gazes met, she eyeball-thanked him for intervening and saving her from the insane cucumber comment. He eyeball-replied, *I got you*, then tossed her a wink.

He returned his attention to her aunt and uncle. "I'm utilizing some of the techniques I've researched about meeting one's life goals to help Phoebe wow the investors at LETIS," he continued, sounding damned knowledgeable.

"He's guaranteed my success," she supplied. "He's given me the Sebastian Guarantee, right?" she said, turning to the man.

"Exactly," he answered, but his tone sounded a touch muted.

"We certainly know Phoebe will be in good hands," Penny gushed. "Libby was right about a shift yesterday."

"You saw Mibby yesterday?" Sebastian asked. "I thought she'd already gone to Rickety Rock."

Penny slapped a wide grin on her lips. "Your stepmom got away for a little while. We had an . . . appointment . . . plans . . . in Denver," she stammered, which was odd for her aunt.

"Have you spoken with your dad since you've returned, Sebastian?" her uncle Rowen asked, shifting the topic, then glanced at a cell phone on the table in front of him.

Sebastian's posture stiffened. "No, not yet. He was already in Rickety Rock when I got home. I'm sure we'll connect when he gets back to the city."

Rowen looked up from the phone. "I know he'd like that. And Phoebe?" the man continued, returning his attention to his cell.

"Yeah, Uncle Row?"

"What's going on with your Info Darling page?"

Phoebe's cheeks burned with mortification. "It was Aria being silly."

"That's a relief," her uncle replied and adjusted his glasses. "Don't get me wrong. I understand you're a grown woman with needs and urges. I was worried that . . . I understand they're your favorite food, but . . ." The man trailed off.

Phoebe's mouth fell open as absolute humiliation set in. She'd sell her soul to the devil if he could guarantee she'd never have to hear her uncle mention her *needs* and *urges* again. She checked the little square on the laptop's screen with her and Sebastian's image. She'd gone full-on ripe tomato. And again, she couldn't help but wonder where that damn sinkhole was when a gal needed it.

"Uncle Row," she yammered. "I would never . . . I'm not attracted to . . ."

What the hell was she supposed to say? Hot dogs don't make me horny?

Penny glanced at Rowen's cell phone. "My goodness, that's quite a description. Then again, Aria is a songwriter. It makes sense she'd be good at painting a picture with words."

When would this end?

Phoebe twisted the collar of the trench coat. "It's a joke—just a joke."

She'd barely gotten the words out when Sebastian started vibrating. She looked over to find the guy on his cracked-to-hell cell phone perusing her Info Darling webpage while shaking with pent-up laughter.

"All of you, stop reading! Get off the Info Darling page. I'll fix it when I have a spare second. That's the problem with websites," she fumed. "They're like the Wild West. You better believe Go Girl won't have those kinds of shenanigans. When it's fully funded, we'll have admins monitoring to ensure it's safe for all ages, and quality control managers to ensure the content is accurate and appropriate. That's the sort of thing I'll share with potential investors at LETIS."

"What about the Munch Match app?" Rowen pressed.

Her brows knit together. "What about it?"

"Investors might be interested in expanding on or delving into the matchmaking side effect. Something about your algorithm works not only for identifying what food truck meal a person is craving but also facilitates love matches. It's quite fascinating," her uncle pondered.

It might be fascinating, but it wasn't how she wanted to make a mark in this world. And she wasn't sure why an app to pick what food one was craving also seemed to be able to match users with their soul mate.

"Don't get me wrong, Uncle Row. I'm beyond happy people have met their love matches with the app, but it's not what I want to focus on."

"Why limit yourself? Nobody says you only have to do one thing. Your father and I worked on both Gale Tech and Gale Gaming."

Phoebe sighed. "And I'm in awe of that. But turning Munch Match into a love match app was a fluke. I don't know how it happened. Not to mention, I'm the last person who should oversee matches. I pick the wrong guy every time. Madelyn said our matches were already made. I remember it like it was yesterday, but I'm not sure if that applies to me anymore," she answered, then peered at her friend's hand clasped around hers—emphasis on *friend*.

"Whatever you do, always know your uncle and I support you," Penny said warmly.

Rowen glanced at his phone again. "Unless it involves what's on your Info Darling page. We're open-minded people, however—"

God help her! "Okay, no more hot dog talk. I've experienced quite enough embarrassment for one day."

"I'm writing a sticky note for your uncle to remember that," her aunt Penny said, dumping out her purse's contents onto the table and plucking a pen from the pile. Her uncle's eyes nearly popped the lenses out of his glasses as he took in the clutter.

Phoebe smiled at the two people who'd raised her and showered her with affection. "I love you both very much. But if I don't end this call, I might combust thanks to an excess of mortification. Buh-bye," Phoebe blurted, then slapped her laptop shut and rested her head on the cool surface.

Sebastian's thumb grazed the back of her wrist. "Your uncle was on the mark with his comments."

She groaned. "Sebastian Cress, not you, too. Please, we're dropping the horny hot dog talk."

"I'm not talking about your hot dog fetish, Pheebs."

She tilted her head to glare up at him but softened her gaze as his expression grew sober.

"Your uncle was right about your parents," he said gently. "You're an amazing woman, Phoebe. If they were still alive, I'm certain they'd be proud of you."

She sat up and peered at a framed photo of her parents on their wedding day. The pair stood in front of a stone altar. She kept it next to the glass canister of coffee beans and a note card with her high school quote tucked inside the frame.

The future belongs to those who believe in the beauty of their dreams.

Reading those words, then taking in her parents' smiling faces, was how she greeted each day.

"They're the reason I'm working so hard—why I insist on building my own business without my family's money. I want to make them proud. I want to be worthy of my last name."

Sebastian's chin dipped as he stared ahead with a wistful look. "I understand that completely."

A fluttery feeling took over. She had to ask the question that had lingered around the edges of her mind and in the depths of her heart. "What happened six months ago, Seb? Why did you—?"

"Throw away everything I'd been working for, blow off my friends and family, and start acting like a spoiled wanker?"

She gifted him with a weak grin and a half-shrug. "Yeah."

The air in her apartment thrummed with anticipation, or perhaps it was her heart beating like a drum, desperate to hear his reply.

The conflicted look he'd had earlier returned. A muscle ticked in his jaw, and he couldn't hide the struggle going on inside. He released a pained breath. "It's complicated."

Chapter 9
PHOEBE

It's complicated?

Sebastian's words hovered in the slice of space between them.

Phoebe observed his body language. With a hardened demeanor and agony welling in his eyes, she didn't want to cause him any further pain. Still, she needed to know what was going on inside his head. She'd spent half of a year racking her brain, wondering what could have triggered her loyal, steadfast friend to lose track of what mattered most to him.

Her pulse quickened. "If you can't tell me why you did a complete one-eighty with your life, can you tell me what brought you back? Is that complicated, too?"

His features softened as warmth returned to his expression. "My mum and . . ."

"Your mom?" she repeated, not meaning to cut him off, but she wasn't expecting that to be the reason.

"I had a dream about her. She spoke to me, and when I woke up and looked at my phone to see what time it was, I noticed the date. It was the day after her birthday. Between the partying, drinking, and the revolving door of women, I'd forgotten it."

She squeezed his hand but remained quiet, giving him space to continue.

"I should have realized something was up. My dad called several times that day. I blew him off. I didn't even listen to his messages. I figured it was more of him telling me to stop '*faffing around like a right git*,'" he said, reciting the last part in his father's accent. A sad smile graced his lips. "My dad and I would always go out for fish and chips, my mum's favorite, on her birthday. It was a sacred date. When I was away at school or for work, we'd do a video chat and eat together. My dad always accommodated my schedule. Sometimes, he'd be eating fish and chips for breakfast or in the middle of the night. And we'd talk. We'd always begin by talking about something we remembered about Mum, but then the conversation would shift." He sighed, the puff of air a mix of hope and longing. "Those were some of our best conversations. It was where I started talking to my dad about leaving the business and branching out on my own. My dad was so supportive, and I got the strangest feeling my mum was with us, too—quietly there, encouraging me."

"I remember your fish and chips dates with your dad," she said, allowing herself to drift back in time. "He used to take you out of school for lunch if her birthday fell during the week." She glanced away. "I always envied you."

Her hand still clasped in his, he stroked the sensitive skin on the back of her wrist. "Why is that?"

She focused on his eyes—blue-green like the open sea. "Because you'd come back bright-eyed and beaming, telling me, Oscar, and Aria some sweet story about your mom or some project you and your dad had decided to do together."

"Why'd you envy that?"

She glanced at the photo next to the coffee beans, then traced an invisible line on the table with her index finger. "I was so young when my parents died. All I have of them is flashes. I've had to rely on the stories people have told me about them. Those have become my memories. When you'd talk about your mom, your descriptions were so vivid. I could see her in my mind. While I listened to you talk, I used to picture myself in those moments—like I'd been an honorary Cress, munching away on fish and chips."

Sebastian shifted the chair so they could be face-to-face. With her knees between his powerful legs, he took both her hands in his. "Phoebe, I'm so sorry I haven't been a good friend these last six months. I've been selfish and distant." He exhaled a pained breath. "I read that text, and in that instant, nothing made sense. I lost my way."

She narrowed her gaze. "What text? Was it from your dad?"

He swallowed hard. "What matters is that I'm back, and I can make up for being a royal plonker by helping you become Phoebe 2.0. I'll be by your side at LETIS, coaching you through every encounter."

That hopeful love seed in her chest soaked in his words like a flower opening to the sun. She was grateful to have him back, but she couldn't monopolize his time. "What about your business, Seb? You said that you met with a potential investor yesterday. But a potential investor is far from a done deal. Don't you need to be prepared to pitch to investors if that opportunity falls through?"

"You're my priority, Phoebe. Don't worry about me. I know what I'm doing."

He sounded like he cared, but she could have sworn she detected a thread of trepidation. It could be nerves, though. Both of their emotions had been running high for the last twenty-four hours.

She pushed aside her worries. "You are the best *friend* a girl could ask for." She meant it, but something about the statement didn't ring true.

"All right," he said, releasing her hands and rubbing his together like a mad scientist. "Let's get started. There's no time like the present. What are your goals for LETIS?"

She glanced at the clock on the wall. "Shouldn't I shower first? Thanks to the martinis, I probably smell like day-old olives. And then I need to pack. We should probably get a move-on if we want to make it to the resort. I'll need time to get ready for the cocktail party tonight."

"You can shower after we talk. This is important. We need to set the foundation for your transformation. It won't take long." He glanced at his cell. "Do you mind if I record this conversation? Once I transfer the information to my notes, I'll delete the recording."

She stared at his phone. "Okay."

He tapped his cell's screen a few times, then returned to her. "I want you to focus, Phoebe. I'll ask you a couple of questions, and I'd like you to say the first thing that comes to mind."

She nodded.

"What's your goal for LETIS?"

"To secure funding for Go Girl." She chewed her lip. "I'd be coming in stronger if I had an organization already pledging to be a part of the community, but I can't let that stop me."

"Optimism is good," he agreed. "Focus on what you can deliver, not on what you're lacking. Now, pick a word. This is the word that you'll whisper to yourself before you go into a business or professional setting."

She gave him a wry twist of a grin. "Capable—like my lips."

He countered with a twitch of a half-smile. "Capable, it is. Now pick a centering word for your personal life."

She cocked her head to the side. "My personal life?"

"Your personal and professional lives are intertwined—two halves of a whole. What's the first word that pops into your head?"

She sat a little taller. "Man-eater."

Sebastian raised an eyebrow. "You mentioned that word last night. You're sure you want to stick with it?"

"Yep, I want to roll into LETIS like a rock star. I want people to look at me and not be able to turn away. I want Jeremy Drewler to see me and wish he hadn't been such a colossal—" She tapped her foot five times for butthole douche nozzle.

"A man-eater is in charge of her sexuality. She's not afraid to embrace pleasure. Is that something you want to explore?" Sebastian inquired.

Hearing the words *pleasure* and *sexuality* drip from Sebastian's lips sent a delicious shiver down her spine. She crossed, then uncrossed her legs. "Go big or go home, right?"

"You don't have to be nervous. There's nothing wrong with sex between two consenting adults who understand there are no strings attached to any physical encounter."

"Uh-huh," she answered as her brain started melting into gray matter mush.

"If the opportunity presents itself at LETIS," he pushed on, "would you welcome the chance to have sex?"

Her lips parted, but nothing came out.

"I'm not asking you these questions to make you uncomfortable. By presenting possible options and scenarios, you'll be better able to react."

She engaged in another bout of leg crossing and uncrossing. "I wouldn't sleep with an investor. That would feel like crossing a line. Still, if I met someone, like another innovator who I found attractive and appealing, I'd consider it."

"Are you a good kisser?" he asked as nonchalantly as someone asking for the time.

Was that something people knew about themselves?

She twisted the cuff of the trench coat. "I assume I'm okay at it."

His gaze dropped to her lips. "You've never gotten explicit feedback?"

She shifted in her seat. "I've never sent out a questionnaire or asked to be rated on a scale of one to five," she blathered, feeling her cheeks heat.

"Kissing is an art, Phoebe," the man purred.

"Mm-hmm." Thanks to the tingle party between her legs, that was all she could get out.

"It's good to get a baseline to know where you're starting. If you want to come across as capable in your business life and sexually assertive in your personal life, you need to know your strengths in both areas. One complements the other." He folded his hands in his lap. "I could help you obtain this information."

Was he saying what she thought he was saying?

"Are you suggesting you'll kiss me?" she shot back as wet heat joined the tingle party.

"It's part of the man-eater transformation. Think of it as a data point."

Sebastian delivered this statement as cool as a cucumber—wait, not a cucumber. He was cool and composed. She needed to be suave and poised. She wanted to give off a vibe that said *I'm in control.* Had the fact that none of the men she'd kissed ever commented on her kissing meant she was bad at it? Maybe she was crap when it came to the physical stuff?

"I can see the wheels in your head turning, Pheebs," Sebastian said, looking way more chill than she felt.

"I'm concerned I'm not very good at the sexy stuff. Maybe that's why I haven't found my match."

He waved her off. "There's no good or bad. There's your starting point and what you need to do to sharpen your skills. Chemistry plays a crucial part, as well. If it's not there, you might as well be kissing your—"

"Best friend," she answered awkwardly. "There shouldn't be any chemistry when kissing your best friend because you're friends, right? You have friend chemistry, which has to be different than sexual chemistry."

Without answering, he took her chin between his thumb and index finger and tilted her head up. Was this the kissing assessment? Had it started? Adrenaline coursed through her veins. She squeezed her eyes shut, scrunched up her face, and puckered her lips—basically her hot-girl face but the eyes-closed version.

Sebastian chuckled. "Please tell me this is not how you kiss."

She opened her eyes. "Of course not. But I've never thought about . . ."

"Kissing me?" he supplied.

Moment of truth—she had thought about kissing him, but she wasn't about to cop to it.

"I have an idea." He stood, scanned the room, then appeared to zero in on a scarf draped over one of the racks Mara had left.

"What are you doing with that?" she asked, watching him pluck the scarlet material from its perch and shake it out.

He assessed the scarf. "I'm blindfolding you."

"Why?" she stammered.

"To reduce your anxiety. You can picture yourself kissing someone else."

"You're serious?" she asked, her voice jumping an octave.

"Right now, I'm not your best friend."

"You're not?"

"I'm the life coach implementing the Sebastian Guarantee.

Think of it like this: it's my job to be completely honest with you about how good a kisser you are."

The man had a point. Still, she didn't want to be the only one in the dark. She sprang to her feet, raked her gaze over the racks of clothing, then snagged a pair of lacy panties from an arrangement of lingerie. "You can cover your eyes with these."

He studied the bit of lace and satin. "You want me to put underwear on my head?"

"Yes, so you can think of someone else."

"If it makes you feel comfortable, I'm happy to oblige." He took the panties from her, then pointed back toward the table. "Sit," he directed.

His no-nonsense, commanding tone did nothing to quell what was going on between her thighs.

"We're doing this at the kitchen table?" She stared at the basic wooden table and the nondescript chairs—pieces of furniture that had never taken on a sensual appeal . . . until this very second.

"It's as good a spot as any." He shrugged like blindfolding women and kissing them at their kitchen tables carried the same emotional weight as a trip to the dentist.

"Right, sure," she answered, maintaining her composure as she returned to her seat. He folded the scarf into a long rectangle, creating a blindfold. He came up behind her. Before she could take another breath, the silky fabric covered her eyes. There was something erotic, titillating even, listening to the sounds of fabric rubbing against fabric as Sebastian tied a knot.

"I didn't tie it too tightly, did I?" he asked softly.

She shook her head. "It's great . . . totally fine . . . I like being tightly tied up."

Oh, sweet Jesus!

"What I meant was," she said, praying she wouldn't disintegrate into a pool of goo, "was that the pressure is acceptable." She could barely think straight, then stilled as she sensed him sitting across from her. She shifted in her seat. "Just to be clear. I won't think about kissing you, and you won't think about kissing me."

"That's right," he replied, his tone taking on a gravelly quality. "Are you thinking of someone else, Phoebe?"

"Yeah, totally, absolutely," she lied. "What about you?"

"Yeah, totally, absolutely," he parroted back.

She concentrated on her breathing. She could do this. It was just an assessment kiss. How many kisses had she wasted on jerks? How many of those men only wanted to lock lips with her because her last name was Gale? How many creeps were only there to use her? Too many to count, and at least this kiss would garner some data.

"Who's going to get the ball rolling on this assessment?" she asked, aiming for a professional air. "Should I because I'm going for the whole man-eater, woman-in-charge-of-her-pleasure vibe? Or maybe you should initiate the kiss because you're the one doing the critique," she yammered, then inhaled a sharp breath as two warm hands cupped her face. A thumb—no, not just *a* thumb, *Sebastian's thumb*—stroked her bottom lip. She hummed as her body tingled beneath his touch.

"Phoebe," he breathed.

She trembled. She couldn't help it. It was an involuntary reaction. Her name had never sounded so alluring or so erotically charged.

"Yes?" she answered, way breathier than she'd expected.

"Let's start slowly and build momentum."

His in-charge energy was working for her. "Wow, you've got a real process for this, like, actual techniques. That's helpful and professional. With Jeremy, kissing was a bit sloppy. Then again, for a guy with the last name of Drewler, being a sloppy kisser might be par for the—" Before she could blabber on, Sebastian's lips silenced her with a whisper-soft kiss. The barely-there contact sent her belly into a wild swirl. Nothing felt real. It was as if she and Sebastian had left the normal versions of their lives and switched to creative mode like an option in a video game.

Creative mode, like an option in a video game.

She pulled back a fraction and pushed up the blindfold. "Seb?"

"Yeah?" he answered with a strip of lace from the G-string barely covering his closed eyes.

She plucked the panties off his head and tossed them onto the table. "Look at me."

He did as she asked. Confusion marred his expression as his brows knit together. "What are you doing?"

She set the blindfold next to the panties. "It just came to me. We can think of the Sebastian Guarantee as a game, and we're playing in creative mode."

"I'm not following. What's creative mode?"

It made sense he wouldn't know. Even growing up, Sebastian had spent most of his time doing yoga or hitting a punching bag. She was the gamer, the tech nerd of their group.

"Creative mode is a gaming term," she explained. "When I was still working for my uncle and aunt at Gale Gaming, we made sure it was an option with every game. It means you get to explore the video game's world without worrying about getting killed or attacked. You're in a safe space, free of danger, where you can experiment and hone your skills without consequences." Her pulse kicked up. "Essentially, nothing counts."

Sebastian's expression grew pensive. "That sounds similar to suspending societal expectations via utilization of role-play techniques."

She didn't understand what he'd just said, but his voice was doing things to her that a best friend's voice should definitely *not* do.

"Um . . . if that's your business-y, behavioral science-y talk for doing whatever you want without repercussions to yourself or others, then yes . . . and," she beamed, "we can think of each other as characters."

Framing the Sebastian Guarantee with a gaming lens could work for her. She had already gotten one gaming element: new skins. Not to mention, she was currently rocking a non-wrinkled, chic-as-can-be designer trench coat. She was certainly dressed to pretend to be a tech-savvy man-eater of a businesswoman. She looked down at her feet, frowned, then peeled off her fuzzy socks.

"Is there a problem with those?" Sebastian asked, gazing at her now bare feet.

"I'm getting into character, and these socks won't do." Dramatically, she dropped the fuzzy white balls and stared off into the distance. Pretending to ponder whatever hot-girl man-eaters pondered, a euphoric buzz took over. She flicked her attention to Sebastian and schooled her features.

And . . . action!

"I'm Phoebe Gale, American Man-eater, and I've got my sights set on the sexiest man on the internet, a sort-of-a-Brit, Sebastian 'Mr. Lickable Abs' Cress. And one thing is guaranteed," she continued, hamming up the off-the-cuff plot of her totally bullshit fictional adult-rated video game.

"Footnote," Sebastian interjected, raising his index finger. "Despite not having an accent anymore, I am still, and will always be, one hundred percent British. And"—he paused as a deliciously wicked grin twisted his lips—"what's the *one thing* that's guaranteed?"

She could barely remain still. His enthusiastic reaction sparked a palpable zing. It surged through her, transforming her tingle party into a hornball hoedown. Emphasis on the *ho*. She sat up, smoothed her trench, then leaned in, getting nose to nose with the man. "What's guaranteed is that one hell of a kissing critique is about to take place." She pulled back and broke character. "See what I did there, Seb? I made the kissing test sound like a good time."

"Phoebe Gale?" he growled in a hot headmaster tone.

She straightened. "Yes?"

"Stop talking."

"Why?"

"Because," he answered, devouring her with his gaze, "Sebastian Cress, aka Mr. Lickable Abs, needs to examine those lips to determine—"

"Their capability as a means for inducing sexual gratification," she answered like she was reading his mind.

That boyish, crooked half-grin cracked his growly demeanor. "You took the words right out of my mouth, lass," he confirmed in a one hundred percent British accent that tipped her libido over the edge.

She sprang from her chair like a revved-up Jack-in-the-Box. She couldn't help it. She was no longer in control. The move was quasi-coordinated. Like they'd majored in chair jumping and flailing-body receiving, Sebastian caught her like a pro and drew her in close. His hands gripped her ass, locking her in place as she straddled him.

And holy titillating tumbling! This situation had gotten crazy-hot crazy-fast.

It wasn't like she'd never touched the man. They'd hugged, cuddled, and held hands, but she'd never mounted him like she was the naughtiest cowgirl at the kissing critique rodeo. But this wasn't nerdy Phoebe and her BFF, Sebby Cress. This was the American Man-eater and Mr. Lickable Abs, and nothing was off the table when it came to advancing the evolution of Phoebe Gale 2.0.

And speaking of evolution—kissing assessment or not, she decided to play by her own rules. She cupped *his* face in *her* hands and captured *his* mouth. Their lips met in a crash of man-eater passion. She went in with no plan or agenda—

simply the yearning to kiss and to be kissed. She gave herself freely, tasting and teasing. The rush of kissing this man was both nothing she'd ever expected and everything she'd always desired. There was no building up momentum. It was as if their mouths had been waiting for this moment, preparing for the very second their lips met.

Another fascinating development: sweet hallelujah, this man could kiss.

She raked her hands through his cropped hair, then wrapped her arms around his neck. Rolling her hips, her body followed the example of her mouth, moving to the beat of her rapid breaths. And it was safe to say Mr. Lickable Abs had noticed her *go get 'em-girl* assessment enthusiasm. He slipped his hands beneath the trench, then froze.

She inched away and studied his face. "What is it?"

"Phoebe, you're missing your knickers."

Knickers. That word had never sounded hotter.

She swayed her hips from side to side, feeling the distinct pressure of skin on skin as his fingertips pressed into her bare ass.

That's right, her *knicker-less* bare ass.

"I took off everything before I put on the baby doll negligee. I've never tried on lingerie before. I figured it all had to go."

He didn't reply. Like he was savoring every second, his gaze inched downward. He slid his hands from her buttocks and took the tails of the trench's belt into his hands. Deftly, he untied the belt. A dirty grin tipped the corners of his mouth as the material loosened. Feeling like a present being unwrapped, she inhaled as her coat opened, exposing the baby doll's pink silkiness cradling her breasts. The smooth, flowy material hugged her curves, and thanks to her current position, the fabric bunched just below her waist.

Playing the seductress, she dipped her left shoulder, then

her right, and allowed the stylish jacket to skim down her arms and drop onto her kitchen floor. She glanced at the discarded item. "That was a hella man-eater move, don't you think?"

He twisted a lock of her hair between his fingers. "That might be the sexiest thing I've ever seen."

Way to go, Phoebe 2.0!

Emboldened by Sebastian's comment, she gripped his shoulders and rolled her hips, finding him rock-hard between her thighs. "Is that what I think it is?"

"I'll tell you one thing. It's not a cucumber," he purred with nothing but brazen filth glittering in his eyes.

This man.

She chewed her lip, breaking character again. "It seems larger than the last time I saw it—like, a lot larger."

He traced his fingertips along the bustline of her negligee. "That last time you saw it, we were ten years old, and you walked in on Oscar and me changing into our swim trunks when we were on your aunt and uncle's boat."

She pitched to her right, losing her balance. "You remember that?"

"Are you kidding?" he replied, steadying her. "I was terrified you'd never talk to me again."

"Because I saw your . . . *penis*," she whispered.

He raised an eyebrow. "You don't have to be embarrassed about saying that word."

She flicked her wrist, going for the opposite of embarrassed. "I'm not embarrassed."

Lie alert! Nerdy Phoebe, in fact, was mortified.

"Then say it," he challenged.

Get in the game, girl.

Man-eater Phoebe 2.0 rocked her hips, slowly building friction between them. "Your *cock* appears to enjoy having me on your lap. It also appears that your penis has grown since I last saw it."

Boom! Man-eater Phoebe was killing it.

It was time to up the ante.

She reached between them and undid the top button on his trousers.

Sebastian's gaze darkened. "Do you know what you're doing?"

Good question.

Did regular Phoebe know what she was up to? Hell no. And man-eater Phoebe? She wasn't totally sure either, but she was going with it.

"What I'm doing is whatever I want," she replied smoothly. She unzipped his fly and . . . "You're going commando, too?" she exclaimed, feeling nothing but cock—a giant, fully-erect *P* to the *E* to the *N*, *I*, *S*.

He looked down, and they took in his manhood. "I was in a hurry this morning when I went to my place. I started grabbing clothes and didn't pack enough pairs of boxer briefs to get me through the weekend. I couldn't wear the same ones I've had on for the last God only knows how many hours. So yeah, you and I are both without undergarments."

"Some people might call that a problem," she said, admiring his beautiful cock. "Man-eater Phoebe calls it an opportunity."

Did she say that out loud?

She must have. Before she could part her lips to ask, Sebastian tangled one hand in her hair and drew her in. She barely had a second to register the raw animal hunger in his eyes before he demolished the slip of space between them and ravaged her mouth, kissing her with the same gusto he did when presented with a giant bowl of ice cream donning a luscious cherry on top. But that wasn't all he was doing. With his other hand, he reached beneath the baby doll lingerie. He trailed his fingertips along her inner thigh, then stroked her most sensitive place. He teased her sweet bud, then inhaled a sharp breath.

And she knew why.

She'd never been more aroused in her entire life.

It was Soaked City down at the Hornball Hoedown.

Working her slick center, he tightened his hold on her hair and deepened the kiss, rolling out the sexy-times trifecta.

Hair pulling? Check.

Lip locking? Check.

Fancy finger work between her thighs? Check, check, and . . . yes, yes, yes . . . check!

She was pleasure putty in this man's hands. Her chest heaved, and Jesus, that baby doll silkiness felt deliciously decadent against her skin as Sebastian had her writhing with wanton desire. Closer and closer, she edged toward orgasmic bliss but wanted more.

"I'm on the pill," she whispered between kisses.

"Tested . . . I'm clean," he rasped.

And holy hell, Houston, they were a go for an X-rated launch.

Was this happening? Was this really happening? Should this be happening? She shut off that part of her mind. She couldn't allow herself to think. Phoebe 2.0 wouldn't hesitate. She'd act. Phoebe lifted her hips, preparing to take every inch of him as Sebastian drank her in. His piercing gaze had her trembling. It was as if the man could see her soul.

What did he see? Who did he see?

Did he see man-eater Phoebe, or was he gazing at the hot-dog-loving, beret-wearing computer geek Phoebe? She couldn't answer that question, or perhaps she didn't want the answer. All she could do was gasp as he shrugged down his pants, then lined himself up with her entrance. Eye to eye, she lowered herself, taking him in, stretching to accommodate his girth.

Excruciatingly erotic, the sweet bite of pain mingled with the heady elation of anticipation.

"Am I hurting you?" His earnest tone nearly had her melting into a pool of swoon.

But this wasn't the time to get sappy. Channeling Phoebe 2.0, she arched her back and pressed her breasts against his chest, taking him deeper into her sweet heat. "You could never hurt me," she purred, playing the part of a seductress.

He didn't reply. With desire glinting in his eyes, he watched her ride his cock. Rising and falling, she moved like sensual waves. He cupped her face in his hands and kissed her with a desperation that struck a chord in her heart. Friction building, a spark ignited between them. He held her close, growling through heated breaths as he pumped his hips.

"Harder," she demanded.

There was no turning back.

"Bloody hell, Phoebe," he ground out, his voice hoarse and gravelly. He rose, taking her with him. She gripped his muscled arms as he rested her ass on the edge of the kitchen table. "Lie back," he commanded.

She glanced at the spot where she ate breakfast each morning. The most action it had seen was when she'd made the mistake of drinking a triple espresso after dinner a few weeks ago and ended up wired at two a.m., then decided to apply a layer of wood wax polish to the table's surface. Now she was about to get polished off, thanks to Sebastian's wood.

She pushed her laptop aside and reclined on the hard surface. He ran his hands down her torso. His touch was electric. Again, she arched her back, aching for his hard length.

"Sebastian," she moaned.

The look of absolute depravity in his eyes let her know her message had been received loud and clear.

He thrust his cock inside her. There was no pause, not even the slightest hiccup. He pistoned his hips, banging the hell out of her like he was born to do nothing else. Her breasts bounced with each powerful movement. Her core clenched around him. He licked the tips of his fingers and worked her tight bundle of nerves.

"You like it like this, don't you? You like it quick and dirty," he rasped, then inhaled a sharp breath. "You're so tight. You feel so bloody good."

And . . . dirty talk? Check!

Within seconds, she was teetering on the edge. "Kiss me," she begged, needing to be closer to him.

He pressed his hands onto the table, one on each side of her head. Leaning over, he moved like a machine, grinding against her. Their lips met in a rush of moans and heated breaths. Ready to burst, she held on to his forearms, reveling in his hard body as they made love like wild beasts, consumed with nothing but chasing carnal release.

"I'm there. I'm so close," she whispered between kisses, losing herself in the rhythm of their bodies.

"Look at me," he answered, pulling back.

She complied and gazed into his blue-green eyes as his cock filled her to the hilt, retreated, then returned to working her body at a dizzying pace.

"I'll tell you when you can come. It's one of the Sebastian Guarantee rules."

She tightened her grip on his forearms. "Don't tease me."

"You know you love it."

She did. Heaven help her. She did.

He leaned in and ran his tongue along the seam of her lips. "You can come in three, two—"

"One," she cried, allowing Phoebe 2.0 to take control. She unraveled beneath him in a pounding rush of white-hot lust. Her orgasm tore through her. It shredded her resolve. It flooded her with ripple after ripple of sublimely toe-curling ecstasy. Unable to control the dirty moans slipping past her lips, she tightened around him and clenched her core.

His eyes awash with desire, he cried out, joining her as they catapulted into fiery carnal oblivion. Her orgasm gripped her like a sea of pleasure. Nothing else existed but the two of them and the sensual slap of skin meeting skin.

Catching her breath, she held on to him. She loved his solidness and treasured the way his hard body melded with her soft curves.

"That was . . ." she began, then froze.

That was knocking out a quickie in the kitchen with her best friend.

A switch flipped, and with the precision of a Swiss timepiece, the realization of what had transpired between them hit. The yearning in Sebastian's eyes made way for utter bewilderment. She didn't need a mirror to know she had the same look slapped on her face.

"I should probably remove my . . ." he began.

"Your appendage," she supplied with a touch too much enthusiasm. "You were going to say you should remove your *appendage* from my . . . *orifice*."

Orifice? Had she ever said that word aloud? No, she hadn't. And honestly, nobody should use that word.

He nodded. "I'm going to—"

"Vacate my primary lower abdominal orifice—aka orifice central," she blurted, repeating the most god-awful words ever spoken—and she'd added *central* to the mix—like it was a cringeworthy location on the planet.

She could hear a train conductor now. *Next stop, Orifice City Center.*

"Pheebs?" he said with a wooziness to the syllable.

"Sorry, I was thinking about"—*do not say orifice trains*—"getting cleaned up," she managed.

"Right, good thinking," he stammered, then gently pulled out.

She sat up and adjusted the baby doll negligee. "About the kissing critique thing—did you get enough data?"

He pulled up his pants. "You passed the assessment. Five stars. Highly recommend." He shook his head like he was trying to activate more brain cells. "What I mean is you're proficient in that area of personal development and we can revisit this facet of your program if the need arises."

"Okay, that's helpful information, I think," she said, not even trying to decipher the Sebastian-sized helping of word salad he'd doled out. She slid off the table. "I should shower . . . in the bathroom . . . where the shower is located."

"I believe most showers are located in that room," he agreed. "Unless it's an outdoor shower—like at the beach." He cringed.

If there had been an awkward meter installed in her apartment, the thing would have blown a gasket.

She clamped her mouth shut to prevent any further word carnage, then padded across her apartment and slipped into the bathroom. The coolness of the room's bright white tile floor sent a shiver through her—or was that just her body reconciling with her head—or her heart—over what had happened? She closed the door, then caught her reflection in the bathroom mirror. Bracing herself on the sink, she studied the face of a woman she didn't quite recognize.

A lump formed in her throat. "Phoebe Gale, what have you done?"

Chapter 10
SEBASTIAN

Sebastian Cress, what have you done?

From the second Phoebe had bolted into her bathroom, that question had been stuck on repeat in his brain like a broken record. It seemed unreal—something akin to a dream. But there was no denying what had happened between them. He could still taste her kisses and feel the warmth of her soft curves as she raked her fingers through his hair. He inhaled and swore he could smell the scent of sex, spicy and fragrant, fused into his pores and blanketing his body in a sultry embrace.

Stop!

There could be no more thoughts of embraces—sultry or otherwise.

He tightened his grip on the steering wheel of Phoebe's Jeep and stared ahead into the inky darkness as they traversed the mountain road headed toward Glenn Pines Lodge. Due to the kissing assessment evolving into a session of sex-fueled revelry, they'd left later than he'd planned. He'd hoped to arrive at the lodge a few hours early and have a chance to settle in and unpack. Now, they'd be lucky if they got there two minutes before the LETIS happy hour kicked off.

Noting the time, they'd decided to make the drive in their cocktail attire. He tried to focus on the purr of the engine and the steady grind of rubber meeting the road.

It was a useless endeavor.

He couldn't get the gorgeous mute woman sitting beside him, dressed to kill in a beaded midnight blue dress, out of his head. A pair of hot pink stilettos, currently resting on the floor beside her bare feet because she hadn't mastered the art of walking in them, perfectly complemented the sexy yet sophisticated garment.

When she'd emerged from her room holding the heels in one hand, she'd looked like a barefoot man-eating femme fatale. Right then and there, he'd made a mental note to create another ten posts promoting Mara and Janelle's shop. The women had curated one hell of a wardrobe for his friend. It took everything he had not to suggest an additional round of *let's defile another flat surface*.

Alas, there was no escape from the torment—no way to get around one inextricable truth.

He'd crossed a line.

He'd banged his best friend on her kitchen table.

No, that wasn't quite it. He'd had *sex* with Phoebe Gale.

No, that wasn't it, either. It wasn't *just sex*.

He'd had plenty of *just sex* in his life. As far as sex went, there was absolutely nothing wrong with *just sex*. He'd sustained himself on the staple exclusively for the last six months. An exchange of mingled breaths and sweaty thrusts, *just sex* had served as a useful distraction.

But what he'd shared with his best friend wasn't a distraction. It wasn't a casual hookup. It wasn't a quick fuck in the loo. It had been mind-blowing, life-altering, smokin' hot sex with his best friend.

His Phoebe.

Every wild revolution of that fact whipping around in his mind rendered him more gob-smacked by the second. He couldn't stop picturing the scene. He couldn't stop imagining her dark hair fanned out in a chestnut halo, dusting her bare shoulders. He squeezed the steering wheel even harder, hoping that would shut off his brain. But it couldn't stop him from contemplating the contrast between her creamy skin and the blush of lingerie wrapping her in silky pink sexiness. When she'd slipped the trench from her shoulders and he'd drunk in her ripe, round breasts and come-hither expression, he'd nearly exploded with pent-up desire.

No woman had ever done that to him.

Under the crazy guise of American Man-eater Phoebe and Mr. Lickable Abs Sebastian, she'd kissed him first, and she hadn't stopped there—not that he was complaining. He wasn't a prude, and he was no virgin. He knew he was good in the sack. But he'd gone into every one-night stand assuming the role of the dominant party. He wasn't a selfish lover, but he also wasn't there to have his world turned upside down.

The truth is, he'd never slept with anyone who'd challenged him and pushed him out of his comfort zone.

A screw was a screw until Phoebe Gale rocked him off his axis.

Once she'd welcomed him into her sweet, wet heat and tightened around his rock-hard shaft, he'd been a goner. He couldn't have stopped even if a runaway train had been headed straight for them, horn blaring and lights flashing. Nothing could have diverted his attention from the woman.

With a white-knuckled grip on the wheel, the blood supply to his head diverted straight to his cock as the words he'd gritted out in the heat of passion flowed through his sex-addled mind.

I'll tell you when you can come.

He'd never spoken like that before. For him, sex had been about releasing steam and getting off. That's not what had happened when Phoebe ensnared him in her web with her beguiling blue eyes. He'd lost himself to the rhythm of their bodies. He hadn't thought before he'd uttered the filthy, possessive command. He'd allowed his carnal desire to take control. At that exact moment, if a genie had offered him one wish, he'd gladly have asked to remain locked in that slip of time, working Phoebe's body like a sex machine and owning every drop of her pleasure. He inhaled a tight breath, recalling the delicious slide of his cock as he watched her writhe on the table, taking every hard inch, thrust after sweaty, breathy thrust.

He swallowed hard. Jesus, what was he doing? He couldn't keep replaying the scene of their first sexual encounter again and again.

No, not only that. He couldn't think of it as their *first* sexual encounter.

It had to be their *only* sexual encounter.

He couldn't slip up. He had to focus for her and himself. But here's what he knew, one shiny nugget of crucial information: the Sebastian Guarantee had helped her harness her confidence. Sure, she'd suggested the whole video game creative mode scenario, which had helped her relax. But he'd never seen her own her sexuality. He'd known her for most of her life. He'd seen the guys she'd dated over the years. There'd been no pop or sizzle between her and whatever douche du jour she was dating.

Had he ever liked any of the guys Phoebe went out with? No! *No bloody way!* Oscar had reminded him of that. Still, he'd never seen Phoebe look at another man like she couldn't wait to be naked and tangled beneath the sheets with him—the way she'd looked at him. His approach, his Sebastian Guarantee, had to have been the catalyst that sparked her inner man-eater. And holy hell, it was one heck of a turn-on.

But he had to keep it professional. Luckily, he'd already started down that path.

When she'd retreated to the bathroom, he'd made sure he heard the shower running before he slipped his notebook from his bag and jotted down a few salient points. He'd started with the basics, compiling a list of Phoebe's personal and professional life traits—pre-Sebastian Guarantee characteristics.

Did it feel cruel to write words like *nerd, socially awkward, and poor at choosing supportive partners and advocating for oneself?* Of course it did. But he hadn't meant it as hurtful or harsh. It was science—behavioral observations required to establish a baseline. His goal was to turn her into a poised, self-assured woman who knew what she wanted and went for it. That's what she'd asked him to do. She wanted to become a man-eater. Their foray into kitchen table sex had been a fluke—an emotional reaction to a tumultuous twenty-four hours. They'd find their working, platonic Sebastian Guarantee rhythm at LETIS. They'd return to being Pheebs and Sebby, two people who genuinely loved and cared for each other as friends.

Repeat: friends, friends, friends, friends.

Still, a whisper from the back of his mind couldn't help but wonder if they were meant to be more than best friends. Just as the thought hit, he tried to imagine what life would be like if they dated and it didn't work out. A dose of clawing anxiety hit his system. His stomach twisted. His heart hammered as if, locked within it, a pendulum gauging his emotions swung wildly between one side emblazoned with the word *friend* and the other with the word *lover.*

There was only one answer.

He couldn't imagine a life without her, and he couldn't risk losing her. The six months he'd kept her at arm's length had been hell. He couldn't fixate on that, though. To successfully coach Phoebe through this weekend and get the data he needed to secure funding for his endeavors meant that he had to pull himself together. Still, when it came to his feelings for Phoebe, wouldn't it be something if the universe was kind enough to send him a sign?

"Sebastian, that's the sign," Phoebe exclaimed, her voice cutting through the quiet like a car alarm piercing the air at three in the morning.

The sign? Had she read his mind? No, Christ, she meant an actual, physical sign-sign. He blinked and caught a flash of a road sign.

Next Exit, Glenn Pines Lodge.

"Hold on!" He jerked the wheel, swerving left, then right. Thank God they were the only car on the road. "Bugger all," he murmured, hitting the brakes and banking hard to catch the off-ramp. Adrenaline exploded into his veins as he flew across two lanes of traffic. He forced himself to take a few deep breaths as the paved exit ramp gave way to an access road. Narrowing his gaze, he spied another sign for Glenn Pines and turned onto a gravel road leading straight into the dark wooded terrain.

"I didn't mean to startle you, Seb. Are you okay? Do you want me to drive?" Phoebe asked. It was the most she'd said in hours.

"No, I'm good. I was just in my head, thinking about . . ." He couldn't confess to the myriad of sexually graphic scenes he'd been playing over and over in his mind.

"What was on your mind?" she pressed.

"LETIS!" he cried like he was calling out bingo. *Take it down a notch, man.* "I was thinking about the game plan and reviewing elements of the Sebastian Guarantee." He glanced at her, sure she'd be able to see through his inane prattling, but she didn't seem to notice. Instead, he caught her wringing her hands.

Jesus, what was wrong with him? He wanted to punch himself in the mouth. She was nervous. This was a make-or-break event for her. He had to stop behaving like a horny teenager and start acting like her life coach.

With the soothing sound of the gravel crunching beneath the wheels, he gestured to the clock on the dashboard. "Looks like we made it. We've got a little over fifteen minutes to spare."

She barely nodded.

He pressed on. "It was a good idea to wear our cocktail hour clothes in the car. I think that was your idea." He sounded like a blabbering fool.

He reduced their speed as they came around a bend and a sprawling lodge emerged in the distance. Flanked by rows of lights, the Glenn Pines Lodge glowed invitingly next to a shimmering lake.

"See, we made it, and this place looks lovely." He wasn't lying. There was something enchanting about coming around a corner in the dark of night to find a mountain oasis shimmering in the distance.

Phoebe shifted in her seat. "Sebastian, pull over."

"But the lodge is only a few minutes away, Pheebs. It's right there. We're so close."

She rubbed the back of her neck. "We need to talk before we check in."

Her voice shook. It was barely perceptible, but he caught it, and it broke his heart. He slowed and eased the car to a stop beneath an iron lamppost. The golden light glinted off the beads and tiny sequins sewn into her dress like she, too, was part of the place's magic.

He could see the wheels turning in her head and decided to make the first move. "Listen, Pheebs, I know what you're worried about. I've been thinking about it, too."

"You have?" she replied, wide-eyed as she returned to

wringing her hands. "You've been thinking about what *occurred* in my kitchen?"

Occurred—now there's a word. But now wasn't the time to worry about semantics.

Be her life coach. No, be more than that. Be her best friend.

He rested his hand on hers. Instantly, she stilled the nervous wringing and inhaled a sharp breath. Maybe touching her was the wrong call. They hadn't even brushed past each other since they'd made love. The contact of his skin meeting hers sent a buzz through his body. He stroked his thumb over her knuckles as if it were second nature.

Focus on the Sebastian Guarantee.

What did he need to do? He knew the answer. He had to reframe what had happened to allow them to move forward. He removed his hand from hers, hating how it left an emptiness in his chest.

Clearing his throat, he went into work mode. "What occurred is in the past. It's not like we did anything wrong. We're adults. We share a comfort level and a familiarity with each other that carries into every facet of our lives. I can still picture your face the first time I saw you through the window when I was sitting in the back seat of Mibby's car."

"You can?" she asked, her voice a scrape of a sound.

Why the hell had he said that? This was absolutely not the time to muddy the waters. He needed to fall back on his knowledge base: business, yoga and meditation, and what he'd gleaned from experts regarding health and success.

"What *occurred*," he continued, "was merely two people driven to be their best, exceeding the standard. In other words, we're the types to go above and beyond and always give it our all. We go all in. And our *all in* with the kissing assessment spiraled into another activity."

Jesus, what a word salad.

"Okay, I think I've got it." She chewed her lip. "When we

went *all in*, what occurred involved your appendage and my orifice, like an extra credit project."

More like an extra, extra, extra credit project, but this was what they got for being two very detail-oriented people. Still, he couldn't go down this orifice-and-appendage road again. The words alone would leave a perma-cringe plastered on his face.

"And we're moving on, mindfully, with open hearts that are prepared to accept exciting new possibilities." Sweet Jesus, he was serving up another helping of word salad with an extra side of word salad slaw.

"Can we also agree," Phoebe began tentatively, "that our *all in-ness* will stay between us? As much as we love them and would never want to keep anything from them, Aria and Oscar won't be privy to the details of the all-in appendage-orifice extra credit occurrence." She cringed.

Winner, winner! They had a word salad spinner winner, and her name was Phoebe Gale.

"Agreed," he said with a relieved breath. "And Pheebs?"

"Yes?"

"I'll need you to stop saying the words *appendage* and *orifice*."

"Yeah, okay, duly noted," she answered, then pressed her hand to her mouth to stifle a flowery giggle.

"They are strangely comical-sounding words," he commented.

She smiled, and damn if it wasn't the smile that only seemed to bloom for him. "No, I'm not laughing about the words. I just remembered another secret we've kept from Aria and Oscar since our college days."

He leaned toward her. "What secret?"

"The grand cake debacle," she announced dramatically.

Straightaway, his anxiety eased as he recalled what she was talking about. "Oh, yes, the time when we decided to bake Aria and Oscar a big-ass cake since their birthdays are only a few days apart." He relaxed into his seat and chuckled. "You know, the grand cake debacle was ninety-nine percent your fault."

She gasped and swatted his forearm. "It was not. I had my earbuds in and was happily icing their birthday cake, listening to music and getting my cake groove on, when you snuck up behind me and scared the living shit out of me."

His chuckle evolved into a full belly laugh. "You spun around and knocked the whole damned cake onto the floor. The chocolate was everywhere, and oh my God, your expression. You were so freaked out."

"My expression?" she tossed back. "You'd gone as white as a ghost and had guilt written all over your face."

There had been a reason he'd looked like that, but it wasn't what she thought. The real reason had nothing to do with cake. But now wasn't the time to divulge that information. He forced himself back into best friend mode. "Maybe that's true. But who solved our problem?" he asked, taking on a cocky edge and pointing to himself so there could be no doubt as to who had saved the day.

That got him another playful slap. "No way! I got us out of that mess."

"What?" he exclaimed. "I went to Cupid Bakery and picked up another cake."

"You did, but . . ." she snapped in that school marm-y tone that never boded well for him.

He reared back. "But what?"

"*But*, I had the presence of mind to take a knife and mess up the frosting to give it an authentic, made by Sebby and Pheebs feel." Her expression grew pensive. She glanced down at her dress, toyed with a bead, then met his gaze. "Are we okay, Seb?"

Emotion welled in his chest, and he took her hand. "We'll always be okay. You're my best friend. And we're in creative mode. Remember, it's like you said: we're in a safe place to hone skills where nothing counts." He'd spoken the truth. Still, he hated the way that last part sounded.

She gave his hand a weak squeeze, then slipped from his grip. "Nothing counts," she repeated, her voice losing the bubbly quality he adored.

A heavy silence fell between them, and he cleared his throat. "We should get a move on." Not sure how they'd gone from awkward to comfortable and back to awkward again, he shifted the Jeep into drive and followed the gravel road toward the lodge.

It only took a few minutes to get there. He stopped the car beneath the building's rustic porte cochere, pulled the lever to pop the back hatch, then got out and jogged over to the passenger side. He opened the door for Phoebe as an older woman with rosy cheeks, donning a wooly cardigan, and a slim young man in jeans and a flannel, pushing a luggage cart, emerged from the lodge.

"Welcome to Glenn Pines," she said, ambling slowly as the man zipped by with the rattling cart. "I'm Mae Edwards, the owner. You must be Phoebe Gale and Sebastian Cress."

"Yes, that's us," Phoebe answered, slipping on the pink heels, then grabbing her purse before Sebastian helped her out of the car.

"You're the last to arrive," Mae explained, handing them each a lanyard with their name and *innovator* written on a card tucked in a clear plastic sleeve. "Go ahead and put those on. The LETIS cocktail hour is taking place at the old boathouse by the lake. They seem to be running a bit behind schedule, so I don't believe you've missed anything yet." She gestured toward a large structure with twinkling lights that looked more like a grand lakeside pavilion than a musty old boathouse. "I'll have my grandson Bruce bring your bags to your room."

The young man nodded.

"You mean *rooms*," Phoebe clarified, teetering as she took a step in the sky-high heels.

And dammit, he'd forgotten that he'd have to build in some time for her to practice walking in stilettos.

Mae shared a look with Bruce, then waved for him to bring the bags inside. She folded her hands in front of her. "We're in the middle of renovating the rooms on the east side of the lodge."

"I'm not sure I'm following you," Sebastian said.

"I must have misunderstood when you called to confirm, Mr. Cress," the owner began. "I got the impression you and Miss Gale were attending together, which was fortunate because you were also the last to confirm you were coming. You were able to secure our last room."

Phoebe wobbled, then clutched his arm to remain upright. "You only have one room available?"

"One room, two keys," the woman crooned, producing the bits of metal from her wooly pocket. She looked between them, eyeing them closely. "That won't be a problem, will it?"

He glanced at Phoebe. Rocking a deer-caught-in-the-headlights expression, her thoughts were plain to him.

So much for keeping it professional.

Chapter 11
SEBASTIAN

One room. This had to be a joke. But their host wasn't laughing.

What the hell was the universe throwing their way now?

Sebastian glanced at Phoebe. She smiled her oh-shit smile —the one that looked like her lips might snap from being stretched like a piece of taffy. But her nails digging into his forearm gave away her true reaction.

Mae looked between them, clinking the metal room keys in her hand. "Your room is quite spacious, and there's a folding cot in the closet."

"I'm sure the room is perfect. We're happy to have it," he replied and accepted the keys. "Phoebe and I have been friends for years. We'll be fine sharing a room."

Phoebe's nails retracted, and she released his arm. They could handle this. There was a cot. They could keep it professional, right?

"Wonderful!" Mae chirped, then peered into the Jeep. "I see you left your keys on the dash. Bruce will take care of parking your car. Now, I'm going to sit by the fire. My quilting group is in town, and we have quite a bit to sew and catch up on. So I'll let you get to your first event." Gifting them with one last smile, she started toward the lodge.

He jogged to get ahead to open the door for her. Peeking inside, he spied three women by a roaring fire. All around the same age as Mae, the group was bent over a table covered with a quilt and patches of fabric. Mae shuffled inside, and he rested his hand on the woman's shoulder. "We appreciate your hospitality, Mrs. Edwards."

"You're very welcome, dear," she answered, then glanced over her shoulder at Phoebe, who was staring down at her pink stilettos, oblivious to the woman's attention. "My goodness, just look at her," Mae said softly as the warmth of her words took on a dream-like quality.

My goodness, just look at her? That was an odd statement. He was about to ask Phoebe if she recognized Mae Edwards when two women, one with short red hair and the other with a long black braid, carrying champagne flutes and wearing LETIS lanyards, breezed past him, exiting the building after Mae entered. He'd barely released the handle when a gasp pierced the air.

"Phoebe Gale?" the woman with a braid blurted.

Phoebe swayed atop the heels but regained her balance. "Yes, I'm Phoebe Gale."

"I owe you a debt of gratitude," the woman crooned. "I met my husband because of your food truck app." She touched the card attached to her lanyard. "I'm Carla Lopez, one of the editors for Techy Times. I wrote about your matchmaking food truck app. This is Tracey, my assistant."

Phoebe lit up. "It's nice to meet you both. Thank you for writing that piece, Carla. I'm so happy for you, and I believe I owe you a debt of gratitude, too. I think your article is what earned me an invitation to LETIS. Perhaps Techy Times nominated me?"

Carla shook her head. "We don't have anything to do with that."

"You don't?"

"No, Zinger was in charge of extending invites to the tech innovators this year."

"I see. I wasn't sure how that worked."

"Are you here promoting Munch Match as a matchmaking app?" Carla asked, then took a sip of champagne. "I'm sure you could make a fortune if you sold the algorithm. Everyone and their brother are looking to launch the perfect dating app. I can't even tell you how many I tried before meeting my husband thanks to yours."

Phoebe twisted a lock of hair nervously, then released it. "No, not exactly. I'm hoping to secure funding to create an online community that connects and empowers girls and women across the globe. I'm calling it Go Girl."

Carla nodded, then took another sip. She glanced his way as he returned to Phoebe's side, then scanned his name tag and frowned.

That was not a good sign.

"Did you come with Sebastian Cress?" the Techy Times editor asked Phoebe in the same tone one would use when enquiring about rancid cheese.

Despite Janelle reporting otherwise, it appeared not everyone had moved on from his Tech Tweens snub.

Phoebe looked between him and the frowning Carla. "I did, and I can see from your reaction that you've seen the viral video."

"I was a Tech Tween," Carla quipped, her scowl deepening as she glared at him. "I cannot believe you'd do that to twelve-year-old girls."

This was not how he wanted to start the weekend. "I never meant . . . I didn't mean," he stammered.

Phoebe rested her hand on his arm. He met her gaze as an

eyeball conversation ensued where she told him to shut his trap. He wasn't about to argue.

"It was a terrible misunderstanding," his best friend explained. "Sebastian was being hounded at the airport. He sprinted away from people filming him and jumped into the first cab he could find. He feels awful about the whole situation and plans on apologizing in person after LETIS. Isn't that right, Seb?" Phoebe eyeball-ordered him to agree.

And he did—wholeheartedly. But this was no small matter. Phoebe had just vouched for him to a heavyweight in her field. Her reputation was as much on the line as his. Not to mention, she'd done the same thing with Tula and Ivy. He couldn't ask for a better friend. But he couldn't have her fighting his battles without backup.

He turned to face Carla's wrath. "That's what happened," he replied. "I have a little sister. I would never intentionally leave children out in the rain."

"The video that's been trending makes it look like you were enamored with yourself, snapping selfies, and that you completely ignored the girls," Carla countered.

"Being women in tech," Phoebe said gently, "we both know that there are usually two or even more sides to any video that goes viral. It's easy to find a clip that paints someone in an unfortunate light. But I can promise you, it was truly a misunderstanding. Sebastian would never knowingly hurt anyone."

His throat thickened with gratitude. But was there a touch of shame sprinkled into the mix?

The Techy Times' editor's expression softened. "That does make more sense," the woman conceded. "The community center I went to back in Chicago when I was growing up was funded by a Cress Family Grant. Your family's philanthropic efforts have helped many kids and teens—me included. I doubt people like your parents could raise a giant douchebag."

His father may have begged to differ, but Sebastian would take whatever goodwill he could get from this woman.

Phoebe squeezed his arm. "I guarantee that Sebastian Cress is one of the good guys."

He smiled appreciatively, but he couldn't ignore the gnawing feeling inside and the little voice in the back of his head. *Was he one of the good guys?*

A chime cut through the air as Carla's assistant slipped her cell from her clutch. The woman stared at her phone. "We need to get back. They're supposed to start the LETIS welcome spiel in five minutes."

"Sponsor duties call," Carla said, sounding a lot less like she wanted to toss his ass into the nearby lake. "Good luck to you both."

"And you might want to be careful," Tracey added and glanced at his trousers.

"Careful?" he asked.

"Your notebook is about to fall out of your pocket," the assistant answered, then followed a step behind Carla as the women made their way toward the boathouse.

He felt Phoebe's eyes on him. He tucked the slim pad deeper into his front pocket. He couldn't have her getting a glimpse. "All right," he said, needing to draw her attention away from the pad. And he knew just how to do it. "It's go-time. First impressions are what matter now. Close your eyes and listen to what I'm about to tell you. I want you to soak in this message before we step foot in that boathouse."

She glanced past him, eyeing the spot humming with activity. "Do I have to?"

"Yes."

She watched him for a beat, exhaled an audible breath, then obeyed the request.

It was time to harness the power of the Sebastian Guarantee. But what did that mean exactly? Sure, he had reams of research, but he'd never broken it down into actionable steps. He'd have to wing it. "You are Phoebe Gale, tech mastermind. You know you've got what the investors want. You're also a man-eater extraordinaire. You're confident. You're most comfortable when all eyes are on you."

The gentle sounds of the lake lapping against the shore tangled with the hum of conversation floating toward them from the boathouse. He watched her. Her eyes were closed. But she wasn't relaxed.

She nibbled on her lip. "What if nobody takes Go Girl seriously? What if all I ever achieve is a food truck finder app that accidentally helped people meet their significant other? I don't even know how it works, Seb."

"With my coaching, I'm certain LETIS is where you'll become who you are supposed to be," he assured her.

She opened her eyes. "And who is that?"

The breeze blew a lock of her hair across her face. Without giving it a second thought, he tucked the hair behind her ear. His fingertips grazed her neck, and he cupped her face in his hand. "You're the brains behind Go Girl. You'll make that dream a reality."

"You believe that?" she asked, her breathy voice stirring a longing deep within him.

He traced the line of her jaw with the pad of his thumb. "I do." He was on the cusp of losing himself in her blue eyes—his friend's blue eyes.

Friend, friend, friend. Remember that! He could not allow himself to blur that line again.

He forced himself to pull away. "But don't worry about getting into the weeds with pricing structures or concerning yourself with analyzing website traffic," he continued. "I guarantee tonight isn't about pitching ideas. Tonight is about . . ." He paused, worried he was dropping too much information at once. "Tonight is about giving them a whiff," he said as the pieces of what he wanted the Sebastian Guarantee to look like fell into place.

Phoebe's jaw dropped, and she teetered back a step. "A whiff, like the sense of smell? Do I smell bad?"

He watched her lift her arm and discreetly sniff, but he couldn't assure her that she didn't stink because her words had sparked an epiphany.

Sense of smell . . . the senses. That was it.

"Phoebe, you're a genius!" he exclaimed.

"A foul-smelling genius?" she asked, giving her other armpit a sniff.

"No, you smell fine. I'm talking about the senses. That's the . . ." He recalled the words from his meeting with Bernadette and Claudette.

"The what?" she asked.

"The unifying concept. The fresh take on life coaching," he answered, barely able to contain his excitement.

She gave him a wary once-over. "I'll let you marinate on your fresh take while I make a pit stop in the ladies' room. I'll meet you at the boathouse."

"I'll be there."

Ideas raced through his mind. He had to get it down. He slipped his notebook from his pocket and removed the little pen from the metal spiral. Setting off on the path toward the boathouse, he thumbed through the pad until he found a blank page. Walking and writing at the same time, he listed the five senses: smell, sight, sound, taste, and touch. He could easily organize his core principles around them. It was relatable and memorable.

The Sebastian Guarantee: Success by the Senses.

There it was!

He laughed to himself as relief and elation coursed through his veins. Thanks to Phoebe, his business plan was coming together.

Standing a few steps from the boathouse, he returned the pen to the spiral binding, pocketed his notebook, then took in the lake. The moonlight shimmered on the surface. And he felt it. There was magic in the air. With his heart pounding, he scanned the cocktail hour participants. He recognized a few health and wellness influencers who also had large followings online.

He continued perusing the crowd when a woman in white caught his eye. She glanced away from the trio of men she was conversing with and nodded to him. His stomach dropped. What was Claudette and Bernadette's associate doing here? Was she there to keep an eye on him? Had the sisters sent her to scope out other health and lifestyle entrepreneurs?

"Ladies and gentlemen," a woman with a glowing ebony complexion said into a microphone, cutting off his spiraling train of thought. "Welcome to—" Before she could continue, an earsplitting alarm pierced the night air, followed by the *bam* of a door slamming. She, along with everyone else, swiveled toward the source of the sound.

His jaw dropped. The source of that sound appeared to be Phoebe.

Standing in front of a door with an *emergency exit only* sticker fixed across the top, Phoebe froze. Mae's grandson Bruce sprinted toward the door, coming in fast from inside the lodge. The kid inserted a key into a box on the door, and the blaring ceased.

Aside from the lapping lake, not a peep could be heard from the LETIS participants. Hopefully, she'd taken heed of his *you want all eyes on you* speech because every single LETIS participant was currently looking right at her—which wasn't a bad turn of events. The lights glimmered off the beads and mini sequins sewn into the dress. Taking on an ethereal quality, she looked every part the sexy, sophisticated siren. She flashed her stretched-taffy smile and didn't move a muscle.

He hurried to her side. "What are you doing, Pheebs?" he asked under his breath.

"I took off my glasses and put them in my purse. I didn't realize this was an emergency exit until it was too late," she answered with a forced grin. "Is everyone looking at me?"

He surveyed the crowd. "Yep."

"I don't hear any laughing."

He drank her in. "It's because you're stunning. They're staring because you're an absolute knockout. Are you okay?"

"My vision is blurry, and my feet are literally killing me. How do women wear these all day?"

"Take my arm and let me do the talking." He surveyed the still-stunned LETIS participants. "False alarm, folks," he said to the crowd, walking at a geriatric turtle's pace toward the lake with Phoebe clutching his arm. He looked around and caught the eye of the young woman in white again. She was on the phone, just like when he met with the Marieuse sisters.

"What an exciting way to open the sixth symposium," the woman with the mic mused, pulling the crowd's attention from Phoebe.

"Thanks for coming to my rescue," Phoebe whispered, leaning into him.

"What are friends for?" There! *Friends.* He'd said it. Now, did that stop the insane, possessive urge to wrap his arm around her so every guy still stealing glances thought she was with him? No. But he fought it.

"Let's start again," the woman with the mic said. "I'm Josephine Carlisle, one of the LETIS board members. I'd like to welcome our innovators and investors and thank our main sponsor, Zinger, and the Glenn Pines Lodge, for making this unique event possible. For the next couple of days, you'll enjoy camp-style activities where investors and innovators can interact in a casual, fun-filled environment. The schedule of events is listed in the folder we've placed in your rooms. In the past, LETIS has fostered many lucrative collaborations. Look around. Your perfect match could very well be standing next to you."

Perfect match?

Phoebe's entire body tensed—or perhaps it was him.

"I'm also excited to announce that we've added a twist to this year's LETIS. We're calling it LETIS Live."

Phoebe tapped his arm. "Did you know about a twist?"

He shook his head. "The confirmation email was pretty light on details. But it did mention something about needing to stay in the area after LETIS ended."

"At the last five symposiums," Josephine continued, "we've announced innovator-investor pairings on the final day. This year, we'll broadcast those partnerships at a live event in Denver three days after our time at Glenn Pines ends. But that's not all," Josephine teased. "If an innovator doesn't connect with an investor during the symposium, LETIS Live will provide one final chance to pitch your idea and wow our handpicked group of unmatched investors. Now, mix and mingle. We wish everyone the best of luck."

"Should we mingle?" Phoebe asked as the hum of side conversations returned. "Everything is a bit blurry. As long as you make sure I don't fall into the lake or open any more emergency exit doors, I should be fine."

He studied the crowd. People were talking in small groups, but nobody appeared to pay much attention to their conversations. They were still tossing furtive glances Phoebe's way.

"No, our work here is done. You've accomplished what you needed to do."

She cocked her head to the side. "I did?"

He nodded. "They got a whiff of you, Pheebs. That's catering to the sense of smell."

"We're back to smell?" she replied, her voice rising an anxious octave. "I thought I smelled pretty good?"

"You do. I'm employing senses as a framework. The whiff-sense-of-smell is the first step. For sight, they get to see you. But you'll leave them wanting. That'll lead to sound—the buzz. You want people talking about you. Do you understand where I'm going with this? These principles work for both your professional and personal goals."

Phoebe's hold on his arm loosened as she relaxed. "Wow, okay, I totally get it, and I'm game. What about taste and touch?"

"We'll get to those." He did another scan of the space. "But we need to make an exit. Everyone knows you're here. And believe me, you caught every man and woman's eye."

"This might work, huh?" She beamed up at him. "Phoebe Gale, Tech-Boss and American Man-eater, is ready to kill it at LETIS, thanks to the Sebastian Guarantee."

Her enthusiasm was contagious. She had no idea how sexy she was when she was bursting with confidence.

"Come on," he said, snagging two champagne flutes from a passing waiter's tray. He offered her a glass. "Let's check out the room and nail down a game plan."

Phoebe took the flute and clinked it with his. "To—" she began, but her lit-from-within light dimmed as she looked past him. "Oh no, I forgot about that."

What could be such a buzzkill?

"What did you forget about, Pheebs?"

She swallowed hard and tightened her grip on his arm. "Even half-blind, I recognize the glasses and the strawberry blond man bun. It's Jeremy Drewler, and he's headed straight for us."

Chapter 12
SEBASTIAN

Sebastian looked over his shoulder. Phoebe was right. He recognized the wannabe hipster techie, Jeremy Drewler, from her social media posts. He also recognized that the white-hot anger roiling through his body might compel him to hurl this butthole douche nozzle into the lake.

Phoebe tapped her foot five times.

"I was thinking the same thing. I read you loud and clear, Pheebs," he murmured. "You've got this. Play it cool. I'll pretend to laugh at something you said, then we'll make our exit. Jackasses like that drool king have no hold on you. You're with me now," he added, not knowing exactly what he meant by that. It should mean he was there as her friend, but again, like God knows how many other times over the last twenty-four hours, it didn't ring entirely true.

In his defense, it was one thing to hear Phoebe describe what the asshat, Jeremy, had said to her. He'd viewed the video of the shitshow after Phoebe had fallen asleep, and that had also pissed him the hell off. But seeing the guy in the flesh brought out a level of protectiveness he could barely contain.

Phoebe nodded. "He's about to get a whiff of man-eater Phoebe 2.0 and have his senses blown away."

"That's the Sebastian Guarantee spirit." He liked her energy. Now he had to keep himself in check. Murdering a LETIS innovator at the welcome cocktail party—even one as despicable as Jeremy Drewler—wouldn't be a good look.

"Okay, laugh," she said under her breath.

He chuckled, then took a sip of champagne. "Phoebe, your razor-sharp wit is hilarious."

Jeremy slowed his pace, then looked Phoebe up and down like he couldn't believe his eyes. *Lap it up, buttercup*. Phoebe Gale was a stone-cold fox, and she was his . . . his friend. He grimaced. How many damned times would he have to remind himself of that? Christ, twice in less than sixty seconds, obviously. But there was no time to concern himself with his struggle with the term *friend* while a befuddled Jeremy stood before them.

"Phoebe, I hardly recognized you. You look different—terrific, gorgeous even," the jackass blabbered, talking like he'd just figured out how his mouth worked.

Phoebe slapped a shit-eating grin on her lips. "Thanks, Jeremy. You look . . . the same."

Boom! Hello, Glenn Pines Lodge. Phoebe, the American Man-eater, was in the house.

Jeremy glanced at him. "And Sebastian Cress," the man stammered like he was still getting the hang of the English language. "We haven't met, but I've heard a lot about you. Phoebe talks about you all the time. I feel like I know you, and of course, you're internet famous. I'd leave those kids in the rain, too. Dog-eat-dog world, right? Anyway, I'm Jeremy Drewler. I'm not sure if Phoebe mentioned me to you."

They'd knocked the butthole douche nozzle off-balance. The guy sounded like he belonged in a padded cell. Another good sign. Then again, there was something slightly contrived in his nervous demeanor. Was he pretending to be nervous?

Sebastian held the man's gaze for a long beat, taking a page from his dad's boxing ring playbook. Looking at a guy a second longer than what was socially accepted was a strategic way to assert dominance. Just when he thought Jeremy was about to shit his pants, he flicked his attention to the lapping lake. "I know who you are, Jeremy."

"Right, because Phoebe and I are . . ." Jeremy shifted his stance and took a step toward Phoebe.

"Are what?" Phoebe mused and raised her hand, signaling the man to stay back. "And by the way, how's your friend Tina doing?"

Sebastian didn't know who Tina was, but it didn't take a degree in rocket science to infer that Jeremy had a chick on the side. He should chuck the guy into the water for Phoebe, this random Tina, and probably every other woman who'd endured dating this tool.

"She's just somebody I know," Jeremy answered, then glanced over his shoulder toward a trio of man-bun hipsters. They must have been Jeremy's tech bros because they sure as hell weren't surveillance specialists. The men were doing their best—and failing miserably—to appear as if they weren't glued to this interaction.

Phoebe took a sip of champagne. "Like I was just *somebody* you knew?"

"Could I speak with you, Pheebs, privately?" Jeremy asked, lowering his voice.

Phoebe reared back. "You've never called me *Pheebs* before."

"Really? I thought I had," the man answered, then flicked his gaze toward the tech bros.

"*Pheebs* is what the people who love me call me." Phoebe took another sip of champagne. "And anything you have to say to me, you can say in front of Sebastian, my best and closest friend."

Sebastian puffed up. "That's right, Drewler. I'm her best friend. And we don't have all night to stand here lollygagging. Speak your piece, Strawberry Man Bun."

Strawberry Man Bun? That sounded like the annoying hipster stepbrother of Strawberry Shortcake, and it was one gem of a response. Phoebe appeared to like it as well. She pressed her lips into a tight line. He knew that face. She was trying her hardest not to laugh her ass off.

Jeremy flashed heartsick puppy-dog eyes at her. "My behavior was atrocious. I didn't mean what I said."

Phoebe tapped her chin and frowned. "I'm confused, Jeremy. You said quite a bit. Let me get this straight. You didn't mean that you were only dating me to get in with my uncle and aunt. Or you didn't mean that I wasn't the kind of woman a man would want by their side. Or perhaps, it was the statement about me only getting invited to LETIS because I have two X chromosomes."

Phoebe Gale wasn't taking any prisoners tonight.

Jeremy toyed with his strawberry blond man bun. "All of the above. I was stressing about LETIS. Like you, I want to succeed so badly. I let that cloud my judgment. I said some terrible things. I'm so sorry—so very sorry."

Sebastian waited for Phoebe to let loose another verbal jab. A few seconds passed, but she didn't make a peep. He glanced down and could barely believe that her expression had softened.

She mustered a weak grin. "The things you said were cruel and hurtful, but I appreciate your apology."

"What?" Sebastian yipped like a flabbergasted Chihuahua. He couldn't help it. How could she fall for Jeremy's fake act of contrition?

"I'll do whatever it takes to make it up to you, Pheebs," the man continued, laying the blubbering on thickly.

And who did he think he was, calling her Pheebs? He didn't have the right to call her that.

A muscle ticked in Sebastian's jaw. He glanced at Jeremy's man bun squad. The trio didn't even try to disguise their interest. This was bullshit. Jeremy was playing her. The man bun audience proved that the douche had something up his sleeve. But what?

"I don't know what to say to that, Jeremy," Phoebe replied, clearly taken aback, and rightly so. The guy had gone from telling her she wasn't worth his time to begging her to forgive him.

"Say you'll let me make up for my bad behavior," he replied, heaping on the fake sincerity.

Phoebe released a pained sigh. With her lips pressed into a slight grimace, she looked downright conflicted. And no, no, no! She could not be conflicted, not over this poser. And she wasn't exhibiting her man-eater demeanor. But he knew what was going on in Phoebe's head—no, in her heart. Phoebe had the biggest heart of anyone he knew. And Jeremy Drewler appeared to also be in on that fact—and damned gleeful to take advantage of it. Still, Sebastian wasn't about to let Mr. Strawberry Man Bun manipulate her. He touched her arm, about to remind her that they needed to blow this cocktail hour, when a woman called Phoebe's name.

"Do you have a second to chat in the lodge?" the familiar voice continued.

He glanced toward the source of the sound and spied Carla Lopez.

"It's Carla, the Techy Times editor," he said under his breath. He was pretty sure Phoebe couldn't make out who was calling her name. "She's by the side doors leading to the lodge.

The non-emergency doors. I'd suggest using that door unless you want to make another blaring grand entrance."

"Very funny," Phoebe replied, sounding more like herself. "Will you both excuse me?"

"Certainly," Jeremy crooned.

"Do you want me to walk you over?" Sebastian asked, ignoring Jeremy as irritation prickled down his spine.

"I'm good. I'm getting the hang of these shoes," she answered, then lifted her high-heel-clad foot.

"I'll meet you inside," Sebastian replied, then threw a pointed glance at the drooler. "I'll be close by. I've always got your back, Pheebs."

Phoebe flashed an appreciative smile, then set off for the lodge. Now he needed to get away from Jeremy before he hurt the guy. Without saying a word, he started toward the building and spied Phoebe through the floor-to-ceiling windows lining this side of the lodge. Carla appeared to be introducing her to a group of men. He entered the rustic space and caught a snippet of the conversation.

A man slipped Phoebe his card. "We're fascinated by your Munch Match app, Ms. Gale, and its application in the dating and relationship sectors. Most dating sites pair couples based on a myriad of psychological assessments. It's intriguing that your app bucks that line of thinking. Can you tell us more?"

Phoebe hesitated, wavering for a second, and he knew why. She was debating whether she should shut down the Munch Match talk and pivot to Go Girl. When he heard her explain the technical nuts and bolts of the food truck matching app, he breathed a sigh of relief.

He wasn't trying to be a jerk. Phoebe wanted to promote her Go Girl concept. He understood that. It was her passion. But this group appeared genuinely interested in another one of her projects. Her Munch Match app could be the quickest route to success.

He hung back, far enough away not to intrude but close enough to hear the conversation float through the cavernous space. He leaned against an exposed timber and casually slipped his hand into his pocket. Anxiety panged in his chest as he felt the slim notepad, but then a realization took hold. Promoting the Munch Match app could also be the quickest route to success—for himself and his case study. Success was success, right? If she had to hold off on Go Girl for a little while, it wouldn't be the worst thing in the world. Even her uncle had told her not to limit herself. As her friend and life coach, he'd guide her toward the fastest path to promoting her business.

Yep, that's what he was doing.

He was helping her. He was helping her and helping himself. Nothing wrong with that. Except, she didn't know about the *helping himself* part. He couldn't get that not-so-little tidbit out of his head. But he'd have to get past it if he wanted to succeed. It wasn't like keeping her in the dark hurt her. He was no Jeremy, was he? No, he couldn't be. He took a sip of champagne to quell his nerves, when the ladies quilting near the fire roused his attention. He soon learned he wasn't the only one keeping an eye on the beguiling Phoebe Gale.

The women tossed curious glances Phoebe's way, then murmured to each other like they recognized her. He'd gotten the same feeling when Mae welcomed them to the lodge. Phoebe's family was from Colorado. That's where her uncle and her birth parents had grown up, but it was a big state. What connection could she have to an old lady who owned a lodge and her gray-haired sewing buddies?

He checked his watch. He didn't have time to worry about a group of little old ladies. He couldn't have Phoebe spending too much time with the investors tonight. Sticking with his new Sebastian Guarantee framework, she'd given them a hint and generated the buzz. It was time to get back to the room to strategize. He took a step toward her, but someone tapped his shoulder.

Not someone—some asshole.

The one and only Jeremy Drewler.

Sebastian shrugged off the man's hand. "Are you lost?"

"No, I'm right where I want to be," the guy answered, losing the earnest edge he'd employed with Phoebe and utilizing a decidedly more devious tone as his gaze raked over her.

Sebastian kept his expression neutral. "Is that so? Don't you think you should be schmoozing with the investors? You droned on about how badly you want to succeed."

Jeremy's lips twisted into a cocksure smirk. "There's an excellent chance I already have financing lined up. This morning, I received an email from an investment group that's very interested in working with me."

"How nice for you," Sebastian served up with a helping of *I couldn't give a flying fuck* laced into his reply. "Are you sure it wasn't some internet scam? A phishing email from a prince somewhere across the globe?"

With a smug air, Jeremy lifted his chin. If he were a rooster, he'd be crowing. "Oh, this investment firm is legit. I checked them out. They have offices in the US, Europe, and Asia. They're called . . . the Marieuse Group."

Chapter 13
SEBASTIAN

The Marieuse Group?

Sebastian's heart leaped into his throat. He swallowed hard, doing his best to appear unfazed by the colossal bomb the drooler had dropped. And if that wasn't enough, the woman in white, the Marieuse Group assistant herself, walked past them with her cell pressed to her ear. The woman caught his eye. He nodded to her, but Jeremy didn't react.

"Do you recognize her?" he asked, trying to discern how much Drewler knew about the Marieuse organization.

Jeremy gave the woman a once-over. "She's got a nice ass. I'd like to know her. Is she your type? Will the lady in white be your next conquest?"

A knot twisted in Sebastian's stomach. "No, forget it. I'm not interested in her like that," he muttered, so damned angry he'd spent the last six months posting his exploits online like a vapid playboy. That, coupled with the news that the Marieuse Group had contacted Jeremy Drewler, had thrown one hell of a wrench into the situation.

"Listen," Jeremy said, leaning in, "I messed up with Phoebe. But you get it, right?"

What was Strawberry Man Bun talking about? On what planet would *getting it* mean he was okay with this loser breaking his best friend's heart? He sized up the man. "No, I don't get it."

Jeremy adjusted his bullshit hipster glasses as a slimy grin leaked across his lips. "I think you do. I started following you on social media the day I met Phoebe. You're with a different woman every day of the week. Don't get me wrong—I'm not judging. Who wouldn't want that life? But seeing Phoebe without that stupid beret and not covered in hot dog condiments would make any man take a second look."

"Is that so?" Sebastian shot back, wishing they were near the edge of the lake.

"Sure, who could have thought that ugly duckling of a tech nerd could turn into a smokin' hot swan?"

Disgusted, Sebastian glared at the man.

"As her friend," Jeremy continued, undeterred, "I'm sure you want her to be happy."

"As her *best friend*," Sebastian countered, "I don't want her to be jerked around by some guy who's only out to use her."

Jeremy Drewler didn't care about Phoebe—not in the way she deserved to be cared for. Sebastian tightened his hand into a fist. Did he want to employ a few well-placed jabs straight to Jeremy's kidneys and maybe a sharp pop to his left cheek? Hell yes. The man's smug expression was begging to be pummeled clean off his face. But he couldn't make a scene. And he didn't want to upset Phoebe.

The slimy grin returned to Jeremy's face. "I get it. We both want what's best for Phoebe. And with that thinking, would you mind doing me a favor?"

Sebastian scoffed. "You want me to do you a favor?"

"Yeah, keep the news of the Marieuse Group between us. I don't want Phoebe or anyone else catching wind that I'm on the cusp of partnering with another investment firm. I wouldn't want her wanting me for my money, you know what I mean? If things go my way, I'll get the girl and have investors clamoring to pay me buckets of cash."

"You're trying to get her back?" Sebastian blasted.

"Look at her. What man wouldn't want her? Besides you, since you're her best *friend*," the man replied, placing an oily emphasis on the last word.

Sebastian schooled his features. "Do you think I'd allow that?"

"It's not up to you, bro," Jeremy replied, puffing up like an overstuffed strawberry blond turkey.

This douche nozzle was walking a fine line.

"I'm not your bro, and Phoebe would never take you back."

Jeremy offered up an aloof shrug. "I don't know about that. You saw her face when I apologized. That sappy stuff turns her into a tenderhearted pile of mush. And then there's our love match."

A muscle ticked in Sebastian's jaw. He knew what was coming.

"We met in line at a food truck, thanks to the Munch Match app," Jeremy answered coolly. "And Phoebe told me about how a matchmaker said her match had already been made. Why couldn't it be me? It certainly couldn't be you, right?"

Sebastian tightened his fist and ground his teeth together. If he wasn't careful, he'd bust a molar. But he couldn't help himself. It was as if he'd been thrust back in time to that damned day. His phone had pinged an incoming text, and the message had gutted him to the very core. But he couldn't let this wanker know he'd hit a nerve. He schooled his features—but he must not have done a very good job of hiding his reaction.

Jeremy's slimy smile oozed wider. "Or do you believe you're

her love match? Do you want her for yourself now that she's a knockout? I wonder how that would make her feel?"

Jeremy Drewler was one slippery snake.

Sebastian hardened his gaze. "What I want is none of your business, *boyo*."

Yep, he'd busted out the *boyo*. He also wanted to throw a few well-placed jabs and knock the smug prick down a couple of pegs. Thank Christ he'd been raised by a master yogi who'd taught him to harness his powerful emotions. Otherwise, this *tech bro* would be walking with a limp for the rest of his life.

Sebastian gestured toward Jeremy's squad. "Why don't you get back to your little man bun-ettes? But before you do, remember one thing."

"What's that?"

Sebastian tapped into his spiritual side and looked the man over. "Your aura is absolute bullshit, and I have the distinct feeling the universe is preparing one hell of a karma cake for you. Word to the wise—don't press your luck with me." He hadn't lied to the man. The guy's vibe was Shit Central.

"Don't you trust Phoebe to make her own choices?" Jeremy sassed.

This guy was a manipulative knob-headed prat.

Sebastian took a step toward the man and towered over him. "I trust Phoebe completely, but I sure as hell don't trust a bloody tosser like you," he gritted out, drifting back into his British accent.

He was done with this fool.

Uninterested in Jeremy's reply and finished with whatever game the man was playing, he walked away. He had to gather himself and focus on what mattered—and that was Phoebe. He needed to find her so they could get to their room and strategize. Did he want to tell her everything Jeremy had said? Hell yes, but he couldn't. He wouldn't allow Jeremy to monopolize their time at LETIS. One mention of the guy wanting her back would send her into a tailspin. She had to stay sharp.

He scanned the lodge and found Carla Lopez chatting with the investors, but Phoebe wasn't with them.

Where had she gone?

He searched the room, combing through the LETIS participants who'd migrated inside. But she wasn't with any of the lanyard-clad clusters chatting and exchanging business cards. He touched his pocket and felt the bits of metal. She couldn't have gone to their room; he had both keys. Still, he knew she hadn't left. He could feel her energy—her bright, bubbly, loving energy.

"Phoebe Gale, you are truly a lifesaver."

His ears perked up, and he wound his way through the maze of people. Two women broke off from a group and cleared the way for him to see across the room. At the sight of Phoebe sitting around the quilt with Mae and her friends, the muscles at the base of his neck loosened. The jittery irritation brought on by his tête-à tête with Phoebe's ex made way for a soothing sense of calm.

He glanced over his shoulder and was relieved to see Jeremy and his man-bun brigade heading back toward the boathouse. He'd have to keep an eye on the man and Phoebe's mind off the conniving snake.

Taking a few breaths to center himself, he focused on Phoebe and strolled toward the group. "What's going on over here?" he asked with a crease to his brow. Now that he was closer, he could see four cell phones on the quilt in front of Phoebe, along with an ancient laptop.

Phoebe looked up at him and gifted him with a grin—the grin she only smiled for him—and the last of his residual anxiety melted away. She'd put on her glasses and twisted her hair into a bun. She looked . . . radiant—her own version of Phoebe 2.0.

"Sebastian Cress," she said, making introductions, "you know Mae Edwards. These are her friends, Enid Timmons, Theodora Sanchez, and Shirley Miller."

He nodded to the women. Dressed in wooly cardigans, the group gave off kindly granny vibes. "It's nice to meet you."

"And so lovely to meet you, the son of the—" Enid Timmons began.

He knew what was coming.

"Boxing's British Beast," he supplied, used to people bringing up his father.

With white bobbed hair and a curious glint in her eyes, Enid was the smallest of the quilting quartet. "No, dear, not your father. I was talking about your stepmother, the creator of the Wham Bam Thank You Libby Lamb vibrator."

Had he not still been standing, he would have sworn his heart had stopped beating and he was dead—dead as a mortified doornail.

Shirley nodded enthusiastically, her ebony skin glowing in the firelight. "It's an excellent device. Top-notch."

"Always my go-to vibrator," Theodora agreed.

Sebastian's mouth opened and closed like a befuddled trout. He wasn't expecting that from the quilting grannies. And was he sweating? Yes, Jesus, he was nervous-sweating all over the damned place. This might be worse than when Mibby and his dad sat him down for the sex toy talk years ago.

"I agree. I love the updated version with the new settings," Phoebe added.

"What?" he eked out. "You've got one of Mibby's vibrators, too?"

"Just about every woman I know either has the Wham Bam or the Rainbow Screamer," she answered, then tossed him a little wink, letting him know she was thoroughly enjoying his pearl-clutching reaction.

His cheeks burned. Yep, this was worse—way worse—than the kitchen table talk.

"Is that what you ladies were doing? Talking vibrators?" he asked, begging the universe for the answer to be no.

"We weren't," Phoebe replied, eyeball-telling him to relax.

"Thank God," he mumbled, then took the seat next to her.

"I was helping the ladies with a tech matter. They were trying to post an image to their website and were having some issues," Phoebe explained, tilting the old laptop so he could see a rudimentary webpage. It looked like it hadn't been updated in decades.

"We asked several people walking by for help," Shirley explained. "But they were preoccupied and ignored us."

"Isn't that something?" Mae commented. "All these savvy innovators in my lodge and none can spare a moment for someone else—that is, until this kind young lady swooped in." She patted Phoebe's hand.

Mae was right. Phoebe had a heart like no other. The thought had barely materialized when a sinking sensation set in. Did he want to change that? Was he working to strip her of what made her who she was? No, it was more complicated than that. She'd demanded he turn her into a man-eater. Why didn't that make him feel better? Dammit, he had to figure out how to silence the gnawing voices in his head.

"Phoebe heard us asking for assistance and excused herself from her conversation to help a few tech-challenged little old ladies," Theodora added.

"Do not call yourself tech-challenged," Phoebe chided gently. "All you need is a little guidance and some time to play around, and you'll be posting images like tech divas in no time." She scrolled down the page and pointed to pictures of finished quilts. "See, Seb, they sell their quilts online."

"And we're having trouble with that, too," Mae chimed, then shared a look with her sewing circle.

He couldn't quite read the ladies. They seemed as if they were holding back, but he couldn't figure out what they were keeping to themselves. Was it simply excitement? Perhaps they were grateful for some friendly tech assistance. Still, the vibe they gave off had an oddly familiar energy. Then again, Phoebe brought that out in people. Within minutes of meeting her, she'd draw you in like an old friend.

Getting back to the issue at hand, he leaned in and scanned the computer screen. "What are your sales issues? Maybe I can help."

"We ask people to mail in checks to pay for their quilts," Shirley answered.

He couldn't remember the last time he'd seen a paper check. "I can imagine that slows down the process quite a bit."

Phoebe clicked a tab and revealed a website featuring the women's quilts with a more modern layout. "I whipped up a new page for them. Something a little fresher."

"She's so good with the computer and did it so quickly," Enid remarked as the quilting quartet nodded.

"This is what I do, and I'm happy to help." Phoebe turned to him. "I wanted to link a commerce feature, but I need your input."

"Are you wondering which digital money management plan would be best?"

"You read my mind," she replied, again gifting him with that smile that sent his pulse racing.

With every word she spoke, he fell further under her spell. He willed himself to shut off that part of his brain, but a lock of Phoebe's hair came loose from her bun and dusted her cheek. Like it was common practice, he tucked the strands behind her ear, brushed his fingertips along her jawline, and stared into her blue eyes.

"The best digital marketplace plug-in . . . you recommend?" she murmured, talking like Yoda, seemingly caught in the moment, just like he was.

He drew his fingertips farther down to the hollow of her neck. "Yeah, uh-huh," he breathed, not sure his mouth and brain were connected. It was like his head had turned into a balloon, floating peacefully atop his body, when a log in the fireplace cracked. He startled as the rustling hiss of the fire snapped him back.

"What do you do with the money after you earn it?" he asked, willing himself to act like a competent human being, not a swoon-struck bubblehead.

"We donate the proceeds to a food bank," Theodora answered.

He knew what they needed. He scooted his chair closer to Phoebe. "Can I drive?" he asked and gestured to the laptop.

"Take the wheel," she replied and nudged the ancient piece of tech his way.

He went to work, tapping away on the keys. "This site is called Pay It Forward. It was designed by STEM Development. They're a solid company. They have several financial applications depending on your needs. They're safe to use," he explained, showing the ladies the site. "It'll integrate with your webpage. Now people can buy your quilts electronically through your site—no mailing and cashing checks necessary. Another great feature of this plug-in is that it doesn't charge a fee for nonprofits."

"It sounds like what we need," Theodora answered with a sly twist to her lips.

Phoebe patted his arm. "Sebastian's the best when it comes to business innovation."

"I'd say you two are quite a team," Mae remarked.

Phoebe leaned into him. "We've been best friends since we were six."

Friends. He bristled internally and stopped typing like he'd been hit with a jolt of electricity. The word shouldn't grate on him. It never had before, but since he'd dreamed of his mother, everything in his life had shifted like tectonic plates in motion, still unsure of where they'd settle.

"Phoebe, dear," Enid began, "I couldn't help overhearing the group of investors ask you about a food app that's also a dating app. Did I hear that correctly?"

"You did," Phoebe answered, losing her easy, flowery tone. "The app helps people identify their food craving and connects them with a nearby food truck selling the cuisine. But it seems to do more than that. People are meeting their matches—their soul mates—while waiting in line to order. It was an unintended consequence. I've looked over the code. I'm not sure why it's happening."

Theodora leaned in. "Have you met your soul mate?"

He froze again, remembering Jeremy's smug words.

"I . . . I've been a fan of food trucks since I was a girl," she replied, dodging the question. "Our friend's dad is a chef who started out making gourmet grilled cheese sandwiches in a food truck and now runs a charity that teaches new chefs how to build their own food truck business. It's safe to say Sebastian and I have been frequenting food trucks together since we were barely old enough to see over the truck's counter window."

He stifled a grin and suppressed the desire to pump his fist. Score a point for Team Cress. Phoebe Gale didn't see her meeting with Jeremy as a love match—or at least, she wasn't sure, and that doubt gave him hope.

"And then," he said, looking up and meeting each of the quilter's gazes like he had a juicy tidbit to offer, "Phoebe learned that food trucks didn't only sell grilled cheeses. There were ones that sold . . . wait for it . . . hot dogs," he added playfully.

Phoebe chuckled, and the easiness had returned to her voice. "I have a thing for gourmet hot dogs," she explained.

"Indeed, you would," Enid blurted.

Theodora, Mae, and Shirley exchanged nervous glances.

"Pay no attention to Enid. She's . . ." Shirley mused, then looked to Mae.

"She's drunk. Enid is drunk," Mae announced.

"Yep, so drunk," Enid agreed, then faked a hiccup.

"Tell us more, dear," Mae said, pulling the attention away from Enid. "We old gals enjoy a good story."

He scanned the group. What the hell was going on with these women? But Phoebe didn't seem bothered by the odd exchange.

Undeterred by the women's strange behavior, Phoebe rested her hand on his arm. "Do you remember when I saw my first gourmet hot dog food truck?"

"How could I forget? I was the one who caught you when you nearly passed out with excitement. Your uncle Rowen had to carry you while we waited in line, and then you ordered eight hot dogs and ate them in one sitting."

Phoebe chewed her lip. "I thought it was four?"

"It was eight," he countered. "I remember my dad saying, 'just another reminder that our Phoebe never does anything halfway. She goes all in every time.'"

All in.

He couldn't refrain from smiling, then recalled the aftermath of that day. "And then our friend Oscar's dad asked the food truck chef for a plastic bag."

"I don't remember that," Phoebe quipped with a little frown.

"It was the bag you used when you barfed up those hot dogs on the way home. We had to roll down the windows, and then Aria, that's our other friend, started gagging. Phoebe's uncle had to pull over. And here's the best part. Phoebe dropped her puke bag in the car, and it landed on my shoes."

"Oh no!" the quilting quartet exclaimed.

Phoebe cringed and pressed her hand to her belly. "Now I remember. What a night! I forgot about your shoes. You'd gotten a pair of boxing shoes like your dad had. I ruined them."

He held her gaze. "It was a small price to pay for getting to spend the majority of my childhood by your side." And then it happened again—that feeling of connectedness, the twist of her life wrapping around his.

"How's that digital marketplace coming, Sebastian?" Theodora asked.

Focus, man! "Almost there," he answered and returned to the keys.

"You were gracious when you explained your app, but if you don't mind me saying," Shirley pondered, "you seemed a bit reluctant to talk about it with the investors."

"Can I share a secret with you?" Phoebe asked.

His ears perked up.

"What's said in the sewing circle stays in the sewing circle," Mae answered.

"While I'm grateful investors are interested in the Munch Match app, and I'm thrilled people have found their love match standing in line," Phoebe began, "my passion is to create an online community tailored to girls and women of all ages. I'm dreaming big. I want to build a clearing house for girls and women to experience the full scope of what's available to them in the tech world. There are more women innovators now, but look around." She gestured to the crowd—the heavily male-dominated crowd. "Girls need a starting point that will support them throughout their life, and women need a consistent community to build and maintain relationships."

"My goodness, that sounds quite comprehensive. What kinds of things would you offer to them in this community?" Theodora asked as the ladies' demeanor sharpened.

He studied the sewing circle. For a group of women with a

website from thirty years ago, they sure seemed interested in Phoebe's idea.

"The sky's the limit. I'd create a whole host of entry points," she answered with the effervescent enthusiasm that drew people in.

"Such as?" Enid asked, looking dead sober.

"Apps to connect like-minded women to foster collaboration, team-based online gaming to promote camaraderie, mentorship opportunities between younger and more seasoned members, ways to apply and be a part of vetted community groups, applications to join tech organizations, chat forums, and an educational component to build skills. My goal is to have girls join Go Girl—that's what I'm calling it—and remain a part of the community for their entire lives. It's got to be flexible and always striving to meet the members' needs."

Shirley narrowed her gaze. "Why didn't you mention this idea to the investors?"

Phoebe shrugged. "The Munch Match app is what people are buzzing about."

"And there's nothing wrong with playing your strongest card," he interjected as he finished setting up the marketplace feature.

"You believe the Munch Match app is Phoebe's strongest card?" Theodora asked. And it wasn't only Theodora. Every woman at the table zeroed in on him.

"I think she should pursue what will bring her success—the fastest route to success. And that appears to be the Munch Match app." It was a sound explanation. Why did he feel like he was on shaky ground?

For what seemed like a century, no one at the table said a word.

"We've taken up enough of your time," Theodora said, breaking the heavy stretch of silence.

"Indeed, we have. Thank you for helping us," Shirley added, her features softening.

The women appeared pleasant enough, but it felt like he'd failed a test. It would have been damned nice if he'd known what he'd done wrong.

He rose to his feet, then turned the laptop toward the ladies. "Enter your banking information here, click save, and you'll be good to go."

"You've helped us so much," Mae gushed, passing the laptop to Enid. "Enjoy your time at Glenn Pines. Feel free to explore the grounds. But I must warn you. Autumn is mud season in the mountains. If we get heavy rain, the trails become impassable until the storm lets up."

"We'll keep that in mind. It was lovely spending time with you," Phoebe said, coming to his side.

The women said their goodbyes, and he pressed his hand to the small of Phoebe's back, leading her away from the lodge's main hall and back toward the wing with the guest rooms. He reached into his pocket, got the key, and checked the room number.

"The women are great, aren't they?" Phoebe commented, her words taking on an uneasy lilt.

"They are."

"It's weird. It's like I knew them, or they knew me." She sighed and took his arm. "I know what you're going to say."

He rested his hand on hers. "And what's that?"

"You'll say that I feel that way about everyone."

"I think it's the other way around, Pheebs. People feel that way about you. You've got a heart like no other, and you let people into it without reservation," he answered as they walked down the dimly lit corridor.

She stopped in the middle of the hallway and took a step back, untangling her arm from his. "A heart that probably shouldn't have accepted Jeremy's apology." Confusion flashed in her eyes as she took another step away from him and leaned against a door. "What's wrong with me, Sebby? It's like my man-eater superpower skills only work on . . . on you."

That was quite a revelation.

"Nothing is wrong with you," he stammered and glanced past her shoulder. "Except . . ."

"Except what?" she squeaked.

"Except you're standing in front of our door."

"Gah, Seb, what am I supposed to do?" she lamented, stepping aside as he unlocked the door and opened it for her. "Maybe I focus my man-eater energy on Jeremy," she pondered, entering the room.

Every cell in his body screamed *fuck no—Jeremy Drewler is a colossal schmuck*. He wanted to shout this to the mountaintops, but he held back his blistering tirade.

Phoebe paced in front of the king-sized bed. "I could lead him on, reel him in, and then drop him like a bag of dog crap." She gasped.

"What is it?" Did she realize that was a terrible idea? Jesus, he hoped so.

"You shouldn't drop a bag of dog poop. It would make a mess and smell terrible. Plus, it's illegal and bad for public health."

He could see the cogs in her brain starting to smoke. She was spiraling.

"How about this?" she continued. "I string him along and drop him like a hot . . . dog." She shrieked. "No, I would never drop a hot dog. But you know what I mean. If I could make Jeremy Drewler fall for me, that would be the ultimate sign that I'd attained total man-eater status. You saw him tonight. My wardrobe, makeup, and hair transformation knocked him off balance. He said he wanted to prove himself to me." She twisted one of the beads on her dress. "What if he meant it and truly did feel bad about what he did? Let's not forget, I'm not completely innocent either. I retaliated with a bottle of Dijon mustard."

He nodded, trying to appear unaffected while his mind worked overtime. He had to figure out a way to make her see Jeremy was wrong for her and a terrible target for her man-eater project. "Jeremy was awful to you, Pheebs. He deserved way more than a little mustard to the eyes. I watched the recording and heard what he said."

"You heard it?" She stopped pacing, then huffed a mirthless little sound. "Of course you did. I sent it to you." She shook her head and continued wearing out the carpet. "I don't want to waste my energy hating him. And I don't want to discount what he said tonight. I understand what stress can do. I want to succeed as well. I want to be the kind of person that would make my parents proud if they were still alive. It's a tall order. That amount of drive and determination can make a person do crazy things. I stress-ate six food truck hot dogs in one day. It was almost seven, but you—"

"Ate it. And it was delicious. The best I've ever had," he answered, and he wasn't kidding.

She leaned against the dresser positioned against the wall across from the bed. "Hank's Franks serves up a mean hot dog," she replied, losing the frantic edge.

"Do you want my professional assessment?" This was the best avenue to take. Keep it about the life coaching.

She captured him with her deep blue eyes. "I want that more than anything."

He stood before her. "Let's role-play."

"Role-play?" she repeated.

"You weren't prepared to run into Jeremy. That was a slip on my part. It won't happen again."

She watched him closely. "And why is that?"

"Because next time you see him, no matter what he says, you'll know what to do to maintain the upper hand. When he approached us, you started off with the right energy. You were assertive and employed the right amount of disregard, but then—"

"I felt sorry for him," she finished, her shoulders slumping.

He tipped her chin up and met her gaze. "You've got to learn to turn off your sentimental side and tap into the man-eating barracuda. You don't need Jeremy Drewler's attention. In fact, focusing on someone else could make him squirm."

That was his angle—his purely professional angle.

Jesus, who was he kidding?

"You might be right," Phoebe agreed. "I wasn't wearing my glasses, but even I could see his expression. Jeremy has never looked at me like that before."

He released her chin and caged her in against the piece of furniture. "What's that look?" he asked, lowering his voice.

Phoebe inhaled a sharp breath. "Like there's nothing else in the world he wanted."

He leaned in. "Like he desired you?"

"Yes," she breathed.

"And how did that make you feel?"

"Powerful."

"Following the Sebastian Guarantee will ensure you're in control—personally and professionally. That's where the senses come in. Tonight, every person at the cocktail party got a whiff of Phoebe 2.0. They got a glimpse of the attractive, poised woman. But you're still an enigma. I'd be willing to bet your name was on every investor's mind and it got them talking. Now, we'll prepare you for what to do when you see your target—personal or professional. They'll be itching for a taste and longing to touch. Professionally, investors will want to get their hands on your ideas. Personally, they'll want to get man-eater Phoebe alone and preferably naked." He shut his trap, not sure where the naked part came from, but there was no taking it back now.

Phoebe's breathing grew audible as the rise and fall of her chest quickened. "Um . . . wow . . . that's quite comprehensive, Seb. And look at me. I haven't even asked about you. Did you meet any investors or see anyone you were interested in? I caught you looking at a woman in a white pantsuit. She was gorgeous. She'd probably look great naked."

He had to get that thought out of her head. He pressed his index finger to her lips, silencing her rambling chatter. "I'm not interested in anything or anyone outside this room. Stop stalling, Phoebe. Let's get back to the Sebastian Guarantee. Pop quiz time—the man-eater edition. Tempt my senses. Make me want to taste you. Make me want to touch you. Tease me until I can't take it."

Chapter 14
SEBASTIAN

Had he just asked—no, demanded—that Phoebe seduce him?

It sure as hell sounded like it.

Was this request related to the protocol? In theory, yes, anything he did was guaranteed by Sebastian because, well, he was Sebastian. Was that one hell of a convoluted life-coaching model? Sure. But Jeremy had his sights set on Phoebe, and he had no choice but to turn her into a vixen and refocus her attention. As her coach, he could be a safe space. They could do as they'd done at her place and enter creative mode.

Was that what he was doing, or was Jeremy correct? Did he want Phoebe for himself—for something more than friendship? *Dammit,* that was complicated. But this wasn't the time to tease out his Phoebe Gale complication conundrum. However, his rock-hard cock knew what it wanted, and she was wearing the hell out of a midnight blue shimmery cocktail dress and standing a breath away.

"What are your words, Phoebe? The words to center yourself."

The sexiest hint of a grin tipped the corners of her lips.

"Kissable and man-eater. Oops," she cooed, eyes glinting with mischief. "I meant *capable*."

She knew damned well the word was "capable." This was good, though. He wanted her relaxed.

He met her sly expression with one of his own. "What does a capable man-eater do when she wants something? What would Phoebe 2.0 do in this situation?"

Phoebe drew the tip of her tongue across her top lip, then schooled her features and pressed her hand against his chest. "Phoebe 2.0 would like you to sit your ass down."

He wasn't about to make her ask twice. He took a step back and sank onto the edge of the bed. She took off her glasses, set them on top of the dresser, then, like she'd been cast in a shampoo commercial, shook out her bun. Carnal urgency tore through him as her chestnut waves dusted her shoulders and framed her face. Although he'd seen her like this hundreds, maybe even thousands of times, there was something different about it now. Something he couldn't quite put his finger on.

Phoebe swept her hair over her shoulder, turned slowly, and presented him with her ass.

She looked over her shoulder. And God help him, she radiated a coy coolness that had his temperature rising. He shifted on the bed. His trousers had gotten rather snug. He drank her in and couldn't stop himself from picturing her on her hands and knees, buck naked as he gripped her hip and tangled his other hand in her hair while he thrust in hard, taking her from behind. The image sent another jolt of lust surging through him.

"Can you help me with the zipper?" she purred.

He snapped back from Phoebe Fantasy Land. "Yeah, yeah, yeah, sure." Jesus, he couldn't be stuttering and stammering. He needed to harness his composure. He was Sebastian Cress. He had millions of online followers. Scores of fans. He could bed any woman he wanted. But he didn't want just any woman.

He brushed away a few errant wisps of her hair, then slipped his fingertips beneath the collar of her dress. She trembled under his touch as he slowly unzipped her dress. Then, taking the utmost care, he parted the sides of the garment and enjoyed the view. Inch by inch, he exposed her porcelain skin. But that wasn't all he'd revealed.

"What are you wearing?" he asked. It was a stupid question. He was peering right at what she had on under her dress, but it still caught him off guard. She'd changed in her room before they left for Glenn Pines. He hadn't seen what undergarments she'd chosen. But he could now, and sweet Christ, she'd picked out the pink lingerie set Mara had gifted her. Unlike the pink baby doll negligee, this selection wasn't billowy and light. It was skimpy, skintight, and smokin' hot—and all he'd seen so far was a sliver of it. The hint of a lacy pink waistband peeked out from beneath the dress. He trailed his hands up her back and traced a line beneath the band of the lacy pink bra.

"Do you like it?" she asked, allowing the dress to fall to the floor and pool at her feet. She stepped out of the confines of the cocktail clothing and took a step back. Swiveling like a high-heel-wearing ice skater, she faced him, giving him one hell of a view. "The bra and panties match my shoes. How about that for man-eater thinking?"

Hopefully, that was a rhetorical question, because he didn't have any words at his disposal. Beautiful, tantalizing, enchanting, and electrifying didn't aptly describe the goddess standing before him. "Phoebe," he breathed. It was the only word he was able to speak, and her name passed his lips in a deep, gravelly whisper.

His caveman reply put a smile on her face. "And what have you got for me beneath your shirt and tie?" Mischief glimmered in her eyes. "And no judgment if it turns out you're wearing the same thing as me and we're twinsies. Pink is your color, too, Sebastian Cress, and don't you ever forget it," she teased—the little minx.

Awestruck, he feasted his eyes on her. How the hell did she do it? She'd woven sweet, silly, and sexy into a tapestry that had him on the cusp of losing control.

And speaking of control, he needed a hit of it, something fierce. He donned his best poker face. "I hate to let you down, but my undergarments are decidedly less alluring."

She walked up to him and stood between his legs. They were nearly the same height, with him sitting on the bed and her in heels. She ran her fingertips down his jawline, then loosened his tie. She slid the fabric from his neck and ran the silky material between her fingers. "Nice," she remarked. She read the tag on the necktie and raised an eyebrow. "Hermès. The brand of the scarf our nanny matchmaker Madelyn Malone wears. Very posh."

He stared at the silk tie, paying particular attention to the color—a deep enchanting shade of blue. He returned his gaze to Phoebe. "Want to know something crazy?"

She wound the fabric around her fingers. "I always want to know something crazy."

"Madelyn gave me that tie. It was a gift for my last birthday."

Phoebe released the rolled fabric and gave the ribbon of silk a swift examination. "Lucky for us, ties can't see, hear, or talk," she said, then flung the stretch of blue onto the bed.

"Why? What are you about to do in front of my Hermès tie?"

One by one, she undid the buttons of his shirt. He shrugged it off. Before it even hit the floor, she unbuckled his belt and started in on his pants.

"Are you in a hurry?" he teased, losing his trousers.

She knelt, then pulled off his shoes and slipped off his socks. Tossing the items aside, she met his gaze as a deliciously dirty grin bloomed on her lips. "Sebastian Cress, you'll want to be naked for what I'm about to do."

And stop the presses! Those might be the hottest words ever uttered in a lodge guest room.

"Is that right?" he shot back.

"Lose the boxer briefs," she directed over her shoulder as she sauntered toward her suitcase perched on the floor next to a narrow fold-up cot.

He couldn't see what she was doing, but she was making a racket. A quick zip, then a bit of rifling, followed by another zip.

She looked over her shoulder. "Don't be weird about this."

What was she doing?

She turned around and returned but kept whatever she'd procured from her bag behind her back. She moved her arms, wiggling a bit, then started buzzing.

Buzzing?

Buzzing!

His jaw dropped. "No way. No bloody way."

"Sebastian Cress," Phoebe announced, eyes twinkling with wanton delight, "meet my Wham Bam Thank You Libby Lamb deluxe vibrator."

"Why do you have that?" he asked, wide-eyed.

She cocked her head to the side.

Jesus, that was an insanely stupid question. In his defense, he was buck naked, gawking at a goddess in lingerie and heels, who held the vibrator his beloved Mibby had designed. There was a very good chance his head was on the brink of exploding.

He cleared his throat. "Why did you bring *it* to Glenn Pines?"

"I don't leave home without my Wham Bam."

"What are you going to do with it now?" he stammered. Was he ready for this?

"I can tell you what we're not going to do with it." She sat next to him, scooted back, then rested her head on the pillow. "We won't be dropping it into the bathtub like we did when we were kids and thought these beauties were submarine torpedoes."

He joined her in bed. "If we're not playing submarine torpedoes, what's the plan?"

"The plan is for me to make myself come while you watch."

Forget what she'd said before. Those were the hottest words ever uttered inside a lodge guest room.

"Watch?" he repeated, spellbound.

She held the device near the hollow of her neck, then trailed the humming vibrator between her breasts and past her navel. "I distinctly recall you growling at me," she began, slipping the Wham Bam into her panties, "commanding me to make you want to taste me." She gasped as the titillating vibrator met her sensitive bundle of nerves. "And make you want to touch me," she moaned, arching her back.

Even if the lodge had been on fire, he couldn't have moved. The damned world could be ending, and he wouldn't have been able to tear his gaze from the woman wrapped in pink lacy lingerie, currently owning her sexuality like a man-eating boss.

"I'm . . ." Phoebe breathed.

He wrapped his hand around his thick shaft. "Yes?"

"Just . . ."

"Uh-huh," he growled, working his rock-hard cock.

She hummed along with the vibrator. "Following . . ."

It was almost too much to take. "What are you following?" he gritted as he masturbated alongside her.

"The Sebastian Guarantee," she moaned. Her eyelids fluttered closed as she flew over the edge. Chest rising and falling and hips rolling, she was glorious. It would be no hardship if he never saw again, and this was the last vivid image ingrained in his mind.

He covered her hand that was working the vibrator and absorbed the titillating beats. The erotic pulse intensified his drive to have her. He pressed her hand, increasing the pressure and lengthening her release. And holy hell, he watched her ride out each wave of pleasure. She sighed a dreamy sound and removed the Wham Bam from her panties.

He'd never say no to watching her get off, but he wasn't about to play second-fiddle to a sex toy either. He turned off the device and set it aside. "The pop quiz is over."

With flushed cheeks and another dreamy sigh, she looked his way. "How did I do, Coach?"

He peeled off her G-string and threw the bit of lace and silk over his shoulder. "A-plus. Objective achieved."

A bit of blue caught his eye, and an idea sparked. He glanced at the black leather padded headboard and studied a decorative element—a slim strip of empty space running along the bottom, interspersed with spindly iron rods. And his idea morphed into a plan.

"In addition to you acing the exam, I've got even better news," he said, baiting her.

"What's that?"

"An extra credit assignment."

The sated look in her eyes gave way to lusty longing. "You know how I love earning extra credit."

Hell yes, he did.

He picked up the blue Hermès tie and dangled it in front of her. "Raise your hands above your head."

Phoebe's gaze bounced from him to the silky strip of fabric.

"You mentioned you like being tied up," he reminded her.

She chewed her lip. "I did?"

He nodded. "Yesterday, when I blindfolded you, you said"—he wrapped the tie around her wrists—"that you like your bindings tight." He crisscrossed the material and pulled the ends of the tie. The silk snapped as he bound her wrists and fastened them to one of the iron rods.

Her breaths quickened. "I don't know why I said that. It must have been nerves. I've never been tied up before."

He covered her body with his and nudged the tip of his cock against her sweet, wet heat. "I've never tied anyone up," he confessed, gazing into her blue eyes—blue eyes that threatened to swallow him whole. He wasn't lying. He didn't do this with other women. For all the sex he'd had, he'd never wandered into light bondage. It required a level of trust he'd never experienced with another person.

The question was, did Phoebe trust him?

He watched her closely.

Her hesitant expression melted away, and the mischievous glint returned to her eyes. She moved her arms, then tugged against the iron rod—the sexual equivalent of kicking the tires to check a car's worthiness. "It appears I do like a tight binding," she purred.

This woman.

She rolled her hips, welcoming another inch of his hard length, and he couldn't wait any longer. He captured her mouth in a searing kiss and rocked into her, filling her to the hilt.

He pulled back and savored the moment. "You feel so good—like we were made to do this together."

She tightened around him, contracting her core muscles. The move triggered a deep, carnal yearning he couldn't ignore. It shredded any last threads of his resolve. He closed the distance and kissed her like he wasn't sure if tomorrow would come. Pumping his hips, he worked her body. With each punctuated, deliberate stroke, their connection deepened. It was as if the tie wasn't only wrapped around her wrists. An invisible thread bound them together, cocooning them inside a secret place meant only for the two of them. Bodies writhing, she opened to him, taking all of him. He dialed up his pace. A sheen of perspiration coated their skin. Slick and gritty, the slap of their bodies coming together provided an erotic soundtrack. He couldn't get enough. He changed the angle of penetration, grinding against her. Panting and moaning beneath him, Phoebe was his captive to tease, please, and devour.

"Oh, Sebastian, just like that."

Her words emboldened him. He strained every muscle, moving to satisfy her, grinding to fulfill her every desire. She cried out, arching into him. The lace of her bra chafed against his chest. The sweet bite of pain was the perfect companion to the slick slide of pleasure.

"Yes, yes," she whimpered.

She tensed, teetering on the precipice of sweet release. He gripped her bound wrists, anchoring himself to her, anchoring his soul to hers.

"Unravel, let go," he breathed against her earlobe. "Fly over the edge with me."

Bodies moving as one, they plunged into a sea of ecstasy. His orgasm gripped him with a ferocity he'd never known. He needed more. He wanted everything. Growling like a beast, tears pricked his eyes as he and Phoebe disintegrated into nothing, into everything, into two people who knew each other inside and out. She was his past and his present. Was she also his future—a future where she wasn't only his friend but his and his alone? Was that even possible?

He exhaled a slow breath and pressed up onto his elbows. "Hey," he said and stroked her cheek.

"Hey," she cooed.

He unfastened the bindings and massaged her wrists. "Do they hurt?"

She shook her head. "No, not at all."

She studied his face. A pang of panic welled in his chest. Did his expression give away his feelings? Could she sense the push and pull going on inside his head?

She wrapped her arms around his neck. But something was off. She looked away and stared at a point past his shoulder.

"What is it, Pheebs?"

"This doesn't count, does it? It's extra credit. The two of us going *all in* in creative mode." She swallowed hard, then flashed a nervous smile.

Was that what she wanted? Should he tell her he wanted more—that he wanted her? No, he couldn't. A declaration like that could ruin everything. There was too much on the line. He couldn't jeopardize their success or their friendship.

He forced himself to nod. "That's what we agreed to, right?"

For a slip of time, they watched each other like they were trying to picture a different path—a path where spending their evenings wrapped around each other in bed, sweaty and breathless, wasn't part of a life-coaching plan but their life, their real life.

"It is what we agreed to, but . . ." Phoebe said, breaking the silence.

Buzzy optimism zinged through his body. "What is it?" he asked, heart pounding and not from the sex.

She wiggled beneath him. "Do you mind rolling over?"

He maneuvered his large frame off her and turned onto his back. Before he could take another breath, she straddled him, then picked up his tie and pulled it taut between her hands. "But now, Sebastian Cress," she purred, then guided his hands above his head, "it's your turn to earn extra credit—in creative mode, of course."

Creative mode, of course. He hated the sound of that. Not knowing what to do about his feelings or what to say to Phoebe about the Sebastian Guarantee, he ignored the voices in the back of his head and soaked in every drop of Phoebe's attention. She leaned over and dropped feathery kisses onto his cheek. They landed like pearls of summer rain.

He smiled, turning his head to press his lips to hers. "I'm all in, Phoebe."

She stilled.

Shit! Why had he said that? He didn't want there to be any unease between them. He didn't want to lose her. He didn't want to ruin whatever this was. And that meant he had to lie. "I'm all in . . . for earning extra credit."

She held his gaze. "In creative mode."

He couldn't figure out if she was making a statement or asking a question.

He knew what he had to do.

Say what she needs to hear.

He swallowed past the lump in his throat. "Yes, where nothing counts."

Chapter 15
PHOEBE

Phoebe yawned. She rolled her head from side to side and sank into the fluffy pillow. With her eyes closed, she stretched beneath the quilt. Had her body ever felt this loose, this sated, this deliciously satisfied? Oh, hell no. Could it have been a dream? That was another hell no. The sweet ache between her thighs served as proof that she'd aced her seduction pop quiz. She'd never done anything like her little vibrator masturbation exhibition. Never in a million years would she have described herself as a nymphomaniac until last night.

An exhilarating tingle danced down her spine. Still riding a euphoric high from hours of sexual escapades was a delightful way to meet the day. She and Sebastian had earned extra credit on the bed, on the floor, against the dresser, and on the wobbly cot, which they'd destroyed. Okay, destroyed might be too strong a description. But their strenuous activity atop it had rendered the hotel staple permanently out of order.

Note to self: never attempt a rollicking, rambunctious bout of bouncy reverse cowgirl with a six-foot-four brick house of a man on an unsteady padded surface. On the plus side, it had, however, led to another round of Sebastian taking her hard and fast from behind on the floor.

Hmm, maybe she should invest in a rickety cot.

No, she couldn't.

They'd merely been adhering to the Sebastian Guarantee. The sex was an assignment, a vehicle to assist her in honing her man-eater skill set. She had to move on. She couldn't relive the events of last night.

Too bad her brain hadn't gotten the memo.

Not a second after she'd tried to shut down her thoughts about Sebastian rocking her body, her traitorous brain went there, big time. Like a movie montage, she pictured Sebastian between her thighs. She could nearly feel his lips pressed to hers as she recalled Sebastian holding her in his arms all night long. She'd fallen asleep with his muscled chest against her back and his warm breath against her neck—that slow, melodic in and out she'd heard more times than she could count. She'd grown up having sleepovers with him. She'd spent holidays bunking with him, Aria, and Oscar. She knew how he sounded when he slept. But she'd never known the bliss of listening to him sleep as she drifted off with his naked body pressed to hers.

She pictured his face—his beautiful, perfectly chiseled face. There was a slip of seconds where he'd looked at her as if she made up his entire universe, like he'd wanted it to count with her, like they weren't role-playing, but instead, were two people completely in sync and absolutely crazy about each other. She could have sworn he was on the cusp of professing his feelings, but he'd blinked, and the emotion in his eyes had muted. Whatever sentiments he'd had bubbling to the surface, he'd tucked them away.

Then again, she could be wrong.

Perhaps it was her sentimental heart, a heart that could mistake lust for love.

Case in point: Jeremy Drewler.

What should she do about him? Had he been telling the truth? Did the man honestly want to win her back? She sighed. She didn't have the bandwidth to worry about him—not with Sebastian's scent on her skin, his taste in her mouth, and the imprint of his hands on her body. Creative mode had allowed them to stretch the parameters of their relationship, but one irrefutable fact remained: he was her best friend.

Did she want more? And if she did and shared this with him and he rejected her, how would they move forward? Thanks to the jerks she'd dated who'd played fast and loose with her affections, her heart had been bruised. But Sebastian's rejection would surely shatter it.

"Quiet down, brain," she whispered.

There was a good chance her runaway imagination was a reaction to a life that had gone off the rails. Over the past few days, every facet of her world had turned upside down and inside out. Maybe she should take a few tips from Phoebe 2.0 and embrace her fierce sexual energy.

She rolled over and cracked open her eyes, expecting to see the man. Instead, she stared at a tray with a plate of cookies and a glass of chocolate milk. She blinked. Was she dreaming? Truth be told, she loved cookies, and it wasn't that uncommon for them to appear in her dreams. She inhaled. They sure smelled like real cookies—her favorite, chocolate chip, to be exact. She reached from beneath the quilt and touched the plate. It wasn't a baked goods mirage. This was the real deal. Sebastian must have gotten them for her. She sat up, plucked a beauty from the stack, and raised it to her mouth.

Before she could take a bite, a squeak, followed by the beat of water pelting off the tile, distracted her from her breakfast of champions. She retrieved her glasses, then peered through the half-open bathroom door.

Her breath caught in her throat. "Mr. Lickable Abs in a

towel."

Her eyeballs were glued to the half-naked man. Sebastian leaned against the sink as billows of steam filled the room. She clenched her core and took a hot minute to drink in his strong shoulders, muscled arms, and his oh-so-lickable abs. She slipped out of bed, hastily threw on his now-wrinkled button-up shirt, then tiptoed toward him.

He hadn't noticed her, but something was weighing heavily on him. He pursed his lips and frowned. What had him so growly? Armed with a cookie, she moved closer. Still unaware he was being stalked by an abs-obsessed woman wielding a cookie, he turned and picked something up from off the ground. It was his notepad. But he had something else in his hands. Two items rested on his palm: his pocket watch with his mother's photo and the blue-green aquamarine stone his stepmom had given him. He set the trinkets on the sink and opened the notepad. She took another step and hit a creaky floorboard.

Sebastian slapped the notebook closed and peered out the door. "I didn't hear you get up."

"What are you up to in there?" she asked, padding through the doorway.

His cheeks grew rosy. "Just work. Making some notes, going over a few results."

"Results? That has to be a good thing."

"Yeah, my data is promising," he replied and stuffed the pad into his backpack.

His behavior was off. It was odd to see Sebastian jittery.

She glanced at the shower, and she put it together. "Seb, you don't have to be embarrassed about working in the bathroom. Some of my best ideas come to me in the shower."

"That's it. That's what happened." He picked up the stone and watch from the lip of the sink and added them to his pack.

"Thinking about your mom and Libby?" she asked,

watching him closely as he zipped up the bag.

"Something like that." He leaned against the sink, eyed the treat in her hands, then flashed her a sexy half-smile. "What do we have here?" he purred, sounding more like himself.

Her core—her now very wet core—clenched, and her nipples tightened at the sound of his gravelly voice. It was time for man-eater Phoebe to take over. She took a bite, then held the baked good to Sebastian's lips. "I thought you'd like to taste my cookie."

Hello, party people! Phoebe 2.0 was in the house.

Sebastian's gaze darkened. "I believe we established that last night." His cocksure grin widened. He took a bite, then hummed his satisfaction. "Delicious, and I'm not talking about the baked goods."

This man. With anyone else, she'd feel like such a total weirdo talking like that. But with Sebastian, it was fun, flirty, and so easy to slip into her alter ego. Then again, nothing was real. She and her best friend had changed roles, donned new skins, residing in creative mode. What would happen when they were back in the real world?

Pushing the thought aside, she offered him another bite, then brushed a crumb from the corner of his mouth. "Did you have these sent up?"

"No, I grabbed the cookies and chocolate milk off the lunch buffet, and Mae was nice enough to give me a tray."

She jammed what was left of the treat into her mouth. "The lunch buffet? What time is it?" she garbled through chocolatey bliss.

"It's almost three."

"In the afternoon?" she shrieked. "Why did you let me sleep all day?"

He looked her up and down with a decidedly mischievous glint in his blue-green eyes. "Lose the shirt, and I'll tell you."

She was not expecting him to reply like that. *This bathroom tête-à-tête just got way more interesting.* "Lose the towel, and I'll *let you* tell me," she countered, carrying herself like the man-eater she was, at least for the moment.

Sebastian's grin widened. With a flick of his wrist, the snowy white towel hit the ground, revealing the full-on god-bod package, complete with one hell of a hard-on.

She gestured to his equipment. "Did my cookie do that to you?"

"No, *you* do this to me."

What was a gal supposed to say when the sexiest man on the internet dropped his towel and doled out a little dirty talk?

Answer: Get naked.

Like she had a vendetta against clothing, she ripped the button-up apart. Buttons bounced, hitting the tile floor as she tossed his shirt next to the discarded towel. "I hope you weren't too attached to that."

He raked his gaze over her body. "I can't think of a more fitting end for a garment."

"Good," she breathed, body tingling and goose bumps peppering her skin.

He took her hand and led her under the shower's warm spray. "Come on, shirt annihilator. I could use a hot shower for my sore muscles, and I reckon you could, too."

Reckon.

She giggled as the water soaked her tangled hair and trickled down her back.

"What are you laughing about?" he asked, soaping up.

She leaned against the tiled wall, taking in the view. "I love it when you do that."

"Do what?"

"Drop little British words and phrases into your American-pie dialect. I *reckon* you don't even realize when you're doing it, mate," she answered in a British accent, because, why not?

He rinsed off and wiped the droplets of water from his face

in a move she would have sworn played out in slow motion, or perhaps her brain was overheating and could only process her vision at a quarter speed.

"It usually happens when I'm experiencing strong urges," he explained, shaking his head and ridding himself of the excess moisture like the hottest golden retriever on the planet.

She twisted a lock of wet hair, playing the part of the coy vixen. "And how strong are your urges now?"

"Off the charts, lass," he said, rocking his toe-curlingly hot accent. He took a step toward her. Inches away, water droplets trailed down his ripped torso.

Feeling a few urges herself, she drew her fingertips down the hard ridges of his six-pack. "We should probably do something about that."

He tilted up her chin and eased in but stopped when his lips were a breath away from hers. "Turn around and let me see that perfect *arse* of yours."

"You're a tease, Sebastian Cress."

"And you love it. Stop faffing around and get to it," he growled, still sounding all British-y.

And heaven help her! She was lucky she hadn't fainted from the amount of raw sexual energy pulsing between them.

Snapping to it, she presented her ass like she'd just won first prize in a sexy wet-ass contest and pressed her hands to the glass. Barely a second passed before she felt his thick shaft against the small of her back. She inhaled a sharp breath, ready to have her body rocked shower-style. But he didn't position himself at her entrance. Instead, he took her hair into his hands and started . . . washing it.

What?

She inhaled the floral scent of the shampoo, confirming that their naughty shower romp had morphed into a game of beauty shop. "In addition to life coaching, do you offer hairdressing services?"

He massaged her scalp, doing one hell of a good job shampooing her roots. "In this situation, yes."

She glanced over her shoulder at him. "Why?"

"Because I'm all for alleviating urges, but we've got work to do."

"Exactly," she shot back. "You should be working my body and making me call out your name."

He chuckled and wiped the excess shampoo from her forehead. "We'll get to that. First, I need to tell you why I let you sleep in."

"Okay," she answered, relaxing beneath the spray and quite enjoying the Sebastian Guarantee shampoo service.

"When I hit up the breakfast buffet," he began, running his hands through her locks to wash out the soap, "I caught snippets of conversations—conversations about you. You're all anyone could talk about."

"You're kidding?" she replied, completely caught off guard.

"You made one hell of an impression, Pheebs." He added a dollop of conditioner to her hair and rubbed it in.

"But I didn't talk to any investors."

"You didn't have to. The Sebastian Guarantee did the trick. The investors got a whiff, and that emergency door debacle—the little peek—turned out to be a genius move. Every person there got a glimpse of you, and that led to the buzz. Lots of buzz."

"Wow," she breathed.

"That's not all," he continued, excitement coating his words. "At breakfast, I heard several lifestyle investors talking about how good you looked and how they thought it would be brilliant to partner with you and connect you with clothing designers. Then there were the tech investors. They were salivating over your Munch Match app. I heard one guy tell another that the online global dating market is an eight-billion-dollar industry. Imagine if your algorithm is the best one. Think of what that means."

Anxiety, thick and thorny, settled in her chest. Despite standing under the warm spray, a chill passed over her. She took a step away from Sebastian and rinsed the conditioner from her hair. "They were talking about Munch Match?"

He held her shoulders and turned her to face him. "It's what you're known for. Carla Lopez had her phone out. She was showing everyone her wedding photos. People want to find their love match, Pheebs, and they'll do anything to make that happen."

She wanted that, too. Did Seb?

"Pheebs?" he said softly, brushing the water from her cheeks—or were those tears?

She mustered a grin. "Yeah?"

He kissed the corner of her mouth. "This is a good thing."

She tried to nod but couldn't. "I'm not sure if it is, Sebby," she replied, her voice barely a rasp. She couldn't divulge her algorithm to just anyone—especially if she wasn't crystal clear about how it worked. Not only that, she had an obligation to protect what she'd created and make sure it was used wisely and prudently. And what about Go Girl? That was her dream.

As if Sebastian could read her mind, he cupped her face in his hands. "I know you've had your heart set on promoting Go Girl with the investors. But the goal of the Sebastian Guarantee is to achieve success. That's what I promised you, and you can have it. Investors are falling arse over elbow for you—and it's happened while you were sleeping."

Arse.

She would have pointed out his Brit slip if she wasn't so conflicted.

"Can you give me a second in the bathroom to get ready? I need some time to sit with what's happening."

"You got it," Sebastian answered. He turned off the

shower, grabbed a fluffy white towel from a hook, and wrapped it around her shoulders. "I'll be right outside." He plucked a fresh towel from a stack, tied it around his waist, then grabbed his pack. "Do you need anything?"

She glanced around the bathroom. "My toiletries pouch. It's in my bag. And maybe a few cookies and the chocolate milk. I could use some sustenance."

"Coming up, Miss LETIS Diva," he said over his shoulder, slipping out of the room.

She'd barely dried off when Sebastian was back. "Here's your bag, blow-dryer, and the tray of goodies. And I've got a few more things." He grabbed something off the bed. "I picked out an outfit for you. It's mountain chic which will be perfect for this evening's dinner. Zinger and Techy Times are throwing a barbecue on the patio," he explained as he hung a rose-colored blouse and slim-fitting jeans on a towel rod before setting a pair of boots on the ground. "And I thought these would work, too." He handed her a lacy bra and matching panties in fire-engine red. "Mara and Janelle really hooked you up."

What was he? Her personal stylist?

"The clothes are great. I won't be long," she said, doing her best to remain upbeat.

Sebastian left, and she shut the door. She stared at the expensive lingerie in her hands and exhaled a pained breath. Her mind raced as she went through the motions of getting ready. What did she want? Should she embrace the interest in Munch Match? That was what Sebastian wanted her to do. And she'd be lying if she said she didn't enjoy being the focus of his complete attention. Did he feel the same way, or was he simply doing his job? There was a good chance her tender heart was seeing something that wasn't there. And speaking of her tender heart, she still had to deal with Jeremy.

Time passed in a blur of teeth brushing, blow-drying, and

makeup-applying. She sat on the edge of the bathtub, zipped up the stylish black leather boots, then stood in front of the mirror and stared at herself, first with her glasses on as regular Phoebe and then with them off as Phoebe 2.0.

Which was the real Phoebe?

The question hung in the air with the scent of the expensive lodge shampoo. She was about to put her glasses on when a muffled knock caught her attention. Had Sebastian left and accidentally locked himself out?

She opened the bathroom door and found Sebastian standing in front of it. She gasped, not expecting to find him lurking like a creeper. "Who's at the door?"

"That's got to be the LETIS mail," he answered, sounding downright giddy.

"What is LETIS mail? Is it like email? Were we supposed to download a messaging app for the symposium?"

"No, it's actual paper mail," Sebastian said, leading her to the door. "They explained it at breakfast. I can't believe I forgot to mention it. It's this throwback thing they do. Investors fill out interest cards, which then get delivered to the room every day around four."

He flung open the door, revealing a young man holding a stack of hunter-green envelopes.

"Phoebe Gale?" he said, meeting her gaze.

"Yes."

"These are for you." He handed her the stack.

There had to be ten envelopes, maybe more.

"Thank you," she stammered, pressure building in her chest.

"And one more thing, Miss Gale," the man said nervously.

"Yes?"

"Will you be coming down anytime soon? People have been asking about you."

She could feel Sebastian nearly vibrating.

"I'll be down in a bit. Thank you for bringing these up."

Sebastian closed the door as she stared at the stack. She'd barely heard the latch click when he scooped her into his arms and twirled her around the room.

"Phoebe, this is amazing," he exclaimed, smiling at her like . . . like she was his everything.

"It's overwhelming," she answered, choosing her words wisely. She didn't want to be a wet blanket, but something felt off.

He set her on the ground, then held her face in his hands. "Pheebs," he breathed, then leaned in.

He kissed her with such enthusiasm and such jubilation it was impossible not to glean some sliver of excitement. Maybe it was a good development. She kissed him back and melted into his touch. There was no denying it. She was falling for him —no, she'd fallen for him. She'd fallen for her best friend, and it was tearing her up inside.

"Way to go, Phoebe 2.0," he whispered against her lips.

Phoebe 2.0. Was that who she was now? Was that who he wanted?

He pressed her back to the door, and she dropped the cards as he gripped her hips and held her close. He deepened the kiss, and she sighed, allowing her mind to empty of its worries. She was a beat away from begging Sebastian to take her against the door when someone knocked.

Sebastian broke their kiss and smiled against her lips. "I bet that's the LETIS delivery guy with more cards."

They stepped away from the door.

Sebastian gestured toward the knob. "Why don't you do the honors? It's your destiny."

She nodded as the pressure in her chest returned. She turned the knob, but the person standing in the hallway wasn't the LETIS delivery guy.

Her stomach dropped. "What are you doing here?"

Chapter 16
PHOEBE

Phoebe blinked, hoping her eyes were deceiving her. But not even a round of rapid-fire lash batting could change what was smack-dab in front of her.

Jeremy Drewler stood before her with a touch-too-wide grin slapped on his face. Before she could utter another word, Sebastian came up behind her, and the overdone arc of Jeremy's smile changed trajectory.

Her ex scowled. "They didn't mention anything about a roommate when I asked the front desk for your room number. Are you sharing a room with Sebastian?"

"She is," Sebastian snarled before she could get a word out.

Jeremy kept his eyes locked on her. "Pheebs?" he pressed.

The way he said her nickname turned her stomach. Then again, she had to cut him a little slack. He was at her door. That had to mean something.

"There was a mix-up, and the lodge put us together."

Jeremy pushed up onto his tiptoes and peered past her into the room. "There's only one bed."

"Damn right, there's only one bed," Sebastian lobbed back. She couldn't see his face, but she could tell from the cadence of his reply that he had a cocky smirk pasted to his lips.

What was he playing at? Was he trying to make Jeremy jealous? Was this part of the Sebastian Guarantee?

"There's also a cot," she added, praying she wasn't blushing like the naughtiest of reverse cowgirls. She wasn't lying explicitly. There was a cot—an out-of-commission cot—but a cot, nevertheless. She schooled her features. "Is there something you need, Jeremy?"

He shifted his stance and raked his gaze over her body. "Well, first of all, you look amazing."

She glanced at the outfit and couldn't deny that there was something empowering about being put together. "Thanks, it's new. The boots, too," she added and kicked up her heel.

He glanced toward her feet, and his eyes widened. "I saw the guy go by with a stack of LETIS letters. They must have been for you."

The LETIS letters.

She crouched and gathered them. "They just arrived. Have you gotten any?"

"No," he said with a touch too much gusto. "But that's not what's important. You're important, *Pheebs*."

She bristled. He needed to stop with the Pheebs overkill.

"That's why I'm here," Jeremy continued. "I wanted to check on you. I didn't see you at breakfast or lunch."

"I slept late."

"She was exhausted—wiped out from *exertion*," Sebastian purred.

He was laying it on thick.

She mustered a grin. "I was exhausted from all the excitement at the boathouse cocktail hour, and I didn't get much sleep."

Jeremy frowned. "Why couldn't you sleep?"

"Wouldn't you like to know?" Sebastian shot back.

She threw Sebastian a pointed knock-it-off glance, then met Jeremy's gaze. "The cot broke." Again, it wasn't a complete lie, nor was it the complete truth, but she didn't have much to work with.

"I see," Jeremy answered, then stuffed his hands into his pockets.

"Don't you need to get back to your man-bunettes or blog about hipster eyewear?" Sebastian tossed out.

"No. Like I said, I'm here for Pheebs," Jeremy crooned like a used car salesman. "I'd be honored if you would allow me to escort you to the main hall."

Escort her? Where did he think they were? Downton Abbey? Why was he talking like they'd been cast in a historical romance? And what was this crazy energy between these two men? Sure, they didn't like each other—anyone with two brain cells could discern that—but there was something deeper, something she was missing.

"Perhaps we could take a walk," Jeremy continued, cutting into her thoughts. "It's overcast, and it looks like it might rain later, but I bet we could get in a stroll. It would be great if people saw us together."

Now she was the one frowning. Even when they'd been together, they'd rarely gone out. "You want to take a stroll with me so people can look at us?" she asked, needing some clarification.

"Absolutely! I overheard people talking about a hike they'd gone on this morning. They mentioned seeing a sanctuary or some stone building in the woods. It's just up the main walking trail, not too far from here."

Sebastian moved around behind her, then returned with his backpack. "A walk sounds great, Jeremy. Nothing like crisp fall mountain air. You don't mind if Pheebs' best friend since she was six years old tags along, do you, drooler?"

Jeremy pegged Sebastian with his gaze. "It's *Drew-ler.*"

"Yeah, sure, that's what I said," Sebastian answered as if he could give a flying fuck, which he clearly didn't, then proceeded to sling his arm over her shoulder.

She flashed him eyeball-speak for *what the hell are you doing?*

"What the hell are you doing, Pheebs?" Jeremy asked.

That better have been a coincidence. She couldn't have both Sebastian and Jeremy in her head.

Sebastian's shit-eating grin spread across his face. "We're talking with our eyeballs. We also talk with our feet. For example, Jeremy Drewler, I believe it's safe to say that you are a . . ." He tapped five times.

Of course he would.

"What does that mean?" her ex barked.

She sighed. This was exhausting. "It's something silly from when we were kids." She looked between the men. If she didn't get them moving, there was a very good chance the next thing to happen would be the two of them whipping out their junk to see which was bigger. "Oh my God," she murmured. *Holy penis problems!* With Sebastian behind her and Jeremy in front of her, a realization hit. She was quite literally stuck between two men, and she was intimately acquainted with both of their naughty bits. "Seb's is bigger. Way bigger," she mumbled.

"What's bigger?" Jeremy asked.

"Don't you know it," Sebastian quipped.

She could feel her cheeks burning. If anyone needed the crisp bite of mountain air, it was her. "Let's go for that walk." She tossed the LETIS letters onto the side table, then channeled the energy of an Olympic speed-walker and busted out of the room like it was on fire, freeing herself from being sandwiched between big dick (and small dick) energy. But the reprieve was short-lived, and the men quickly caught up to her.

"Phoebe, would you like to hang out at the barbecue tonight?" Jeremy asked, trying to take her hand.

She crossed her arms. "I—" she began, but Sebastian swooped in.

"She'll be too busy strategizing with me and weighing her investor options. I saw you at breakfast and lunch, Drewler," the man continued. "You know as well as I do that investors are salivating over her."

"Then you can scamper off," Jeremy shot back. "I'm sure my tech knowledge and guidance would be far superior to whatever you do. I'm not sure international playboy is an actual profession that could offer Pheebs any solid advice."

"I'm not a playboy, and Pheebs doesn't need tech guidance. If you haven't noticed, she's a tech genius. What she needs is strategic business advice from someone who genuinely cares about her, holds a business degree, and has been instrumental in expanding an actual business."

Jeremy smirked. "Your family business. I believe they call that nepotism."

These two were bickering like an old married couple as they entered the main hall.

Phoebe's pulse skyrocketed. "What I need is—"

"An offer to invest in the Munch Match app," a short, squatty man interjected, charging toward her.

If another man interrupted her, she would scream.

She stared at the guy. "Who are you?"

"Don't bother with him," a lanky older gentleman bellowed, edging his way in front of the short guy. "I'd like to speak with you first. Did you get my LETIS card?"

She took a step back. Men migrated toward her like the investor version of a zombie movie, and it appeared as if she were the zombie main course. She needed an escape plan. She peered up at Sebastian but found him as giddy as a schoolboy.

He rubbed his hands together like a mad scientist. "What did I tell you? You're the belle of the ball."

Ball was right—no, more like *balls*. Men were coming at

her from all sides. It didn't take a genius to deduce that the big and little dick energy was nearing catastrophic levels. Panic tore through her as a crowd formed.

"Phoebe, are you interested in modeling the latest fashion trends for sponsors?"

"Phoebe, we'd love to partner with you. Are you willing to wear a bikini?"

"Phoebe, we're willing to pay top-dollar for Munch Match."

"Phoebe, you could be a millionaire by tomorrow if you work with us."

"Phoebe, Phoebe, Phoebe!"

"Water?" came a woman's smooth voice, cutting through the chorus of male mooing.

Phoebe swept her gaze through the mass of men and caught the eye of a tall woman in a white turtleneck with a bottle of good old H2O in her hand. It was the same woman in white Sebastian seemed to recognize.

Whoever the hell she was, she offered hydration, and that was a godsend.

"Thanks," Phoebe stammered, accepting the item. She twisted off the cap, tossed it into the tittering swarm, then chugged it like she'd majored in keg stands in college.

Sufficiently hydrated, she surveyed the scene as her water angel disappeared behind a wall of men. This was too much. She needed to get out of there. But how would she disperse these dudes?

Then it came to her. Woman-speak was the answer.

She cleared her throat. "Excuse me, make a path. Woman experiencing menstrual cramps coming through."

Was she suffering from menstrual cramps? No, but she recalled her uncle's face when, years ago, she'd asked him to explain menstruation and female reproduction. He'd turned the color of dirty dishwater and referred her to take up the topic with her aunt. And it worked again on these guys. Just like the menstruation proclamation had sent her uncle heading for the hills, the male investors parted like the Red Sea—pun absolutely intended.

"What are you doing, Pheebs?" Sebastian asked.

"Lady stuff," she blurted, but she couldn't take refuge in the restroom. They'd wait her out. She scanned the main hall and found her getaway route. Dropping the water bottle, she took off toward the doors that led to the boathouse. Bursting through, a chilly pop of air hit her face, followed by . . .

Dammit! A blaring siren.

Wee-ooh-wee-ooh!

She'd used the freaking emergency exit *again*. And again, every pair of eyes fell on her. With her heart ready to explode, she surveyed the outdoor area and spied the quilting ladies working at a table under a canopy near the water's edge. Mae, Enid, Shirley, and Theodora looked up from their work as she sprinted toward them.

Phoebe skidded to a halt. "If a gal needed a little space, where would you suggest she go?"

"You could always scope out the trails," Mae suggested, then glanced at the gray, overcast sky. "But be careful. The trail could wash out if we get a lot of rain."

Phoebe glanced over her shoulder as the men closed in, with Sebastian and Jeremy leading the pack. A hike wasn't the answer. They'd follow her. She needed something better. "I'm not feeling like a walk. Any other suggestions?"

"Try a paddleboat—a little Zinger perk we've got here. There's nothing like the peacefulness of a placid lake to calm one's frayed nerves," Mae replied.

"Paddleboats," Phoebe repeated, her heart hammering as the blare of the alarm ceased and a chorus of male voices called to her.

Theodora pointed to a long wooden dock not far from the

boathouse. A trio of two-seater hot pink paddleboats sporting Zinger's Z logo bobbed on the water's surface.

"Better hurry," Enid remarked, then gestured with her chin toward the lodge. "It appears you've got some admirers."

"Yeah, but it's for the wrong reason," she bit out over her shoulder as she set off for the dock.

The wood planks creaked beneath her feet as she traversed the wobbly path to freedom. She eased into the first paddleboat, threw the rope tethering it to the dock aside, then pedaled like her very life depended on it. Unfortunately, as far as watercraft went, paddleboats could be classified as ridiculously slow as molasses in the speed department. Nonetheless, she was moving away from the shore, and nobody could bombard her with questions or offers.

"Phoebe!" Sebastian called.

"Pheebs!" Jeremy belted.

She looked over her shoulder. *Ugh!* How could she have forgotten about the two remaining Zinger boats? With Sebastian in one and Jeremy pedaling away in the other, the men made a beeline for her. And to add insult to injury, Mother Nature decided to contribute to the calamity. The sky opened up. Beads of rain danced on the surface of the lake, dampened her blouse, and accumulated on her glasses.

Layers of frustration built in her chest, and she glared at the sky. "Seriously?" she yelled at the universe and nature and the male race and whoever had decided *not* to add a motor to the back of paddleboats. Before she could think of someone or something else to blame for her predicament, Jeremy and Sebastian were hot on her tail.

"How did you guys catch up to me?" she yelled, pedaling faster.

"You're a slow pedaler," Sebastian answered.

"What?"

"You've always been. When we were kids, Oscar, Aria, and

I would rock-paper-scissors it out to see who'd hang back with you when we were riding bikes."

"Argh!" she cried.

"Pheebs, what are you doing? What about our stroll?" Jeremy hollered.

"Drewler, forget the stroll. Phoebe is on the precipice of success, and you're distracting her."

"Distract this," Jeremy barked, followed by a *thunk* of hardened plastic ramming into hardened plastic.

"Did you hit me on purpose, Strawberry Man Bun?" Sebastian shot back.

"You bet your playboy-ass I did."

Phoebe looked over her shoulder as two grown men repeatedly whacked their paddleboats into each other like two deranged goats headbutting—the slow-motion water version.

Thunk, thunk, thunk!

"Wait a bloody second! I'm taking on water."

"So am I," Jeremy howled.

"Pheebs!" the men cried.

"We're sinking! Save us!" Jeremy called.

She chewed her lip and pondered the situation. Would it be that bad if they sank? Sure, the water was cold, but they weren't that far from shore. Wasn't a girl's sanity worth the price of a few shipwrecked—or paddleboat-wrecked—dudes? She took off her glasses and pinched her nose.

"Phoebe," Jeremy whined.

She wiped the rain out of her eyes and put on her glasses. Shaking her head, she nixed the sanity sink-or-swim plan. "I'm coming," she called and pedaled backward, reversing course. She got to Sebastian first. "Get on."

"What's going on with you?" he asked like she was the crazy one.

"Are you kidding me?"

He settled into the seat with his backpack in his arms. "Phoebe, the success you want is at your fingertips."

She stared at her best friend. "Sebby, I'm not sure—"

"Phoebe," Jeremy wailed, cutting her off. "Hurry, I'm sinking!"

She flicked her gaze from Sebastian and eyed the blubbering man. "Jesus, Jeremy, you can literally see me. We're ten feet apart. Give me a second." Maneuvering past Sebastian's out-of-commission boat, she sidled up to Jeremy, then checked the slim deck behind her seat. It wouldn't be comfortable, but her ex was the smaller of the two men, and he could fit if he sat with his legs extended. "Get onto the back shelf. It's not ideal, but it'll do."

The horn-rimmed-glasses-wearing man pouted as the rain flattened his man bun. "Why does Sebastian get the front seat?"

"Because I'm the manlier man here," Sebastian growled, shielding his eyes from the rain. "Bunettes ride in the back."

Jeremy hemmed and hawed, then pulled himself onto the back shelf. "I still don't think it's fair."

"Stop acting like a crybaby," Sebastian muttered.

Jeremy shifted his weight. "I'm not acting like a crybaby."

"You are!"

"Am not!"

"You are!"

"Am not!"

"You—"

"One, two, three," Phoebe snarled on the brink of losing her mind, "eyes on me!" she finished, stealing a line from her first-grade teacher's playbook. The men complied, and she exhaled an aggravated breath. "There is no talking on the paddleboat. Anyone who talks is going into the lake. Don't say a single word. Nod if you understand."

Blessedly, the men must have detected the thread of homicidal maniac in her voice. Both nodded, and neither said a word as she steered them toward the dock, cutting a painfully slow line across the lake's rain-pebbled surface. All she wanted was a minute to herself. But that wouldn't be happening any time soon. Her stomach dropped. A crowd had gathered. Armed with umbrellas, gawking men and women spilled from the boathouse onto the dock and along the rocky shoreline. And to make matters worse, her stomach was at it again. This time, it growled as the scent of grilled hot dogs cut through the air. The staff had set up a canopy near the water's edge, and chefs were grilling the evening's meal beneath it.

If anyone on the planet needed a hot dog, it was her.

Hungry and fed up, she eased alongside the dock. She secured the watercraft, then sprang onto the wooden planks and set her sights on the only thing that could bring her comfort: a table piled high with condiments, buns, and trays of freaking hot dogs.

"I'll get you a towel, and then we can talk," Sebastian called.

"Woman with menstrual cramps coming through," she belted, ignoring the man as she charged down the dock, passing by Jeremy's snickering buddies. Soaked to the bone, she ignored them as well because she'd passed the point of no return.

She was truly a woman with no fucks left to give.

Entering the bustling food tent, LETIS participants edged away from her, murmuring softly like they were accommodating a bear emerging from hibernation. It wasn't that far from the truth. Her belly growled, and she pursed her lips, surveying the scene. Hot dogs, hamburgers, and boxes of Tech Tween chocolate chip cookies lined the main serving table. She plucked a basket from the stack, loaded it with four hot dogs, then grabbed a box of chocolate chip cookies and shoved it under her arm. She could feel all eyes on her. How was that for giving everyone another *glimpse*, another *whiff*? She'd surely piqued everyone's senses by now.

She ignored the whispers and focused on her tray of food. She took a breath to help slow her hammering pulse. What she needed was solitude. She could barricade herself inside her room and pray Sebby was smart enough to give her some space. That's what she'd do. She made her way to the condiments table and picked up a bottle of Dijon mustard, ready to dress her dogs and haul ass back to her room, when a voice caught her attention.

"Pay up, Drewler, you lost the bet. You said you'd have Phoebe crawling back, begging to date you again. It looks like she's the one trying to get away from you."

Bet?

"I'm happy to pay," Jeremy balked. "Phoebe Gale is certifiable. It might have been worth taking her back since she's hot and was on the brink of making a fortune. But she's bat-shit crazy. Even with a last name like Gale, nobody will want to partner with her. She's not even worth stringing along as a side piece. What do I need her for? I've already got an angel investor waiting in the wings. Pretty soon, I'll be loaded, and she'll be some loser trying to build a website for chicks that nobody cares about."

He'd been gearing up to use her again—as a joke, as entertainment for his douche canoe friends—and she'd nearly fallen for it. She should have seen through his saccharine-sweet demeanor. The man didn't care for her—he'd never cared about her. He was out for himself. She could stomach that. She could also bear the sting of being made to look like a fool. But she couldn't allow him to belittle Go Girl.

She lifted her chin, and a peculiar calm descended. She set down the Dijon, eyed a container of Sriracha, then slid her gaze to a fire-engine red bottle of hot sauce with flames on the label.

Bingo!

She palmed the bottle, assessing its weight, as a cunning smirk twisted her lips.

The container was full—but not for long.

She peered through the crowd and locked in on her target, standing beneath an umbrella with a trio of men rocking man buns.

Sauntering out of the tent, she came up to the men just as Jeremy doled out soggy one-dollar bills to his douche canoe crew. She couldn't feel the rain, couldn't feel her blouse plastered to her wet skin, and she could no longer hear the murmurs of the crowd. "I've got a bet for you, Jeremy," she cooed.

"What?" the man stammered, eyeing the bottle. He took a step back toward the water's edge.

She assessed the condiment. "I have a feeling this will burn. But we'll let you be the judge."

"Phoebe, I—" he began.

With his stupid jaw nearly hitting the ground, he gave her the opening she required. Just like she'd done at the bistro, she raised her arm and let the hot sauce rip. She'd aimed for his face when she'd tagged him with Dijon. Tonight, she zeroed in on his big fat lying mouth like a condiment marksman. And bull's-eye, baby! She filled that sucker like she was manning a fire hose.

"Water, water!" Jeremy garbled, sticking his tongue out like a toddler and flapping his hands.

"I can help with that," Sebastian offered, coming out of nowhere. He tapped the juddering and jerking Jeremy. The man took another step back, then another, then . . .

Splash!

Jeremy Drewler hit the lake.

The crowd released a collective gasp.

He thrashed in the shallow waters, spitting and hacking.

"You can squirt hot sauce or mustard or whatever the hell condiment you can get your hands on at me, but you're the one who let me treat you like crap. The day we met, all I did was talk to you in line at the food truck. Guess what? I hadn't used your dumb app. I heard the food truck guy call you Phoebe Gale. That's the only reason why I asked for your number. But you loved it. You ate up the attention. You even thought I was your match. You texted it to Sebastian the night we met six months ago and told him that."

"You looked through my phone?" she bit out.

He shrugged like an insolent child. "You left the chat open when you went to the bathroom."

"You're a terrible person," she shot back, adrenaline surging through her body.

"I'm an opportunist. But you're the one who answered my one a.m. texts, and you're the one who considered taking me back. Was I an ass for betting I could get you back? Maybe, but you're the one who makes it so easy to trample on your heart."

Jeremy Drewler might have been the worst of the worst, but he wasn't wrong. Her gut twisted. Humiliation thickened in her throat. In that flash of shame, she thought of her parents. What would they think of their daughter? Their daughter was no man-eater. She was a doormat. Swallowing past the emotion, she willed herself not to crumble. Right or wrong, she would not give Jeremy Drewler the satisfaction.

"Want me to hit him or throw him into a deeper part of the lake?" Sebastian seethed.

"Go ahead," Jeremy sputtered, waving off Sebastian as he dragged himself out of the lake. "But don't try and play the hero, Cress. You're no better than me, and after our little discussion last night, you know it."

She pegged Sebastian with her gaze. "What's he saying? What did you two talk about? Is there something I need to know?"

Jeremy removed his glasses and shook off the excess water. "Your best buddy here, Mr. Six-Pack Internet Playboy, is into you because you aren't traipsing around in those stupid overalls and that dumb beret anymore. It was written all over his face last night. He's not your best friend, Phoebe. The guy wants you for himself," Jeremy griped, then marched up to Sebastian. "Do you deny it?"

Barely able to breathe, she turned to her friend—her best friend. What had he said to Jeremy behind her back? Sebastian couldn't be so shallow he'd only want her because she had an upgraded wardrobe and donned sexy lingerie. But as the thought crossed her mind, she pictured his socials over the last six months—his *shallow*, playboy-lifestyle posts where beauty and status reigned supreme. He'd said he wanted to change and put that behind him, but was that a lie?

She didn't know what to believe.

Feeling like an exposed nerve, the mountain air assaulted her soaked body. It whipped through her hair and sent a shiver down her spine. "Sebastian?" she breathed, her teeth chattering.

"Answer the question, Cress. Yes or no? Do you want Phoebe?" Jeremy spat.

Agony flashed in Sebastian's eyes as rain trailed down his cheeks. "Yes, I want her."

Chapter 17
PHOEBE

Crunch, crunch, crunch!

"Phoebe, the weather's only getting worse. We have to go back to the lodge. It's not safe out here."

A blistering crack of lightning followed by thunder roared above her head. It illuminated the billowy clouds and mountainous terrain. The wind hissed through the aspen leaves as towering evergreens loomed, shadowy and imposing. Another roll of thunder grumbled, and the pelting beads of rain turned to sheets of icy moisture. But Phoebe didn't flinch. It didn't slow her down. Soaked inside and out, she kept her gaze on her feet.

"Phoebe, say something!" Sebastian pleaded.

She could hear him calling. He'd been hot on her trail since she'd dropped her dinner tray, abandoned the box of cookies, and taken off running for the path carved into the side of the mountain.

"Phoebe, stop!"

She narrowed her gaze. There was no way she'd comply with that command. Even if she wanted to, she couldn't stop.

Every beat of her heart pushed her—no, forced her—to keep going.

Crunch, crunch, crunch!

Sticking to the patches of gravel, she hopped over thick grooves in the trail. Cut by the rain, the watery channels snaked downhill like tentacles crisscrossing through the stones and mounds of mud.

"Phoebe, talk to me, please!" Sebastian called, now a few paces behind.

The man could catch up to her if he wanted to. She could barely run a mile. Sebastian Cress practiced Pun-chi yoga. He was as fit as a fiddle and strong as an ox, but at this very moment, he had the good sense to give her space as she wound her way deeper into the forest.

Did she have a destination?

No.

Between Jeremy's salty confession and Sebastian's sobering admission, she only had one choice. And that choice was to run. Or, in her case, speed walk, or speed hike, or speed trudge—which probably wasn't even a thing. But it didn't matter what she called her escape. She had to get out of there. If Sebastian wanted to follow her like a lost puppy, that was his choice.

Another rumble of thunder vibrated through the saturated evergreen landscape, and she exhaled a pained breath. With each step, her heart endured another fracture, another crack, as a heartbreaking realization set in. She'd loved Sebastian Cress since she was a girl. She'd loved him when he was a scrawny kid. She'd loved him when he was an awkward preteen. She'd loved him regardless of what he looked like or what he'd achieved. She also knew that her love for him had changed.

She'd felt the shift the minute their lips touched. She'd tried to deny it, tried to hide behind excuses like saying nothing counted because they'd agreed to co-exist in a wishy-washy, sex-fueled creative mode or deem their intimate encounters as quasi-academic man-eater training exercises. But that was bullshit, complete bullshit, a veneer unable to hide the glaring truth. Barely a handful of days ago, she'd opened her heart to him, not as a friend, but as a lover.

It wasn't like she hadn't fallen for men in the past. She'd just never expected Sebastian to be so reckless with her heart. Whatever had transpired between her ex and her oldest friend had opened Pandora's box. Where did they go from here? How was she supposed to see him as a friend now that she couldn't hide from the truth—the truth that she loved him and he only wanted satin-and-lace Phoebe 2.0?

"Phoebe, stop! There's an animal ahead."

That exclamation warranted a reaction.

She flicked her gaze from the ground, shielded her eyes, then froze. In a small clearing, no more than twenty or thirty feet ahead of them, a fox sat in the center of the path. Its bushy tail curled inward as the animal held its ground. She scanned the area, checking to see if the woodland critter was alone, then spied a stone structure through the trees just off the path.

Sebastian came to her side. He took another step and put himself between her and their new friend. "It's a fox," he said like he was the end-all and be-all authority on mountain wildlife. "We need to make noise to scare it away."

Who did he think he was talking to?

She pushed him out of the way. Fox or no fox, she was tired of men thinking they knew more than she did. "Of course we have to make noise," she bellowed, her voice rising above the pounding rain. "You only know about foxes because, growing up, you went with *me* to Bergen Adventure Camp every summer." She stabbed her finger into his chest. "Every year, I was right there by your side when the counselors went over trail etiquette. You and I have been all over the entire state—and all over the world together."

Salty tears and rainwater pricked her eyes. Anger and frustration had her wound up so tight she wasn't sure if she was on the cusp of breaking down or parting her lips and screaming like she'd been cast to create sound effects for horror movies. Adrenaline pumped through her veins. It was fight-or-flight time. She hardened her features and went into fight mode.

She eyed the animal. "I do not have the time or the patience to be mauled, bitten, or attacked. Do you hear me, Mr. Fox? I will harness every ounce of energy to banish you from this trail, from this state, from this earth. This is your warning, you bushy-tailed bastard," she bellowed, raising her hands like she was calling the corners to cast a spell. "Get. Off. This. Path!"

The words screeched past her lips a second before a lightning bolt rocketed toward the earth. It struck a rock jutting from the trail a few feet from the animal as a bang of thunder shook the mountain.

She screamed and stumbled backward. Turning away from the jagged flash, she pitched forward and slipped on a slick patch of mud. But she didn't hit the ground. Sebastian caught her in his arms. She held on to him as he guided her off the trail. Beneath a canopy of golden-leaved aspens and a trio of boulders providing respite from the wind, he wrapped his arms around her. She should have rejected his touch, but she couldn't fight him. She needed his strong embrace to hold her together. Trembling, she pressed her head against his rain-soaked chest and exhaled like she'd been holding her breath for the last hour.

But what about the fox?

Panic shot through her. "Did I kill it?" she yelped. "Did I summon a lightning bolt to barbecue a fox? I'm so sorry, fox. I'm sorry, creatures of Glenn Pines. I didn't mean to be such a

. . ." she whimpered and tapped her foot five times. "Only a douche nozzle butthole threatens a fox," she sobbed, bunching the fabric of Sebastian's shirt in her hands as she clung to him.

He tightened his hold and threaded his hand into her mass of wet hair. "Easy now, you're not a douche nozzle butthole. The fox is okay. He took off like a shot into the woods."

"Was he intact? Did he lose an ear or his tail? Did he escape with all his appendages?"

He pulled back and tipped her chin up. "Trust me, the fox is fine. And I thought," he added, mustering a weak grin as rivulets of rain trailed down his beautiful face, "we agreed to never, ever use the word *appendage* again. And don't even ask me about the fox's *orifices*, because I sure as hell didn't get a look at any of those. Did an offshoot of the lightning bolt hit his ass orifice and send him off with a little more zip? I don't know, Pheebs. I reckon it's possible."

This man. Even when she wanted to throttle him, he was there beside her, making her smile.

Her tears mixed with the rain as she melted into him, holding on like he was the only thing keeping her tethered to the ground. "What do we do now, Sebby?"

He rested his chin on the crown of her head. "You let me talk, and you listen to me for one bloody second," he bit out, his voice taking on his old accent.

She took a step back. She had some questions first. "Before you say anything, tell me what you and Jeremy discussed."

Sebastian scrubbed his hands down his face. "He came up to me last night when you were talking with Carla and the investors at the cocktail party. Your transformation took him by surprise. He said he had time to devote to winning you back because he'd been contacted by an investor yesterday morning."

She scoffed. "Wow, nice to know I play second fiddle to a potential investor."

Sebastian swallowed hard and looked away.

"What else?" she pressed. "Did he mention the bet?"

"No, he just looked at me, smiled that smarmy smirk, and said he knew."

"What did he know?"

Sebastian's features softened. "How I felt about you. How I feel about you."

"No, not me," she corrected, shaking her head. "How you feel about Phoebe 2.0, Phoebe the lingerie-wearing man-eater."

"You're wrong, Pheebs."

"How am I wrong?" she fired back. "It's black-and-white. Up until a couple of days ago, I was your good old buddy, Phoebe, and then I put on a baby doll negligee and you couldn't keep your hands off me."

"No," he rasped, shoulders slumping as he shook his head.

"Sebastian, don't lie to me."

He cupped her face in his hands. Trembling, he leaned in. "Phoebe Gale, I'm not lying to you. I would never lie to you. I want you. I've wanted to be more than your friend for more than six bloody months. But I didn't want to lose you. I didn't want to ruin our friendship—a friendship that sustains me. It completes me. It guides me. You're my true north." He wiped the water from her cheeks. "And you're also the reason my life went to shit. And the only way I knew how to numb the pain was by being the opposite of what you made me want to be."

She balked. "Are you blaming me?"

"No, I'm the guilty party here. What I'm telling you is that the day you sent that text, it broke me."

She stared at him as the pieces came together. "The text about Jeremy being my match?"

"I read it, and nothing made sense anymore because . . ." He stroked his thumb across her bottom lip. "Because you couldn't meet your match."

She pushed him away. He wasn't making any sense. "You don't think there's anyone out there for me?"

"No, just listen. You couldn't meet your match with an app or on a blind date or at some coffee shop, because you've already met your match. Madelyn Malone was right. Our matches had been made. You met your match on a summer day. You'd barely been introduced when you made him call you Phoebe, Princess of the Hot Dog Fairies, Bearer of Cookies, and Eater of Pizza."

"Sebastian," she whispered, her heart swelling as the little love seed in her chest bloomed.

He gathered her into his arms, smiling that boyish grin that made her weak in the knees. It didn't matter that she was soaked to the bone. The cold and wet disappeared as she closed her eyes. Her entire body craved his kiss. Her heart pounded. Sweet anticipation electrified the air. She could sense the energy and feel the ions dancing around them. With his lips a breath away, a tingle danced down her spine. She smiled, ready to be kissed into a soggy oblivion, when another bolt of lightning sliced through the atmosphere, landing not five feet from where the fox had nearly been barbecued.

She screamed and nearly jumped out of her skin. What was the name of this trail? Killer Lightning Alley?

Another round of rolling thunder grumbled, and the clouds crackled with threads of electricity.

"Listen, Pheebs," Sebastian said, eyeing the sky warily, "I want to kiss you until I can't feel my lips, but we can't do it here. We have to go back to the lodge."

"No, the trail is too waterlogged," she replied, recalling Mae's warning. "We'll get stuck. I saw a stone building just past where the fox was sitting." She pointed to a spot between a trio of aspens. "It's our best option."

"I see it," he said, taking her hand.

They darted up the wet trail, avoiding the slick spots, and

came upon a fork in the path where a narrow limestone walkway branched off the muddy trail. Hand in hand, they sprinted toward the pale yellow and burnt orange stone structure. The rocky oasis looked like something out of a mountain fairy tale, with a pitched, pointy roof and an arched wooden door.

"Is this somebody's house?" she asked as they scaled the few steps to the door.

"I'm not sure." Sebastian knocked, then pulled on the handle, but the thing didn't budge.

A blustery gust of wind sent the rain sideways, and a sharp set of bangs cut through the pounding rain.

"Let's check the back," he called as the banging continued.

"Do you see that?" she called as the wind opened and closed a weather-beaten door.

"We're going in," Sebastian called. "We can take shelter here."

He held the door for her, and she slipped into the darkened space. She inhaled the comforting scents of rain and cedar wood, grateful to escape the downpour. Sebastian entered a second later, then pulled the door shut behind him.

She felt around, searching for a light switch, but stilled when Sebastian came up behind her. "I'm looking for a l—" she began, but he didn't let her finish.

He dropped his backpack onto the floor. It hit with a wet thud. In a fluid motion, he gripped her hips and spun her to face him. He gathered her into his arms. "I can't wait, Phoebe. I need you now. I need to be inside you."

Arousal and adrenaline coursed through her veins. Surrendering to desire, she pressed up onto her tiptoes. He ducked his head and kissed her, devouring her with an urgency that had her breathless within seconds. Deepening the kiss, he lifted her into his arms, holding her wet body flush with his. She wrapped her legs around his waist and threaded her fingers into the hair at the nape of his neck. She hummed her pleasure as the velvety warmth of his mouth had her near-delirious with desire.

This was no slow and sultry make-out session. Sebastian was positively ravenous—and he wasn't alone. Desperate for more, she arched into him. With his hands palming the globes of her ass, she rocked her hips, feeling him thick and hard between her thighs. He took a few steps and stopped when they bumped into what must have been a ledge or a shelf with something soft, possibly tablecloths or blankets, piled high.

"Are you okay?" he asked.

"Shelf . . . blankets . . . all good," she whispered between kisses, then reached back and pushed aside something smooth and solid—perhaps a leather-bound book.

But the last thing on her mind was conducting an inventory. With Sebastian rolling his hips in time with her, the friction teased her most sensitive place, rubbing her at a pace that had her roaring toward an orgasm.

Sensing her heightened arousal, he tightened his grip on her ass. "You like that. But you want more, don't you?"

Hell, yes, she did. She ached for his cock. "You know what I want."

He set her down and knelt before her. He pulled off her boots and tossed them aside. Unbuttoning her jeans, he peeled the soaked denim past her thighs, then slid her panties down to join the fabric at her ankles. She shivered as the cool air met her wet skin.

"Let's warm you up," he growled, coming to his feet. "Hold on, lass," he added in that accent that had her clenching her core.

She turned and gripped the edge of whatever the hell was against the wall, listening as he unzipped his pants. Then it dawned on her. She'd never done anything like this. Could someone find them at any moment? Possibly. But something inside her knew they were supposed to be here—like this place had been waiting for them.

She closed her eyes and focused on the sound of Sebastian's breath. It mingled with the torrent of raindrops battering the roof. Then he was there, kissing her neck, holding her close. She brushed her ass against his cock.

"I will never get enough of you." He guided himself inside her and inhaled a sharp breath. Nipping at her earlobe, he slipped his hand past her hip and massaged her tight bundle of nerves. Rocking into her, he caressed her most sensitive place, making love to her as he pleasured her with his hand. "This is me wanting you and only you. This is me," he rasped, "taking what's always been mine. When I'm done with you, Phoebe Gale, you won't be thinking of me as your friend anymore. That word won't even exist in your vocabulary."

"You think you can screw a word right out of my head?" she asked, amazed she could still form a coherent question.

He dialed up his pace, taking her fast and hard. "I bloody guarantee it."

His breathy words, hot against her skin, washed over her, bathing her in a fiery euphoria. She squeezed the fabric on the shelf and closed her eyes. Her entire universe contracted around the sway of their bodies, the slide of his cock, and the beat of their hearts. She hovered in that sensual space, a raindrop suspended in the air milliseconds before crashing to the ground.

"Phoebe, I love you. I've always loved you."

His words snapped the last strands of her resolve. Wrapped in his warmth and drunk on his affection, she cried out, letting go and catapulting into a sea of bliss and love.

Love.

Sebastian held her close and followed her over the edge. Pistoning his hips, he cupped between her thighs, not letting up and demanding she feel every ripple, every pulse, and every sensual swell of their release. Breathing hard, she allowed him to support her weight as she leaned into him.

"Pheebs," he breathed, "that was—"

"Something we should have started doing a lot earlier. I love you sex is out of this world," she finished with a coy lilt to her voice, chest heaving as every muscle in her body relaxed.

He chuckled and kissed her neck. "Remember the cake we destroyed in college—the one for Oscar and Aria?"

"After everything that's happened, you're thinking about cake?" she asked, still catching her breath.

"Bear with me."

She caressed his cheek, loving that he was still buried deep inside her. "Okay, yes, I remember the cake *you* destroyed."

He kissed her temple. "That's still up for debate, but that's not why I'm thinking of that cake."

"All right, I'll bite. Why, after making love in the dark in some random room in a little stone building, are you thinking of cake? Then again, cake does sound pretty good. All right, go on."

"After it was a heap on the floor, you bent down and ran the tip of your index finger through the icing on the top part that hadn't touched the ground. Then you slid your finger into your mouth. Do you remember doing that?"

She racked her brain. "No, but I'm not one to let sweets go to waste. Not to mention, eating cake off the floor sounds like something I'd do, so I'll take your word for it. What made you think of that?"

"Jesus, you were so sexy, Phoebe," he answered, his voice deepening as he traced the line of her collarbone. "I couldn't tear my eyes away from you. Then you looked over your shoulder with your finger still in your mouth and caught my eye. And bloody hell, I was hard instantly."

This was news to her.

"All I wanted to do," he continued, "was press your body

against the counter and screw your brains out until we both couldn't see straight."

"Sebby, I had no idea."

"I hid it. I didn't know what to do with those feelings. I put it out of my mind because we were best friends, but now you're more than that to me."

"What am I?"

"You're all mine."

"All yours," she repeated, heady with the prospect of life with this man as not only her best friend but her lover—her love of a lifetime.

Needing to face him and seal this conversation with a kiss, she shifted her hips, and he pulled out. She started to turn in his arms but forgot her ankles were bound by wet denim and soaked lace. She pitched backward. "Oh no!"

Sebastian held her hips, working to keep her upright, but he was in the same pants-at-the-ankles predicament as she was. She reached for the shelf, grasping for anything solid, and snagged the cloth and whatever that big leather-covered thing was. Sadly, neither item kept her from crashing into Sebastian. They hit the floor like two half-naked ankle-bound sacks of potatoes.

"Pheebs, are you hurt?"

She sat up. "I'm okay."

"I'll try to find a light switch," he said, coming to his feet.

She pulled off her jeans and panties and stood in her wet blouse. Her eyes had adjusted to the dark, and she watched Sebastian pull up his pants, then feel around the confines of the room. With a click, a single bulb hanging from above lit the room in a dim glow. She squinted and took in the space. They were in a mudroom or a small storage area with a door across from the one they'd entered. The shelves were lined with vases and candles. She eyed a clear canister piled high with what appeared to be pink silk-flower rose petals.

"Here," Sebastian said, digging in his pack. He removed his cell and the slim pad he'd kept with him, then pulled out a Sebastian-sized hoodie and handed it to her.

"So prepared," she said, peeling off her shirt and bra. "I'm impressed."

"Always have a change of clothing with you in your waterproof pack when you're in the mountains," he said, draping their wet clothes on a folding chair in the corner. "That's a little nugget I picked up, thanks to my girl, Phoebe, who dragged my pasty British arse to summer camp, year after year."

My girl, Phoebe. Her heart fluttered.

She put on the dry hoodie, which looked more like a puffy dress on her, and inhaled Sebastian's scent from the heather-gray fabric. She sighed, then stared at the heap of wet clothing dripping onto the floor. "I don't think I've ever been that wet," she remarked, twisting her damp hair into a bun.

Sebastian removed his jeans, pulled on a pair of sweats and a T-shirt, then sauntered over, looking all casual-sexy. A wicked grin spread across his face. "Is that a challenge?"

Hello, Swoonville!

"Damn right, it is," she replied, taking a step toward him, but she stubbed her toe on a giant leather-bound book. She pitched forward, and again, Sebastian caught her. She eyed the items strewn about the floor. "We should tidy up."

"What is this place anyway? A storage facility?" he asked, picking up the book.

She gathered the quilt into her arms and eyed the others lining the shelves. "Why do you think these are here?"

Sebastian ran his hand over the material. "Blankets are good to have around to wrap exposed outdoor pipes to keep them from freezing. I thought I saw a gravel road past the clearing. We might be near a trailhead. The one in your hands has bits of flowers on it. They might leave this place open so people can stop in and borrow a blanket for a picnic. Mae and her friends probably donated them."

She nodded as she studied the squares on the quilt in her hands and raised an eyebrow. She was no quilting expert, but this wasn't your typical-looking quilt with geometric designs or flowers made from shapes. On this quilt, each square contained a different stitched item. A computer, a microscope, mathematics symbols, beakers, gears, planets, and a square at the bottom right corner with six words sewn into the material. She stared at them, not sure she could believe her eyes.

Made by STEM in Stratlin, Colorado.

"I get that STEM stands for science, technology, engineering, and math, but where's Stratlin, Colorado?" Sebastian asked and touched the letters.

"It's a small town on the way to the Eastern Plains, an hour or so from Denver."

"Have you been there?"

"No." She looked up at him. "I only know of it because my mom grew up there. She lived with her grandmother."

"Isn't that something," Sebastian replied, absentmindedly turning the leather book over in his hands.

She caught a glimpse of the cover and gasped. "Hold the book upright for me."

"What is it?"

"Glenn Pines Chapel wedding registry," she said, reading the title embossed in faded gold letters on the deep mahogany-colored cover.

"Pheebs, didn't your uncle say that your parents got married at the Glenn Pines Chapel?"

"He did."

"That's what this place must be—a chapel. Let's see if we can get in." Sebastian slung his pack over his shoulder, tucked the book under his arm, and went to the interior door. He turned the knob. The latch clicked with an upbeat squeak, like the knob was grateful to be of use. "After you," he said, holding the door.

Barefoot, she entered the cozy chapel. With six polished wood pews and a raised altar at the front, the simple space had a sacred feel. She walked down the aisle and sat in the center of the last pew. Her chest welled with emotion. Despite never having set foot in this place, she recognized the view. She admired it every day when she made her morning coffee. First, she'd read the note card with her high school yearbook quote about the future belonging to those who believe in their dreams, and then she'd gaze at the picture of her parents on their wedding day.

And now she was in the chapel. She stared ahead and imagined her mom and dad standing mere feet away, gazing into each other's eyes as they exchanged vows.

"When did they get married, Pheebs?"

She kept her gaze trained on the altar. "June twenty-second, five years before I was born."

Sebastian set his pack on the pew and slipped in next to her. "I found them. They signed the book," he said softly, then rested the ledger on her lap.

Melanie Funke and Andrew Gale.

She ran her fingertips across her parents' signatures. "What do you think my mom and dad would want me to do, Sebby? Partner with an investor on Munch Match or hold out for Go Girl?"

Sebastian wrapped his arm around her. "I think they'd want you to succeed in your field. Munch Match is your ticket to do that."

She chewed her lip as the signatures on the page grew blurry.

"You said it yourself a few days ago," Sebastian continued. "For Go Girl to work, you'd need a major organization to partner with you. You don't have that."

She slid her gaze from the book and concentrated on the empty altar, wishing she could have one minute to see her parents in flesh and blood. She'd ask for their guidance and tell them how much, even in death, they'd enriched her life.

"I guaranteed that I'd help you find success, Pheebs. You've got your pick of investors for Munch Match. Take my advice, not as your friend, but as your life coach and the person looking out for your business interests."

Conflicted, she exhaled an audible breath. "Maybe you're right."

A bang from the back room echoed against the stone walls.

"That's got to be the door. The latch must be broken. I'll take care of it," he said and headed toward the source of the sound.

She returned her gaze to the book, smiling at her mother's loopy handwriting and her father's sharp, slanted lines. Even in their writing, they complemented each other. She should take a picture. *Shit!* She'd left her phone at the lodge. But Sebastian hadn't. Opening his pack, she took out the notebook and set it on the seat next to her, then proceeded to sift through the bag, searching for his cell. The book on her lap shifted as she moved the bag, and the pad fluttered open and fell to the floor. She set the backpack aside and glanced down. The breath caught in her throat as she read the words highlighted in neon yellow.

Objective: Collect data on Test Subject 1 to demonstrate that the Sebastian Guarantee techniques produce a successful outcome. PUSH THE FASTEST ROAD TO SUCCESS. This is imperative. Per potential investors, no convincing data means no investment funds.

Her stomach dropped, and her breathing grew ragged. She turned the page, then the next, skimming Sebastian's notes.

"The rain stopped, but the wind is still blowing," Sebastian remarked, coming toward her, then skidded to a dead stop. The color drained from his face. "What are you doing with my notes?"

"I was looking for your phone. I left mine at the lodge. I wanted to take a picture of my parents' signatures. I figured I'd use yours. Your pad fell out, and I . . ." She trailed off.

"It's not what you think it is, Phoebe."

But she knew better. "It's exactly what I think it is. I'm your Sebastian Guarantee case study test subject."

He didn't answer.

She turned a page of the notebook. "Before following the Sebastian Guarantee protocols," she read, her voice void of emotion, "the subject was flailing professionally and personally. Subject could be described as nerdy, socially awkward, and unconcerned with presenting herself professionally—for example, wardrobe choices."

"Phoebe," Sebastian called.

She waved him off. "There's more, but you know that, don't you?"

He didn't reply.

"Subject also lacks direction regarding career trajectory," she continued. "Subject makes poor choices when it comes to dating and relationships. Subject leads with her heart and not with her head." She closed the notebook. "That's what you think of me?"

"Pheebs," he eked out, his voice a cracked husk of a sound.

"Answer the question, Sebastian."

"My plan was to help the both of us. The investors I met with asked for proof that my life-coaching protocols worked, but I didn't have any. The day you texted me about meeting your match was the day I was supposed to set up trials and recruit test subjects."

She narrowed her gaze. "You used me."

"It's not like that."

"It is. And here's the ironic part. I would have let you. I would have happily volunteered. I wouldn't have even needed to think it over. If you'd come to me and told me the truth, my answer would have been yes. I would have done anything for you because I love you. You *were* my best friend."

He flinched. "Were?"

"You're no different than Jeremy. No," she breathed through a mirthless laugh, "you're worse than him. For all his selfish faults, at least he copped to it. I can see the wheels turning in your head. You're still trying to convince yourself that you did this for me."

"You asked me to turn you into a business-savvy man-eater. That's what I did. I did it for you."

"*And yourself.* Don't forget that piece. And you didn't tell me, because a part of you knew what you were doing could hurt me. It's so clear now. Pushing me to pick an investor to expand Munch Match wasn't about my success. It was about your data. It was about you getting your win so you could follow your dreams."

He sank into the pew across from her. "I never meant to hurt you. I wanted to help you."

"Then you don't know me. Because if you knew me, and if you loved me, you would have been honest with me. We would have done this as a team." She gazed at her parents' names and smiled a bittersweet smile as a tear trailed down her cheek. She knew what she had to do. It wouldn't be easy—far from it. But there was no alternative.

She rose and studied the man seated across from her—the man whose life had been intertwined with hers since she was a girl. She stood before him, not as Phoebe 2.0, but simply Phoebe, the nerdy, awkward woman who led with her heart and not her head.

She kissed his cheek. "Goodbye, Sebastian."

Chapter 18
SEBASTIAN

Sebastian zeroed in on the target.

Pop, pop! Pop, pop!

Jab, cross. Jab, cross.

The beat of his fists against the heavy bag echoed through the studio, but it couldn't drown out the voice in his head—the voice whispering one name again and again.

Phoebe, Phoebe, Phoebe.

He'd dreamed of her every night for the last three nights. In those blissful hours, he'd gazed upon her sparkling blue eyes and a smile that rendered him speechless. He dreamed of everything that could have been, that should have been—holding her hand, waking her with kisses, and basking in her radiant glow. But he'd ruined it. He'd made an unconscionable mistake. He'd betrayed the woman he loved—the woman who made him whole, who lifted him up, who defended him when he was down. He was a bloody fool.

Pop, pop! Pop, pop!

Jab, cross. Jab, cross.

She'd left him in the chapel. Like he'd been living in a fog, he'd heard the door to the stone sanctuary slam. The ripples of that crack of a sound still vibrated in his chest, or maybe that was his heart breaking over and over again. He wasn't sure how long he'd sat in that pew, staring ahead at the empty altar, wondering what the hell was wrong with him.

Goodbye, Sebastian.

He could hear the steely certainty in her voice and feel her lips against his cheek.

Had he lost her forever? He couldn't answer that question. He wouldn't do it. He'd never imagined a life without her. He wasn't ready to throw in the towel. He couldn't accept defeat. There had to be a way forward. Unfortunately, his addled mind hadn't devised a plan to win her back.

And time was ticking away.

When he'd finally emerged from the chapel, the storm had passed. He'd followed the mud-spattered, moonlit trail back to Glenn Pines. Even before he'd opened the door to the guest room, he'd known she was gone. He could feel her absence like a piece of his heart had broken loose. He'd sat on the edge of the bed, unable to stop the onslaught of memories. His limbs ached as he remembered what it was like to hold her in his arms, to feel her curled into him, to trail his fingertips along the contours of her body, and to know, in those moments, ripe with perfect harmony, that she was his.

With her scent and her spirit imprinted in the space, he had to get the hell out of there. He'd packed his bags and ended up in the main hall. The place had cleared out. By then, it was either very late or very early—he didn't know which. He'd spied Mae sitting in one of the lodge's over-stuffed armchairs, sipping a steaming cup of tea. She hadn't appeared surprised when he'd asked to check out. He'd wanted to inquire about Phoebe, but he hadn't, and Mae hadn't brought up the subject either. When he'd asked her to recommend a car service to get back to Denver, she'd waved him off and handed him the keys to one of the lodge's pickup trucks, telling him she'd be in

Denver in the next few days and would pick it up when she was in town. It was a kind gesture. The only thing he could do was offer a weak smile, load up, and head back to the city alone and utterly broken.

But he hadn't remained idle—it wasn't in his nature. He'd thought about falling back into his playboy ways. Liquor and women had numbed the ache before. But when he'd woken up in his childhood bedroom, he hadn't hightailed it to the nearest bar. Instead, he'd put on a shirt and tie and begun visiting the Pun-chi yoga studios across the state.

And why had he done that?

The short answer: he wasn't sure. The auto shop had returned his car to his parents' place while he was at Glenn Pines. Not needing to rely on Tula's sparkly scooter, he'd gotten in his vehicle, started driving, and ended up at the first location his dad and Mibby had opened years ago when he was a boy. It was housed in Helping Hands, a community center and shelter in the heart of the city. He'd gotten there as a class had ended, and they'd recognized him immediately. He'd spoken to the instructors and fielded questions from the class participants. He hadn't officially been with the company for a year, but they'd greeted him with open arms and made him feel useful.

Was this another distraction of sorts? Possibly.

But this was different.

Maybe he'd gone to Helping Hands because he had to prove he wasn't a complete screwup. Perhaps he needed to be seen as more than the sexiest man on the internet. Perhaps in a quest to be the kind of man who'd make his mother proud, he'd forgotten who he was, forgotten the true meaning of something his mum had believed in—serving others without an agenda.

From there, he traversed the state, stopping into studios to say hello and asking if they needed help with their books or business plan. He'd suggest a tweak here or a deviation there, but the Pun-chi yoga studios were running like a well-oiled machine.

And that's where he'd ended up today—another studio. After visiting a few centers in the outlying suburbs, he'd returned to Denver to check on a location that was a few weeks away from opening in the Baxter Park neighborhood, not far from his parents' place in Crystal Acres. The crew installing the hanging punching bags had finished early. He'd told them he'd stick around and lock up. Instead of turning off the lights and slipping out the door, he'd balled his hands into fists and put one of the new bags to use.

Pop, pop! Pop, pop!

Jab, cross. Jab, cross.

"Tuck that chin, *boyo*. It's sticking out so far, I could land a bloody 747 on it. And tighten up, mate. You're wobblier than a twelve-year-old sneaking his first pint."

Despite not knowing if the man speaking in the gritty British accent wanted to curse him out, throttle him, or all of the above, he couldn't help but smile at the sound of his father's voice.

Sebastian rested his hand on the bag. "I didn't hear you come in, Dad."

"I'm stealthy like that. Your old man's still got it," Erasmus Cress said, knocking out a few shadow-boxing moves, then stilled and gave him the once-over. "Bare knuckles? We've got a real British brawler here," the man added with a curious lilt to his tone.

After all the messages and Briggs's warnings, Sebastian had expected his father to be cross with him. He studied the man—the boxing sensation, the husband and father, the fighter who'd been his hero for as long as he could remember. The lines at the corners of the man's eyes had deepened. Over the years, his brown hair had welcomed a touch of gray near his temples, but he was no less imposing in his solid stature. It was like looking at the gray-eyed older version of himself.

Sebastian gave the bag one last hit. "Did you guys just get back from Rickety Rock?"

"Yeah, we left this morning and made it home an hour ago. Tula's got an activity nearby this afternoon." He touched Sebastian's tie. "Are you starting a new type of posh boxing, something for corporate types?"

Sebastian eyed the blue fabric, and his throat grew thick with emotion. He hadn't even realized he'd chosen the tie Madelyn had given him—the tie he'd used to bind Phoebe's wrists. "I drove to Boulder to check out the studios near the Flat Irons. I wanted to look professional."

His dad nodded. "I heard you were making the rounds."

"I figured it wouldn't hurt to stop in and say hello. You don't mind, do you?"

"Not at all. A few instructors reached out. They were thrilled to see you. What's your assessment of how the business is doing?" the man asked, watching him closely.

Sebastian took a few steps, gathering his thoughts. "It was hard to find any faults. The studios are performing above expectations. They're gaining new members. Attrition is low."

His dad leaned against the stark white wall. "And why do you think that is?"

"Pun-chi yoga is a solid fitness program."

"A solid fitness program," his dad echoed, "that had expert direction from our former employee in charge of business development. Are you thinking of returning to the family business, son?"

Sebastian tapped the bag with his fist. "Is that why you're here—to offer me my old job?"

"I'm here because the installers called to let me know they were ahead of schedule and mentioned you'd popped in."

"You didn't come to talk Pun-chi yoga, though, did you?

And you're not only here because you were in the area for Tula's thing."

His father pegged him with his piercing gray gaze. "You were always a sharp lad."

"You don't look like you want to put me through the wringer," Sebastian replied, attempting to interject a thread of humor, but it fell flat.

"From what I hear, Phoebe's already done that to you, *boyo*."

"You know what happened with Phoebe?" he asked, unable to conceal the pain in his voice.

"I talked to Rowen earlier. He said you two had a falling out. He didn't have much more information. He added that Phoebe was tight-lipped about it, even with Penny."

"Did he tell you how Phoebe's doing? Is she okay? Or does her uncle want to . . ." Sebastian trailed off.

"Does he want to strangle you?" his father supplied with a cheeky smirk.

Sebastian shrugged. "I'd deserve it. She won't answer my calls or reply to my texts. I went with her to this event and cocked it all up."

"LETIS, right?" his father tossed out.

"Yeah."

"Briggs told me about it. The invitation-only shindig matching investors and innovators."

"Phoebe got invited, too. We agreed to go together. She wanted to put her best foot forward and be more business savvy and . . ." He paused. He wasn't about to drop the man-eater sex-machine bomb. "She wanted to be more confident professionally and in her personal life."

His father raised an eyebrow, reading between the lines.

"I told her I'd help her," Sebastian continued. "I promised I'd coach her through the event using everything I'd learned about business and success. I even gave it a name: the Sebastian Guarantee."

"The Sebastian Guarantee," his dad repeated. "It's catchy."

"That's all it is. I thought I had it figured out. I met with some investors before we left for LETIS. They were interested in working with me, but they asked for data on my life-coaching protocols. I didn't have any, and then Phoebe asked me to help her change. So I decided to use her as a case study."

"And you didn't tell her," his dad supplied, connecting the dots.

"She saw my notes. I wrote some brutal things—not because I thought there was anything wrong with her, but because I needed to show a shift from ineffective practices to successful performance. But it wasn't just that. She thought I was directing her toward another opportunity to get a quick success, not keeping her best interests at heart. She accused me of putting my prospects above hers."

His father met his gaze. "Was she right, lad?"

A crushing weight returned to Sebastian's chest. "She was. I got carried away. I lost focus. But the one thing I'm crystal clear about is that I love her. I love her, Dad. I ruined everything, and I don't know how to make it right."

"You blurred the lines in your relationship with her?" his father asked.

"Yes."

A knowing grin graced the man's lips. "I know a thing or two about that."

Sebastian waited for his father to dole out a nugget of wisdom.

Instead, the man checked his watch. "Are you hungry, lad?"

"What?" Had his dad not heard him? Did the man not realize the magnitude of the situation and how badly he needed advice?

"Let's walk. We're meeting your sister and Mibby at the sports fields next to the Baxter Park Community Center. There's supposed to be food."

Flustered at his father's cavalier response, Sebastian followed him toward the exit. "We?"

"Yeah, Tula saw your stuff in your room. She went through your pack, nosing around. She's worried about you and wants to see you. She's like Mibby. They just know things. It drives me bloody bonkers sometimes, but they're usually right."

"What about my dilemma? What should I do? I'm in a world of shit, Dad," he said, locking up the studio. He pocketed the keys and jogged to catch up with his father. "When I say that I love Phoebe, I don't mean as a friend. I want to be with her. I want . . . I want to marry her." The words tumbled out of his mouth. But he meant it. He absolutely meant it.

"It's crazy when it hits you like that, isn't it? Beautifully brutal, yeah?" his father replied, glancing over at him as that slight hint of a grin returned. But his features grew pensive. "I need to ask you a question. And I'd like you to be honest with me."

"Okay."

"What made you miss your mum's birthday?"

Sebastian sighed. "I was gallivanting across the globe like a knob-headed plonker."

"I know a thing or two about acting like a knob-headed plonker, too, but something or someone altered your course. I reckon that someone was Phoebe."

It was a relief to finally talk with his dad about something that brought him such shame. "Phoebe texted me and said she might have met her match. It threw me for a loop. In the back of my head, I always knew I loved her. But the thought that maybe I was wrong, maybe there was somebody else out there for her, sent me into a tailspin. It went downhill from there."

They walked a half-block in silence before he spoke again. "Can I ask you something, Dad?"

"Anything."

"I know how you and Mibby got together."

A grin spread across his father's face. "The nanny love match."

"But how did you know you were supposed to be with Mum? How did you know she was your match, too?"

"Lightning—with your mum and with Mibby."

"You're kidding?" Sebastian repeated, thinking of that poor damned fox.

"I am not. Two strikes when I met your mother, then two strikes the first time you, me, and Mibby went to Rickety Rock all those years ago."

"And then you knew it was meant to be?" he asked, now feeling damned grateful he and Phoebe had nearly been electrocuted. That had to be a sign.

His father chuckled. "No, I was hard-headed. I messed up. I made mistakes. I let my ego get in the way. But those trials and tribulations got me to where I needed to be. I've been blessed, son. Your mum and Libby have made me the man I am today. They forced me to look at myself and decide who I wanted to be in this world. I'm exactly where I'm supposed to be, supporting the woman I love."

"What do you think Mum would think of me?" There it was. The question that had been in the back of his mind ever since Phoebe had walked out of the chapel.

"What do you think of me, Sebby?" a little girl's voice bellowed, cutting short his conversation with his dad.

He looked up as a kid-sized hot dog charged toward him. "Tula, is that you?"

The skipping hot dog waved. "Yeah, it's me."

"Why is Tula in her Halloween costume, Dad?" he asked under his breath.

"She wanted to start wearing it straight away ages ago. Mibby and I made a deal with her. We told her she could wear it in October, just not to school. She put it on the second we got home. We probably should have put a few more restrictions on where she could wear it," his dad said, shaking his head, but that didn't stop the man from beaming at the bobbing frankfurter headed their way with Mibby a few steps behind.

"Hi, Daddy! Here I come, Sebby," Tula called. She tried to jump into his arms, but the adult-sized, tube-shaped costume that came to her ankles didn't accommodate the movement. Instead, she pitched forward like some processed-meat lumberjack had called out "*hot dog timber*."

Luckily, he caught the kid before she did a face-plant.

"Hey, Big Foot," his sister said, her little face peeking out of a hole in the frank part of the costume.

"Sebastian, namaste, sweetheart! It's good to see your face on this physical plane," Mibby said. How he'd missed her and her yoga-mystic speak.

He set Tula upright on the ground, then kissed his stepmom's cheek. "Have you been seeing me on another plane, Mibbs?"

"When we were meditating a few days ago, we both saw you, Sebby," Tula chirped. "But it wasn't the usual you. Your aura was . . ." She scrunched up her face like she'd gotten a whiff of dog shit, then tapped her foot five times. "It was bad. I could tell you felt like a butthole douche nozzle."

"Tula!" he and his parents exclaimed.

"Oops, I forgot I wasn't supposed to say that part out loud," the kid replied, then brightened. "But Sebby looks better, huh, Mibby?"

His stepmom gifted him with a warm grin and patted his cheek. "He's getting there," she answered.

His dad's cell pinged. "It's the contractor," the man said, growling at his phone. "He's at the new Baxter Park Pun-chi yoga location. We must have missed him. There's an issue with the lighting. He wants our opinion before he has the electrician install them. The guy wants to start working tonight."

Mibby nodded. "We should head over. I know they're on a tight schedule."

"Do I have to go, too?" Tula asked, drooping like a soggy hot dog.

"You can't stay on your own. You're not quite old enough yet, lass," his father replied, then tapped the little girl's nose.

"Mibby, Daddy, I don't want to listen to adult talk. Can Sebby take me to the Jamboree, please, please, pretty please?" Tula pleaded, batting her eyelashes. "And then he can get me a food truck hot dog, so I can be a hot dog eating a hot dog."

"I'd be happy to escort Miss Tula the Frankfurter to her event," Sebastian said, grateful to be with his family.

"Sebastian, you're a lifesaver," Mibby cooed. "We'll catch up with you in a bit."

Tula took his hand, and the pair started down the path. Baxter Park was hopping. He knew the place well. He, Phoebe, Oscar, and Aria had attended a few summer camps here as kids. But today, the area had been transformed with tents and tables. Food trucks lined the streets adjacent to the open space. Groups of young girls hurried past them in ruby-red T-shirts with *TT Denver Jamboree* printed on the back.

TT Denver Jamboree?

The hairs on the back of his neck stood at attention as he watched a trio of girls a bit older than Tula hurry past them—a trio that looked oddly familiar. But where would he have seen three random girls? Still, a foreboding sensation spider-crawled down his spine.

"They're selling cookies to go on a trip," Tula remarked as they passed a sign that read *Chocolate Chip Cookie Fundraiser for TT Disneyland Trip This Way.* "We should buy a box or two."

"Yeah, sure," he said to placate his sister. He couldn't worry about a kids' trip to a theme park when he had the distinct feeling that he was walking into the lion's den. On high alert, he peered at the grassy sports fields and basketball courts teeming with girls in groups of three and four standing around small metal and plastic creations. No, not creations, robots.

"Tula, is this the Tech Tweens Denver Jamboree?" he asked, lowering his voice and wishing he'd worn a ball cap and grown a beard as they walked down a grassy strip between the groups of girls.

But his sister didn't have a second to answer.

A child with golden braids, one of the girls he thought he'd recognized on the path, glanced up and scowled. "I was right. That's him. That's the guy. He's here. Fire up the secret weapon!"

Chapter 19
SEBASTIAN

As if he'd accidentally kicked a beehive buzzing with red-faced, red-shirted twelve-year-olds, Sebastian wasn't about to wait around to see this Tech Tween secret weapon.

He squeezed Tula's hand. "Come on, let's get a move on."

"Why is everybody looking at you like you ate their hot dog?" his sister pressed, then gasped. A disapproving scowl puckered her face. "You haven't apologized to the Tech Tweens, have you?"

Like a horror movie, an eerie quiet swept the field as girls stared—no, glared—at him.

"I haven't gotten around to it, T. I've been busy," he replied, feeling every pair of tween eyes locked on him.

His sister's scowl deepened. "Busy making Phoebe upset?"

His jaw dropped. "How do you know about that?"

"I heard Daddy on the phone with her uncle Rowen. Adults always think they're sneaky when they talk on the phone, but I heard every word."

"What did he say?"

"Lots of *uh-huh, uh-huh,*" Tula recounted, mimicking her

father's voice. "Then he said, 'you're right, nerd, *she* mentioned it could get worse.'"

"Who's the *she* Dad was talking about?" Sebastian pressed.

The little hot dog shrugged. "How am I supposed to know?"

"You're not getting a vibe or a message from another metaphysical plane?"

She tapped her chin. "I see red."

He glanced at the tween mob amassing around them. "Every T-shirt here is red."

"That's all I got, Sebby. Red and flappy," the child remarked with a take-it-or-leave-it flick of her wrist.

The words had barely passed his sister's lips when something small hit his back, and he didn't have to guess what it was. "Tula, we've got to make a run for it," he said as a smattering of baked goods tagged his arm.

"Sebby, they made a robot cookie launcher with a big spatula thing on it," Tula exclaimed, looking behind them.

A robot cookie launcher with a spatula?

Not wanting to look, but knowing he had to, he peered over his shoulder. His eyes nearly popped out of his head as he observed children dumping boxes of chocolate chip cookies onto precisely what Tula had described: a spatula cookie catapult robot.

"Ready!" a blond girl with braids and a tablet in her hands called.

"Aim!" a little redhead snarled.

"Fire!" a girl with dark pigtails cried.

It was like something out of a dystopian children's book. If pissed-off twelve-year-old girls weren't waging a baked goods assault on him, he would have taken a second to appreciate the craftsmanship and innovation it took to design and construct a motorized weapon of cookie warfare. If he'd had more time and Phoebe acknowledged his existence, he would have snapped a pic and texted it to her. She'd love this. But he didn't have a moment to spare.

"Hold on, Tula! We're making a break for it," he exclaimed, lifting his sister into his arms. Thanks to the costume's tubular design, he had to carry her like he was holding an actual gargantuan hot dog.

Tula giggled as a cookie landed on her hot dog belly. She picked it up and took a bite. "These are great. Thank you, Tech Tweens!"

This wasn't great! Was his sister insane?

He glanced over his shoulder. There had to be twenty, maybe thirty little girls parading behind the kid with the golden braids. And their robot was no joke. Low to the ground and about the diameter of a hula hoop, with a rake-sized spatula affixed to the top, the metallic machine hummed, chewing up the ground as the group continued their pursuit.

"We'll head for the pavilion. It's got stairs. I don't think the cookie catapult can traverse steps," he said as cookies pelted the back of his head.

"Direct shot!" a child cried.

The girls cheered like a horde of bloodthirsty mercenaries.

"I've got to pick up the pace, Tula. Are you okay?"

"Be careful! I can't bump around too much. I've got something important in my little hot dog pocket. I took it from Daddy's closet, and I can't lose it."

"I'm doing my best, T!" He weaved through a hailstorm of cookie carnage. Chocolate chips and crunchy crumbles rained down on them as they raced past a line of food trucks.

His sister started waving. "Hi, Mr. Hank's Franks! That's Phoebe's friend who has the hot dog food truck."

Sebastian did a quick check. Tula was right. It was the older guy who'd called to him from the food truck after his first Tech Tweens cookie attack. He grimaced. Bloody hell, what kind of terrible life choices did a person have to make to be attacked not once but twice by children?

Unable to stop and chat, he nodded to the food truck vendor, then set his sights on the pavilion. Scaling the three steps in one leap, he whipped around to assess the situation. His heart was ready to beat itself out of his chest, and he wanted to punch himself in his big stupid head. The pavilion looked out onto a pond. With a body of water on one side and a throng of fuming tweens on the other, they were trapped.

He set Tula down as an unnerving silence set in, laced with only the grinding hum of the robot. It was safe to say their gooses were cooked.

"All-terrain mode on," golden braids snarled.

Those bloodthirsty tech girls had built one hell of a machine. Four metal rods pushed the contraption up several inches. One by one, the cookie spatula catapult robot negotiated the steps.

"Wow," Tula breathed.

Wow, was right! He watched in awe as the spectacular weapon of total cookie destruction inched toward them.

"Step away from the big jerk, little hot dog girl. We don't have any beef with you," golden braids called.

Tula didn't budge. "This is Sebastian Cress. He's not a jerk. He's my big brother. If he's going down in a cookie blaze of glory, then so am I."

At eight years old, his sister was a real badass.

"Suit yourself," golden braids replied, then flicked her gaze to the tablet. "Ready!"

"Wait, wait!" he cried, raising his hands defensively. "Before you fire more cookies and cookie-bomb me into oblivion, I'd like to apologize." He surveyed the blond girl with the tablet. A dark-haired girl in pigtails and a redhead stood beside her. "You're the girls I cut in front of at the airport, aren't you?"

The scowls etched onto their faces told him he was right.

"I took your cab. I left you in the rain, and you missed an important activity."

"And our robot got ruined. We had to build another," the dark-haired girl hissed.

He took a cautious step toward them. "I'm so sorry, truly, I am." He gazed at the innovative robotic creation. "Can I ask you a question?"

The girls exchanged glances, then nodded.

"Did you also see me a few nights ago in Denver and throw cookies at me on the street?"

The redhead nodded. "Yeah, it was us. We had a couple of other Tech Tweens with us, too."

"You didn't have a robot that night, did you?"

Blond braids lifted her chin. "We decided to build a cookie spatula catapult after that."

"We used spare parts from other Tech Tweens," the pigtailed girl clarified.

"You built that robot in a matter of days?" Sebastian asked, thoroughly impressed.

"They did. They were quite motivated," a woman answered, weaving through the mass of girls.

He took a step back as the woman in white, Angelique, the associate from the Marieuse Group, now clad in a red Tech Tweens T-shirt, ascended the steps.

"Do you know her, Sebby?" Tula asked.

"Kind of, yeah." He turned to the woman. "What are you doing here?"

"Along with STEM Development, the Marieuse Group sponsors the Tech Tweens. I'm their volunteer director."

"This is the guy, Miss Angelique. He's the one who jumped the taxi line and left us in the rain," blond braids explained.

"That's true, but isn't he also the person who sparked your idea for Mr. Cookie Combat?"

That was quite a name.

"Yeah, I guess," the girl replied.

"You had a problem and worked together to create a solution. Isn't that what Tech Tweens is all about?" Angelique pressed.

Tula touched the edge of the spatula. "And you'd have to be super smart to build that robot. How did you do it?"

"We used what we know about robotics and coding," the redhead replied.

"Don't forget about force and motion. We had to figure out how to set the catapult to get the cookies into the air," the girl with the dark pigtails added.

"These girls are amazing and so smart," Tula exclaimed. "What are you guys going to build after Tech Tweens?"

The girl with blond braids shrugged. "I don't know. Our school doesn't have a robotics program."

"I think there's a club where they send you stuff in the mail and you put it together," the dark-haired girl mused.

The redhead's shoulders slumped. "I heard that it's a rip-off."

"There's got to be something you can do," Tula lamented. "You can't stop."

And there probably was something—a program out there perfect for these girls once they aged out of Tech Tweens, but these kids didn't have a cohesive community to rely on for that information.

"My sister is right," Sebastian began. "You can't stop. We need more women leading companies, starting businesses, and forging the path ahead." He pictured Phoebe when they were twelve. Clad in overalls and a black beret, she'd spend hours coding, glued to her computer as she munched on cookies and hot dogs. "I'm lucky enough to know a woman who was very much like you when she was your age. She's the smartest person I know. We need people like you and her in charge. I'm sorry for what happened at the airport. I should have been more observant. I was only thinking about myself. I'm going to change that. I'll find a way to do better. Will you accept my apology?"

"What do you say, girls?" Angelique asked.

The girls huddled, then blond braids met his gaze. "Yeah, we can forgive you."

Tula waved him down. "That was good, Seb. Now you need to do something nice for them."

"Like what?" he whispered back.

"Buy the cookies they need to sell to get to Disneyland. That way, they'll be happy, and then they can't throw more of them at you."

He peered at his whip-smart sibling. "You are one clever frankfurter, Tula Cress."

"I know. I'm smart like Phoebe."

The kid wasn't wrong.

He surveyed the group. "And as a gesture of our gratitude, my sister and I would like to purchase your remaining boxes of cookies."

"You're going to Disneyland," Tula announced.

"We're going to Disneyland!" the trio of girls shrieked as the other tweens cheered.

The redheaded girl walked up to Tula. "We're doing another round of catapult testing on the basketball court. Do you want to come with us, hot dog kid?"

Tula's face lit up. "Can I go, Sebby?"

"You bet, but make sure you can still see me, and don't leave the park."

"We'll keep an eye on her," the girl with blond braids said, taking Tula's hand as the foursome headed toward the blacktop and the mass of Tech Tweens dispersed.

"That was quite a speech," Angelique commented.

"I meant every word of it."

"We can tell."

"We?" He'd barely uttered the words when a cell phone rang.

Angelique slipped the device from her pocket, pressed it to her ear, then met his eye. "The Marieuse Group investors would like to speak with you."

"At their office?"

"No, now," she corrected. "They're here at the Tech Tween Jamboree."

"They are?"

"I told you, they're one of the two major sponsors. They always attend the Tech Tween Jamboree."

"Are they interested in my life-coaching business?"

"They're interested in you, Mr. Cress."

What did that mean?

She gestured toward a table beneath a red pop-up canopy not far from the blacktop. "I'll let Tula and her new friends know where you'll be."

He narrowed his gaze as he headed over. He could make out Bernadette and Claudette in their matching black turtlenecks, but a third woman sat with her back to him. The breeze picked up, and the woman's red scarf flapped, dusting her shoulder.

A red scarf.

Red and flappy. That's what Tula had said, and there was no question as to the woman's identity.

As if on cue, Madelyn Malone, the famed nanny matchmaker, looked over her shoulder. "I see you're wearing the tie I got you for your birthday," the woman commented in her flowing Eastern European accent.

He pressed his hand against his chest. In the crazy melee of the day, he'd forgotten he had it on. "It's my favorite."

"Here, take a seat, Sebastian. Sit with us," she said, then

eyed the tie. "The color is what drew me to it. It's the perfect *match* for you."

His ears perked up as he sat, noting how she'd phrased her reply. "It's so good to see you, Madelyn. You look fantastic." She did. The woman had to be pushing ninety, but she barely appeared to have aged a day since they'd met years ago when he was a boy. Her mass of dark curls, with a lone silver streak, framed her face and highlighted her dark, perceptive eyes.

She twisted her lips into a coy smirk—a signature expression he recalled from when he was younger. "Matchmaking keeps me young. Love is its own fountain of youth."

He didn't doubt it. "I had no idea you were in town. Are you in Denver to meet with a client?"

"I am," she replied as her eyes glinted with mischief.

He looked between the Marieuse sisters and the matchmaker, and a revelation hit. "Are you the silent investor, Madelyn?"

Madelyn and the twins exchanged a round of curious glances.

"No, no, dear," Madelyn said with a chuckle in her rich vibrato tone, "my work is in matchmaking, but I am a facilitator of fate, and that affords me the opportunity to meet many people in my pursuits. I've known the Marieuse sisters for a long time. My dear friend, their silent partner, introduced them to me years ago when I was in Denver doing a little background research for a nanny match. And there's my friend now," the woman added, peering past his shoulder. "Mae, I'm so glad you could make it."

Mae?

And holy twist of fate! It was Mae Edwards from Glenn Pines. Was she the silent partner? No, that couldn't be.

"Are you here to get your truck?" he asked, his mind working overtime to figure out what the hell was going on.

"No," Mae said, suppressing a grin, then greeted the women and took a seat next to Claudette.

"Are you here for a quilting event?" he tried.

"No," the woman repeated.

"Sebastian, I told you who she was," Madelyn supplied, looking pleased as punch with herself. The matchmaker patted Mae's hand. "Our Sebastian is having quite an eventful day. I promise you, dear, he'll lose the deer-in-the-headlights look as soon as he figures it out."

What was this? A setup?

Sebastian gazed around the group of women. Madelyn was wrong. He absolutely felt like a deer in the headlights, and he didn't see that feeling letting up anytime soon.

"Oh, I know he will," Mae remarked. "He's a smart one, and he's a fan of my work. Well, my work with Shirley, Theodora, and Enid. That speaks volumes."

"Mae is the silent partner?" he repeated, his brain feeling as nimble as a bowl of three-day-old oatmeal.

"It's coming," Madelyn cooed.

He held Mae's gaze. "You have a company with Shirley, Theodora, and Enid?"

"Yes," Mae replied.

"Something in addition to selling quilts?"

"Warmer," Claudette chimed in with a sly smirk.

"He's so close I can feel it," Bernadette added, mirroring her twin sister's expression.

"Shirley, Theodora, Enid, and Mae." He repeated the names of the quilters. There was something about the four of them that he was missing. He turned to Madelyn. "How do you and Mae know each other?"

"I met Mae and her friends after I was hired to find a nanny match for Rowen Gale and his niece, Phoebe. You see, I learn as much as possible about my clients, which meant learning about Phoebe's parents and the people who knew them. Her father, Andrew Gale, is from Denver and her mother, Melanie Funke Gale, grew up in—"

"Stratlin, Colorado," Sebastian supplied. "The quilt." His pulse kicked up. "Phoebe and I found the chapel. Inside, there was a quilt with *STEM* and Stratlin, Colorado stitched into the corner. That's you," he said, not sure he could believe his eyes. "You're STEM. You're STEM Development. You're a tech mogul. Your online financial tools are second to none," he finished, his mind blown.

"I like this one," Mae remarked and tossed him a wink.

"STEM Development also holds a ten percent stake in Zinger," Claudette added.

"Ten percent of a company estimated to be worth a trillion dollars? Whoa," he breathed.

Mae chuckled. "My friends and I invested at the right time, but before we founded STEM Development and began partnering quietly with investors, we were teachers at Stratlin High School. Theodora and I were the computer science instructors, and Enid and Shirley taught graphic design. Melanie Funke was our star student."

"Phoebe's mom," he said, recalling the signature in the wedding log.

"My heart broke when we learned of her and her husband's deaths. She was bright, vivacious, and one heck of a coder. She didn't let anything hold her back. We didn't have many resources at Stratlin High. When Phoebe's mom was our student, Melanie coordinated a fundraiser to supplement the tech budget. She planned a cookout near town hall and sold—"

"Hot dogs," Sebastian answered as the pieces came together.

"And chocolate chip cookies."

"I had a feeling you'd recognized Phoebe. Why didn't you tell her? Why did you pretend you didn't know how to set up a sales page on your website? Why were you working at a lodge?"

"Shirley, Theodora, Enid, and I purposefully keep a low profile. Extreme wealth can alter one's perspective. We agreed years ago that we'd invest anonymously. You learn a lot about people when they only see you as a little old lady doing needlework or running a lodge. We'd asked several LETIS participants for help. The two of you were the only ones who offered assistance."

"That was all Phoebe," he answered.

"And you," Mae countered. "You were right there beside her. I meant it when I said that the two of you worked well together."

"That might be true, Mae, but I hurt her, and I don't know how to win her back."

Mae patted his hand. "I figured as much when she checked out with tears staining her cheeks."

Sebastian flinched, hating himself for losing perspective and breaking Phoebe's heart.

Madelyn pegged him with her gaze. "Do you want to help Phoebe, dear?"

"More than anything. I love her. She's got to be my match, right?"

The matchmaker folded her hands in her lap. "That's not my call to make. My job is to set things in motion. The rest is fate. But I do have a feeling your boxing knowledge and a special person from your past will help you figure out what to do."

Boxing knowledge and a special person from his past?

He was about to ask what she meant by that when a memory came to him. He was young—three, maybe four years old—as he sat on a little stool next to his mum, watching his dad train in the ring. And then the image of his dad's last fight played in his mind. His mum wasn't by his side—Mibby was, and so was Phoebe. Quirky and open, accepting and abundantly kind, Phoebe Gale was pure magic.

All his life, he'd been surrounded by women—accomplished, intelligent, caring women. He lifted his tie and studied the hue of deep blue. He understood why it looked familiar. "This tie is the exact color of Phoebe's eyes and . . ." He gasped.

"I think he's got it," Madelyn said softly.

He stared at the matchmaker as he recalled the dream that had snapped him out of his six-month playboy stupor—the dream where his mother had drifted into his subconsciousness. In it, she'd spoken one word. *Fight.* He'd figured the utterance was his unconscious mind weaving in boxing terminology. But she wasn't telling him to fight in a ring. She wanted him to fight for love. And in his dream, his mother was wearing a dress that happened to be the same color as his tie.

"How would you know about the dress?" he asked the matchmaker, disbelief coating his words.

"What dress?" the woman replied with her signature all-knowing twist of her lips. "Now, tell me, what does Phoebe need?"

"Someone in her corner. Someone who's got her back. Someone who'll fight for her." Conviction flowed through him. He'd never been more sure of anything.

Madelyn smoothed her scarlet scarf. "Now you understand."

He did—and he had to get to work. He glanced around the table. "LETIS Live is tomorrow, right?"

"It is," Bernadette affirmed. "The Marieuse Group will be in attendance. We're always looking for investment opportunities."

Her reply sparked another question. "Speaking of investment opportunities, do you mind me asking about your interest in Jeremy Drewler?" He needed to know how the douchebag factored into the equation.

"I can answer that," Madelyn purred. "Our interest in Jeremy Drewler could be classified as a side pursuit."

He raised an eyebrow. "I thought you set things in motion and let fate do the rest?"

"When an obstruction is a person who is in need of a comeuppance and happens to be a real"—Madelyn turned toward him and tapped her foot five times—"there are times when one must work within their network to intervene appropriately."

He suppressed a grin. "I see."

"There's no place in this world for misogynistic wankers," Bernadette supplied.

These women were undeniably formidable.

"I couldn't agree more," he said, in awe of the group, then spied Tula out of the corner of his eye.

"I'm back, Sebby," his sister chimed as she bobbed toward them in her frankfurter glory. "Hi, Miss Malone," she exclaimed, hugging the matchmaker. "Hi, ladies!" She plopped onto his lap.

"This is my sister, Tula Cress."

"Tula," Madelyn began, "these are my friends, Mae, Bernadette, and Claudette."

"It's nice to meet you," Tula answered brightly, then turned to Madelyn. "Mibby said she was so happy to see you the other day. She showed me the picture she took with you, her, Penny, Harper, and my friend Ivy's mom, Charlotte. You were holding up fancy triangle wine glasses. They had little sticks with tiny balls on them, and they're called bikinis."

"The word is *martini*, Tula, dear, and yes, it was lovely seeing old friends."

"Martinis?" he repeated, recalling Phoebe's bender that had been conveniently covered by an anonymous benefactor.

"I hope you're hungry," Tula continued, "because I brought everyone a love-match hot dog."

Love-match hot dog?

He eyed his sister. "What are you talking about, Tula?"

"I went with my new friends to get a food truck hot dog from Hank. He got excited about his new hot dog and wanted to talk to you. Tell 'em, Hank."

The tattooed food truck vendor strode toward them with a tray crammed with hot dogs. "These are my newest bestsellers. A Hank dog with ketchup, mustard, and a heap of lettuce. Phoebe came up with it. I got the name from her, too. She told me the person who ate her love-match hot dog would be the one for her."

The one.

Tula had also called Phoebe the one.

"It's the one you ate," Hank said, handing him a hot dog identical to the one he'd inhaled while Phoebe was in the dressing room at the boutique. "Remember, I called out to you when you were helping Phoebe get home? You said it was everything you didn't know you wanted."

That's right.

"And I almost forgot to give you this, Sebby," Tula said, slipping a metallic ball from a little pocket hidden beneath a patch of fabric mustard. "I found it in your backpack. I put something inside it. Open it and see what it is."

He loosened the layers of tinfoil. "Tula," he breathed, eyeing the item he hadn't seen in many, many years.

She leaned into him. "I thought you might need it. I don't think Daddy will be mad."

From lightning to love-match hot dogs, the signs were unmistakable. Phoebe Gale was his match.

"No, I don't think he'll be mad at all," he replied, feeling his mother's presence. He gazed at the matchmaker. "How do you do it?"

The woman didn't answer. Instead, she flashed her coy twist of a grin, plucked a Hank dog from the tray, and took a bite.

"What are you guys talking about?" Tula asked, choosing a Hank dog for herself.

"We're talking about how much I love Phoebe and how I'm going to prove to her that I'm her match. But I'll need your help to do it, T."

"I'm all in," the child replied.

All in.

There it was—another sign.

"One question remains, Sebastian Cress," Claudette said, sharpening her gaze.

"And what question is that?"

"Do you have case study data to share with us?"

It was a very apt question and one he could easily answer.

It was time to make his mark on this world. He surveyed the grounds, taking in the Tech Tweens—the future innovators of tomorrow. He glanced at the item cradled in silver foil, then molded it back into a ball.

"T?"

"Yeah, Sebby?"

"Tell your new Tech Tween friends to hold on to the cookies we just bought. I have a use for them."

"You bet," she answered, wiggling off his lap.

"Enjoy the hot dogs," Hank said and turned to leave.

But Sebastian couldn't let him go. He stood and rested his hand on the man's shoulder. "Hank, I need you to stay a moment longer."

He watched his sister waddle away in her costume, knowing what his mother would want him to do. He met Claudette's gaze straight on. "I don't have any data to share, but I do have a doozy of a new proposal, and I *guarantee*, everyone at this table will want in."

Chapter 20

PHOEBE

> You have not been matched with an investor. Please join us at LETIS Live. Be prepared to pitch your idea. The event starts in two hours and is being held at the Denver Amphitheater.

Phoebe stared at the text, turned over her phone, and slumped into the diner's booth. She traced the handle of her coffee mug and peered into the half-empty cup, feeling completely and utterly stuck.

How could LETIS Live be today? It didn't feel like days had gone by since she'd left Glenn Pines. Then again, nothing had seemed real from the moment she'd kissed Sebastian's cheek and spoken the words that shattered her heart. She'd floated through the hours, going through the motions, spacing out in front of her laptop, and asking herself the same question over and over.

What was she supposed to do? What path did she take—and would she be walking it alone?

In two hours, there was a very good chance many innovators' lives would be changed, and the picturesque Denver

Amphitheater was an apt location for new beginnings. She knew the spot well. The open-air venue wasn't far from her aunt and uncle's place in Denver's Crystal Creek neighborhood. Situated next to a large swath of open space with the Rocky Mountains in the background, this time of year, the foliage would be bursting in the autumn hues of gold, red, and orange. The mid-sized amphitheater would certainly be a quintessential mountain-chic setting for a live event.

Did she plan on attending?

It didn't seem likely. This wasn't because investors didn't want to get their hands on the Munch Match app. No, they wanted it. A stack of green envelopes had made it clear that many were chomping at the bit to get their greedy little hands on her source code. But whether she got from point A to point B within two hours was purely a logistical issue. Her point A was currently one hundred miles east of Denver.

She hadn't expected to wander so far from home. Not long after she'd awoken today, her uncle and aunt had stopped by with a hot dog delivery—her favorite. But she'd taken one look at it, wrapped in tinfoil, and another piece of her heart had shattered. Mustering a grin, she'd thanked them for thinking of her, but told them she didn't have an appetite. She should have come up with another excuse. She could see the concern in their eyes. Since she'd returned from Glenn Pines, she'd only had a few conversations and text exchanges with them. They knew something was up and guessed her current semi-zombie demeanor had to do with her relationship with Sebastian. She affirmed their assumption but didn't go into it, and fortunately, they didn't push for more information.

It hadn't helped that her phone had pinged and dinged during their brief visit. She didn't have to look to know who was texting and calling. Sebastian had been trying to reach her nonstop. But there was nothing he could say to heal the hole in her heart. She loved the man. She'd loved him for nearly her entire life, but she'd have to figure out how to live without him. How could she look at him the same way, knowing he'd lied and used her? He didn't believe in Go Girl, which was tantamount to not believing in her. She couldn't figure out a way to fix them, to get them back to what they were before. Sebastian was right about one thing, though. He'd banished the word friend from her mind—just not in the way she'd thought he would.

But her problems weren't limited to matters of a broken heart.

She had a decision to make regarding her professional life. She was stone-cold broke.

She'd ventured out on her own with Foot Tap Studio, dreaming of creating Go Girl. Had that been a mistake? Was she better off putting her heartfelt aspirations on the back burner and going back to work for her aunt and uncle? Was that what her parents would want for her?

She stared into the coffee cup and narrowed her gaze, searching the dark liquid for the answers.

"Need a warm-up, sugar?" came a woman's singsong voice.

Phoebe blinked, snapping out of her stupor, and looked up to find the waitress smiling at her. With a faded name tag sporting the name Val clipped to a pink apron, heavy makeup, and her white-blond hair piled on top of her head and saturated to shellac-level with hairspray, the woman looked like she'd been sent from central casting to play the part of the middle-aged, small-town server who'd been dishing out decaf, delivering plates of the daily special, and shooting the breeze with locals for the last half-century.

"A what?" Phoebe stammered, taking a second to engage with the real world.

The waitress slipped a pen behind her ear and held up a steaming pot. "A warm-up for the half-cup of coffee you've been staring at for the last hour. Let's get you topped off. And it's your lucky day, sugar. I've been told I make the best cup of joe in all of Stratlin, Colorado."

That's right—Stratlin, Colorado. Her mother's hometown.

She hadn't planned on setting off on a mini road trip. She'd run out of coffee, which had been all she could manage to consume these last few days. When she'd found the canister empty, she'd stared at her parents' photo. She'd had no intention of leaving her apartment, but a strange feeling came over her as she gazed at their smiling faces. Like she'd been issued marching orders, she'd grabbed her tote, thrown in her laptop, and gotten in her car, thinking she would zip to a coffee shop to get her next hit of caffeine. But that wasn't what happened. Instead of popping inside or breezing through the coffee place's drive-thru, she hit the gas and hit the road. She'd jumped on the highway and headed east until the sun-beaten sign for Stratlin, Colorado, caught her eye.

"Got a lot on your mind, sugar?" the waitress probed as she filled the cup. "Man problems?"

Phoebe chewed her lip. "Um."

The woman raised an eyebrow. "Job troubles?"

"Well . . ." Phoebe sputtered.

The waitress stepped back and looked her over. "Are you from around here, sugar?"

Phoebe could answer that one. "I'm from Denver."

"A big city girl. But why do I think I know you?" the waitress mused, then walked a few tables down. "Clem, Amaryllis, take a look at this big city gal. I swear, I've seen her before."

"I've never been to Stratlin. I'm sure of it," Phoebe called, hating to cause a ruckus and interrupt a couple on her behalf.

This Clem and Amaryllis scooted out of their booth and ambled over. The elderly couple peered down at her. Clem, a slim man, wore thick glasses, a faded ball cap with a red fox embroidered on it, and the words *Stratlin High School* stitched beneath the animal.

At the sight of the fox, she couldn't help but think of Sebastian and the poor animal who'd nearly met his maker on the day her life had gone from something out of a dream to the stuff of nightmares. She couldn't help herself. Her heart hadn't caught up with her head. It ached for the man who'd professed his love in the pouring rain. It had felt so real, so genuine. Sure, most declarations of love weren't sandwiched between lightning strikes and near-animal electrocutions. Still, as hard as she'd tried these last few days, she couldn't banish the image from her mind of Sebastian, gazing at her like she was everything he'd always wanted and never knew he could have.

She returned her attention to the couple. They stared at her like she was an attraction at the zoo, but there was warmth in their eyes.

"You know why you think you know this young lady, Val?" Clem said as a grin cracked his wrinkled face.

Val adjusted her apron. "I'm all ears, Clem."

"Because she's the spitting image of Melanie Funke," Amaryllis answered before the man could continue, then gifted her with a warm grin.

Val cocked her head to the side. "Good gravy, she sure is."

At the sound of her mother's name, Phoebe's throat tightened. She sat there, dumbstruck, staring at the trio. "I'm Phoebe Gale. Melanie Funke Gale is my mom—she was my mom. She passed away with my father . . ."

"Coming on twenty years ago, give or take a few years," Clem supplied, his features growing solemn.

Phoebe swallowed past the emotion. "Yes."

"We were heartbroken when we heard the news. She doesn't have any kin left in Stratlin. Her granny passed not a year after Melanie graduated from high school. But we loved her like family when she was with us," Amaryllis offered, her expression matching Clem's.

Phoebe steadied herself. "How did you know my mom?"

"You're looking at Stratlin High School's former principal and school secretary, Amaryllis and Clem Wagner," Val said, nodding to the couple.

"You were the principal?" Phoebe asked Clem.

"My wife was the principal," the man answered and beamed at Amaryllis.

Phoebe felt her cheeks heat. "I'm sorry. I made an assumption—a clearly knobheaded assumption."

Amaryllis tossed her a wink. "We've got to keep on keeping on when it comes to advancing women into positions of power. I'll admit, it was harder back in my day. But even after all these years, women still have a way to go."

"I agree," Phoebe said, feeling the warmth in her cheeks dial down a few degrees.

"Amaryllis and I got to Stratlin when we were newlyweds, barely twenty-three years old. We served the Stratlin community in that very building across the street for nearly seventy years," Clem added and pointed out the window toward the school.

Phoebe stared at the building. It was strange and oddly enchanting to think of her mother as a girl. "You both remember my mother?"

"We might look a touch past our expiration dates on the outside, but we're sharp as tacks up top," Clem replied with a sly grin as he tapped his head.

"What brings you to Stratlin?" Amaryllis asked.

"She's got a lot on her mind, Mr. and Mrs. Wagner," Val chimed. "Trouble with a boy and worried about work."

Phoebe opened and closed her mouth as she tried to think of something that didn't make her sound like a hot flaming mess. But nothing came to mind. "That's the truth," she conceded with a weak grin.

Amaryllis nodded. "Sounds like you've found yourself at a crossroads and you're stuck deciding what to do."

"How about we get your mind off your troubles for a bit? Come on over to the high school with us. We'll show you around," Clem proposed.

Phoebe waved him off. "I would hate to take up your time."

"You'd be doing us a real favor." Clem offered her his hand and helped her out of the booth. "We love having a reason to stop in."

"And you can see where your mama discovered her love of computers and coding," Amaryllis added.

"I thought she got into coding when she was in college?" Phoebe replied, hardly able to believe she'd stumbled upon this couple. She slipped a bill from her tote and left it next to the coffee mug.

"Oh no, she was coding in high school, and she was a big part of helping the teachers raise funds for the Stratlin High computer lab. It's still going strong today."

Phoebe stared at the school as they left the diner. "I had no idea."

"Oh, yes, Melanie was one of the brightest kids to come out of Stratlin," Amaryllis asserted as they crossed the street. "Back in high school, during this time of year, she and four of her teachers would set up down the block in the town square. She'd haul her granny's grill through town and cook up hot dogs and sell chocolate chip cookies to earn extra money for the school. I believe it was Melanie's idea."

"It was my mom's idea to sell hot dogs and chocolate chip cookies?" Phoebe repeated.

"Yes, ma'am," Clem replied. "I think there was a year in there that she added pizza to the mix."

Amaryllis chuckled. "That's right. She did. Melanie was always thinking up something. That mother of yours had a mind like no other."

Phoebe glanced down the block, imagining her mother serving up hot dogs and selling cookies. "That's amazing."

"What's amazing, Phoebe?" Clem asked.

"Hot dogs, cookies, and pizza are my favorites, too."

"You should probably get in a vegetable every now and then, but you look like you're doing okay," Amaryllis replied with a cheeky grin.

"My uncle would agree—my father's brother. He and my aunt raised me. He's a pretty big health nut, but I wore him down as a kid."

"Tenacious like your mom," the woman tossed out.

The couple's words were like a salve to her broken heart.

"Welcome to Stratlin Public High School. This is the original building from 1908," Clem explained, gesturing to the two-story, red brick building with a bell tower.

Phoebe drank in the charming structure as Clem got the door. "We won't be interrupting the school day, will we?"

Amaryllis shook her head. "School got out an hour ago. The kids who are still here stay for clubs and sports."

Phoebe studied the space. To the naked eye, there was nothing overtly grand about it. White tiles on the floor. Navy blue lockers with nicks and scrapes lining the hall. But to her, it was as if she'd stepped back in time. Her mother had walked through this very door. She'd graced the halls. A warmth filled her chest. She didn't remember much about her mother, but at that moment, a memory long tucked away resurfaced, and she could hear the woman's laughter—that sweet, rhythmic flow like water through a babbling brook.

She exhaled a slow breath when she caught movement in her peripheral vision.

A round woman with her dark hair in a bun headed toward them. "Clem, Amaryllis," the lady called and waved a file in her hand. "I was about to give you a ring."

"How can we help, Sue?" Clem asked.

The woman blew a stray hair out of her face and opened the file. "We've been having trouble finding the paperwork for when the boiler was last replaced. It has to be going on fifteen or twenty years. I need to check the warranty. I thought it was with the maintenance paperwork, but I can't find it. Can you spare a few minutes to check the files with me?"

"Absolutely," Clem replied.

"Phoebe," Amaryllis said and touched her arm. "Why don't you take a look around? Get a feel for where your mother went to school. We'll catch up with you after we've got Sue sorted."

"Sure, no hurry," Phoebe replied, grateful to have a few moments to herself. The last ten minutes had turned into quite a whirlwind, yet there was something calming and familiar about the place.

Clem and Amaryllis went in one direction, and Phoebe meandered down the other, listening as the trio's footsteps against the tile flooring faded. She adjusted her tote on her shoulder. Drawing her fingertips along the row of lockers, she made her way down the hall. She couldn't help but remember her high school days. Aria and Oscar were involved in the arts. They'd shared a locker near the auditorium, while she and Sebastian had their locker home base near the computer lab and the library. Those days seemed so long ago.

It had always been the four of them. What would happen now? Were those days over?

She pushed the thought out of her head as she approached a large glassed-in cabinet housing trophies and framed photographs. She surveyed the images of smiling students. From the hairstyles and clothing, many photos looked like they'd been snapped decades ago. She was about to continue walking the halls when she saw a picture of herself. No, not herself. Melanie Funke. She leaned in and read the caption.

Melanie Funke's hot dog and cookie fundraiser earns thousands for Stratlin High.

"Hi, Mom," she whispered and pressed her hand against the glass.

She stared at the woman—a woman she knew through photographs, stories, and video clips. She studied the photo. The resemblance was uncanny. They even wore similar black-framed glasses. She slid her gaze from her mom and peered at the entire composition. Her mother wasn't the only one in the shot. Four women were with her, two on each side, smiling at the luminous Melanie Funke. Phoebe narrowed her gaze as she scanned the others in the shot. Had she seen them before?

"Eloise," came a girl's voice from a classroom down the hallway. "I found another application for the Munch Match code. Look, it works for narrowing down college choices. Boy, do I need that."

Phoebe froze. Whoever that was, they were talking about her software.

"It's got to be what we thought, Shelby," came another girl's voice. "The application weighs each question, and the artificial intelligence written into the algorithm becomes more attuned to the user after each use."

Tiptoeing down the corridor, Phoebe followed the sound of the girls' voices to the computer lab, then peered in through the half-open door.

"It doesn't matter what the user is trying to narrow down. The algorithm is always learning and adjusting. That's why I think people are meeting their love matches, but it requires the user to answer eight or more questions. Everything we tried with eight or more questions has homed in on a match. Less than that, and the program doesn't evolve."

Holy teenage hackers! These kids had thwarted her security protocols, hacked into Munch Match, and discovered the secret behind her algorithm. They'd done what she hadn't been able to do.

Slack-jawed and still undetected by the high school lady hackers, Phoebe stood in the doorway, observing the girls. Eloise had auburn curls in a high ponytail, and Shelby sported a dark swath of jagged bangs that brushed against the frames of her glasses. Seated side by side on a giant hot pink bean bag near a bank of windows that looked out onto an empty sports field, each girl had a laptop propped against their legs.

Eloise turned to her fellow hacker. "Do you think Phoebe Gale knows this?"

Phoebe couldn't stop herself. She burst into the room. "Phoebe Gale absolutely doesn't know this."

The girls shrieked and sprang to their feet. Shelby lost her glasses in the movement melee.

"You're Phoebe Gale! Oh my God, it's you," Eloise blathered. Her eyes looked ready to pop out of her head. "Are we in trouble? Are the police here or the FBI? Do you think they'll let us go to homecoming before they lock us up?"

Phoebe raised her hands defensively, then lowered herself to the ground and retrieved Shelby's glasses. "Here," she said, slipping them on the girl's face.

The kid squeezed her eyes shut. "I don't want to see the FBI storm the room. Eloise, my mom is totally going to take away my phone. We're sorry we hacked Munch Match, Miss Gale. We were just messing around."

"You can open your eyes and relax. And please, call me Phoebe," she said, keeping her tone even. "Nobody's going to jail or getting picked up by FBI agents, which, FYI, are actually a lot cooler than you'd think when they come to your elementary school after you've accidentally intentionally broken through their firewall."

"You hacked into the FBI?" Eloise pressed, awe coating the question.

Phoebe bit back a grin. "On the record, no, I did not. That would be bad, very, very bad and very illegal." She waved the girls in. "Off the record, yeah, totally. It was super cool."

"You're super cool," Shelby replied, grinning from ear to ear.

Eloise remained pensive. She twisted her ponytail around her finger. "So, you heard us talking about hacking your app?"

"I did, and I'm impressed."

"You are?" the girls yipped.

"You bet. I have some questions for you. Let's sit," Phoebe suggested and gestured to a table. She sank onto the plastic seat and set her tote aside as the girls joined her, one to her left while the other took the chair to her right. "Show me how you got into Munch Match, and then bring up your modified algorithm. I'd love to take a peek."

Shelby opened her laptop. With a few key strikes, the Munch Match code appeared on the screen. "We got in with a backdoor hack. The lines of code that data mined for the words *hot* and *dog* were vulnerable."

Taken down by a hot dog.

"That makes sense," Phoebe replied, shaking her head. "Now show me how you modified the algorithm."

"First, we were able to match a person to a shelter dog. We altered the algorithm to scrape trait information from different dogs' descriptions on animal shelter web pages. Then we added lifestyle questions about the person—like whether they're active or more of the homebody type. As we input more information, the algorithm was able to narrow down the choices and make a match."

Phoebe studied the screen, eyeing the coding changes. "That's a phenomenal way to use Munch Match."

"It worked, too. We got a match," Shelby continued. "Eloise's dad said she couldn't get a dog, but we had her dad take the Mutt Match survey."

"Love the name," Phoebe chimed.

"And now we've got Rosie, a Great Dane and Great Pyrenees mix. Check this out." Eloise removed her phone from her pocket and pulled up a picture of a beaming older gentleman and an adorable black and white dog.

"I'm impressed by the both of you. Your names are Eloise and Shelby, right?"

"Yeah, that's us," Eloise replied. "Shel and I have been best friends since elementary school."

Phoebe eyed the teens. "Are there other girls at your school who like to code?"

"No, it's just us. Most girls in our high school only use their phones to post videos of themselves making duck lips," Shelby answered and rolled her eyes.

Phoebe suppressed a grin. "I'm not a big fan of duck lips either," she answered, then glanced into her tote and removed her beret. She put it on, feeling more like herself. "I'm a fan of walking to the beat of your own drum."

"So are we," Eloise replied and shared a smile with her best friend.

"Have you joined any groups online to find kids like you?" Phoebe tossed out, curious to hear their answer.

"You hear 'girls in tech' and 'girl coder groups' thrown around so much, you can't tell if it's a decent program or click-bait or worse," Shelby offered with a shrug. "You never know which groups have real actual girls interested in tech or if it's creepers and trolls looking to cause trouble. We stay away from those places online."

"I get it," Phoebe agreed. These girls, and others like them, needed a trusted place, vetted and monitored, where they could connect with like-minded young women. They needed Go Girl.

Eloise glanced at Shelby's laptop. "Do you want us to delete everything we've done with your code, Phoebe? We promise we won't tell anybody about it. We just wanted to figure out how it worked."

Phoebe gazed at the screen, taking in the altered source code—her altered source code. She'd been so worried about what an investor would do if they had gotten ahold of her algorithm. She didn't want one investment group to profit off it and potentially harm the food truck vendors she'd helped—or worse, sell it to a company that would shelve it to reduce competition. She couldn't let that happen. These girls had proved that the Munch Match algorithm's possibilities were endless.

And all at once, she knew how to protect what she'd created.

She grabbed her laptop out of her bag and logged into her Foot Tap Studio files. "I'm about to do something a little bit crazy." Her fingers danced over the keys, and again, she got the distinct feeling she wasn't alone. Yes, the girls were with her, but something else was driving her forward, a presence reassuring her. She finished typing, rested her hands in her lap, and stared at the screen. "It's done. Go to the Foot Tap Studio website and check for an update."

The *tap, tap, tap* of the girls typing on their keyboards punctuated the expectant air. And then, it was quiet.

"No way! No freaking way!" Eloise exclaimed. "OSS, Munch Match is OSS!"

Shelby gawked at the screen. "You made the Munch Match app open-sourced software. Anyone from anywhere in the world can download your code and modify it however they see fit. Your algorithm is out there for free."

"And that means young women like you can use it to help animals and find the best fit for college and whatever else you can dream up," Phoebe answered as a lightness took over.

"This is so cool! I'm going to post about it on my socials

and on the big tech message boards," Eloise chirped. "Phoebe Gale, you're our hero."

Phoebe chuckled. "I'm no hero. I'm just a nerd—a slightly awkward hot-dog-loving nerd." Like her mom, but she kept that part to herself.

"Do you care if we keep playing around with it?" Shelby asked, vibrating with excitement as she gestured to her laptop.

Phoebe sat back. "Get to it. It's all yours."

The giddy girls returned to the giant pink bean bag and started tossing out ideas to test. Phoebe watched them, then thought of Tula and Ivy—little girls she adored. Girls and women needed a place that allowed them to connect to a supportive community. She knew this, but was she the person to create it? Was her dream to build Go Girl too big? Could she do it alone?

"Here you are," Amaryllis remarked, walking into the computer lab.

The girls greeted the former principal, and Phoebe met the woman's gaze.

"It sounds like you've made some friends," Amaryllis continued, coming to the table with a large hardback book in her hands.

Phoebe closed her laptop and slipped it into her tote. "Just a little tech talk among girls," she answered and came to her feet.

"I have something decidedly less high-tech to show you." The former high school principal handed her the book. "I thought you might like to see this. It's the yearbook from your mom's senior year. I found her picture. It's marked with the slip of paper."

Reverently, Phoebe touched the cover. She cracked open the book, inhaling the scent of the old pages. She scanned the rows of smiling faces and found her mother.

"I still can't get over it. The resemblance is uncanny," Amaryllis commented.

"My blue eyes come from my father, but every other feature from the slant of my nose to the curve of my cheek comes from my mom." She ran her finger over the photo, then skimmed the few lines below the picture and read her mother's senior year quote.

The future belongs to those who believe in the beauty of their dreams. ~Eleanor Roosevelt

She gasped. "It can't be."

Amaryllis watched her closely. "Everything okay, dear?"

"This was my senior yearbook quote, too," Phoebe answered, her voice barely a whisper. "It's probably a coincidence, huh?"

"I've been around long enough to learn a thing or two about coincidences."

Phoebe ran her fingertips across the text. "What have you learned?"

"There's magic behind most of them, if you know where to look. I'd say that yearbook quote is a message meant for you that was years in the making. A seed made of pure love, planted before you were even born."

"A love seed," Phoebe repeated.

"A mother's love is timeless, Phoebe, and it appears this coincidence is your mom reminding you to believe in yourself and follow your dreams."

Amaryllis was right. Phoebe knew it with every breath she took and every beat of her heart. She had to follow her dream, not only for herself, but for girls like Eloise and Shelby. And that dream was Go Girl. Did she want to do it alone? No. She thought of her aunt and uncle, who complemented each other in every way. Their partnership had taken Gale Gaming to the next level, and their love for each other touched every facet of their work. She'd wanted that, too, but she wouldn't let it hold her back either.

"The future belongs to those who believe in the beauty of their dreams," she said, reading the words aloud.

It was time to believe in herself. That's what her parents would want for her. And that started today with a pitch at LETIS Live.

"Phoebe," Eloise called, "you're trending. Everyone's posting about the Munch Match algorithm becoming open-source software. Your website says it's been downloaded fifty thousand times, and it's been less than ten minutes."

"That's fantastic," Phoebe replied in a daze as her mind raced. She glanced at the clock on the wall. There was only an hour until LETIS Live. "I have to get back to Denver," she said, but she was a hundred miles away from the city. Even speeding her ass off wouldn't get her back in an hour. Maybe there was another way, another route. She dug around her tote, feeling for her phone. She could check the navigation app and see if there was a country road she could take to bypass the highway. It was near rush hour. Traffic in Denver alone would be at a standstill.

"Do you hear that?" Shelby called. "I think it's a helicopter."

A helicopter?

Shelby jumped to her feet and ran to the window. "It is! And it's landing next to the school."

Mid-navigation search, Phoebe dropped her phone into her bag and stared out the window. Dust swirled as bits of earth and dry grass created a hazy whirl around the sports field. The rotor blades stopped moving, and the door opened.

"No way! No freaking way," she whispered, borrowing Eloise's words.

"Am I seeing things, or did somebody in a hot dog costume

get out of that helicopter?" Eloise asked as she joined her friend at the window.

Phoebe couldn't answer. She couldn't do anything but stare out the window, completely gobsmacked.

Amaryllis patted her back. "Looks like your mom came through for you, Phoebe Gale. I have a hunch that helicopter is your ticket to making your dreams come true."

Chapter 21
PHOEBE

Phoebe's gaze ping-ponged between her mother's yearbook quote and the helicopter in the middle of a sports field. She closed the yearbook. "Could I . . ." she began, then slid her gaze back to the window and watched as the hot dog danced around the field.

"Could you take the yearbook? Yes, dear, you're welcome to take it with you," Amaryllis supplied.

"I'll return it. I promise."

Stratlin High's former principal waved her off. "No need. The school likes to keep one copy of every yearbook it puts out. Funny thing about the year your mother graduated—it appears there are two copies."

"Two copies," Phoebe repeated. What were the chances of that? Then again, what were the chances she'd get in her car, end up in Stratlin, mosey on into a diner where a waitress just happened to recognize her, meet Clem and Amaryllis, share the Munch Match algorithm with the world, and then learn that she and her mother had picked the same yearbook quote? She should probably consider picking up a lottery ticket at some point.

So utterly grateful, she squeezed Amaryllis's hand. "Thank you." She held the book to her chest. "I feel like I should thank you and Clem for more than just talking with me about my mother and gifting me this yearbook."

The woman glanced out the window. "I can tell you what you won't be thanking me for."

Phoebe's brows knit together. "And what's that?"

"If you and your hot dog friend don't get that chopper off the field in two minutes, you'll be dealing with the local sheriff."

"Oh my gosh! Okay," Phoebe replied on a sharp exhale and snapped into action. She grabbed her tote and waved to the girls. "Thank you for helping me see Munch Match's true purpose and potential."

"You're the coolest nerd girl in the world," Shelby said.

"Yeah, you go, girl!" Eloise cheered.

"Go girl," Phoebe repeated. A smile bloomed on her lips. She glanced at the yearbook, getting her mom's message loud and clear.

But there was no time for gazing at books. There was no doubt that the helicopter was for her. And come hell or high water, she would insist it take her to Denver. Not wasting another second, she tore out of the room. Sprinting down the hallway, she hit the doors with a clatter and bolted toward the field.

The dancing hot dog whirled around. "Hey, Phoebe, what do you think? I wanted to show you *my* hot dog costume first," Tula called.

"I absolutely love it," she answered. "But what are you doing here? Are you by yourself?"

No helicopter pilot in his right mind would ferry an eight-year-old out of the city, right? Or was this the cherry on top of a crazy-day coincidence sundae? The door to the chopper slid open. Phoebe squinted as surprise number—oh, forget it, she'd lost count at this point—peered out of the aircraft.

"Uncle Rowen?" she called.

"Let's go." Tula took her hand. "Your uncle says the cops are on the way, and we gotta hop to it."

Amaryllis wasn't kidding.

In a flurry of movement, Phoebe helped Tula into the helicopter and climbed in after the child. *And hello, high-end helo.* Sporting white leather bucket seats and a plush milky gray interior, this was no bare-bones chopper. And she soon learned that Tula and her uncle weren't the only guests riding along. Sebastian's dad, Erasmus Cress, was with them.

"How did you know I was here?" she asked, sinking into the seat next to her uncle as the helicopter rose above the high school.

Rowen clucked his tongue. "Phoebe Gale, I taught you better than that. You know how many apps are tracking your mobile devices at this very moment."

She eyed the man. "Is that uncle-speak for 'I hacked your phone'?"

Her uncle cleared his throat and adjusted his glasses. "There are overarching circumstances today. Plus, your aunt said I could do it," he added with the hint of a grin.

"Where is Aunt Penny?"

"Day drinking."

"Day drinking?" she echoed. That wasn't like her Aunt Penny. Sure, the woman had a few glasses of wine or a cocktail or two when everyone got together, but day drinking? "Why is she day drinking, Uncle Row?"

"She's meeting up with an old friend who demands a certain cocktail when they get together," her uncle answered with a very cat-who-ate-the-canary smirk.

"Are you going to tell me who?"

"No need."

There was way more to this story, but she wouldn't be getting anything about it out of him. Maybe Tula would spill the beans.

"What brings you to Stratlin, Tula? Is there something going on with our families?"

The little girl looked to her father. "Can I tell her, Daddy?"

"Yeah, petal, you can."

"We're here because Sebby said he acted like a . . ." The child tapped her foot seven times.

Seven?

Phoebe racked her brain. "What do seven taps mean?"

"*Sup-er butt-hole douche noz-zle,*" Tula clarified, enunciating each syllable. "I added the *super* part."

Phoebe looked between her uncle and Erasmus. "You're here on Sebastian's account?"

Tula wiggled with excitement. "We need to get you back to Denver because Sebby's been so busy with—"

"Tula," Erasmus chided.

What were they hiding?

Her uncle knew she and Sebastian had a falling out. It was safe to assume Sebastian's father understood the circumstances of what had transpired between herself and his son as well.

"Is he busy partnering with an investor—the one who contacted him?" she asked, willing herself to keep her voice even.

"That depends on you, Phoebe," Erasmus answered.

"On me? I don't understand."

"He's been working on his pitch," Erasmus continued, seeming to choose his words carefully.

She sat back in her seat. "He's pitching at LETIS Live?"

"Yes."

"To the investors he met with before the event?"

"Something like that," Erasmus answered.

"And that's why you're here? You want me to see Sebastian

pitch an idea?" she said a touch more sharply than she'd meant. Maybe there was a disconnect. Perhaps in the helicopter excitement, she'd missed something.

"Yep, that's why we're here," her uncle Rowen confirmed.

What the hell?

"Well, he's not the only one with a pitch," she asserted, lifting her chin. "I need to get back to Denver for LETIS Live, too, for my own pitch to the investors."

"We know," her uncle answered.

Dammit! She was back to being totally confused. "Uncle Row, what's going on? How could you know what I'm pitching?"

He held out his phone. He'd pulled up Foot Tap Studio's webpage. "I know it's not Munch Match."

"No, it's not," she replied, softening her sharpened demeanor as she stared at the page's download counter. The open-source software had garnered over one hundred thousand downloads. "I posted the source code. It's free for anyone to use however they like." She swallowed past a lump in her throat. "I'm pitching Go Girl. I believe it's what my mom and dad would want me to do." Her voice cracked as an overwhelming sensation washed over her. She glanced away and blinked back tears.

"Hey, Tula," Erasmus said gently and waved his daughter over to the windows. "Let's see if we can spy our house from up here."

He was trying to give them a little privacy, and she appreciated it. She wiped her cheek and steadied herself.

Her uncle Rowen glanced at the yearbook on her lap. "Is that what I think it is?"

She opened the book to the page with her mother's picture and handed it over. "I met the former principal and school secretary from my mom's high school at a diner. They remembered my mom, and they gave me this."

Rowen studied the page. "You chose the same quote for your yearbook, didn't you?"

She nodded. "Crazy, huh?"

Now her uncle was the one with tears welling in his eyes. "I'm sorry I never brought you to Stratlin, Phoebe. Your mother and father were very important to me. I got to know your mom first as Andrew's girlfriend and then his wife. She didn't have any living relatives. We were her family. After your parents passed away and you came to live with me, I focused on our life in Denver. But I should have done more. I should have taken you to see where your mom grew up."

She took his hand in hers. "You don't have to apologize, Uncle Row. I know with all my heart that today was supposed to be the first time I visited. But I'm still not totally sure what you're doing here."

The man's gaze grew glassy. "I need you to trust me, kid. Can you do that?"

She held the gaze of the man who'd loved her like a father. They'd had one rocky beginning. Barely six years old and a hellion at that, she'd tested his patience and run the poor guy ragged. Then Penny came into their lives, and everything fell into place—and it still did. She adored her aunt and uncle.

She glanced at the picture of her mother. "The future belongs to those who believe in the beauty of their dreams," she said, reading the quote. "You and Aunt Penny always believed in me. My parents trusted you to raise me and love me. I couldn't ask for more." She bit back a grin. "So, yeah, I trust you," she replied, then tapped her foot twice, like she used to do as a kid when she would secretly call him a butthole.

The man shook his head.

She chuckled. "I was a handful, huh?"

"Phoebe, Princess of the Hot Dog Fairies, Bearer of Cookies, and Eater of Pizza, you are still a handful," he teased, but behind his bifocals, his eyes were as teary as hers.

"I see our house! Phoebe, that's my house, and that's the big pasture and our barn for when the donkeys are with us in Denver. But they're back in Rickety Rock," Tula called, bobbing back and forth in her hot dog suit.

"Oh, yes, I know your house well," Phoebe answered.

A ping vibrated through the ritzy cabin.

"Buckle up, please. We'll be landing shortly," the pilot announced over the intercom.

Phoebe pressed her hand to the window and focused on the ground. "We're landing in the Cress's backyard?"

"And there's the party bus," Tula chimed. "Look at the flashing colors."

Phoebe saw it, too. It was hard to miss. "Why is there a party bus at the Cress's place? I need to get to the Denver Amphitheater. Can't we land there?"

Her uncle rested his hand on top of hers. "You'll need to go with the flow."

Go with the flow?

"I'll need a little more information than that, Uncle Row."

"Remember how I asked you to trust me on this?"

"Yes."

His eyes were full of love and pride as he squeezed her hand. "That starts now."

Chapter 22
PHOEBE

"Phoebe Gale, welcome to the party bus!"

And hello to the day-drinking crew.

Phoebe stepped onto the party bus and found herself face-to-face with Aunt Penny, Libby Lamb-Cress, Aria's aunt Harper Presley-Paige, and Charlotte Elliott, Oscar's stepmom. Despite not knowing what would come next on this roller coaster of a day, she couldn't help but smile as a warmth emanated from her heart. These were her aunt and uncle's best friends, but they might as well be family. It wasn't strange to see them together. This wasn't the first time she'd been alone with her aunt and her best friends. They'd done girls' trips together—many of them. But they'd never picked her up in the cheesiest party bus she'd ever seen. With hot pink furry seats and multiple disco balls reflecting off neon flashing lights, it was as if someone thought it was a good idea to design a traveling seizure-inducing mobile. And that wasn't all. There was a bar with two bartenders—a man and a woman. Wait! She recognized the woman.

"Madelyn Malone, you're here, too?"

"Come, come, Phoebe, dear, take a seat. We're on a schedule," the matchmaker purred like it was commonplace for her to be milling about a party palace on wheels . . . And was that a stripper pole?

Phoebe shielded her eyes from the luminous light blasts. "What is going on here?"

Her aunt tapped a panel on the wall. The flashing lights switched to a less vertigo-inducing neon glow. "We needed a way to get you from the helicopter to the Denver Amphitheater."

It appeared everyone in her orbit was in on this cooked-up scheme.

"You didn't consider having the helicopter land at an airport? There's a regional one ten minutes from Crystal Creek. Not to mention, we could have landed on that swath of open space next to the amphitheater, or you could have used a mode of transportation that didn't contain four disco balls."

"There's five. See the one over the bar?" Charlotte answered.

"And did you see the pole? They're great for strength work. Almost as good as yoga," Libby chirped.

Phoebe steadied herself. There was a decent chance she'd end up with whiplash from the pendulum of shifting emotions. "Listen, I appreciate whatever this is. I do. But I need to get to LETIS Live. I know what I'm pitching. I can't miss this opportunity."

Harper Presley-Paige, the sassiest of her aunt's best friends, pointed to one of the hot pink fuzzy seats at the shiny black lacquer table. "Do not be a party pooper, Phoebe Gale. Get your beret-wearing ass over here. We've got this disco beauty rented for another fifteen minutes, and I plan on enjoying every second." Harper never disappointed with her razor-sharp commentary.

"All right, disco bus it is," Phoebe replied, then sank into the furry chair.

The bus started down the street, and they were off.

Libby closed her eyes and raised her hands. This wasn't an uncommon behavior when the spiritual maven of the group felt a message coming on—and nine times out of ten, her advice was worth following. "Phoebe won't be a party pooper, girls. I'm reading her vibe, and she's spiritually centered, even cleansed." Libby opened her eyes. "And that aura! Phoebe Gale, you're either prepared to accept the opportunities the universe has to offer you, or . . ." Sebastian's stepmother paused.

Phoebe leaned in. "Or what?"

"Or you've been getting a lot of use out of the Wham Bam deluxe vibrator."

God help her! Forget calling this vehicle a party bus. Mortification transportation was a better title. And please, universe, do not let this woman pick up on the fact that Sebastian had taken part in the Wham Bam sexy-times.

Sebastian.

She pictured his face and imagined his eyes drinking her in. His lips pressed to her skin. His tongue tasting the hollow of her neck. And then, she experienced a lightening. The piercing anger and resentment she'd harbored these last few days shifted. Had she forgiven him? *No, hell no!* But her time in Stratlin and the conversation with her uncle seemed to have ushered in a quiet strength, a serene sense of purpose that softened the sharp edges of her anger and heartbreak.

"What is it, Phoebe?" Harper pressed, her gaze glinting with mischief. "Are you enjoying the new Wham Bam as much as . . ." She turned to Libby. "How many have you sold?"

"Seven million nine hundred thousand."

"Are you enjoying it as much as nearly eight million chicks?" Harper inquired.

Phoebe grimaced. "Um . . ."

Libby gasped. "Hold on. I'm refining my reading. Phoebe

is open to new possibilities with quite a bit of sexual energy on the side."

"What are we talking about here, Libbs?" Harper probed. "Like eighty percent open to possibilities, twenty percent Wham Bam?"

"I'm thinking sixty-forty," Libby clarified.

And mega-ugh! Phoebe was damned sure her cheeks had gone from pink to beet red. This was worse than dreaming about being naked in public. Scratch that. This might be worse than actually being naked in public.

"Smile!" called Charlotte, then snapped a picture with her camera.

Phoebe cradled her head in her hands. She loved these women. It was like having four aunts, which was great—until they rented a puffy-pink stripper pole party bus and instigated an interrogation.

"Ladies," Madelyn said, like a judge calling court to order, "let's allow Phoebe to take a breath and tell us about her day."

How would Madelyn know that?

"Yes," her aunt Penny agreed. "Tell us about Stratlin."

Phoebe couldn't help but smile. "I met the former principal and school secretary at my mom's high school—the wife was the principal, and the husband was the secretary."

"Busting the patriarchy. Woot, woot!" Harper interjected.

"They showed me around the high school and gave me this." Phoebe removed the yearbook from her tote, opened it to her mother's page, and set it on the table. "You'll never believe this, but my mom and I had the same senior quote."

"The future belongs to those who believe in the beauty of their dreams. Eleanor Roosevelt," Charlotte read.

"Why did you pick that quote, Phoebe? I don't think I ever asked you," Penny commented, touching the page.

Phoebe watched her aunt closely. "You and Uncle Rowen

gave me a book of quotes from notable women in history for one of my birthdays. I think it was for my thirteenth."

"No, honey," her aunt answered with a furrowed brow, "that book wasn't from your uncle and me. I would have remembered giving it to you."

"Then who gave it to me?" Phoebe asked, glancing at Charlotte, Harper, and Libby. "It was on my desk in my bedroom. I remember seeing it wrapped in shiny silver paper with a red bow."

Madelyn adjusted her scarlet scarf. "It was from me."

"It was?"

"Yes, and it wasn't for your thirteenth birthday. It was a year before, when you turned twelve."

Phoebe stared at the matchmaker. "Did you know my mother and I picked the same quote? Did you want that to happen? Is that why you gave me that book?"

Madelyn maintained a poker face, giving nothing away. "Your mother's maiden name is Funke."

Phoebe reared back. That was one hell of a pivot in the conversation. "Yes, Melanie Funke."

"Funke is German. It translates to *spark* in English."

"Okay," Phoebe answered, stretching out the word. Where was Madelyn going with this?

"And that's what you are, Phoebe. You're the spark of the group," she explained without explaining anything.

"I don't understand."

Madelyn folded her hands in her lap. "When I came to Denver many years ago to make four nanny matches, there was a reason your uncle was the first to be matched in the group."

"I'll bite. Why did you match Uncle Row first?"

"You, Phoebe. You were the reason."

Phoebe cocked her head to the side. "Was it because I was such a giant pain in the ass and my uncle needed the most help?"

That remark cracked the matchmaker's demeanor, and the woman chuckled. "You liked dominoes when you were a girl."

Another pivot.

"Yes, I like them because of my uncle. We played them all the time when I was growing up."

"You started the domino effect, dear—well, more like the nanny love-match effect. I believe it was you who told your uncle you wanted Penny to be your nanny."

"I did," Phoebe answered, meeting her aunt's eye. "I still remember when my uncle came to pick me up at school and you were with him. You were meant to be with us. I felt it here," she said and pressed her hand to her heart.

"I did, too," Penny replied, then brushed a tear from her cheek.

"And do you remember meeting with me before you met Penny?" Madelyn continued.

Phoebe nodded. "Yes, you came to the house with a box of cookies. We played dominoes, too. Wow, I forgot about that."

"The moment I met you, Phoebe, I knew you'd decide the trajectory of the four Denver matches. You were the spark. When you chose Penny, that led me to Charlotte, then to Libby, and finally to Harper. It set off a series of actions and reactions that have gotten us to this place, right here, in a disco party bus with a stripper pole," the woman finished with a ghost of a grin.

Phoebe stared at the matchmaker. Her mouth opened and closed like a flounder before she could form words. "But I was only six, Madelyn. How could you know I'd make the right choice?"

"Even then, dear, you were adept at something many people never master."

"What is that?"

The matchmaker held her gaze. "Trusting your heart."

"And that's what we want you to do now," her aunt Penny

added, her eyes shining with tears. "Trust that part of you that brought this group together. Trust the wise, loving heart you inherited from your mom and your dad."

Phoebe wiped the tears from her cheeks, so grateful to have her aunt and these women in her life. Then, for a beat, maybe two, it was as if her parents were with them in this traveling party palace. What a place to commune with the dead! She chuckle-sobbed, which she hadn't even known was a thing until now.

"Do you feel that energy, Phoebe?" Libby asked softly. "It's all around you."

"I do."

"And do you know what it is?" the woman pressed.

Phoebe nodded. "It's them. It's my mom and dad, or maybe it's not them exactly. It's their love."

For a moment, no one said a word.

"Are we supposed to cry?" Harper sobbed, breaking the silence. "Because I'm crying. I feel like we should be crying. This is our Phoebe. Our first nanny love match kid. And we didn't mess her up. Do you hear that, ghosts of Phoebe's parents? We didn't screw her up. Yay us!"

The women broke into teary laughter as Aria's aunt's comment lowered the pulling-at-the-heartstrings temperature and the party bus slowed to a stop.

Phoebe glanced out the window and saw the sign for the Denver Amphitheater, then noticed something else. There were people everywhere—and lots of kids. Droves of girls in pink T-shirts milled around. Was something in addition to LETIS Live going on? Perhaps an event in the open space next to the venue?

"Before you go, Phoebe, I insist you have a drink with us," Madelyn said, then nodded to the bartender.

Phoebe studied the man. "Do I know you?" She cocked her head to the side. "I do. You're the waiter from the bistro."

"I'm a bartender, too," the man replied as he set a tray of drinks on the table.

"And he's available for private events," Madelyn added, then handed her a drink. "The perfect dirty martini. Three olives, no more, no less. You recently enjoyed a few of these, if I'm not mistaken?"

Phoebe held the martini glass as another whopper of a revelation hit. "It was you, Madelyn," she said wide-eyed. "You sent the drinks to my table and paid for me to get hammered after I squirted mustard all over Jeremy Drewler."

"It was the five of us, dear," Madelyn replied, nodding to the women at the table.

"And you were glorious," her aunt Penny added.

"Way to use that Dijon," Harper cheered, still crying as she raised her glass. "That was straight out of something I would have done back in the day."

"How did you know I'd be there?" Phoebe pressed.

"I can't give away every matchmaking secret," Madelyn confided. "Just know that at the end of the day, I'm simply—"

"A facilitator of fate," Penny, Harper, Libby, and Charlotte supplied, then clinked glasses.

Phoebe stared at her martini. While she appreciated their love and support, there was one item she had to address. "Madelyn, you said that my match was made years ago, and I have a feeling you think my match is Sebastian, but you might be wrong."

Madelyn raised an eyebrow. "And why is that?"

"I can't be with someone who doesn't believe in me. I love Sebastian. I do. But he doesn't support my dream to create Go Girl. That's what I'll be pitching at LETIS Live."

Madelyn took a sip of her drink, then glanced out the window. "Are you sure about that?"

Phoebe followed the matchmaker's line of sight. The woman had zeroed in on a group of girls. They held signs with two lightning bolts framing two words: *go* and *girl*. "Holy shit," she whispered, then reached for her martini and downed it in one gulp.

"Here, honey, finish mine. I have a feeling you'll need it," Harper offered, sliding her martini across the table.

"Thanks." Phoebe downed the second cocktail like a seasoned day drinker. She sat back, set the martini glass on the table, then peered out the window to find a giant hot dog waving to her. She blinked. Was she seeing things? "These drinks weren't made with magic mushrooms, were they?"

"No way," Harper assured her. "I'd know if they were."

Phoebe nodded but couldn't pull her gaze from the life-sized hot dog. "Is that who I think it is?" Her heart skipped a beat.

"Why don't you *go, girl*, and find out," Madelyn purred.

"Go, girl?" Phoebe repeated.

"Go, girl!" the ladies exclaimed.

Message received. And this was it. Go Girl or bust. Like she'd slipped into a dream world, Phoebe rose to her feet. She floated off the party bus, took a few steps, then stopped in front of a six-foot-four-inch hot dog. No, not just any six-foot-four hot dog. A six-foot-four hot dog with Sebastian's face framed by the fabric of the costume frank.

"What the hell are you doing?" Honestly, she was impressed she could muster an actual question in the presence of Sebastian Cress dressed like a giant wiener. The guy was all about looking good—only giving the masses a whiff and a taste of the abs-tastic, social media sparkly version of himself. He'd been voted the sexiest man on the internet. One could assume donning an adult-sized hot dog costume was the polar opposite of maintaining that facade, and yet, if anyone could wear the hell out of a frankfurter ensemble, it was him.

"I figured it out, Pheebs," he said earnestly. "I owe you an apology. You were right. A part of me knew keeping the Sebastian Guarantee data a secret from you was wrong. And that wasn't the only thing I was wrong about. I couldn't figure out my purpose in this world. I thought I knew how to make a name for myself. I thought I had it figured out, but I was wrong about who I was meant to be. I'm not confused anymore. I know where I belong."

Check out Sebastian 2.0.

Phoebe stood there awestruck—or she was dead, or those cocktails did contain some hallucinogenic substance.

She pinched herself. "Ouch!"

"What are you doing, Pheebs?" he asked, taking her hand. "Did you hear what I said?"

"I must be asleep. I'm asleep, or maybe the helicopter I was in earlier crashed and I'm in a coma experiencing a fever dream or . . . I'm dead. I could be dead," she sputtered.

He smiled that boyish grin that turned her brain to mush. "You're not dead. You're awake, and this is very much the real world."

She looked him over. "Why are you dressed like that, Seb?"

His smile twisted into a sly smirk. "It got you talking to me, didn't it?"

The man had a point.

"It's surprisingly hard to be furious with a frankfurter. But seriously, what are you doing? What's going on here?"

"I'm helping the girls sell hot dogs and chocolate chip cookies. They're partnering with Hank's Franks and a few other Denver-based hot dog vendors to earn money."

Phoebe surveyed the open space teeming with kids in pink T-shirts. "Who are these girls?"

"Hey, Sebastian!" a trio of—speak of the devil—*girls* called. Like the others, they had on hot pink shirts printed with two lightning bolts and *Go Girl* in the center, like the sign.

"Hey, Jana, Christy, Clarissa! How's Mr. Cookie Combat?"

Mr. Cookie Combat? Forget being dead. Had that bus transported her to a different dimension?

"We added eight feet," a little redhead answered.

"Amazing!" Sebastian exclaimed, fist-bumping the kids as they walked past him.

Phoebe studied the trio. "Why do they look familiar?"

"They're part of the Tech Tweens group who ambushed us with cookies outside the clothing boutique."

Well, that's not something you hear every day.

Her jaw dropped. "And now you guys are best buds?"

"Yeah."

"Did the Tech Tweens ask you to dress up in a hot dog costume? Is this some weird punishment for what happened at the airport?"

"It was my idea, and it's part of my pitch. Also, I think I look damned good. What do you think of the T-shirts? I tried to call you to get your input, but you didn't pick up. I had a few questions about the color choice, but I winged it because the printer needed the logo. It turned out great for a rush job, don't you think?"

She'd just picked up her jaw from the floor, and it was back down there again. "You designed a logo for Go Girl?"

"I did." The man positively beamed. "You're wearing your beret."

She touched her felt hat. "Yeah."

That sexy-as-hell boyish grin returned. "I love it. I always have."

"Sebby, what is this? Why did you design a Go Girl logo and make T-shirts for the Tech Tweens? You wanted me to put Go Girl on the back burner."

"I know, but do you like the logo?"

She threw up her hands. "I do. I was struggling to come up with one, but—"

"Here's the hot dog you asked for, Sebastian," another kid

in a Go Girl T-shirt said, interrupting their conversation as she handed him a bag.

"Thanks, Cassie."

And there was another surprise. Why were the Tech Tweens selling hot dogs and cookies like her mother used to do? "What's with the choice of cuisine?"

"Madelyn suggested it."

"Madelyn knew about this?" she shot back.

"I think Madelyn knows about everything." He handed her the hot dog and tossed the bag into a nearby trash can. "I figured you'd be hungry or freaking out when you got here. Either way, I knew if I had a hot dog on hand—or four food trucks' worth—we'd be good." He peeled the foil and handed her the half-wrapped dog.

She stared at it. "Ketchup, mustard, and lettuce."

"Your love-match hot dog. Hank says it's his bestseller."

This was too much, and barely anything the man was saying made sense. Why had he gone to all this trouble? She hadn't secured funding for Go Girl. She checked her watch. She had less than ten minutes before LETIS Live started.

"Sebastian, I've got to go. I'm pitching Go Girl. There's no more Munch Match. Well, that's not completely true. Munch Match will continue to exist, but the algorithm isn't just mine anymore. I made it open-source."

He tucked a lock of hair behind her ear. "I know. I had about thirty-seven tech-savvy girls explaining what that meant. They were giddy with excitement."

Phoebe cocked her head to the side, unsure how to unpack that statement. "Shouldn't you be preparing for LETIS Live, too? Your dad told me you're pitching an idea. I figured it was . . ."

"The Sebastian Guarantee?"

She nodded.

"In a way, it is."

She couldn't handle any more cagey, bizarro-world answers. "Listen, I don't know why you're dressed as a hot dog. I don't understand why these kids are wearing shirts with my concept on them. I haven't even pitched the idea."

"Yes, you have," came a woman's voice. "And it was one heck of a pitch."

Phoebe recognized it and spun around. "Mae?" But it wasn't only Mae Edwards from Glenn Pines heading her way. The whole quilting crew was with her. "Enid, Theodora, Shirley—what are you doing here?"

"We're LETIS sponsors," Theodora answered.

Phoebe chewed her lip. "Your quilting group is a LETIS sponsor?"

"Quilting is our hobby," Enid explained. "We picked it up when we lived about a hundred miles east of Denver."

Phoebe's pulse raced. "The town of Stratlin is about one hundred miles east of Denver."

"That's right," Shirley replied.

"Oh my gosh," Phoebe breathed. Her heart was ready to beat itself out of her chest. She studied the women as the image from the glass case at Stratlin High popped into her head. Two women were standing on her mother's right and two on her left. Phoebe took a step back. It was as if she was looking at the future version of that photo. "Shirley, Theodora, Enid, and Mae. *S, T, E, M.*" Phoebe gasped. "You're the STEM teachers in the picture with my mother, and I have a sneaking suspicion you're also the minds behind STEM Development."

Mae patted Sebastian's arm. "She put that together a heck of a lot quicker than you did."

Phoebe slid her gaze to the giant hot dog.

"That doesn't surprise me. Phoebe Gale is the smartest woman I know," he answered.

"And this must be Phoebe! *Trés jolie*! Very lovely!" came

another voice—with a French accent—and a woman dressed to the nines joined them. "And look, Claudette, she is wearing a beret. *Trés chic.*"

"It is like it was meant to be, *n'est-ce pas*?" a carbon copy of the first woman crooned. "Nice work, Sebastian."

Where the heck did two stylish French women fit into the mix?

Phoebe glanced between the identical twins, then jammed the hot dog into her mouth. Sebastian was right. She sure as hell needed a freak-out frank. She swallowed the colossal bite. "Do I know you?"

"We have not met. I am Bernadette Marieuse, and this is my sister, Claudette Marieuse."

Phoebe looked between the women. "Marieuse?"

"*Oui*," the women replied in unison.

"I may be a little rusty—I took French in high school—but doesn't your last name translate to *matchmaker* in English?"

"You are correct. But we are not matchmakers when it comes to love. We're matchmakers when it comes to investing. We are the Marieuse Group, an investment firm. We partner with STEM Development. We're quite interested in Go Girl."

"You are?" Phoebe breathed.

"Did you say Marieuse Group?" a man barked.

And holy irate man bun! Phoebe knew that petulant, peevish tone. "Jeremy?"

With his strawberry locks poufed on top of his head in a—yep, you guessed it—man bun, Jeremy Drewler elbowed his way through the growing crowd. He marched up to them and eyed the sisters. "Your firm emailed me. You expressed an interest in my concept. But you haven't returned any of my messages. Now I'm stuck pitching at LETIS Live."

Bernadette and Claudette didn't bat an eyelash at the man-bun-baby tantrum.

"After careful consideration and a deep dive into your background, Mr. Drewler," Bernadette began, "while we expressed an initial interest in you, we came to the conclusion that our philosophies do not mesh."

Claudette nodded. "Our values are more in line with Miss Gale's Go Girl vision."

"What?" Jeremy yipped, going full Chihuahua. "Once I secure funding, my Man Bun Nation app will revolutionize hipster men's grooming. You're passing up on that to work with Phoebe Gale?"

"Hold on," Sebastian said, suppressing a grin as he turned to her. "This guy's innovative concept is an app about man buns?"

Phoebe bit back a grin of her own. "I didn't tell you?"

"Oh, I would have remembered something as ridiculous as that."

"The man bun will define this generation of men," Jeremy grumbled.

"Yeah, good luck with that," Sebastian shot back, unable to stop himself from laughing.

"You know what the problem is?" Jeremy barked, glancing around at the crowd, his words dripping with contempt.

Phoebe slapped a syrupy-sweet grin on her face. "Enlighten us, Jeremy."

"Women don't belong in tech. They should step aside and let men who know what they're doing lead the way."

As if the man had awakened a sleeping giant, the energy shifted. A feverish buzz cut through the air as a mass of pink T-shirts closed in on them.

"Did you say that women should stay out of tech?" a blond girl with a tablet in her hand demanded.

"You better run, Strawberry Man Bun," Sebastian cautioned. "The future of tech is coming after your ass."

"What?" Jeremy blathered.

The buzz intensified to a grinding hum as a miniature tank

of a robot sporting a catapult arm loaded down with cookies headed straight for Jeremy.

"Meet Mr. Cookie Combat," a girl in pigtails snarled.

"Ready, aim . . ." the tablet girl called.

"Fire!" a gaggle of Tech Tweens cried.

"Help!" Jeremy squealed.

Cookies soared through the air. Jeremy bolted, but he wasn't getting off easy. A throng of children and one hell of a cookie-flinging robot ran his misogynistic booty clean off the property.

"If that's not a sign that women will usher in the new age of technology, I don't know what is," Sebastian mused as Jeremy disappeared, running into the sunset like the little crybaby cream puff he was.

"We agree. Women must play a major role in tech development," Mae replied. "But the road to providing girls an opportunity to join the industry isn't as clear-cut as one would like. There are many good programs for girls, but currently, they're like quilting squares. They're important, but they're only the pieces. What's missing is the binding, the structure that holds the squares together." Mae paused. "'The future belongs to those who believe in the beauty of their dreams.' That was your mother's high school yearbook quote. I understand it was yours as well."

Phoebe swallowed past the emotion in her throat. "Yes."

"We believe you have the drive to lead this endeavor, Phoebe. We'd like to invest in Go Girl. It would be an honor for us to work with the daughter of the woman Enid, Shirley, Theodora, and I held in such high regard. We see so much of her in you. Would you consider partnering with us?"

Feeling her parents' presence, Phoebe pressed her hand to her heart. "I couldn't imagine a better fit. Thank you."

Mae gestured to Sebastian. "You might want to thank him as well. Sebastian has been in talks with the Tech Tweens organization. It's my understanding that, once your company is up and running, they'd like to join as one of the first Go Girl sponsors. He also planned this hot dog and cookie sale to help them raise funds to expand their organization to include younger girls."

"They want to call it Tech Tinies, and I can sign up," Tula chirped, joining the group in her big-brother-matching hot dog suit.

Now that was a sight.

"When did you get here, Tula?" Phoebe asked, patting the girl's cheek.

"We've been here a while."

Phoebe glanced past the child and found their friends and family standing together.

"We're here for the press conference," Tula continued. She pointed toward the open space where men and women with cameras and microphones clustered around a raised stage.

"Press conference?" Phoebe repeated, then eyed Sebastian.

"Business rule number one: strike when the iron is hot. LETIS Live is a big tech draw, and we've got food trucks. Thanks to the Munch Match app, that'll bring in the community. It's the perfect place to announce Go Girl." That self-assured glint sparked in his eyes. "It also doesn't hurt when the sexiest man on the internet posts about a new tech endeavor on his socials."

"I bet it doesn't," she answered, hardly able to believe everything Sebastian had accomplished in such a short amount of time.

"Shall we?" Claudette gestured toward the stage.

"You're okay with looking like that for the world to see?" Phoebe asked Sebastian, keeping her voice down.

"This isn't the only thing the world's about to see," he answered with a wink.

What else did he have up his sleeve?

Sebastian nodded to the investors, then stepped forward. "Thank you for joining us. I'm Sebastian Cress, and I'm happy to be here today, dressed like a hot dog, to call attention to a fundraiser supporting girls in technology. The event is going on now, and it's being held adjacent to the Denver Amphitheater. We invite everyone in the city to come on down and enjoy cookies and hot dogs from local food truck merchants. We also have another major announcement."

The journalists and reporters edged closer to the stage.

"We're here to celebrate the partnership between tech innovator Phoebe Gale, the Marieuse Investment Group, and STEM Development. They'll be working together to create an online community supporting girls and women in technology. This sweeping endeavor is called Go Girl."

"Will you play a part in Go Girl, Mr. Cress?" a reporter called.

Sebastian flashed his social-media-ready, panty-melting grin. "That's a great question, and it's a question that I'd like to address right now with a guarantee for Go Girl's mastermind, Phoebe Gale." He took her hand and brought her to the front of the stage.

"What type of guarantee are you talking about?" she asked.

He took her hands in his and gazed into her eyes. "I guarantee I've loved you since I was six years old and I will love you every day for the rest of our lives. You're a part of me, Phoebe Gale. You, with your amazing brain and slightly concerning lifelong hot dog addiction, are intertwined with my soul. I want to live my life by your side. This is what my mum would want for me. I can feel her smiling down on us. Let's give Go Girl everything we've got."

"Let me get this straight, Sebastian Cress," she said, working to keep her voice from cracking as camera flashes peppered the air with bursts of light. "You're in love with me. You want to be with me, and you want to work for me?"

His lips quirked into a cocky grin. "I'm not trying to brag, but I've already done one hell of a job. You'll be the president, of course. I'm thinking chief executive officer for me."

This man.

She schooled her features. "I'll be CEO *and* president. I can offer you a position as vice president."

Hello, girl boss ball-buster!

"Vice president?" he repeated, weighing the words.

"Mm-hmm," she hummed, suppressing a smirk.

"I accept, Miss Gale. Now, if you don't mind, I need to do something as my first official act as VP."

"I'm not stopping you," she tossed back, then stiffened. "Wait, I am stopping you." She swallowed past the lump in her throat. "You need to know something. This is me, Seb. Nerdy and awkward Phoebe. You're sure this is what you want?"

"I want everything. All of you."

"I'm not Phoebe 2.0. I don't want, nor do I need, to be a man-eater. I like myself just the way I am."

"You realize that statement is chock-full of man-eater energy, don't you?"

He was right!

"It appears the Sebastian Guarantee protocols did work." She glanced at the media, who appeared to be eating up this public display of affection. She leaned in toward him. "There is one thing I'm keeping from my days of being Phoebe 2.0," she whispered.

"What's that?"

"I'm wearing them beneath my clothing. Turns out base model Phoebe likes a little satin and lace."

He cupped her face in his hands. "My God, I love you, Phoebe Gale."

Before she could take another breath, he kissed her. Their

lips met, and she melted into his hot dog embrace as the crowd applauded. She wrapped her arms around what she hoped was his neck. It was hard to tell. That costume was hella bulky. She giggled, then pulled back. "You've been busy, Vice President Cress."

"I'm behind you one hundred percent. I believe in you. But there's more."

"More?"

His cheeks grew pink.

Was he nervous?

"I've got a pitch to run by you."

"What are you pitching?" she asked, tightening her hold on her hot dog.

"Whoa!" a guy bellowed, sidelining their little moment. "The Info Darling page was right about you, Phoebe Gale!"

She peered into the crowd and spied the golden-haired mophead dude from the food truck line. "What are you doing here?"

"Who is that guy, Pheebs?" Sebastian asked.

"I met him in a hot dog food truck line the day I got invited to LETIS."

"Phoebe Gale's Info Darling page says that she's attracted to hot dogs," Mophead called.

Phoebe rested her head against Sebastian's chest, which also doubled as a fabric squiggle of mustard. "I totally forgot Aria did that to my page."

Sebastian stepped back, wiggled around in his costume, then produced his cell phone. He stared at the screen and started typing.

"What are you doing?"

"A little webpage tweak. Don't worry, boss. It's part of my VP duties." He typed a few seconds longer. "And we're good," he murmured, then pegged Mophead with his gaze. "Refresh Phoebe's Info Darling page."

Mophead looked at his phone. A grin spread across his face. "Congratulations! But you probably want to hold on to that costume, though. The heart wants what it wants."

Sebastian chuckled. "Noted."

"What did you do on my Info Darling page?"

"You're about to find out." He looked out into the crowd. "Tula, I'm ready."

"Catch!" The girl raised her arm and threw a small metal ball to her brother.

Sebastian snapped it out of the air, but it wasn't a ball.

She stared at the crinkled silver. "Is that a hot dog wrapper?"

"It's the wrapper from the love-match hot dog I ate while you were in the changing room. You told Hank that the person who ate that hot dog would be your match."

"I did."

"You were right." He dropped to a knee and peeled open the foil ball, revealing a sparkling diamond ring.

She gasped. "Is that what I think it is? Is this what I think it is?"

He held up the ring. It glinted in the afternoon light. "My dad proposed to my mum with this ring."

"Sebastian," she breathed as another wave of emotion threatened to overtake her.

Dressed as a giant hot dog with love and tears in his eyes, he exhaled a shaky breath. "This is the pitch I've been waiting a lifetime to make. Phoebe Gale," he began, slipping into his British accent, "Princess of the Hot Dog Fairies, Bearer of Cookies, and Eater of Pizza, will you marry me?"

Holy hot dog proposal! She couldn't have dreamed up something so perfect. Surrounded by love, she gazed at the man who held her heart in his hands. Smiling through her happy tears, she knew there was only one way to answer. "Sebastian Cress. Mr. Lickable Abs. I'm all in."

Epilogue

SEBASTIAN

"Pheebs, six more organizations signed on to partner with Go Girl. We're up to thirty-eight in four days. Four days!"

Sebastian waited to hear the love of his life shriek with joy but got nothing. He craned his neck. Peering out of her bedroom, he checked the living room but didn't see her. And yeah, he was working in Phoebe's bedroom. He'd moved in with her. They hadn't even talked about it. It was a given. She was his fiancée. Jesus, he loved the sound of that. But they wouldn't be living here for long. Go Girl was on the cusp of taking the tech world by storm, and the makeshift office in Phoebe's living room wouldn't cut it. And it didn't have to. They were flush with cash and committed to spending every dollar on building their business prudently.

That's right. *Their business.* When it came to Go Girl, he was all in.

The future belongs to those who believe in the beauty of their dreams.

He couldn't agree more with Eleanor Roosevelt. His passion and his purpose were clear. He would be by Phoebe's side, creating a tech community like no other.

They'd hammered out contracts, secured office space

across town, and signed a lease on a quaint bungalow not far from Go Girl's new headquarters. To say the last handful of days had been one hell of a roller coaster would be a colossal understatement. Besides the business odds and ends and scoring a kick-ass job, he'd figured out what mattered most and got the girl. He could safely guarantee it couldn't get any better than this.

Well . . . actually, it could.

Here's the thing he'd never realized. The deep, soul-satisfying love he and Phoebe shared hadn't happened overnight. It had happened minute by minute, day by day, and year after year. A layering of friendship, love, and laughter that revealed an undeniable truth. Phoebe knew him better than he knew himself, and their love was meant to be. From the moment he'd laid eyes on her, the match had been made, but the friendship that bloomed between them through the years was what made this moment so sweet.

He checked his watch. And speaking of making sweet things, they needed to hop to it. They were entertaining this afternoon.

While the world had watched him propose, he and Phoebe wanted to throw a barbecue to celebrate with their close friends and families—or it was Phoebe coming up with another reason to grill hot dogs and nosh on baked goods. No matter the reason, their guests were coming over this afternoon. Between calls, he'd been helping her set up in the complex's courtyard for the last hurrah at her first apartment.

"Pheebs?" he tried again.

She was probably wearing her earbuds. He set his laptop on a stack of moving boxes, then sauntered out of the bedroom. Inhaling the scent of chocolate, he'd only taken a few steps before he found her in the kitchenette. His cock twitched at the sight of his fiancée. Shaking her ass with a spatula in her hand, Phoebe Gale jammed to the beat of her own drum—or whatever she was listening to. Probably one of Aria's new songs.

He tiptoed toward her and surveyed the scene. She'd baked a few batches of chocolate chip cookies. They sat cooling on the counter. But she wasn't working on another batch. He drank her in as she dipped the spatula into a bowl, then shimmied to the side, revealing another culinary confection. And now he was rock-hard.

While he'd been locking in Go Girl partner organizations, Phoebe had baked a cake and was in the process of icing it. It was like college, except now he wouldn't have to spend the next month taking cold showers to get the image of the woman out of his head. Moving stealthily, he stalked his prey.

One step, two steps, three steps.

"Hey, Pheebs!" he called at the top of his lungs.

She gasped, spun around, and whacked the bloody hell out of the cake with the spatula. The block of chocolatey goodness teetered on the edge of the counter.

Come on, universe! Let's wreck a cake.

The freshly frosted delight toppled over and smacked the kitchen floor with a satisfying thud. He whooped and pumped his fist like a baked-goods bandit.

Phoebe removed her earbuds. A devilish twist of a grin graced her lips. "You couldn't help yourself, could you?"

"No, ma'am, I could not."

"What's the time?"

He glanced at his watch. "We've got seventeen minutes until our guests arrive."

"Seventeen minutes. That's plenty of time to *clean up*," she replied with a devious glint in her eyes.

"Uh-huh, and we should start with the frosting."

"One little taste wouldn't hurt." Like she'd read his mind, she lowered herself to the ground and—wait a second—she wasn't wearing her tried-and-true sneakers.

He eyed the hot pink footwear. "Are you baking in high heels?"

"Uh-huh."

"Did you know I would try to make you knock over the cake?"

"Just go with it, Mr. Lickable Abs."

"Oh, I will. I love it when you use your super-smart brain to seduce me with baked goods and the possibility of sex."

She dragged the index finger of her left hand through the icing like she had the last time this happened. There was, however, an addition to the mix. The diamond engagement ring glinted in the light as she trailed her finger through the chocolatey goodness, then tasted the cocoa catastrophe.

"Is it good?" he asked, unbuckling his belt.

"So good," she cooed, then resumed sucking the chocolate off her finger.

He unzipped his jeans. "Is it creamy?"

She closed her eyes and hummed a dirty little sound. "So creamy." She removed her finger from her mouth, dipped it into the frosting, then rose to her feet.

He noticed something else. While he'd been glued to his laptop, she'd switched out of her overalls and into a skirt.

"You changed."

"I did."

"Overalls make it tricky for a quickie."

"They do."

"This is very man-eater Phoebe of you."

"I have to let her have a little fun every now and then." She leaned over and flashed what was beneath the skirt—or what *wasn't* beneath her skirt.

He inhaled a tight breath. "You seem to have misplaced your knickers."

"Oops, it's so time consuming being a tech genius. I must have forgotten to put on panties." She dipped to the ground and brushed her finger across the chocolatey surface again. Replaying the college scene, she sucked her fingertip, looked over her shoulder, and hummed her delight.

"Damn, that's hot."

She repeated the sexy dip and frosting scrape maneuver. Taunting him, she wagged her chocolate-covered finger at him. "Would you like a taste?"

"That would be a hell yes."

He shrugged his pants and boxer briefs to his ankles and came up behind her. Pressing his hard length against her ass, his cock wept, aching for her. She brushed her chocolate fingertip against his bottom lip, then eased it inside his mouth. He sucked like he was auditioning to play the part of a human vacuum.

"Somebody's all in," Phoebe remarked, taking notice of his enthusiasm.

He licked his lips. "Not yet. Bend over."

She gripped the lip of the counter and bumped something with her elbow. It tittered and buzzed along the flat surface. "Oh dear! How did my Wham Bam end up in the kitchen?"

Like he said, he was the luckiest guy on the planet. That was the other thing about falling in love with your best friend. They knew each other inside and out. That meant they were comfortable when it came to dialing up the freaky factor.

He picked up the pulsing sex toy, then lifted her skirt. Lining up his cock with her entrance, he held the vibrator against her most sensitive place. Peppering her neck with kisses, he worked her sweet bud, wham-bamming the hell out of her. Emboldened by her sultry sighs, he reached beneath her T-shirt and massaged her breasts. She moaned, growing slicker by the second. He rocked his hips and nudged the tip of his cock inside her.

"Pick up a cookie," he demanded over the hum of the vibrator.

"A cookie?" she panted.

"Then take a bite."

This was the first time they'd drifted into food-porn sex, and he was there for it.

She plucked one of the sweet confections from the cooling rack and complied with his request. "Oh my God, Sebastian," she groaned.

"Is it delicious?"

"Yes."

He thrust his hips. Filling her to the hilt, he inhaled a sharp breath, savoring the moment.

"Your turn." Her voice was a sexy wisp of a sound. She held the treat to his lips. He inhaled the buttery, chocolatey scent, then took a bite. The sex and cookies combo was the real deal. "Jesus, that's good! From now on, every time we eat sweets, my cock needs to be buried deep inside you."

"Every time?"

"Every time."

She arched her back. "I'm good with that."

With the scent of sex, cookies, and a demolished chocolate cake in the air, he pumped his hips. Their kitchenette escapade escalated, going from zero to sixty as he dialed up his pace. He couldn't stop himself. There was no slowing down. He could feel the frantic pulse of the Wham Bam as he worked his fiancée, taking her hard and fast from behind while applying the sweet buzz to her sweet bud.

They'd barely been at it a few seconds when Phoebe bucked against him, moaning and panting, writhing against him. Wild and unconstrained, she cried out. "I'm so close, but I . . ."

"What is it?"

"The photo. I can't come with my parents watching us."

He glanced at the canister of coffee beans and then slid his gaze to the picture of Phoebe's mom and dad. Was her dad glaring at him? He didn't want to find out. He grabbed the frame and flipped it over. "Better?"

"Yeah. Oh, Sebastian," she breathed, meeting him blow for blow. "I'm so close," she exclaimed for the people in the next town over to hear.

It was probably a good thing they were moving out.

Between his cock and the pulse of the vibrator, she was on the brink of losing control. But she wasn't the only one teetering on the precipice of bliss. He was close, too. She was tight and so wet for him.

Near delirious with need, he knew what to say to drive her into orgasmic oblivion. "Phoebe Gale," he growled, resurrecting his accent.

"Yes?" she cried—again amplifying her voice for everyone in a fifty-mile radius that hadn't heard her the first time.

"Princess of the Hot Dog Fairies . . ."

"That's it, just like that," she panted.

He twisted his hand in her hair and pulled hard. "Bearer of Cookies . . ."

"Damned right," she moaned.

"And Eater of Pizza . . . I bloody love you."

And he did. He loved this woman with a ferocity he'd never known he possessed.

She reached back and threaded her fingers in the hair at the nape of his neck. In a whirlwind of heady vibrations and bodies gyrating, she tightened around him and plunged off the cliff into a carnal abyss. And he was right on her heels. Losing himself, his release tore through him. Surrounded by scattered cookies and a lump of chocolate cake splattered on the floor, he let go and gave in, giving Phoebe Gale every part of him. Like a leaf floating to the ground, their bodies slowed, coming down from the cocoa-fueled copulation.

"That was . . . wow," she said, catching her breath.

"Yeah, it was . . . wow." He set the vibrator on the counter, then glanced at the floor. "So much for having cake."

She chuckled—a sweet, sated sound. "That was the second cake. The first one I made is in the fridge. You were on the phone wheeling and dealing when I iced it."

"You made two chocolate cakes so I could live out my college fantasy?"

She craned her neck to look up at him. "I have the ingredients to make a third. That's how much I love you."

Yep, he was a lucky, lucky man.

She relaxed into him, drawing lazy circles against his neck with the pads of her fingers, when a rhythmic thumping caught his attention. "Do you hear that?"

Phoebe cocked her head to the side. "I do."

"Hey, Sebby! Hey Phoebe! Me and Ivy are here," Tula sang as the pounding of the girls' feet got louder.

Phoebe stopped the lazy circle action. "They're outside. They can't find us like this. And I need to clean up. I can't have you-know-what running down my legs while we make small talk with our families."

Jesus, he could just imagine the looks on everyone's faces. "Hurry, get to the bathroom."

She shimmied out of his embrace. In a clickity-clack of movement, she high-heel sprinted out of the kitchen.

"Are you guys in there?" Ivy called and banged on the door.

"I bet they've got their headphones on. But don't worry, Ives," Tula said. "I know the code to get in."

He was screwed.

Executing the putting-on-pants-while-walking movement, he grabbed the vibrator, then stumbled toward the bathroom door. "Does Tula know the code?"

"Yes, I told her a few weeks ago when I took the girls to a

tech expo. We stopped by my place, and Tula asked to enter it."

Shit!

Beep, beep, beep, beep!

The latch released.

He fastened his belt as Tula and Ivy blew into the apartment like a hurricane.

Hot dog costume-wearing Tula and Ivy Elliott stared at him as he stood in front of the bathroom door with—*God help him*—a Wham Bam in his hand.

"It's one of those submarine torpedoes we found at your house, Tula," Ivy chirped, twisting one of her auburn braids. "Remember, your dad's face turned super-white like a ghost, and then he said they were toys."

Tula beamed. "Yeah, submarine torpedoes."

If Sebastian hadn't been a grown-ass man holding a sex toy in front of two little kids, he would have laughed about his dad recycling the submarine torpedo moniker.

"Is Phoebe in the bathroom?" Ivy pressed.

"Yes, I'm in here, girls."

"I know what's going on," Tula said, nodding to Ivy.

"You do?" he stammered.

"Phoebe must be taking a bath, and you were bringing her a submarine torpedo to play with," Tula supplied.

He plastered a grin on his face, then pulled it back a fraction. The last thing he wanted to be was some dude smiling like a pervert while holding a sex toy in front of two kids. "That's it," he said, finding his voice. "I thought Phoebe might like a toy in the tub."

Phoebe opened the door and joined him. "But your silly brother forgot that I wasn't taking a bath. I was brushing my teeth."

"You've got cookie crumbs all over your face," Ivy remarked.

Tula narrowed her gaze, scrutinizing him. "You do too, Sebby."

"It's a new cookie-flavored toothpaste," Phoebe lied.

The eight-year-olds stared them down. He shared a look with Phoebe. Pure terror glinted in her eyes. How the hell were they going to get out of this?

And then it came to him. "How about ice cream? I owe you four scoops, right, T? Let's make it five. I'll bring it to the picnic table outside. Ivy Elliott and Tula Cress will be the first kids in the history of cookouts to get five scoops of double chocolate fudge supreme."

"That's awesome!" the girls cheered.

And God bless ice cream.

"There's a badminton net out by the picnic tables. Could you girls set it up for us while we get your ice cream?"

"Sure thing, Phoebe," Tula called.

The girls clasped hands and skipped out of the apartment.

"That was close," Phoebe said, wiping the cookie crumbs from the corners of his mouth.

He did the same for her. "Imagine if your uncle Rowen or my dad had walked in on us having cake sex." He wrapped his arms around Phoebe just as the breeze blew open the front door. Two large forms loomed outside.

"Is this something I'll have to read about on your Info Darling page, Phoebe?"

Sebastian winced. Dammit, he'd spoken too soon.

"Uncle Rowen! Erasmus!" Phoebe exclaimed.

"Everyone is in the courtyard," his father said, suppressing a grin. "The nerd and I were sent up here to see if you needed any help. And you might want to put away the submarine torpedoes."

Phoebe plucked the vibrator from Sebastian's hand. Like a star quarterback, she launched it across the room. The sex toy sailed through the air, and his dad nearly jumped out of his skin. He'd never seen the man move that quickly—even in the ring.

"Easy there, lass," the freaked-out former heavyweight champion yipped as the Wham Bam landed in an open moving box.

"That's taken care of," Phoebe said, dusting off her hands.

"Are you coming?" Rowen asked.

"In our kitchen?" Sebastian eked out. Rowen couldn't be talking about the naughty kind of coming, could he? "Nobody is coming in the kitchen. Not me. Not Phoebe, my fiancée, who happens to be your niece, and this is getting awkward."

"Are you coming to the cookout? We're ready to fire up the grill," Rowen clarified.

"Right, and yes, we're coming like two people who know how to come," Sebastian said, and dammit, he'd done it again.

"Can we carry something down? Penny and Libby sent us," his dad said, tossing worried glances at the box where Phoebe had chucked the Wham Bam. The guy had gone toe to toe with hard-core boxers but appeared to still be recovering from the flying vibrator shock. What was that all about?

"Here," Phoebe said, springing into action. She piled the cookies onto a plate, then grabbed the hot dogs and buns. She handed the items to her uncle and his dad. The men turned on their heels and bolted.

"What's cake sex?" Phoebe's uncle asked as the men headed out.

"That was rough." His fiancée shook her head and loaded him up with the tub of ice cream and the scooper.

"They'll have to get used to it. We're not kids anymore."

"No, we most certainly are not. We are grownups who like to have sex and eat junk food."

Phoebe grabbed a veggie tray and a bag of chips, and they left the apartment. It was a perfect fall day—cool with plenty of sunshine. Laughter floated in the air as they took the stairs, and he surveyed the scene. There was nothing new about getting together with their patchwork family, but everything felt different. He glanced at Phoebe. She smiled up at him, giving him the smile that was just for him. He saw her as a girl, then a teen, then a woman. He knew her every season. He'd been by her side for holidays, birthdays, and school events. And soon, she'd be his to have and to hold forever and ever.

"What are you thinking?" she asked as they got closer to their friends and family.

"Just how much I love you," he replied and set the ice cream on the picnic table.

"All right, lovebirds," Harper said, taking the chips from Phoebe and ripping open the bag. "I was told there's chocolate cake but it's on the floor. Have I taught you nothing about the necessity of protecting baked goods at all costs?"

"Pay no attention to Harper," Aria's uncle Landon crooned, eyeing his wife. "She's worried about Aria."

"I'm not worried. I'm calmly concerned. I've texted her and haven't heard anything in a few days. It's not like her. She always responds."

Phoebe chewed her lip. "I've texted Aria about the engagement, but I haven't heard back either."

This was getting a little concerning.

"We can't figure out where Oscar is," added Mitch Elliott, Oscar's dad, as he joined the group.

"I've called him a bunch over the last week," Charlotte added. "It goes to voicemail each time."

Before they could continue discussing Oscar and Aria's apparent escape from the face of the earth, a sleek black town car pulled up. A driver opened the door, and Madelyn Malone emerged from the back seat.

"Madelyn, we're so happy you could make it," Sebastian said, jogging to the woman and offering his arm.

Madelyn patted his hand, then studied the group. "Harper,

Landon, Mitch, and Charlotte look upset. Did something happen?" the woman asked with a distinct cat-who-ate-the-canary bend to the question. "And where are Oscar and Aria?"

"No one can get ahold of them."

Madelyn nodded. "Is that so? Are they together?"

He peered at the woman, and then it clicked. "Are Aria and Oscar a match? No way! They can't be. Aria's dating some guy in a band." Then he remembered Oscar tearing out of town to help *a friend*. Could that friend have been Aria, and if it was, why wouldn't he say that? "Madelyn," he pressed, "do you know what's going on with them?"

"I, of course, am simply a facilitator of fate. But knowing Oscar and Aria, I can guarantee one thing."

It wasn't lost on him that she'd chosen to use that word. "And what can you *guarantee*?"

Madelyn smoothed her trademark red scarf. "Our brooding artist and our rock star diva are in for quite a wild ride."

Thank you for reading The Sebastian Guarantee.
Don't miss a new release.
Sign up here:
https://bit.ly/ConnectWithKrista

Also by Krista Sandor

The Nanny Love Match Series

A nanny/boss romantic comedy series

Book One: The Nanny and the Nerd

Book Two: The Nanny and the Hothead

Book Three: The Nanny and the Beefcake

Book Four: The Nanny and the Heartthrob

Love Match Legacy Books

Stand-alone books featuring characters from the Love Match World.

The Sebastian Guarantee

The Oscar Escape

Mistletoe Love Match

The Bergen Brothers Series

A steamy billionaire brothers romantic comedy series

Book One: Man Fast

Book Two: Man Feast

Book Three: Man Find

Bergen Brothers: The Complete Series+Bonus Short Story

The Farm to Mabel Duet

A brother's best friend romance set in a small-town

Book One: Farm to Mabel

Book Two: Horn of Plenty

The Langley Park Series

A suspenseful, sexy second-chance at love series

Book One: The Road Home

Book Two: The Sound of Home

Book Three: The Beginning of Home

Book Four: The Measure of Home

Book Five: The Story of Home

Box Set (Books 1-5 + Bonus Scene)

Own the Eights Series

A delightfully sexy enemies-to-lovers series

Book One: Own the Eights

Book Two: Own the Eights Gets Married

Book Three: Own the Eights Maybe Baby

Box Set (Books 1-3)

STANDALONES

The Kiss Keeper

A toe-curlingly hot opposites attract romance

Not Your Average Vixen

An enemies-to-lovers super-steamy holiday romance

Learn more at

www.KristaSandor.com

Acknowledgments

Readers started emailing me after the first Nanny Love Match book, The Nanny and the Nerd, came out asking if Phoebe would get her own book.

At the time, I was like, simmer down now—we've got three more Nanny books to go.

But the readers were right.

The kids deserved to have their stories told.

I also knew that I wanted to expand this Nanny world. That's when the Love Match Legacy was born. These are standalone stories with a connection to the Nanny Love Match world, and I have many people near and dear to my heart to thank for making this dream a reality.

My friend, author SE Rose, has been with me from the beginning. She's always just a call away. Through the ups and downs, she's there for me. I'm so grateful for her friendship.

I have a talented group of eagle-eyed women who comb through every line. I know I say this all the time, but I always think I've nailed it when I do my author edits. I'm like, there's no way they'll find anything to fix. I'm always wrong. Carrie, Erin, Marla, and Tera are my editing angels. Thank you for putting care and love into your work to make my stories sparkle and shine.

The stunning cover photo comes to us from Wander Aguiar. My love and heartfelt gratitude go out to Wander and Andrey. Your images are breathtaking, and I love working with you both.

The mastermind behind the gorgeous cover design is Najla

Qamber from Qamber Designs. Najla and her staff are true professionals. It's always a pleasure collaborating with them. *And wowza!* This cover is perfection!

I have to thank my review team—my trusted readers who read early-release copies and help spread the word. Your love and support mean the world to me. Thank you!

A special shout-out to Thomas Costen. Thomas is a narrator and language coach. He helped me understand the uniqueness of Sebastian's situation. He's also the reason I was able to slip some of Sebby's spicy British accent into the book.

To my oldest son—who also helped craft the twist in The Nanny and the Nerd—thank you for again helping your mom with the tech parts of The Sebastian Guarantee and helping me develop the perfect twist at the end. Unfortunately, my son won't see this. I've told him he can't read my books until he's at least thirty, maybe forty. I better be safe and make it fifty.

And last but not least, I have to thank my dog, Rosie. We adopted her a few months ago and can't imagine life without our Rosie Good Girl. Did you catch the part of the book where I slipped her into the story?

Thank you, dear reader, for taking the time to read my book. None of this would be possible without you.

About the Author

If there's one thing Krista Sandor knows for sure, it's that romance saved her sanity. After she was diagnosed with Multiple Sclerosis in 2015, her world turned upside down. During those difficult first days, her dear friend sent her a romance novel. That kind gesture provided the escape she needed and ignited her love of the genre. Inspired by strong heroines and happily ever afters, Krista decided to write her own romance series. Today, she is an MS warrior, living life to the fullest. When she's not writing, you can find her running 5Ks with her husband and chasing after their growing boys in Denver, Colorado.

Never miss a release, contest, or author event! Visit Krista's website and sign up to receive her monthly update.